1

Treecastle Books
115 Fish and Game Road
Cherry Valley, NY 13320

Cover design by Charles Harvey
Silhouette used with kind permission
of Dana Pomeroy www.danapomeroy.com

ISBN 978-1533374653

MERCHANT OF DREAMS

Anita Briggs

With love for Charles Harvey,
who made it happen.

MERCHANT OF DREAMS

"We are the music makers,
and we are the dreamers of dreams."
Arthur O'Shaughnessy, Ode

The music:

Goldberg Variations, J.S. Bach

Flute Concerto in D major
Il Gardellino
Antonio Vivaldi

Piano Concerto # 21 in C major
W.A. Mozart

Concerto for Harp in E minor
Carl Reinecke

Feerie for Harp
Marcel Tournier

Piano Concerto #1 in D minor
Johannes Brahms

Piano Concerto # 3 in D minor
Sergei Rachmaninoff

≫ CHAPTER 1 ≪

The road was a ribbon of moonlight over the purple moor.
Alfred Noyes, The Highwayman

Ever since I read that damned *Secret Garden*, I thought dismally, I've dreamed of seeing Yorkshire, and now all I can think of is my beastly stomach. And my wretched head. The Dalesbus rounded a bend and I opened my eyes briefly, trying to recapture some sort of equilibrium. I saw with dull surprise that it was dark outside the window; I hadn't dared look out for the last ten miles.

The remnants of a month-long bout with flu, compounded by a wearisome flight across the Atlantic, the madness of the airport, and now, to cap it all, this lurching bus, had brought me near the final stages of motion sickness. The standard over-the-counter preventive worked its usual compromise, keeping active nausea away at the cost of marrow-melting weakness and disorientation.

Why hadn't I had the good sense to stay in Lynton? I thought longingly of the village in the hills, and of my serene and beautiful Greek Revival house.

Your deadly dull village, whispered an interior voice.

At that moment I would have traded my nausea for a century of dullness.

The bus braked to a stop. I buttoned my cape with shaking fingers, gripped my handbag, and stumbled past the three remaining passengers. The driver steadied me as I lurched down the steps.

"Someone meeting you, Miss?"

So this was the Yorkshire Dales. I saw with dismay

that the tiny station was dark, and the road empty. No village was in sight.

"Yes, thank you. Are we on time?"

"Five minutes early. That's why your people aren't here, I expect."

"Is there a telephone... just in case?"

"It's locked up in the station, Miss. Took out the booth; vandals, you know, even out here. Your party will be along, though. We're running a bit early, that's all."

I looked at the darkened building, trying to collect a shred of commonsense. "I'm staying at Denham House. Do you know how far that is?"

"Yes, Miss, it's about a mile and a half up that way." He pointed toward the left, where a single-track road snaked upwards, pale in the moonlight. "You'll see the sign, if you should have to walk. You're lucky, it's a lovely night! No snow—we had a good thaw last week." I could see the concern in his weathered face.

"I hear it's an elegant place," he went on, in a rallying tone. "A baronet's estate—they say it's been done up beautifully. You'll have a fine holiday." He nodded and swung himself up the steps.

After a glance in the direction of the road, I sank onto a narrow wooden bench, head in hands. How on earth was I going to survive a car ride up that winding track? Well, only a mile and a half, the driver had said. Five minutes at the outside.

The bus pulled away and the noise of its engine receded into the night. I leaned my head weakly against the clammy stone wall and closed my eyes. It usually took eight hours for the sickness to wear off. I longed for a hot bath, a soft pillow, and a steaming cup of peppermint tea.

I must have dozed for a moment; fleeting and inconsequential dreams chased one another through my head. Coming awake with a start, I found I was shivering uncontrollably in the "lovely night." The biting air was a

8

relief, but a few minutes of inactivity had chilled me to the bone. It was darker now, as the rising wind drove silver-rimmed clouds across a moon just waning from the full.

With an effort that felt heroic, I got to my feet, pulling up the hood of my cape. Except for the wind the night was silent, the bus long gone out of hearing. I shook my head, trying to clear it, and moaned as my stomach responded with a violent lurch.

Why hadn't the hotel sent someone to meet me? Once more I tried to be sensible, to push away the haze of nausea and childish panic. How bad could it be? They'd lost my message, or misread the time of arrival. I certainly didn't intend to spend the night on a freezing station bench, and the hotel was no great distance away. I'd hiked fifteen miles in a day, often enough.

Mercifully I'd sent my luggage ahead, having learned long ago that traveling with only a handbag got me to the longed-for bed much faster. Perhaps the brisk wind and the walk in the cold would dispel my sickness; either that or kill me, I thought wryly. At least the odds on being mugged in rural Yorkshire must be slim. Had the driver really said "vandals"?

Drawing a deep but cautious breath, I turned and set my feet on the twisting lane. My store of bravado was scanty enough as it was. If I'd suspected where that road was taking me, it would have been scantier still.

It was a single track of white gravel, winding up over the low beginnings of the moor. The wind gusted keenly about my head, blowing long bangs back against my hood. As I walked, I began to feel a little better, and for the first time realized how hungry I was.

Food may help your stomach, said the little voice. *But it won't fix what you're getting into. How in the world do you think you'll carry it off, with your open face and your compulsive New England honesty? You're seeing yourself as the heroine of all your beloved books and pictures, you idiotic Anglophile. Mary Yellan, striding across the Cornish moor. Jane Eyre, returning from posting her letters up a dark and icy lane.*

I shut my mind to the irritating thoughts. As the effort of the climb warmed me, I began to feel stronger and to revel in the excitement of this blustery night on the moor, one moment faintly lit by the moon, the next plunged into blackness by the passage of clouds.

Excitement had become a rare commodity of late. After a whirlwind of eventfulness in the teens and early twenties, my last few years had been characterized by a slow descent into apathy. I'd somehow tricked myself into believing that apathy was something to be desired: I called it "serenity."

The wind tore at my cape, and the skirt gave a resounding flap. The cape! I stopped in my tracks when I realized what a mistake it had been to wear it–my brain must have been dimmed by the flu. I'd certainly have to take it off before I reached the hotel. I'd fold it over my arm, and with luck it would look like a coat. It struck me, with rueful humor, that they'd think me one of those compulsively robust Americans who never carried umbrellas or sported proper outerwear.

My amusement evaporated as a low roar broke the night's silence. It grew louder with alarming speed, and a yellow-white glow swelled above the crown of the hill. Lord, it was coming fast! As the car crested, I was pinned in a blinding glare of undimmed headlights. Pain shot through my head as I jumped for the side of the road. Could it be transport from the hotel? If so, I would most assuredly walk. Brakes bit metal with an ugly scream, and the lights went out as the car skidded to a stop.

I had just time to see that it was sleek and black, and not a van, before the driver was upon me, seizing my shoulders and slamming me against the low door. Incredulous shock lanced through my body as violent hands were laid upon me for the first time in my life. Through the awful jerking of my heart I heard him curse. His voice was low and filled with hate.

"You! My God–alive! What rotten game are you playing now?" His rage intensified. "Jesus Christ! Are we never to be rid of you?"

He gave me a vehement shake, reawakening my nausea. I clung frantically to reason. Muggers didn't speak in BBC accents; even anger couldn't distort the unmistakable civilization of this voice. It was all some horrible mistake. Unless, I thought with a new surge of terror, the man was a psychopath.

The chilly moonlight slanted out again, illuminating his white sweater. I saw that he was taller than I and that his hair was black.

The growing light had told him something too. As he drew an audible breath, a hand relinquished its savage grip on my shoulder and moved to tilt my face up out of the shadow. "But..." There was the beginning of doubt in his voice. He pushed my hood back with an uncertain gesture.

The moon, freed of cloud, glared fiercely white, hurting my head and intensifying the scene's surreal aspect. His eyes were unreadable, and I fought down panic. Then quite suddenly, and for another reason altogether, I was coldly furious. The paralyzing fear was gone as if it had never existed.

"Will you please," I said in my best outraged schoolteacher voice, "take your hands off of me. Are you completely mad?"

His hands dropped away as if they'd been scorched. "I must be," he whispered. "Who are you?"

Reaction hit with a vengeance, and I turned blindly away, retching.

His black shadow merging with mine, he supported my sweating forehead with a firm hand, offering a handkerchief. The pure and gentle knight, I thought,

11

cynicism leering through my misery.

"God forgive me," he muttered under his breath. "You're right, I must be mad." He closed his eyes for a moment and drew a shaken breath, forcing calm on himself. Then he turned to face me. "I'm terribly sorry. I've had a bit too much brandy, I'm afraid, and in the headlights, for a moment, you looked like someone I once..."

"Not someone you were especially fond of, I gather," I cut in acidly, through the silly tears that always accompanied the resolution of my nausea. "Though how would you know? Seen at that speed I might have been a giant hedgehog. What were you doing, seventy?"

"Only about sixty, if we're speaking of miles per hour," he replied, "and no one ever walks these roads on winter nights. I was late; the estate wagon had a breakdown over in Ripon and I was on my way to pick up..." His voice trailed off. "Dear heaven," he continued softly. "It's you, isn't it? The American girl for Denham House? I knew you were American when I heard your voice, of course."

"Of course," I replied with undiminished bitterness.

"Well." He took a long, shuddering breath. "Come along then, get in. I must be mad indeed, to keep you standing here in the cold."

I stepped back, and he looked at me in puzzlement. "I'll drive you to Denham House at once. Oh... I see. Would you rather stay somewhere else? That's certainly understandable, given the circumstances."

"I don't know," I responded childishly, and to my horror burst into tears again, swabbing at my eyes with his crisp handkerchief.

"Well, you must do as you like. There's a small hotel a few miles beyond the station. I'll drive you there instead. You can tidy up, have a look, and book in if you wish." He'd recovered his composure, and there was a hint of impatience in his stance as he held the door open for me.

I hardly noticed what a tidy solution this presented to

my earlier worries. At the moment all I felt was a lash of anger at his overweening arrogance. He didn't even realize that a lone woman, assaulted on a dark road, would hardly leap joyously into the car with her assaulter.

My silence and immobility reached him at last, and he made a small deprecatory gesture. "Ah. Of course you must have doubts about riding with me. What can I say to reassure you? You must have corresponded with the manager of the hotel, Robin Denham? Well, I'm his cousin, and quite sane, despite appearances to the contrary."

I knew that far better than he could have imagined, but I had to play out my role. After all, he had behaved like a madman, and I'd been badly frightened. So I turned away and shook my head.

"Please. I can't leave you here. It's getting bitterly cold and you're ill."

I glanced at his face. When had I last seen it–on a poster outside Philharmonic Hall?

"All right. But I don't want to arrive at Denham House looking like this." I pressed icy hands to my face.

"Then we'll go to the Shepherd's Crook and let you wash up." He handed me into the car, and I sank wearily into sleek leather upholstery. An Aston-Martin, I saw without surprise. Two hundred thousand at a guess.

He slipped under the wheel, lowering a lighted mirror as I took a hairbrush from my purse. From the corner of my eye I saw him scrutinize my features with fearsomely quick intelligence. I turned to face him, and the searching look changed to one of uncertainty. He hadn't the faintest notion who I was. My recognition of him, on the other hand, was complete and irrefutable.

He backed the car onto the dead grass of the verge, turning it neatly. With a little spurt of gravel we were back on the road, retracing my path from the station. He drove steadily and sensibly, slowing around the curves, and I could see no evidence of the alleged surfeit of brandy.

13

"Your nausea and faintness, now," he inquired. "Does that all go onto my account?"

"No," I admitted grudgingly. "I'd been feeling pretty shaky. I was, well..."

"Had you been drinking? Or–"

I laughed. With my history of motion sickness, I had been through this far too many times to feel offense.

I recalled New Year's Eve dinner in a Vermont inn at the end of a long and winding road. I, the only member of the party who hadn't had a cocktail, staggered upstairs between consommé and wild boar pâté, fleeing the righteous stares of the other diners. So young to be so drunk!

"Not drinking, no. Just abusing an esoteric substance: Dramamine."

"Oh." Blankly. "You mean you suffer from *mal de mer*?"

"*Mal de mer, mal de* air, *mal de* road. *Mal de* anything that moves, or causes me to move. A month of flu didn't help, either."

"But the drug didn't work for you?"

"Never does. Just makes me weak."

"Why take it, then?"

"Social pressures only. It staves off the moment of truth."

He laughed. "I see. Sorry I misjudged the situation. On the fringes of my profession one sees more than Dramamine abused, and I suppose I'm too quick to jump to conclusions."

"Your profession?" Tell me about it, I thought sardonically. And don't leave out the violins.

"Apologies are in order. I should have identified myself right away." With your hands at my throat? "I'm John Denham's brother. He owns the hotel; I'm not really associated with it. I just stepped into the breach tonight when the estate wagon broke down and there was no one on hand to meet you. I'm actually a musician; my name is Richard

14

D'Annunzio."

"Richard D'Annunzio? Surely not..." Be properly, girlishly awed.

He nodded a bit curtly.

"I... I know your name, of course. I've actually seen you conduct."

We were drawing up to a low, rambling stone building, its sign creaking in the wind. Yellow light shone from the windows, and gusts tore streamers of smoke from clustered chimneys.

Yes, I had seen him conduct, I thought as he came around to open my door. My mind flew back to the last time. It had been his own monumental composition, *Faustus*, based on Christopher Marlowe's demonic masterpiece.

In my head I could hear the superb orchestra, the Metropolitan baritone soloist, the battery of electronics with which D'Annunzio had then been engrossed. The heart-wrenching, appalling terror of that tortured phrase: "Adders and vipers, let me breathe awhile!" was etched into my memory as if with acid. The music, dissonant yet lyrical, seethed with desperate urgency, and powerful amplification shook the arms of the seat under the grip of my hands. I had sat in my box long after the thunderous applause had subsided, staring into the pit at the horrors of Marlowe's hell, which I had never, in half a dozen readings, perceived with such searing clarity.

I stumbled as he helped me out of the car. Whether it was due to weariness, shock, or the memory of that staggering music, I didn't know.

He steadied me, and said, "Are you sure you're all right?" Reaching into the back of the Aston, he pulled out a jacket.

"I'm fine. I was just looking at the demoralized sheep on that sign, and fell over my own feet. I'll go proceed with repairs right away."

In the rosy light of the chintz-curtained powder room,

15

I washed mouth, face and hands, touched makeup over my pallor, and sprayed on scent. Twisting my dark hair back into a low knot, I took special care to comb bangs over the prominent widow's peak. There. That was better; though surely I was far and away the most bedraggled female ever escorted anywhere by Richard D'Annunzio.

So you're going to Denham House after all. You really are a fool.

Maybe, I countered my own better instincts. But at least it's a change from Turnerville Elementary.

I slipped off the damning cherry red cape, smoothed my sensible grey woolen dress, closed my eyes tightly for a moment, and entered the dining room, head high.

≪ CHAPTER 2 ≫

Oh, what a tangled web we weave
when first we practice to deceive.
Sir Walter Scott, Marmion

The eagle suffers little birds to sing.
William Shakespeare, TitusAndronicus

He was waiting by the fireplace, and gave me an appraising glance.

"Back with the living, I see."

A hostess seated us at a table with a softly shaded lamp. Brandy stood ready, reflecting the light in its amber depths.

"Sip it slowly," he cautioned. "It should be restorative. May we complete our introductions now?"

"Certainly. I'm Felicity Godwin," I said with perfect truth. When I saw that the name meant nothing to him, I relaxed a bit. Then, in deliberate rebellion, I took a long sip of brandy. As he raised an eyebrow, I continued with a barefaced lie. "I can handle the brandy."

A beaming young waiter put menus before us. "Good evening!" he exclaimed with irritating cheer. "I'm Doug, and I'll be your waiter for the evening. The specialty tonight is flambéed pheasant with sauce Cumberland and potatoes Pojarski. The pheasant is raised by a local watercolor artist who also does marvelous macramé. I can personally recommend the crab, and the rack of lamb is superb tonight!"

I scanned the card, locating my usual panaceas. "I'll just have the watercress soup and some wholemeal rolls, thank you."

"Nothing for me," added Richard. "I dined earlier."

"Oh." Deflated, seeing his big tip from the famous man take wing, poor Doug gathered the menus to his bosom, summoned a pathetic smile, murmured, "Thank you, Maestro D'Annunzio," and melted away.

"I don't believe it," I whispered. "What's a rural Yorkshire inn doing with American management?"

"Oho!" he laughed. "You detect a ring of familiarity in our Doug's set speech?"

"I never expected to hear it in the Dales. Ten to one when he brings the soup he'll say, 'Enjoy your dinner!'"

"Yes, I'm sure you're right. The dining imperative: enjoy your dinner–or else. And you're absolutely on target about the management. The Shepherd's Crook is American-owned. My cousin Robin managed the restaurant for a while, but John lured him to Denham House when he opened it as a country house hotel."

"Was that a difficult decision for your brother?"

"Not when he considered the alternatives. You're familiar with our tax structure?"

I nodded. The brandy was beginning to warm me. How long had it been since I'd drunk brandy, or sat in a firelit restaurant with an intelligent companion?

"Well, this decides me. I'm definitely going to honor my reservation at Denham House. I just came from the States, and there are plenty of American-run B and B's there."

He turned the glass in his supple pianist's fingers, crystal glinting in the lamplight. For a long moment he was silent.

How brown he is, I thought, stealing a glance at the strong, civilized face, immediately recognizable to anyone with the smallest knowledge of classical music. His heritage was half Italian; he had taken his mother's name. Yet he was tan beyond the natural olive of his skin, and in February. Where had he been this time? Skiing at Chamonix, or

18

Gstaad? Boating in the Caribbean?

His voice broke in on my thoughts. "So you've just recovered from the flu. And now you've come to sunny Yorkshire, in mid-winter, to convalesce?"

For the first time in two days, I felt blood come into my cheeks. "I'm quite well now," I said, a little more sharply than I intended. Control, Felicity. "It was more a matter of–nervous exhaustion. I've always been in love with the idea of Yorkshire, and when I read a New York Times article about your brother's country house, it... well," I finished mildly, "it seemed the perfect place to vegetate and rebuild my strength."

"As indeed it is. Though you'll need to be careful not to catch a chill." A pause. "Nervous exhaustion. You have a demanding job, then?" He fixed me with an inquiring eye.

You're ready for this, Felicity, I told myself without much conviction.

"Are you by chance a musician yourself?" he persisted. "You did know my name, after all."

I sipped brandy, but set my glass down carefully when I saw how the liquid quivered. Under the sanctuary of the tablecloth my hands met in a fierce clasp.

"I imagine most educated people know your name. But yes, I'm a pianist of sorts." That, too, was true enough. "And... and I'm substitute organist at my church. I play a little guitar," I rattled on, feeling a fool. All at once I was desperate with embarrassment at the sham I was acting in front of this great man. "And I teach..." I wound up lamely.

"Ah. Privately? University level?"

"No. Elementary school music."

His courtesy was almost sufficient to hide the boredom. "You must find it gratifying, sharing your music with children. There's a great need for gifted teachers."

"Yes, I love it," I lied enthusiastically, thinking of the quarts of chocolate milk I'd mopped off the floor during kindergarten cookie break.

19

"And where did you study?" Still the careful courtesy, very gallant and Italian now. Let her feel like somebody; don't denigrate her little effort.

"Oh, in the East." Skating on thin ice, Felicity. Then, disparagingly, "A small private college." That, at least, they couldn't take away from me. A little demon of rebellion stirred and I hid a smile in the brandy.

"And the piano... you still keep it up?" My God, was he going to ask me to play a duet?

"Oh, yes!" The demon, nourished by brandy, swelled to epic proportions. I was overdoing it dangerously, but he'd stung me on the raw. "*Clair de lune*, and *Rustles of Spring*. I play lots and lots of Mendelssohn–*Consolation* and some of the other *Songs Without Words*, the easier ones, of course. And I do adore Gottschalk, don't you?"

He'd elevated the eyebrow and opened his mouth to speak when the waiter set a plate of soup in front of me.

"Enjoy your dinner!" he intoned with practiced heartiness. We watched him out of hearing behind the kitchen door before we exploded into helpless laughter.

Fruit and coffee followed the soup, and we were back to brandy, having skipped the wine. The polite inquisition had mercifully ceased, and conversation centered on the attractions of Yorkshire. To my surprise I found that I was feeling fine, and astonishingly relaxed.

"If it's not out of line, I have a question too. What are you doing in this... well... capacity? Surely you don't often spend time ferrying Denham House guests about?" Against my will I felt a large and genuine diffidence.

"No, it's not my usual line of country," he laughed. The teeth flashed in his dark face, and I wondered again, irrelevantly, where the tan had come from. Like many of the new breed of international musicians, he was, I knew, an ardent skier, sailor, and horseman.

"Are you staying at Denham House?" My voice

sounded convincingly offhand.

"No, I have my own place."

Thank God, I thought. He's made it livable, and he's moved in. Richard D'Annunzio was too sharp by half for continued contact. I no longer doubted my ability to carry this evening's encounter through, but even brief chance meetings in the future could push my luck.

"It's located on the estate, over the fell from Denham House. I'm restoring it a bit at a time. Nothing grand, just a big old farmhouse, but it's a welcome retreat. I need a quiet place to compose and practice. I've done precious little of either lately," he continued ruminatively. "The conducting's like a ravenous beast; it eats one up. But I'm not answering your question. I'd stopped by to see if my brother was in this evening. He'd gone to London, but my cousin Robin called while I was there, panicked because the transmission had gone out on the estate wagon when he was over in Ripon, and he had no way to pick you up in time. It's the off season and they're understaffed, you see. So I was conscripted. It's been a new experience for me."

For me too, I reflected, wondering at the apparently unconscious irony of his words. He lifted the brandy, and the remarkable eyes, long-lashed, the light grey irises startlingly rimmed with black, met mine over his glass. I dropped my own glance quickly. Good grief, I thought. No wonder they have to sweep the little blue-haired ladies out of the aisles when he steps onstage.

He set his glass down, somber now. "In any event, I try to be in Yorkshire whenever it's possible because of my brother. I suppose you should be told: we've had a death in the family. Because of that and the renovations, John is keeping activity at the house to a minimum."

"I'm so sorry. I knew the hotel was being redecorated, and felt lucky to get a reservation at all. But I hadn't realized there was family trouble." Under the table my fingers were crossed: that childhood talisman against retribution for the sin of lying. "If it would be better for me to stay here instead..."

He hesitated, and I could almost hear my heart beat. Now that the matter was out of my hands, I regretted speaking. Had I come all this way for nothing?

"Of course not. It happened six months ago, and if you're booked in there can be no question. Robin has things well in hand. And John lives quite removed from the hotel activities, except for an occasional appearance at tea or dinner. His antiques business keeps him in London and on the Continent for the most part." He frowned at his empty glass, and for the first time since we'd entered the restaurant I saw a trace of the man who'd seized me so brutally on the road.

"John lost his wife, you see." He spoke slowly. "They'd been married only a year. It was a boating accident, at night, and she was alone. They never found her body." He picked up his glass again and looked straight at me.

I said a silent prayer of thanks for my professional training. I needed every atom of it to suppress the shiver coursing down my spine.

"You may have heard about it, since you're in music yourself, though you probably wouldn't have associated it with John's name." His voice was quiet, controlled. "It was in the newspapers and on television at the time. She was a concert harpist–one of the great ones. Ciara Rossi."

He pushed back his chair. "And now I'd better drink up–no, you've had quite enough, my good woman–and get you to Denham House."

The Aston was gliding slowly through the night, snowflakes darting at the windshield. The cloud cover had closed in and the road was frosted with a rim of white. Mercifully, D'Annunzio took the corners at a snail's pace.

Illness, nausea and shock seemed far behind in the safety of the warm, dimly lighted capsule. The food and brandy had first revived me, then made me ridiculously sleepy, and the incident on the road seemed as remote as a bad dream. It raised many questions, but I could best explore them stone sober, I decided with owlish wisdom.

"Better?" asked Richard D'Annunzio, glancing my way.

"Inexpressibly."

I leaned my head contentedly against the cushioned leather. He reached over and switched on the stereo, and the clean lines of Baroque music arced through the night.

After a moment he said, as if to himself, "Rameau, of course. *Castor et Pollux?*"

"Mmm, no." I murmured on a yawn. *"Les Indes Galantes."*

I was immediately awake and could have bitten off my tongue. At this rate, you imbecile, you'll be back in Lynton within the week.

In the glow of the dash I saw him throw me a very keen look indeed. But he only replied, "You're right, of course. I'm off my stride tonight."

I found I hadn't the wit or energy to concoct a plausible explanation for an amateur's spontaneous identification of an obscure work. I closed my eyes, swearing to volunteer no more cultural information.

Moments later, to my intense relief, we turned into an avenue lined with ancient beeches, their bare bones ghostly in the rush of headlights. We ran between them for a surprising length of time, at last drawing up before a glowingly lighted Georgian house of arresting loveliness. Richard held the door open for me, and we stepped into a soaring walnut-paneled hall. The room smelled of wood fires, beeswax and potpourri.

A youngish man rose from behind a Chippendale desk and hurried to meet us. He was wiry of build and a bit shorter than Richard, but resembled him strongly. His eyes were blue, rimmed with black like Richard's, and his energy fairly crackled in the quiet room.

"Richard, you dog! We thought you'd absconded with our guest. Welcome to Denham House, Miss Godwin." His handclasp was firm and heartening.

Richard turned to me. "My irrepressible cousin Robin Denham, who runs this place so superbly. Rob, did you get the wagon back from Ripon?"

"No such luck. It's in the shop for a couple of days. I cadged a ride home with Barry. But thanks for pulling me out of the soup. Did you miss your bus, Miss Godwin?"

Richard intercepted the question smoothly. "No. Miss Godwin was a bit under the weather from her trip, so we revived her with a brandy and some American soup at the Crook."

If Robin Denham thought it odd to drive a distressed traveler twelve miles out of the way for a brandy, he didn't say so. "Yes, I know only too well," he laughed ruefully. "I used to preside there. I hope you enjoyed your dinner?"

I smiled, responding to his easy banter. "Dr. D'Annunzio told me you fled from the Americanization of Yorkshire. Wise move," I finished. I hadn't spoken Richard's name before, and found that doing so stirred strange emotions.

"Indeed it was; it's heaven here, you know. But you must be exhausted, Miss Godwin. Would you like to go up to your room? Your baggage arrived yesterday, and Merrin has put everything away. I'll send her up with tea and biscuits. You do understand we're short of staff? Most of the bedrooms are being redone, and we won't be operating normally until April."

"Of course. It doesn't matter. I'm grateful that you're able to put me up at all."

"Oh, we can accommodate a token number of guests. We have an American couple here, by the way, as well as a few lodgers from the Continent." We were moving down the hall toward a stairway that divided at the landing, sending

24

lovely twin curves up to the second floor.

I must say goodnight to Richard, I thought, and pray that I won't see him again. My words of thanks trailed off as I glanced through an impossibly tall double door standing open at my left. In spite of my knowledge, I stood stock-still. It was a room of classic proportions, carpeted with softly-colored Aubusson rugs and lighted by standing lamps. A two-manual harpsichord was placed opposite the nine-foot grand. At the right of the scrolled marble mantelpiece, rich gilding illumining its silent dignity, stood a superlative concert grand harp.

And over the mantel hung a portrait of Ciara at her most ravishing: gowned in deep emerald velvet that accented the green of her eyes (her tinted contacts, I thought, and immediately berated myself for pettiness), the brilliantly smiling face framed by the cloud of black hair that swept up from a widow's peak. I swallowed hard.

Richard broke the silence. "Miss Godwin is a musician, Robin. I'm sure John would want her to have free access to the music room." He turned to face me. "You can practice your... er... Gottschalk on the Bösendorfer. And with your facility on instruments–you said you played organ, and guitar? Who knows? Perhaps you can teach yourself the harp."

Goaded, I couldn't keep the acid from my voice. "I had friends at music school who studied the harp, Dr. D'Annunzio. They assured me that it's the most technically difficult of all instruments. I hardly think..." I drew a deep breath. "Thank you for the offer. And for supper." On impulse I added, "If you're serious, and if Sir John and the guests don't object, I would like to practice the piano when everyone's out."

Richard nodded. "Of course. You can play at any time; the room's virtually soundproof. John will be delighted to have the instrument used. He respects the idea of music, though he's a born monotone, like our late father. Robin, though," he smiled at his cousin. "Robin is the harpsichordist of the family."

I turned in surprise.

"Long retired from the field," said Robin lightly, and started up the stairs.

"Good night. I hope you'll have a good rest. I'll be in touch, Rob."

Robin was waiting for me on the landing, a quizzical look on his neatly bearded face.

"So you're a musician?"

"The merest dilettante," I replied, and followed him up the stairs.

≫ CHAPTER 3 ≪

Success is counted sweetest by those who ne'er succeed.
Emily Dickenson, Success is Counted Sweetest

Lying sleepless in the peony-curtained bedroom, I stared at the fireplace, embers pulsing red and black. The unsettling events of the night were a strange substitute for the peace I'd come seeking. Adrenalin was still racing through my veins, and try as I might, I couldn't turn off my brain. It ranged now, without my volition, back over the past five years.

Richard D'Annunzio. It was obvious that, by the mercy of God, he hadn't the least remembrance of me. Perversely, that vexed me a bit. Well, why should he? I had been twenty-two, just out of the Curtis Institute of Music with a diploma in harp performance. And (I winced at the memory) I was blonde.

I'd been playing on a professional basis with the guidance of my teacher, Leon Lemaitre. He'd placed me under the aegis of one of the most respected agencies in New York, and I was well launched into what promised to be an international career. It seemed that all doors were opening for me. And having an aunt who was indisputably the most successful harpist of her time certainly did me no harm.

Leon was satisfied with my musical development, to a point. But for years he'd fretted over a matter he considered potentially damaging. When I was eighteen, he confronted me squarely with it.

Closing my eyes against the glow on the hearth, I could see the sleek black head, the hawk-like features; hear the precise, rather high-pitched French voice.

"You must be logical, not emotional, Felicity. It is time for you to step out of Ciara's shadow. Stop trying to be her! Yes, yes, you may admire her, but never copy her!"

The authoritative voice spoke on, the words evoking the same curiously humble thrill that they had all those years ago.

"I tell you, before God and man, that you are the greatest natural talent I have ever taught." He sounded stern, almost angry. "But you are submerging your musical identity in hers! You are killing your own gift, and I will not have it. I forbid you to listen to her recordings. Stop trying to phrase as she does! You have enough of your own to say."

In spite of inveighing against emotionalism, he was getting excited now, as he always did, the Gallic temperament burning at white heat. He held me at arm's length, looking at me critically.

"You are beautiful, yes, but your beauty... pah! It is nothing to me. Your music, it is everything." He let go of me and began to pace the room, restless and driven as a captive lion. "But this absurd physical resemblance to Ciara–" He struck his forehead. "Hah! We will change all that, we will break this tyranny of cookies, stamped out in a row. We will make a transformation!"

So my time had come, I thought resignedly.

"And your name. Felicity Godwin." His voice had dropped and every syllable was spoken with gently chiding derision. Then, briskly, "Ridiculous for the concert stage! Impossible! It sounds like–like a Sunday school teacher!"

He was right about that. But even if it hadn't he probably would have wanted to change it. Leon loved to play with names. Ciara Rossi had been plain Clara Ross before he'd gone to work on her. Name changes and "complete transformations" were almost as important to Leon as his teaching. He adored the Pygmalion role.

He strode to his desk and seized pen and paper. How

many young women had he rendered unrecognizable to their astonished parents, I wondered. To Leon, English or American names were anathema. The surname, at least, had to sound Continental. Would I emerge as Peach Melba, I mused, as he shot me a speculative look and scribbled with a fresh burst of energy? Or why not, I thought wildly, Shrimp de Jonghe?

"Felicity... Fe - li –ci - ty... ah! *Lissa! Voila! Mon Dieu*, it is perfection!" he beamed. "And now, now I will do something very special for you, something I have never done for anyone else: I, Leon Lemaitre, I give you my own name!"

"But... what about Leona?" I ventured.

"Bah! Leona!" His voice dripped contempt. "Phut! Do not speak to me of her. She is finished. It is immaterial; she plays like a hectic cat. She is no longer Leona, she is only Geraldine."

Geraldine Bloom had been transformed into Leona Vincenzi at about the same time she became Leon's mistress. And she was indeed now finished, at least as far as he was concerned. She had decamped with a jazz saxophonist and brought forth twins, forfeiting both her career and her nomenclature.

I had no fears of Leon from that quarter. He'd always treated me as if he were my firm yet lovingly indulgent father. His respect for my musicianship filled me with astonished gratification, and I was confident in his disinterested affection.

Satisfied with his inspiration, Leon was benign again, eyes twinkling with as much pride as if he had created me out of clay. "Now you are Lissa Leone, my spiritual child. And we will dress you like Isolde... like Melisande! Ciara is earthy. She exudes sexuality. You will be ethereal." He fingered a strand of my hair.

"But as you are, you are only a pale shadow of Ciara. Where her eyes are green," he murmured musingly and not quite accurately, "yours are grey. Her hair is raven black, yours is brown." Under the pressure of his falling inflection, "brown" became a mildly disparaging word.

I stole a glance at his own hair, dyed monthly to a uniform glossy black, and sighed internally. Oh well. It could have been worse. He could have prescribed fiery red.

And so I became a blonde. The family widow's peak was concealed under subtly layered bangs. It was done beautifully, at a staggering price, and looked as if I'd been born with it. But it always made me feel I was acting a charade.

Leon, however, was triumphant. He would stop my fellow students in the halls and cry, "Have you seen Lissa? She is completely transformed!" My bone structure, so like Ciara's, was beyond even his ingenuity, but he altered my stage dressing to evoke Arthurian fancies. I was by Burne-Jones out of Edward Arlington Robinson, and in truth I loved it.

And so commenced my weaning from the physical and artistic image of Ciara.

Ciara. At that time she was already famed as a performer of peerless technique and interpretation. A great and mesmerizing beauty, she might have have chosen a film career.

And though I barely knew her, she was also my adored aunt.

Ciara was ten years older than I, a contemporary of Richard D'Annunzio's. She had been nine when her only sister, aged eighteen, had married my father, who was just out of Yale. I had been born in the following year.

Though already a superb pianist in her early teens, Ciara had gone on to study harp, win a scholarship at Curtis, and sweep the international competitions. As if that weren't sufficient, she'd also managed to catch the imagination of the public.

The harp was a rather esoteric instrument. Although most people enjoyed hearing it played in lounges or symphony orchestras, it didn't have a familiar solo repertoire. Laymen tended to describe it as "sweet" or "relaxing," terms that stirred murderous thoughts in serious harpists. In this age of classical superstars, there had been no recognized harpist with mass appeal. Ciara had flared into the firmament and stuck there, held in the public eye by impeccable musicianship, superhuman technique, and nerves of steel. Movie-star glamour and sheer wattage hadn't hurt, either. Ciara Rossi's physical appearance, like her musical performance, was stunning. She also possessed, in every sense of the word, a savvy agent who paired her with internationally famous and very salable stars, saw to it that her CDs bore sultry and luscious portraits, and fostered her acquaintance with the rich and musically influential.

I punched my pillow irritably. Be fair, Felicity. She was one hell of a musician. No sour grapes, if you please. Besides, she inspired you to start playing. Encouraged you to go to New York for lessons. Put you into Leon's hands, when you were ready, so you fell into a scholarship at Curtis like falling off a log. Won your own international competitions when you were virtually a child.

Fat lot of good that did me, I thought bitterly.

Conscience spoke again. *You'd better believe it did! Otherwise you'd be baking cookies for cub scout sales. Volunteering in the Lynton library. Chairing Woman's Club meetings.*

When in fact I've ended in a burst of brilliance, teaching "Oats, Peas, Beans and Barley Grow" to Turnerville's second graders?

Sarcasm's no answer. You have resources, haven't you? You've been a fine musician. You still are. Someday....

Never. No. I would never again subject myself to that agony, cut my breast open and lay my heart on the table for general and public dissection.

A scratch at the door brought me out of my reverie. It was a sound familiar from my childhood. I switched on the lamp and padded across the soft rug. Opening the door, I saw a streak of white tear across the room and vanish under the bed.

"All right," I laughed, leaving the door cracked. "If you're going to be coy, you needn't think I'm going to go poking about on hands and knees after you."

I switched off the light for a moment and pulled the curtain aside. The wind had abated, but it was still snowing lightly. My room faced the front of the house, and I could see flakes sparkling like mica as they drifted through the light of the coaching lamps. For all of Yorkshire I'd seen today, I might as well have stayed in Connecticut. But tomorrow I'd put on my warmest things and strike out over the moors, fells, downs—I'd never been sure of the terminology.

I propped myself against the pillows and turned the lamp on again, pulling up the silky comforter. I was punchy with exhaustion and the aftermath of nausea, but still strung tight with excitement. There was so much to work out. I wasn't thinking logically, but I couldn't stop my mind's frantic thrashing.

Ciara dead. Well, that was why I had come here, under a name John Denham wouldn't be likely to know. Certainly I had no notion of playing the detective. Her death was simply a grotesque, shockingly wasteful accident. But Ciara had been my only living relative and my last tie, albeit a tenuous one, to my parents. All through her life, she'd moved too fast to maintain family relationships.

Of course I knew that coming to this Yorkshire house was madly illogical. It was unlikely she'd spent much time here. But lying ill with the flu, it seemed like a wonderful inspiration to recover in a countryside that had held such fascination for me in books; above all, in my loneliness, simply to be where Ciara had been. I'd made a firm resolution not to impose on John Denham by claiming any family tie. That seemed the height of presumption, particularly to an anglophile with an overdeveloped diffidence toward the titled rich. I'd never been an assertive person, and anonymity was truer to my natural reserve. Arriving as a grieving relative smacked too much of the crass American, hoping to hitch a ride on the coattails of the upper class. It was extremely unlikely he was aware of my existence, anyway. And the notoriously awful winter weather of Yorkshire didn't even occur to me.

But I had reckoned entirely without Richard D'Annunzio. Surely he should have been in London, Luxembourg–anywhere but the remote and rural Dales.

The mattress gave under the weight of a compact body, and I looked up into two round eyes of cerulean blue. "Oh, it's you," I murmured. I had completely forgotten about the cat. "Looking for a warm bed tonight?"

With his stub of a tail held erect, the white Manx cat stepped tentatively onto my lap. He had extra toes like thumbs, and the multitude of claws looked formidable. I hoped fervently that he had no intention of using them on me. My fears were allayed when he set up a noise like a distantly approaching Harley-Davidson.

Turning off the lamp for the last time, I slid down under the covers. Well, here I was. Yorkshire. I stroked the cat's fine white fur. Ciara was gone, and her harp stood mute in the great salon below. The irrevocable passing of her vital presence was still difficult to accept. No easier to accept was the fact that Richard D'Annunzio, conductor, composer and pianist of international repute, had attacked–there was no other word for it–attacked me on a deserted country road tonight. After the first shock, I'd never doubted that he believed me to be Ciara. In the illumination of the powerful headlights, wearing the trademark red cape she'd passed down to me (and what a stupid oversight that had been!), with my hair, grown dark again, blown back from the widow's peak that was the twin of hers and my face ashen with illness, I must have looked like Ciara's ghost. Leon's "pale shadow," indeed.

Richard's reaction had stunned me. He'd actually

33

believed, for a moment, that Ciara was alive. That was so irrational as to be inconceivable. And he hadn't wanted her alive. In all my protected life, cloistered first in a loving New England household and then among a community of dedicated artists, I'd never before experienced violent hatred. I had seen and felt it tonight.

Did he know who I was? I thought not, even though he had, for a moment, believed that I was my own aunt. He'd never seen me, in New York or Philadelphia, until all traces of my resemblance to Ciara had been carefully and professionally effaced. He'd known Ciara's niece as a cheerful, confident, softly rounded young woman, her distinguishing widow's peak concealed by a slanting fall of blonde hair. Tonight he had assaulted–and courteously escorted to an inn–a shrewish brunette, thin to the point of emaciation. He might suspect I was some unknown relative of Ciara's, but there was nothing to identify me as the vanished Lissa Leone. Not if he didn't know I was a harpist, and there was no way he could discover that.

No. There was nothing left to equate me with that girl; nothing but the ashes of dreams and aspirations. And those were not for him to know.

A trilling murmur broke the silence, and I felt paws with too many toes gently kneading my shoulder. But no claws. I lifted up the edge of the cover and the little Manx slipped under, curling into the curve of my shoulder. He considerately positioned his nose by my ear so I could hear him purr.

Like a miniscule mouse, something was gnawing at my brain. Exhausted, I pushed it away.

"All right, love," I sighed, gently stroking the kitten's head. "Let's call it a night."

In a disorienting flash, memory flung me back to the scene on the road. Was that an instant of terror I'd seen in D'Annunzio's eyes? I dismissed the thought as absurd. Yet as sleep dropped its dark curtain, I heard that tormented voice crying, "Jesus Christ! Are we never to be rid of you?"

❧ CHAPTER 4 ❧

We make ourselves a place apart
behind light words that tease and flout,
But oh, the agitated heart
Till someone finds us really out.
Robert Frost, Revelation

It was late morning when, roused by a quiet tap at the door, I reluctantly opened my eyes. Soft light filtered through the curtains, lending radiance to the white walls. I murmured a sleepy response and sat up as a young woman entered the room. She was tall, with the strong bone structure passed down to many Yorkshire folk from their Viking ancestors. Her eyes were blue, and dark blonde braids looped cleanly back from a face glowing with good health. I put her at about twenty-three.

"Good morning, Miss Godwin. I'm Merrin. I hope you rested well? Mr. Denham said you had a rough journey."

"Yes, I had a wonderful sleep, thank you. I feel fine now."

She placed a brass-handled rosewood tray on my lap, and I exclaimed in pleasure. It was laid with an ivory cut-work cloth; a Limoges plate boasted two golden croissants. A perfect rose of butter, a pot of blackberry jam, and a tiny pitcher of milk were arrayed around a bunch of hothouse violets. Next to a translucent cup a small silver teapot steamed alluringly.

"Robin–Mr. Denham–said tea, because you weren't feeling quite the thing last night, but if you'd rather have coffee..."

"Oh, no! This couldn't be better. And thank you for leaving the mint tea and biscuits last night while I was in the bath."

"I hoped they helped. Mr. Denham said you were awfully pale."

"I was a wreck, and they were lifesavers. Oops!" I steadied the tray as the Manx cat shot out from under the covers. Crossing the rug in three bounds, he squeezed through the door.

"Oh! Hishi!" Merrin looked startled. "But surely...he didn't stay in with you last night?"

"Yes. I–I'm sorry. Should he not have been in the room?"

"Oh, no, it's not that. But how ever did you manage to get him in? He's very shy with everyone except Sir John and Dr. D'Annunzio. Mr. Denham says Hishi hates women, but then Mr. Denham hates cats!"

"Truly? Well, I really didn't lure him. He scratched at the door and I let him in. He seems very affectionate. But if Mr. Denham hates cats, why does he allow---Hishi, did you say?--- to stay?"

"Well, Hishi is here because Sir John is fond of him, I suppose. Actually, he was Lady Denham's cat, although..." Merrin broke off and crossed the room to open the curtains. "Look! Sunshine! Well, it was sunshine, for a moment. But you might have a nice walk today; the snow didn't stay on because of the wind. It's too bad the horses aren't here. They're boarded for the winter, except those belonging to the family. If you're planning a long stay, they might be back in time; mid-April, I should think."

"I'm not sure how long I'll be here, but I hope at least a month." Drawing a slow breath of contentment, I looked across the tray at the lovely, comforting room, and out the long windows to the buff-colored hills. Yes, I would stay. My body and spirit needed the healing I felt implicit in this beautiful spot, a healing I couldn't find in my own shadow-haunted house. And though I had my share of problems, a shortage of money, fortunately, was not among them.

"Well, I'll leave you to your breakfast," said Merrin. "Ordinarily we serve it downstairs beginning at eight, but as you were so tired last night, we thought you'd like a tray."

"Thank you, Merrin. That was very kind."

"Now don't forget your woollies if you go out!"

The door closed behind her. I took a sip of fragrant tea, swung out of bed, and hurried to the window, enchanted by the prospect before me. Little clouds were scudding before a sharp wind; when the sun gleamed briefly between them, its light turned the hills pale gold.

An hour later, showered, shampooed, and dressed in warm wool pants and jersey, I ran down the stairs. I was filled with a wonderful sense of physical well-being, last night's illness forgotten.

The great house was as entrancing in the fitful sunshine as it had been by lamplight. The rooms were marvelously proportioned and decorated. Furnished with museum-quality eighteenth century pieces, they were warmed by the comfort and luxury of fine paintings, inviting chairs and sofas covered in soft florals, and age-faded Oriental and Chinese rugs. Arrangements of fresh flowers lent color, and polished brass and silver gleamed. The house had an expansiveness that lifted the spirit, yet for all its high ceilings, impressive mantels and tall windows, it maintained a human scale.

I settled into a flame-stitch chair by the drawing room fire and picked up the morning's London Times. Through the window I could see Robin standing in the driveway, pointing out something on a map to a middle-aged couple. The map fluttered in the wind and he folded it firmly, helped the woman into the car, and with a wave, walked briskly back to the house. Looking in at the door, he saw me sitting beside the fire, and greeted me cheerfully.

38

"Miss Godwin! You've apparently had a miraculous recovery; you're positively radiant this morning."

"Thanks. I should be–I spent ten comatose hours in a most excellent bed." I gestured to the coffee tray at my side. "Will you join me?"

"With pleasure. I'll steal the time." He pulled a chair up to the fire. "Have you been to Yorkshire before, Miss Godwin?"

"Never, I'm sorry to say. But I've dreamed of it for years. I'm a Brontë addict, and I've been steeped in it, literarily speaking, since childhood."

"There's so much for you to see. The Brontë parsonage, of course, and Sterne's house, and the abbeys and villages. But I'm afraid this isn't the most hospitable time of year. I'm trying to recall your letter; aren't you planning an indefinite stay?"

"Yes. I'm a teacher, but I've taken leave for the rest of the year. And I don't really want to travel extensively. I'd like to get a good rest and just get to know one part of England. I've always wanted to see the spring here... and I don't want to miss the new lambs."

"Ah. In Yorkshire, they're hard to miss, especially with an automobile." He grinned wryly. "But yes, the spring is indeed glorious, when and if it arrives."

His brilliant blue glance held a sharp, almost wary intelligence that formed a counterpoint to his open good cheer. For a moment I felt a nudge of recognition, but it was gone before I could grasp it.

"Do you think you might be here that long?" he continued. No doubt he was wondering how a schoolteacher could afford the tariff for an extended stay.

I'd already made my decision. "Yes, definitely, if you can put me up. I've been longing to do this for years, and now that I've survived the trip, I mean to make the most of it."

"Good." He spoke with energy. "I only hope you

won't be annoyed by the all-too-audible carpentry." He gestured toward the rear of the house, from whence came the faint arhythmic sounds of multiple hammers. "It's mostly a matter of remodeling the bedrooms and putting in baths. Yours was finished last month. Thankfully, almost all the work on the public rooms is done. John–my cousin Sir John Denham–has planned for a long time to furnish the entire house with antiques from his London business. The pieces are coming in a few at a time, and we've been easing the Victoriana towards the attics. The final shipment of furniture and bibelots will be here in a few weeks, in time for the gala reopening in April. You might enjoy that."

The fire crackled comfortably, and a fugitive sunbeam struck a bowl of dark red carnations. The blossoms warmed into radiant life, then cooled as a cloud swept across the sun.

"I have a high tolerance for percussion." Oops, that was not smart. "And a gala opening," I hurried on, "that sounds like great fun! I'm going to need your advice on sightseeing, by the way," I continued. "I do want to see Haworth, of course, and Whitby, when it's warmer, and I want to walk and walk."

"As a matter of fact, I was going to suggest that you join us for a day trip next Monday. I'll be taking everyone in the house–only five, at that–to York early in the morning. We'll lunch in town, and dine on the way back. Home about nine. It would be a good introduction to Yorkshire."

"I'd love to, but... do you know," I laughed, "although I'm feeling positively reborn, I'm not sure I want to get into a moving vehicle again quite so soon. This stupid motion sickness seems to be worse since I had the flu." All true, but I also felt reluctant to commit myself for a whole day to the company of six people I didn't know.

"You're wise to decline, I'm sure. There'll be time enough for sight-seeing when the weather improves. Merrin will do your lunch that day. Oh–but Monday is her evening off and she'll be leaving at four–can you settle for some cold supper? You'll have to hold the fort unaided. You won't be nervous in the house by yourself?"

An abrupt pang of excitement hit me in the stomach. I would be alone in the house from four until nine.

Alone, with that beautiful instrument standing silent in the music room. I felt like a starving man who's been vouchsafed the prospect of a banquet.

I smiled at Robin, trying to keep the sudden wild joy out of my voice. "No, of course not. I'm used to living alone. And as for cold supper, after six months in a school cafeteria, it sounds like heaven to me."

There was a whisper of tires on gravel and the sound of a car door slamming. Cold air swept around the corner from the outer door, and as Robin got to his feet, Richard D'Annunzio strode into the room. He was evidently in a great hurry.

"Rob, if John gets back before I do, tell him that Marjorie is in charge at Hawthorns, will you? Oh, hello, Miss Godwin." The gracious smile never reached his eyes, which were clear and cold as lead crystal. "Feeling better this morning? Well, I'm off to Bruges. Take care."

He was gone. Robin murmured a brief apology and followed him out.

I rested my cheek on my hand, staring into the fire. Where was the mercurial enigma of last night? This business-suited man, with his chill gaze, seemed another person entirely.

A memory leapt out across the years. It had been one of the summer holidays I'd spent in Colorado with Mother and Daddy. On a solitary hike one day, I'd started climbing beside a slender, almost vertical waterfall which seemed to burst out of the intensely blue sky. The green bank was so steep and slippery that in the end I'd had to climb in the fall itself: a giant's stairway, its sunlit spray effervescing like good champagne.

As I struggled upward I held a vision of what it would

41

be like on top: a flower-starred meadow with the shallow crystalline stream singing across its bosom and tipping merrily over the edge to begin its breakneck journey down. Panting, I pulled myself over the last ledge and saw, with a sense of disorientation, that I was standing in a dark and cramped little canyon, filled with snow and blue ice. I was cold, all at once, the breeze chilling my wet jeans under the shadowing walls. I turned and made my way down with more haste than prudence, shivering in spite of the sun.

That had been the source of the brilliant, living stream: that heart of ice. Why had I thought of it, for the first time in years, when I looked into Richard D'Annunzio's unsmiling eyes?

I was aware of a movement at the door and glanced up blindly. Robin was standing there.

"Richard has a solo recital tonight." His voice was uninflected. He seemed to shake off his thoughts, and continued brightly, "You really should walk over to Hawthorns sometime. It's an old stone farmhouse across the fell; Richard's redoing it. No telephone or electricity laid on yet, though. That's why he has to deliver messages personally."

And who was Marjorie, I speculated. Marjorie who was "in charge." I visualized a willowy blonde set up in the ancient farmhouse. Would she willingly forgo electricity, and the telephone? Most certainly, for Richard's sake.

Wondering why that was an uncomfortable thought, I bade Robin good morning and set out for the beckoning hills.

≪ CHAPTER 5 ≫

Enter a gentleman.
William Shakespeare, King Lear

On my third day in Yorkshire Sir John Denham returned from the Continent. Robin had confirmed that he was seldom in residence, as his antiques business kept him in London and abroad. He kept a suite of rooms in the north wing, and spent what little time he could spare from work here at his family home.

It was a mild afternoon, the thin sunshine diffusing its light from an opalescent sky, and I was exploring the house and grounds. Today I particularly wanted to see the stables.

I'd been luxuriating in the leisure to nap, take short walks, read, and practice the piano–very carefully at first. Richard had said, on my arrival here, that Robin was a musician himself. I hadn't ventured to ask Robin about it, as he'd seemed to back away from the subject. Anyway, it suited me very well to retain the rôle of amateur pianist.

So I'd played a little Mendelssohn–fortunately, I remembered some of the Chants sans Paroles—and sight-read from the library of scores in the salon, slowing my tempos deliberately. How I longed for a Gottschalk piece to flaunt before Richard D'Annunzio, if he should happen to come into the house while I was playing! *The Banjo*, or, better still, *The Dying Poet*.

Postponing the visit to the stables, I entered the music room. I decided I might allow myself some Preludes and Fugues; surely every music student played Bach? Once warmed up with a few scales and octaves, I launched without

43

conscious decision into the Goldberg Variations, their intriguing complexities leading seductively from one section to the next. I thought with amusement of the French writer Colette's description of Bach's music as a heavenly sewing machine and laughed, exhilarated, at Bach's inexhaustible invention. The lines sang out with transparent purity in the quiet salon. For the hundredth time I breathed a silent prayer of thanks for Leon's perseverance in making me continue my piano studies. "Never neglect the piano, Lissa," he had admonished earnestly. "That is where the true music lies."

A cadence rang out decisively. What glory! On impulse I turned to the harpsichord. Why not? I'd had a few lessons one summer, enough to accustom me to the differences of touch. I hurried across to the other instrument, slid onto the bench, and started the Goldberg again, relishing the metallic clarity of the sound and the ease of playing the crossed-hand passages on two manuals.

I was halfway through the twenty-sixth variation when I noticed Robin standing at my side. I threw him a quick smile, including him in my joy, and suddenly it hit me. Oh, Lord, I'd done it this time. Caught up by the relentless energy of the music, and reveling in the technique that had never yet failed me, I was playing a Goldberg that would have passed muster in a concert hall. I was obviously incapable of maintaining any role other than that of chief dolt.

As if it were being performed by someone else, I heard the variation hurtle on to its conclusion. I turned to Robin, wondering what to say, and was startled by the white and strained look on his face.

"Oh... Robin!" I managed. "Are you all right?" I added idiotically, "Anything wrong in the kitchen?" and could have struck myself.

His mouth tensed fractionally, but he brought forth a wry grin. "Shipshape all around. No, I'm only a little tired. How very well you play, Miss Godwin. So you're a harpsichordist as well? I don't think Richard mentioned that."

"Oh, no; miles from it," I protested. "Six weeks of summer lessons; mere dabbling. But I love the sound. You're the genuine article, I hear. I wish you'd play for me." I rose from the bench.

"Someday, perhaps," he answered lightly. "I haven't had much time to practice of late. The kitchen, you know, and all that."

Again I cursed myself for my insensitivity. We left the room together, chatting brightly, but the incident left a curious little ache of regret and uncertainty. I knew I had hurt him, and blown a battleship-sized hole in my cover has well.

It didn't help that I perceived my masquerade more clearly and critically with every day that passed. I realized now that it was both childishly melodramatic and totally pointless; the product of a literally fevered imagination. In my brief time here I had seen no signs of Ciara save the harp, the portrait, and her white cat. There was none of her music in the salon; she'd probably kept most of her things in the London house. I knew for certain that she'd owned at least two other harps, but they were probably sold by now.

Nor could I feel the gently melancholy yet reassuring presence of a blood relation that I'd yearned for on my sickbed in Lynton. Now that I was actually here, I couldn't even begin to imagine Ciara's exotic glamour in these bucolic surroundings.

With a sigh, I turned through the doors under the stable clock and was immediately greeted by a soft whicker. There in a loose box piled with fresh straw stood a big and glossy chestnut hunter. "Oh, you beauty!" I whispered. I felt a wave of loneliness for my own Juniper, boarded with a neighbor for the duration of my trip. The gelding thrust his head over the stall door and I stroked his velvet nose. A deep, cultured voice spoke behind me.

"Are you fond of horses?"

I turned to see a tall, slightly heavy man of about fifty, his pleasant, handsome face framed by greying hair. His eyes widened a bit as he studied me. I forced a smile and replied, "Yes, very."

"You must be Miss Godwin. I believe that makes three Americans we have just now."

I laughed. "Is it that obvious, in only two words?"

"Of course not." His own smile was charming, though just a bit cautious. I could see a resemblance to Richard, yet this face was unmistakably English. "I should have said you're our only young lady, with the exception of Madame Bonnet, who's undeniably French and inextricably glued to that new husband of hers. I'm John Denham, Miss Godwin." He extended a large, well-manicured hand.

"I'm happy to meet you, Sir John," I responded with a cheer I was far from feeling. "And I'm so grateful to be here. I'm just getting over an illness, and Denham House is such a haven of quiet and beauty."

I was at a loss with this man who had, so recently, been Ciara's husband. Had she ever mentioned me? Or her sister and brother-in-law? I felt it unlikely; Ciara was not apt to talk about her American background, preferring to maintain the fiction of having spent most of her life in some unspecified but highly sophisticated spot on the Continent.

The silence lengthened, and I finished feebly. "Well... I'm feeling healed already."

He seemed to rally himself, and spoke with warmth. "Good! Good! Ah, Miss Godwin, you must see Yorkshire in the spring. Do you know, when I decided to turn this big, empty old place into a country hotel, I never dreamed what a pleasure it would be to share my part of England with the guests. I'm seldom here, but when I am, I enjoy seeing my own love of the country reflected in those who are here for the first time."

The wary curiosity had faded from his eyes, replaced by enthusiasm for his subject. He must have assumed that the resemblance was mere chance. I was wearing soft bangs and had my hair pulled back in its customary knot. Ciara, I knew, would never have confined her superb mass of black hair.

Determined to keep the conversation on the hotel and away from myself, I continued his theme. "How wonderful that you can have that pleasure. And it must be exciting, furnishing your marvelous house with antiques of the period. Are you doing a literal restoration?"

He laughed a bit dryly. "No, I'm afraid my tastes are more eclectic than that. And my purse smaller. Anyway, I doubt all twenty bedrooms were originally furnished to perfection, even in the house's heyday. Mostly we're just trying to move the Victorian pieces out. Are you interested in antique furniture, as well as horses?"

"Yes, I am," I replied. I must be careful not to get confused; just so much truth, but not too much. "It's in the blood, I guess. My mother kept a small antique shop in the summers; she was an art teacher." I wondered again whether Ciara had ever mentioned her sister. The evidence of my lies was there in my bone structure for all to see. In my guilt and agitation, so much more acute than I'd anticipated, I felt my face was as garish as Medusa's head dangling from Perseus' brawny young arm.

"Well," he remarked blandly, "you seem a young woman of many gifts. Robin tells me you play the piano, too."

"I do hope I haven't been a nuisance, Sir John. I met Dr. D'Annunzio on my first evening here and he was kind enough to say I might practice. I assure you I'll treat the Bösendorfer with the greatest respect!"

"Oh, my dear..." he made a gently dismissive gesture. "If Richard approves, I'm sure it's in good hands. He's always after me about how valuable it is. The fact is, I know less than nothing about music, although Richard of course is a great success, and Robin... well, he had his little career too."

47

He hesitated, his light blue eyes meeting mine. "I'm a terrible duffer, quite tone-deaf, can't sing the hymns at church, you know, without having prayer books hurled at me. And yet, it's strange: I've been surrounded by musicians all my life. My beloved stepmother was an opera singer, and my late wife was a musician as well. Quite a famous one. Her name was Ciara Rossi. That's her harp in the salon."

"Dr. D'Annunzio told me. I'm so sorry you've lost her." I was feeling worse and worse. I hated spinning a web of lies for this bluff, kindly man.

"Yes. Thank you, Miss Godwin." He glanced upward, squinting his eyes against the pearly sun, and drew a jagged breath. "It was a stupid, tragic accident. She'd just finished a concert, and she could never sleep afterward. Too wound up, I expect. So she went out in a boat; damn fool thing to do at night alone, but danger meant nothing to her. Well. That's that, you see."

He gave the chestnut an affectionate pat on the neck, and resolutely returned to his earlier subject.

"Odd, isn't it. I'm supposed to be something of an expert on antiques; paintings I know and love, and literature... but music." He shook his head. "Always a closed book to me. Now, tell me," he went on in an indulgent tone. "Do you ride? You're not one of those Western cowboy riders, are you, elbows all flapping?"

"Good heavens, no," I laughed. "My father and I were members of a riding club, and I've done some show jumping; nothing spectacular, though."

"Well, Miss Godwin, Fiametto isn't one of our hire horses, as a matter of fact he's my own old boy, but if you'd like to ride him, he needs the exercise. I'm here so seldom, and hardly have the time when I am. Robin's too busy, and he isn't an ardent horseman anyway. Then Richard, if he ever gets a moment, has his Niniane. But I'd like to see how you ride. Would you be offended if I vetted you?"

"Certainly not! In your place I'd do the same." The

prospect of getting my legs around a horse again had taken the edge off my worries. "I haven't any proper riding clothes or boots with me, but I can remedy that when I go to Harrogate. Would you like me to ride him now?"

Fifteen minutes later I was cantering the well-mannered Fiametto slowly around the ring, doing figure eights and lead changes and generally showing off my rather moth-eaten skills.

"Excellent, Miss Godwin. I see that Fiametto, like the Bösendorfer, is in safe hands. Ride him whenever you like. I'll tell the stable boy; he only comes in mornings and evenings through the winter. There's good terrain on the fells. Beware of rabbit holes, and of course, ice, when we have another snow; it seems clear enough now."

I was surprised and touched by his generosity. As he put away the tack and I rubbed Fiametto down, I thought again of how agonizingly embarrassed I would be if he were to discover my kinship with Ciara.

The evening was an embodiment of everyone's dream of a country house hotel. In the elegant dining room with its pale apricot walls, tangy sorrel soup and roasted fowl were followed by quince sorbet. Sir John joined us for coffee and brandy in front of the library fire, and regaled us charmingly with varied anecdotes of Yorkshire farmers and the international antiques trade. The Andersons, a fortyish couple from New Jersey, hung on his every word, while white-haired Miss Stanley from Uist listened with one ear, her needles clicking over an afghan of hideous green. And the honeymooning Bonnets, perched appropriately on a love seat, exchanged lingering glances of soulful significance.

But the brandy's sting reminded me too sharply of the night I arrived at Denham House and of Richard D'Annunzio, and murmuring something about an early bed, I soon slipped away and up the stairs to my room.

≈ CHAPTER 6 ≈

The past is never dead. It's not even past.
William Faullkner, Requiem for a Nun

I was stretched out on the rug in front of my bedroom fire, lamps out. Hishi lay squarely on my chest, purring his asthmatic purr. The little flames painted his white fur rosy on the hearth side; the shadows on the other side, away from the fire, turned it a cool blue.

I hadn't really felt like bed, or even a book, when it came down to it. My thoughts were in a turmoil after the encounter with Sir John.

What was I doing here? Given his easy warmth, why hadn't I identified myself as Ciara's niece? And how, above all, could I justify this harmless but shabby deception? The unwillingness to impose upon nominal kinship was valid enough. Nonetheless I'd longed to be honest with John Denham. Yet some unidentifiable feeling, something stronger than the fear of humiliation, had kept me to my original plan of anonymity.

I stirred restlessly. Hishi opened round eyes and gave his little inquiring chirp. No, there was no trace of Ciara here. So much for my chief motive in coming. Only the stunning portrait; the harp, whose presence was torture, forbidden to me as it was; and this benign beast on my chest. Well, I should have anticipated that. Ciara was too much the jet traveler, too much the international artist to settle anywhere, far less to immure herself in the remote countryside of Yorkshire.

And you could have been that, too. You were well on

the road.

Unwillingly I thought back, trying through the pain to remember when fear and doubt had first crept in.

From my debut recital at twelve, I had been what Leon called a joyous performer. I wasn't entirely without nervousness, but even that took the form of exuberant anticipation. I'd never doubted my technique; I knew it to be natural, comprehensive and formidable. Years of hard work, the work that was a joy in itself, had seen to that. And I had at last developed my own musical personality, cutting loose from slavish imitation of Ciara's every nuance. Leon's happiness with my artistic development was palpable.

Leon... surely I had never doubted myself when he was alive? He'd been striding down Fifth Avenue one winter day when his heart simply stopped. Though years had passed, the loss still left a small hole in my own heart. After his death, the changes in my playing must have been so insidious, so creeping, that I hadn't even been aware of them.

Then it had begun: promised engagements that failed to materialize; a cooling of professional relationships; and finally, unbelievably, actual cancellations.

Hurt and anger boiled up in me. I felt a sharp stab in my chest and rolled over. Hishi leapt for the hearth, viewed me with reproachful blue eyes, and started to wash.

I found I was trembling, reliving the molten fury of recognition that had swept over me under Richard's hands in that dark moment on the moor. It was an emotion that had nothing to do with his own irrational violence. This rage had been born five long years ago.

He was already well established. Triple-threat musicians were rare and generally rather spurious, but he was the genuine article: virtuoso pianist, respected composer, brilliant conductor. He was appearing in New York and, at Leon's behest, attended one of my chamber music recitals. To my surprise and gratification he came backstage, quick and lithe as a cat.

"Leon's been telling me what an extraordinary musician you are. You won the Israel competition, didn't you, and the Brussels as well? Your playing is wonderful, Lissa. Look, I'm directing the Mountbarrow Festival next summer, and I want to do an all-Debussy program." His accent was emphatically British. Though his mother was the Italian singer Gianna D'Annunzio, and he'd done much of his musical study in the U.S., his boyhood had been spent in England on his father's estate.

He continued, intense, obviously in a hurry. "Would you be interested in playing the *Danses Sacre et Profane* and the *Trio*?"

I was bubbling with excitement and triumph. "I'd love it! Oh, thank you..."

"All right. I'll be in touch. I can reach you through Leon? Plan on the first week in August, please. Two rehearsals." With a nod, he strode away.

"Lissa!" Joannie, the volatile, Brooklyn-born flautist in the just-performed Ravel work, was peering at me through her thick lenses. "My God, some people have all the luck. I'd drop dead in my tracks if he just turned his eyes in my direction. Can you believe he came to your recital? And you're going to play under him!"

"Lissa, you'd better watch this guy. He's big trouble."

This cheering remark came from Tim, who looked like a farm team recruit and played the cello like an angel incarnate. He tossed back straight blond hair, dropping into an execrable imitation of an English accent.

"'Leon has been telling me about your great gifts, my dear.'" He gave me a brooding look. "Seriously, Lissa, the man is the biggest womanizer since Franz Liszt. Did you say 'play under him,' Joannie?"

"Spot of envy, old top?" she grinned.

The shaft struck home, and Tim's fair complexion

reddened. He'd been dogging my footsteps since our last year in Philadelphia, exasperated to the limits of endurance by my determination to keep our relationship a casual friendship.

"Envy, hell!" he burst out. "It's not just his reputation with the women, Joannie. You know what Blumberg told me?" Egon Blumberg was Tim's long-time teacher and mentor.

"He knows the family, too. Says they're really crossed up. The father was English, some kind of a Lord or Baron or something, and the mother–well, you know, she sang at the Met. She's Italian and Lebanese, but an American citizen, and D'Annunzio has dual citizenship–"

"So where's the crime, Tim?" inquired Joannie, glancing at me in concern as she saw my euphoria fading. "Anyone who reads *Time* magazine can tell you all that."

Tim's mouth tightened. "Hang on, I'm coming to it. D'Annunzio dropped out of Juilliard midway through. No one knew why."

"Doesn't seem to have suffered. Maybe he'd learned enough!" interjected the irrepressible Joannie.

"May I please finish? Apparently he decided to serve his adopted country, ho ho. But not in any ordinary service, not our Richard. He's not an ordinary guy, don't you know. So he went into intelligence–worked in the Middle East. All the PR says he was a linguist, but actually he was what they call a covert operator. That means he did some other little jobs on the side, such as making people disappear."

"What people?" I asked skeptically.

"People who weren't so convenient for our government to have alive," Tim said in flat tones. "From what Blumberg says, he was just a high-class assassin."

We hooted with laughter.

Tim's face grew redder, and his voice went up a notch.

"For Christ's sake, do you know what they called him? What people who knew him back then still call him? Though

53

not to his face, you'd better believe. *'Le marchand de sable'*–the Sandman. Or, to paraphrase," he went on deliberately, "the merchant of dreams. Among a certain elite government group, as I understand it, 'Sandman' is a euphemism for hit man. You might as well say death merchant. Or, from what I've heard lately, merchant of drugs. Because when he'd had enough of the excitement, he did us all the favor of returning to music. Well, why not? Composer, conductor, pianist–what a cover. And in the meantime he'd learned things in the CIA that had to be useful to his family connections in Italy." He gave a short laugh. "Mafia, through his grandfather."

"The Sandman?" I said incredulously.

"The Sandman," repeated Tim coldly. "And he's got the drugs to bring the dreams."

Somehow that shocked us into momentary silence. Then Joannie spat out, "What a bunch of bullshit! Tim, you can't really believe that garbage." Her normal good nature had turned to ferocious mother-hen protectiveness. She fixed him with her streetwise glare. "Anyway, why are you trying to spoil Lissa's triumph, even if you do swallow that nonsense?"

She put her arm around me in a sympathetic hug.

I said, "Go back to your narc meeting, Tim," and immediately regretted it. I walked away, unbelieving, but with my elation sadly diminished.

Then, in the next terrible week, Leon had died. He was only in his early sixties, and I'd never imagined myself without his guidance. When I'd recovered somewhat from the shock and loss I began working, half-heartedly at first, on the Debussy pieces. As the winter weeks passed, I began to wonder why I hadn't received a letter of confirmation from Richard D'Annunzio. Belatedly, I remembered that he'd planned to contact me through Leon, and sent a message to him via his agent.

In two weeks' time I had a polite reply that hit me like a blow in the chest. Another harpist had been engaged. He regretted that the plans were changed, apologized for the delay in notifying me, thanked me for my interest, and hoped, noncommittally, to hear me play again at some future date.

First doubt, then fear, flooded through the gap in my confidence that his rebuff had opened. I played, and played well, my remaining winter engagements, but things began to slow down for me. At first it seemed like mere bad luck. We all suffered disappointments, and broken promises were certainly not uncommon in the musician's world. But soon I thought I perceived a coolness, a lack of commitment from conductors and fellow artists. That perception grew from a nagging worry into a source of panic, and my playing grew more cautious, more sterile, with far less risk-taking.

I'd been scheduled to tour with Leon that spring, in Europe and South America. Of course that was off. Now I found many of my engagements for the coming fall were canceled as well. New doubts shouldered in. Had Leon been my Svengali? Was I indeed brilliantly accomplished? Could it be that I was too insecure to continue my career without his constant dynamic guidance? I had never been as aggressive as Ciara, and I was absolutely no good at selling myself. A worse thought struck me. Had the powerful Leon, blinded by his fondness for me, pushed me into bookings where I wasn't wanted? That hardly seemed possible; Leon was as clear-eyed about musical worth as any other musician of the first rank, and he had the respect of the greatest musicians of our time. But I was so shaken that I could believe anything.

Then the first physical signs appeared: dry throat, unsteady fingers, lack of concentration, and incredibly, that little jolt of the heart that in mid-performance says, "Dear God, what comes next?"

I went home at the end of the season, convinced that what I needed was rest, Mother and Daddy, horses, the smell of clover and the sound of a stream. I played a benefit that summer, an important one, and for the first time in my life had an actual memory lapse in performance. I covered; I don't think anyone realized, but I felt ill for days afterward. I stopped writing to Ciara, stopped sending her my programs and reviews. Indeed, there weren't that many to send. How could I face her from my welter of failures, when she was going from triumph to infallible triumph?

I was trying to think how to tell my parents I wouldn't be returning to New York in the fall when they left to visit an old Yale classmate of Daddy's in Maine. The delay was a relief to me. I was an only child, and they'd always been so proud of their daughter. Daddy had been raised in a church-run orphanage on precepts of hard work and self-determination. He was one of their successes, and had served on their board as far back as I could remember. My own success was a source of fierce pride to him.

There were only the three of us. Mother's father had been killed in Korea, and her own mother had died years ago, a victim of the smoking that had been so much a part of her era. I'd always missed the grandparenting that many of my friends enjoyed. Yes, there was Ciara, but she moved in a different world, and didn't visit what she jokingly referred to as "the sticks." It was a little like being related to a movie star, remote and unimaginably glamorous, though she had taken such a benevolent and helpful interest in my early career.

When the helicopter crashed in a fog near Mt. Desert, killing both my parents and their host, the rushing free-fall of my life slammed to a black conclusion. My dreams were shattered, and everyone I loved was gone. Only Ciara was left, and I hadn't seen her for four years, not since she'd moved to London. She wrote a warmly sympathetic letter, regretting that she couldn't come to the funeral. I wasn't surprised; she and Mother had been too far apart in age to be really close, even if their lives hadn't taken such different directions.

Daddy's lawyers were kindly reassuring, not knowing

that their words meant nothing to me. My bright and delightful father had commuted to the New York Stock Exchange for the past twenty-odd years. There would always be ample money, it seemed, money I had little use for with the two of them lying under the laurels in the shady churchyard.

There followed a fall and winter that I'd rather forget. I spent it in the empty Greek Revival house among the maples on the hill, unable to go through Mother's and Daddy's things, unable to practice; unable, it seemed, to do much besides sit immobile in a chair before the fire. I couldn't bear to look at the brilliant autumn colors, which had always been so exhilarating to me. This year they looked garish, tasteless; hysterical, even. I was glad when snow settled over the village and I no longer had to force myself to go out.

Other than Janina, our Polish housekeeper, I saw almost no one. My parents' friends were kind and sympathetic, but I didn't know any of them well enough to feel intimacy. Except for holidays, I'd lived away from home since I was fifteen, and had no friends of my own age in our tiny village; they'd all migrated to cities long ago. Under Leon's benign but totally dominant tutelage, my romantic life had been confined to a few dates at school, Tim's puppy-like devotion, and an ardent, painful affair with a tenor which ended when I finally realized that the magnificence of his singing had nothing to do with his imperious but ultimately petty character. Putting a finish to it had left me feeling relieved but faintly debased. Leon never knew. My awe of him and his plans for me made me feel, perhaps wrongly, that he wouldn't have approved of any relationship until I was firmly established.

At last spring came, late and wan, permeated with the smell, so newly exacerbating to me, of things sprouting from the cold wet earth. A whole year had passed since my life started to fall apart. I began going out to church. I even started practicing, simply because it was what I'd always done, and my only emotional outlet. I managed to block the work off completely from any thought of performance. I gardened a bit, and rode my beloved Juniper.

Almost unconsciously, I let my hair grow out to its natural chestnut brown. I dined sometimes with my parents' friends, who after the first awkward inquiries tactfully avoided all mention of my career, and I even went once to the Boston Museum, though I stayed away from New York and turned carefully past the music reviews in the Times. I made no attempt at all to contact my former musical classmates and colleagues.

In October of the following year, I had a telephone call from Mrs. Nichols, superintendent of the school system in which my mother had taught art. Turnerville Elementary, five miles across the pine and maple clad hills, had lost its music teacher to a young oil company executive. Having presented her with a diamond that was, according to Mrs. Nichols, knocking eyes out in the faculty lounge, he now planned to spirit her off to Saudi Arabia. Could I fill in?

"Oh, dear, Julia," I replied absently, with an eye on the grape jelly simmering on the stove, "I don't think so. I've never worked with children, or even baby-sat. And my degrees are in performance, anyway; I haven't had a single hour of music education classes. It probably wouldn't even be legal."

"But Felicity." The precise Boston accent compelled me to attention, and I laid down the spoon. "We're in a desperate situation. Such a hard time of year to find anyone. Besides, you're so kind and gentle, the children would love you. If you'll help us, I'm sure we can arrange for an emergency certificate. Please, dear?"

The "filling in" had stretched out to two years and five months, with summer courses to remedy my "deficiencies." Although I was certain that God had never cut me out to be an elementary school music teacher, I found myself far less depressed when I had to measure up to responsibility.

So I presided at a surprisingly good piano in the brown brick schoolhouse near the river. I loved the children, hated the work, except at rare moments. I would have relished taking all those little people on a picnic, teaching them to knit or ride. But though their wide-eyed eagerness and unintentional humour entranced me, I was bored to desperation by the necessarily limited nature of the music and the repetitious character of the classes.

Twice a year, before Christmas and in the spring, I brought my harp to school in the back of Daddy's old station wagon and played for an assembly. To the children it was magical, and one couldn't be panicked about playing for an elementary school.

But in the spring of the year just past, my own quiet resignation and undiminished passivity had begun to scare me. I was becoming a different person; it was like being on Valium without taking the pills. I'd made no attempt to travel out of New England or seek new friends. The teachers I saw daily in the faculty lounge, mostly young married women, were all good people, but we had no common ground. As far as I was concerned they might have come from a different planet. They seemed seriously absorbed in their conversations about shopping, housekeeping, and television shows.

As the months passed I realized how far my intensive training, discipline, and single-minded aspiration had distanced me from "reality."

Feeling that I was living in a trance, I retreated into even longer hours of practice at the harp and piano, starting after an early supper on school days and often continuing past midnight. The weekends were spent in the same way. For whatever reason, I forced myself on, aiming at the superlative virtuoso level of Leon's playing. I ordered and learned ridiculous amounts of new music, always wondering, with some bitterness, why I was doing it.

59

With a wrenching effort, I even made myself reserve a ticket for a performance in New York–the premiere of Richard D'Annunzio's *Faustus*. I will never know through what twisted impulse I subjected myself to that baptism by fire. I checked in at the Plaza, coiled my brown hair up into a knot and feathered some bangs to conceal my widow's peak–Ciara's widow's peak. There were still those in New York who remembered me as I was in pre-transformation days. I prayed that I wouldn't see anyone who recognized me, and of course I didn't.

I sat through the spectacular performance, mesmerized by the force of the music, stunned by the grief for my lost career, and under it all feeling a curious kind of pity for the composer who could weave mere notes into such stabbing expressions of terror and anguish.

When it was over I checked out of the hotel and caught the late train back to Connecticut, canceling my city plans for the following day. And on the way home, on the lurching train, I'd had my first attack of motion sickness since childhood.

Hishi was kneading my back with velvet paws, and the embers were burning low. As I rose to slip between the sheets, I wondered why my memories, whether they began in New York, Colorado, or Connecticut, always seemed to finish with the unfathomable man who had triggered the downfall of my career.

≈ CHAPTER 7 ≈

It is yonder, out yonder, the fly-away horse
speeds ever and ever away.
Eugene Field, The Fly-Away Horse

Friday dawned bright and warmer, and I rose early, longing for a canter across the fells. I'd just have to make do with sneakers and jeans; anyway, there was no one to see or care.

When I reached the stables I saw a sleek grey hunter standing in the yard. I spoke to her, stroked her nose, and reached in my pocket for the tack room key that Robin had given me. But the door was open, and there in the mote-filled rays of the morning sun stood Richard D'Annunzio, booted and jodphured, wearing a dark jersey and a leather jacket. He looked up casually as I entered the room.

"Going for a ride?" he asked, with a doubtful look at my shoes.

I flushed. I was fully aware of the snobbery of the experienced rider, having indulged it myself in my teens.

"Sir John gave me permission–" I began, and stopped short. Why did I have to justify myself to this man? "Yes," I said decisively, and bit my lip in annoyance at his amused smile.

So I went on the offensive. "Stealing tack?"

"Not just precisely, though you're close. Let's call it borrowing." He was sorting through a box of leather pieces. "I want a lip-strap; mine's split. Ah, here we are. Are you enjoying your holiday from school teaching, Miss Godwin?"

Would he never stop his blasted patronizing?

Grudgingly, I remembered I'd set myself up for it. It was, after all, the sum of his knowledge about me.

"Oh, yes," I said in dulcet tones. "But I do miss the children so."

"I'm sure you do," he rejoined equably. "Though perhaps your piano practice will take your mind away from that. Robin said he heard you play some quite good Mendelssohn–The Spinning Wheel, I think it was."

I turned quickly and began to search for a saddle.

"May I hope that one day you'll let me hear your Gottschalk?" continued the pleasant voice.

I picked up the nearest saddle and started blindly for the door.

"No, no–you have the Miller. Fiametto goes with the Gieffert. And you'll want the egg-butt snaffle. Here, allow me."

Concealing the urge to strangle him under what I hoped was a grateful smile, I followed him to Fiametto's loose box. He thoughtfully handed me a brush, and swung himself up easily to sit on the stall door as I began to work on the chestnut's glossy coat.

Damn it, I thought. With him watching me I'm not even sure I know how to groom a horse.

"Don't let me keep you, Dr. D'Annunzio," I murmured with polite concern. "You're losing the best part of the day; it always seems to cloud up later in the morning. And you must be very busy," I added hopefully.

"Not at all," was the lazy reply. "Now that Bruges is done, I have all of today and most of tomorrow before I set off again."

"Where this time?" I asked, fascinated in spite of myself.

"Milan. I studied for a while at the Giuseppe Verdi Conservatory, so it's a homecoming in a way." The banter came back into his voice. "And I practiced diligently before I left Bruges, so I'm awarding myself the whole morning."

I settled the saddle onto Fiametto's gleaming back, buckled up the girth, unfastened his halter, and slipped the snaffle into his soft, willing mouth. "You are a love," I whispered.

"John tells me you've ridden in competition."

I laughed. "That's stretching it a bit. The usual teenage routine: lessons, local shows, a little jumping. I must get some proper boots," I finished, self-conscious again.

"There's no one on the fells to care, I assure you," he said.

I led Fiametto out into the courtyard, Richard following. The wind gusted viciously and I smoothed my bangs into place.

"Miss Godwin." He was serious now, and faced me with a sort of dogged resolution. I felt a twist of apprehension. "There's something I need to say. I still owe you an explanation for my behavior the night we met. And–"

"No!" Panic swept over me in a hot flood. "I–I don't want to talk about it. Please. You don't have to explain. Believe me," I lied, "I haven't given it another thought."

I'll have to leave here at once, I thought, in a frenzy of embarrassment and fear, before he exposes me for the fool I am. I saw with painful clarity that my whole plan could have come straight out of a supermarket pulp romance.

"Well, I have, many times," he rejoined, taking my arm in a gentle grasp. "And I think we should–"

"Take your hands off me!" I echoed my former words to him in a high, hysterical voice that shocked me. "I've told you I don't want to hear about it!" I vaulted into the saddle and set the startled Fiametto into a canter along the path that led up the moor.

"Damn Richard! Damn Richard! Damn Richard!" I muttered to the triple rhythm of Fiametto's hooves, as we moved handily up the smooth slope. I was furious to find my hands shaking on the reins. "Good boy," I said tardily, and patted the gentlemanly gelding's neck. When I realized that

Richard wasn't following us, I eased Fiametto into a walk. Now what?

I'd lost all my tentatively held poise. Could I hope he'd think it was only emotional reaction to the memory of that frightening night?

But he wouldn't let it drop. He'd seemed so grave, so determined. I must certainly leave here tomorrow–so much for my Yorkshire idyll. Well, I had only my own blindly romantic self to blame. The sentimental search for Ciara had yielded nothing, anyway. Yes, I'd leave tomorrow. But wait: he was going to Milan tomorrow night; if I lay low tonight and in the morning, surely I could give myself one or two more days in this heavenly place before getting back on the hated airplane. It never occurred to me, at that moment, that there were other places in England where I could resume my holiday.

I would hire a car and drive myself to Leeds. I was leery of the right-hand drive in heavy traffic, but the bus held painful memories of my arrival as well as the prospect of an early start on nausea. I'd go in two days, or perhaps three; I'd try to find out from Robin when Richard would be returning.

We were at the top of the fell, its level golden length beckoning. Fiametto, fresh from the confinement of the stable, was fretting at the bit.

"All right, horse," I sighed. "I know you want to run. I do, too." My pent-up tensions were crying for release into reckless physical action. I stroked the satiny neck and signaled a canter. We warmed up for the length of the fell, turning back in a wide arc. The wind whistled by as we stretched into a gallop, and a sort of wild ecstasy took hold of me. I leaned forward a little and Fiametto surged forward at full speed. There was a blur of blue sky and russet grass; the motion of the horse felt as exhilarating as playing Bach. Then the world turned upside down and I was hurtling to the side, with just time to think "Dear God, no!" before I landed with a sickening jolt in a patch of heather.

I lay there, stunned and fighting for breath. At last I managed a sitting position and took stock of my injuries. My back hurt, my lip was cut and bleeding, and my right cheek very tender; I'd rolled against a rock when I landed. Hands, arms, and legs, thank God, were undamaged except for some scrapes. Slowly and painfully I got to my feet, feeling ninety years old.

Fiametto, the saddle hanging under his belly, was placidly cropping the dry grass a few yards away. What on earth... surely the leather girth hadn't given way. With a mild curse for my aching back, I hobbled over to the big hunter and removed the saddle. There was the culprit: a broken off-side billet strap. That was why I'd fallen to the left. Well, it happened sometimes; the saddle wasn't new, and in my anxiety to get away from Richard I'd omitted to check it over. Oddly, the leather didn't look cracked or worn. But it was common enough. I'd broken reins and girths straps before.

Then I saw what I'd missed in my dazed state. Like all English saddles, it had three billet straps on either side, only two of which were used at a given time for buckling on the girth. This was so the third could be used as backup in case of breakage, which was not infrequent in the field during a jump, or if a strap had not been properly cared for and the leather cracked. The two on the mounting side were fastened, as I'd seen to when saddling Fiametto. But on the off-side, which was usually left buckled except for cleaning, and where one wasn't as likely to check, only one strap–the one now broken–had been secured. That meant that all the stress had been on the weak strap, and the two other straps, lying innocently near the broken one, had been left deliberately unbuckled.

I set the saddle behind Fiametto's withers and moved slowly to the off-side, every bone and muscle protesting. There were still two perfectly good straps for fastening the girth, and the ones on the near side were intact. As I did up the buckles I wondered why the word "deliberately" had sprung to mind. That was ridiculous, of course; mere reaction to pain and shock. Very likely whoever last cleaned the tack had simply been interrupted in the task of replacing the girth and had omitted to fasten the off-side buckle.

But no–that wouldn't do. This was the saddle I'd used the past afternoon–wasn't it? And surely it hadn't been cleaned since, unless Sir John had sent someone to do it after our meeting. I felt and sniffed the leather but could detect no fresh scent of saddle soap or oil. Yet there was the faintest whiff of some odor that stirred recollection. It lurked in a corner of my brain, but when I tried to grasp it, skittered away like a bead of mercury.

I shook my head impatiently. I couldn't pin it down. Anyway, I was beginning to ache too much to think about it now, or even to care very much. With a painful effort I hauled myself into the saddle and we started our slow journey down to the stable.

Robin was at his desk when I limped in, and he sprang to his feet, full of alarm at my battered appearance. He helped me up the stairs, eliciting an account of the accident with short, anxious queries. With gentle care he settled me onto the bed and rang for Merrin, crackling with indignation that someone would have been careless enough to leave the girth unbuckled. I insisted it was my own fault; I'd certainly had better training than to omit a final check of the tack. Assured that I wasn't seriously injured and dissuaded at last from calling a doctor, he went away to supervise dinner and create a tray of delectable food for me.

It was no hardship to stay out of sight that evening, though it was totally unnecessary; Richard didn't appear at Denham House. I was more shaken and bruised than I'd realized, and grateful to have my dinner in bed and hide out until I knew he was on his way to Milan.

Late the next morning Sir John tapped at my door, full of concern. I was sitting in a chair by the window with a book, the wan winter sunshine playing across its pages and lightening the subtle colors of the rug. He exclaimed in consternation at the sight of my bruised cheek, and it was with difficulty I convinced him no harm was done.

I begged that the incident wouldn't prompt him to prohibit my riding, as it was due simply to my oversight in checking the tack. We made a few jokes about insurance and he was laughing as he took his leave, adding that he'd be in Paris until Tuesday, and looked forward to seeing me on his return.

Knowing I'd be gone, I bade him a farewell he may have thought inappropriate in its warmth. But his kindness and approachability had been such a comfort to me that I found myself wishing he were my own blood kin.

When the door closed behind him, I lay back in my chair and stared at the ceiling. I must–really must–make plans for getting away from here. Perhaps I'd stay in London for a while. Then I remembered: day after tomorrow was Monday. As I started to prickle with the anticipation of getting my hands on that beautiful harp while everyone was in York, all other thoughts receded from my mind.

≈ CHAPTER 8 ≈

Strange power, I know not what thou art —
murderer or mistress of my heart.
To Memory, Mary Elizabeth Coleridge

I stood at the open door of the front hall, waving at Merrin as she biked down the drive in the waning afternoon light. Robin, with the Andersons, the Bonnets and Miss Stanley in tow, had left early in the morning, and the day seemed to stretch out to eternity.

Returning to the drawing room, I dropped into a wing chair with a sigh, savoring my freedom. The years alone in my own home had accustomed me to solitude. To be in this beautiful house by myself, with the pale declining sun laying its long rays across polished floors, the fragrance of hothouse flowers scenting the room, was a joy indeed.

The thought of leaving was a physical pain.

Soon after the departure of Robin with his group, I'd called and reserved a car. I would invent some emergency in the morning and be on my way. I'd be safely out of this humiliating tangle of my own devising, with no one the wiser. And I would never have to see Richard D'Annunzio again. Another sigh, this one of resignation, escaped me. I'd hoped to stay a month or two in this wonderful place. Well, *che sera, sera,* as Marlowe had Faustus say.

Of course, I thought sardonically, he had also uttered the words *"Homo, fuge!"*. ...."Flee, oh man!"

My thoughts moved, as if magnetized, to the harp, and I made myself finish my coffee, postponing the walk down the long hall as one pauses for a last savoring moment before meeting a lover.

Putting my cup down, I rose from the chair and approached the salon with steps that hastened in spite of myself. Merrin gone, Robin and the guests gone. Sir John in Paris. Richard D'Annunzio safely out of the way, thank God, in Milan. Only Hishi to hear me, wherever in this spacious house he might be. He had slept with me again last night, curling warm and confiding against my neck.

I pushed open the right half of the salon door, flipped a switch, and the chandelier sprang into glowing life. Ciara smiled brilliantly at me from her golden frame.

Slipping the tuning key from its slot on the belly of the harp, I sounded the C flat. It was amazingly close, considering that it couldn't have been tuned in the last six months.

Of course the humidity, like the acoustics, was probably perfect in this jewel of a salon. Slowly I went over the strings, pulling up the octaves, checking the fifths, and silently thanking God for the gift of perfect pitch. When the harp was tempered to my satisfaction I sat on the bench and tilted the great Rococo instrument back. It settled sweetly onto my shoulder and I felt a pang of expectation. Gently now... not because I feared a listener–the house was echoingly empty–but because my fingertips had softened from disuse through the weeks of flu. So, something really easy at first. Irish harpers' songs? The haunting, poignant strains of "*My Thousand Times Beloved*" pierced the air. The sound of the concert harp in the lovely room was glorious; even these simple chords seemed to expand and fill the space, shimmering in the air. I stopped and pulled up a flat F string. Growing bolder, I launched into the first movement of the Handel B Flat Concerto. I was thoroughly sick of it after so many performances in student days, but it was a good warmup. I was a little creaky, but it was coming–it was coming. A trill scintillated with indisputable clarity and I smiled: yes, I was warming up!

After a while I realized that I was playing almost in the dark. When the sun dropped behind the moors the light went quickly; it was like my house in the Connecticut hills. The chandelier gave little illumination in the great room. Setting the harp erect on the floor, I drew the brocaded curtains and switched on the lamps. The mantel clock showed me that I had at least three more hours of safety. Still... better not to push it. Anyway, my fingers were beginning to sting ominously. But this would be my only chance to play until I was settled back in Lynton, and I was starved for it–greedy, ravenous.

Somehow, as I ran my hand lovingly over the gilded scrolls painted on the soundboard, I never thought about its being Ciara's harp. It was, at that moment, simply the gateway to all fulfillment and delight.

I lost myself in the Hindemith Sonata, the Ravel *Introduction et Allegro*, the Villa-Lobos Concerto. Thoroughly warmed up, I tore into my favorite, the Reinecke Concerto, the best German Romanticism the repertoire had to offer. A quick check of the clock told me I had time for just one more: a piece by Tournier that I'd worked on before my illness, harboring vague, disquieting thoughts of playing it with a local string quartet for a library benefit. So far had I fallen: stage fright over a library benefit! The piece was called *Féerie*–Fairyland–and was hardly a profound work. Compared to the Reineke Concerto, it presented no emotional or technical challenge. Yet it was great fun to play, and a far cry from the usual insipid musical characterization of the subject. There was something dark and urgent about the ending of this work, I mused, as I played the quiet opening passages. Soon I was launched into the pyrotechnics of a thousand tiny descending wings. Thank God, the technique was still there, in spades! Then the waltz in a minor key, building into a bacchanalian frenzy.

I forgot Ciara, forgot fear and self-doubt, even forgot Richard, as I careered toward the end, the passages pearling fluidly out from under my fingers, my senses on fire with exultation. The final clashing chords rang out in an insistent pagan cry.

I let the harp drop back to its standing position, steadied it, and closing my eyes, leaned my cheek against the cool, satiny wood. I felt hot to the point of fever, and my fingertips burned as if I'd been playing with coals. But I was myself again. For this one moment, I was Leon's own Lissa.

Tired and contented, I opened my eyes, tilted my head, and glanced at the clock. Eight-fifteen. Its ticking was silvery and impersonal in the wake of the harp's tempestuous voice.

Then breath was driven from my body. At the periphery of vision something shocked my heart with a sickening jolt. I turned, blood singing in my ears, and stared in paralyzed disbelief at Richard D'Annunzio.

He sat in a Queen Anne chair near the Bösendorfer, very still in his black suit, the dark face carefully expressionless above a white shirt.

"Tournier, isn't it?" he asked softly. "The *Féerie*, I believe. I've heard Ciara perform it." This with a nod toward the portrait. "You play it rather better than she did. Not as flamboyantly, perhaps, but you actually make music of a fairly lightweight piece. It's fathoms deeper, and several shades darker. I wonder why?" he ended, gbetting to his feet. He moved noiselessly across the Aubusson. Tim's words of long ago flashed into my mind. *Le marchand de sable*, I thought blankly.

He bent over me and lifted my left hand from the soundboard. A moment ago it had been so strong, with tendons of flexible steel. Now it felt boneless. He turned it palm up, and gently touched the tingling fingertips.

"Painful?" he queried, lifting an eyebrow. "A beginner needs to practice more cautiously, so as not to get burned. But of course, someone who learns instruments with such astonishing facility could hardly be expected to follow the rules."

His mildly sarcastic tone released a rush of fury, wrenching me out of my paralysis as good honest anger always will. I snatched my fingers away from his grasp.

"You can stop playing cat and mouse now, Dr. D'Annunzio," I snapped. "You know very well that I'm a professional harpist, or was, and probably who I am, and what a ridiculous deceit I've been practicing on you and your brother to boot."

"To answer you in order: kindly remember that I'm not the one who began this cat and mouse game. Yes, I know you're a harpist–a harpist without peer, I should say. And you may have deceived my brother, but not me–or at least not for long."

I turned to face him fully, assuming a defiant look, while I clamped my knees together to stop their knocking. He gave a short exclamation. "What–? What happened? You're bruised, Lissa."

It had been years since anyone called me that. A cruel hand squeezed my heart.

"I had a fall, riding," I muttered. "The day you left," I added accusingly.

"A fall–from old Fiametto? And you an expert rider?"

Then it was true, I thought with surprise. People actually did grind their teeth.

I disengaged mine and replied, "I forgot to buckle one of the billet straps." Let him think me incompetent in this as well, I raged. That is, if he didn't do it himself.

The thought struck me into silence. This man, with his towering musical reputation, his almost daily triumphs– would he be capable of such petty, pointless malice?

"And you're all right, otherwise? Well, now that you've blown your so very thin cover, my dear, shall we go somewhere and sort things out? Robin's batch will be back soon, you know, and I assume you don't want to be found sitting on Ciara's harp bench."

The Aston glided to a stop on the brow of a hill north of Denham House. Richard doused the lights and the untrafficked road was swallowed up in blackness. He left the quiet motor running and the heater on.

I hadn't opened my mouth since we left the salon. Nor had it occurred to me to refuse when he escorted me to the car; I'd only paused, mutely, to grab a jacket from the hall closet.

"I should have tumbled to it at once, of course," he began quietly. "The resemblance is extraordinary: the strongest I've ever encountered, far too strong for chance. And at first I thought you *were* Ciara."

A fleeting image flashed on my mental screen: that odd glimpse of fear I'd seen at our first encounter.

"You seem so very different from that girl I'd met in New York. Your hair is darker now, and–"

"And I'm older," I cut in bitterly.

"Younger, I should almost have said. More vulnerable now than then."

"Less confident?" I asked in a brittle voice.

"Perhaps. But my dear girl, why on earth didn't you let us know you were Ciara's niece? She and I had our outs, God knows, but John would have welcomed you. For all his sophisticated exterior, he's a good and simple man."

"I know that," I rejoined wretchedly. "And I have no excuse. I was alone, ill... I wanted to be where Ciara had been. It was my last family tie." I stopped short at the self-pity in my voice. "I have no real relationship to your brother. He probably doesn't even know of my existence. I didn't want to impose myself on a distinguished man who happened to have been married to my dead aunt, that's all."

"Lissa, you didn't come here with the idea that there was something wrong about Ciara's death, did you?"

"Of course not! I'm not such a fool as that. A stupid, tragic accident, that's what your brother called it."

"There are those who wouldn't agree it was tragic, I'm

73

afraid. No," he went on as I turned to him in anger. "I'm sorry. But Lissa... Felicity. I don't want to revive old hurts, but what really happened in New York? You were the rising star, flaming along like a comet, and then–"

"Surely you of all people don't have to ask," I broke in flatly. "You were the first to see it. I wasn't able to continue without Leon. It was as simple as that."

"Rubbish." He spoke rudely. "No one ever doubted your gifts. But I heard you'd had an emotional breakdown. Was that it?"

All at once I was very tired. My bones still ached from the fall, and my fingers were smarting furiously. "Oh, God, I don't know. Yes, I suppose so. When Mother and Daddy died, I guess I really cracked. But no, you mean the playing. That started before..."

"And yet you were performing brilliantly when I heard you."

"Well, I was at the top of my form. Leon's death set me back. But..." Abruptly I was angry again. Why was I humiliating myself, telling Richard these lacerating things? Restraint flew out the window. What if he was one of the foremost musicians of his time? I didn't give a damn if he was the Grand Panjandrum.

"Look," I ground out in exasperation. "What's the point of all this? You know exactly how and when it started. Yours was the first cancellation, and the others were quick to follow; I don't suppose you lost any time in getting the word around. How do you think it feels, anyway, having booking after booking fall through when you know you're playing your best? When you're staring at an empty schedule without knowing why? And anyhow," I finished with staggering inconsequence, "you're supposed to be in Milan."

"The concert was last night," he said absently, and fell silent. After a moment he turned to me. "Lissa..." In the dim starlight I could sense, rather than see, his look of consternation. There was real compassion and bewilderment in his voice, and I hated it.

"Ciara said you'd had serious memory lapses, breakdowns, pretty consistently all winter. You couldn't have been unaware of it."

"All winter? In the late spring, you mean, and it was never an actual breakdown. Besides, what in blazes did Ciara know about it? She was on the Continent."

"But she said she'd heard..." He trailed off. "Wait. Felicity, are you telling me that your failure of nerve started *after* I called off the Debussy performance?"

"Of course. If that's what you want to call it." I was, quite unfairly, incensed by the name he'd put to it.

He sat motionless for a moment. "I see. I should have figured that one out, too. My God, I seem to be suffering from atrophy of the brain." His voice was level in the darkness.

"Felicity, Ciara wrote me a warning letter, a very regretful one. She said you'd burned out; that you'd been pushed too hard and too fast, that your playing had become erratic and undependable. She blamed herself for having a hand in it, for creating an image you couldn't live up to. You must see that I thought I simply couldn't risk it."

"You're lying!" I cried. "I told you I was playing my best. Besides, Ciara would never do that. She was my aunt, and she loved me. She encouraged me from the very beginning!"

"Yes," he said thoughtfully, "until your star grew a bit too bright. You don't know what a real cat and mouse game is, Lissa. It wouldn't have been the first time she'd undermined a career, you know. In your case, because of your extreme closeness to Leon and her fear of his power, she had to wait until he wasn't there to protect you before she made her move. It must have rankled terribly."

"I won't listen to this. And I would have heard if anything like that was going on. There was never the least rumor!"

"You would have heard? From whom? Think, Felicity. Everyone knew she was your aunt."

Yes, she was my aunt. The warm smile of the portrait, so like my mother's, swam up before my eyes.

"Please, I want to go back to the house."

"Lissa..."

"Please!"

"All right."

We were silent on the short drive back. Made vulnerable by my joy in playing, I was newly overwhelmed by grief for my lost career, and totally at sea about Ciara. I was glad that darkness hid the tears pricking at my eyes.

He pulled the car to a stop before the door.

"I suppose your brother will be back tomorrow," I said, looking straight ahead. "I'm sorry to add to his pain, but I think I'd better tell him. Before," I added pointedly, "he hears it from someone else. He's bound to sooner or later, and I don't think it's right to sneak away and leave it to come out afterward. Then I'll be on my way."

"You needn't, you know," he said with sudden gentleness. That broke my thread of control, and without another word I fled into the house, to a haunted bed and a sleepless night.

Sir John Denham's Bentley purred into the drive at about eleven the next morning. I'd been sitting in the drawing room, watching the window. Mercifully the other guests were off on a morning jaunt to a farm museum.

I knew it was selfish of me to assail his ears with my ridiculous tale the moment he arrived, but I simply couldn't stand any more of this nervous apprehension.

So I met the poor man on his own doorstep.

"Oh, Miss Godwin!" He smiled a bit abstractedly. "Enjoying the fine weather? Going out for a walk? All recovered from your bumps and bruises, I hope."

"Yes, thank you. Sir John, forgive me. I know you've

just arrived, but could you spare a moment? It's rather urgent."

"Of course, my dear. Something Robin can't handle? And please, call me John, everyone does, you know. Makes one feel less a national monument. Besides, when all the stagehands called Lord Olivier 'Larry,' what's my hope of keeping up the forms?"

"But your title is inherited," I said, distracted in spite of myself. "Surely that makes a difference."

"Not to me—Felicity, isn't it? Anyway, if you're staying into the spring, we'll save a lot of time by dispensing with the formalities."

He looked first into the library, where two workmen were refinishing the paneling. Turning, he took my arm and ushered me into the salon.

"That's what I wanted to speak to you about," I ventured. "You see, I'm not staying; as a matter of fact, I... I'm packed and leaving this afternoon."

He looked mildly puzzled, wondering, no doubt, why I was burdening him with such inconsequential news.

"I'm very sorry to hear it. I hope it's not because of your injuries. Not because of the construction noise, is it? I know it can be fierce at times. We should probably offer you a refund. Have you spoken to Robin?"

"Oh, no. No. It's not that. I'm perfectly well. And... and I love it here and don't mind the noise in the least. It's just that..." I realized that I was literally wringing my hands. Another cliché proving itself.

I gathered my nerve and plunged ahead.

"Sir John," I said as firmly as I could. "I've come here under false pretenses." How melodramatic it sounded! "I'm leaving to spare you and your family needless embarrassment."

Nonplussed, he looked at me askance, probably wondering whether I was a prostitute or a murderess.

I opened my mouth but the words wouldn't come. I

was standing under Ciara's portrait. In desperation I pulled the leather clip from my hair, letting it tumble around my shoulders, and pushed the bangs savagely back from my forehead. I stood dumbly, waiting for him to speak.

At last he did. "My God," he breathed slowly. "I see. Yes." The blood had left his ruddy face, turning it grey. "It troubled me when I first saw you; I thought I'd gone a bit mad. Then, when we talked together, I dismissed it as fancy—you were so different. But it's all there: the bone structure, the widow's peak... everything but the coloring." His brows drew together. "Who are you, then?"

The words reminded me of Richard's anguished question. Sir John had been Ciara's husband, yet he was far calmer than Richard had been. Well, it was broad daylight now, and he was cold sober.

"Sister? Not daughter, that's not possible. And your name's not Rossi. But perhaps it isn't really Godwin."

I laughed shortly. "Ciara's name wasn't Rossi either, until she had it legally changed from Clara Ross. Yes, my name really is Felicity Godwin, though I was known professionally as Lissa Leone. We do seem to fool around with our names, don't we? I'm a harpist too, Sir John. Ciara never mentioned me, or her sister Ellen?"

He shook his head slowly, like a man who's taken one punch too many. I forgot my own nervous despair in guilty concern for him.

"Sir John, I'm Ciara's niece. My mother was her sister, Ellen Ross, and my father was William Godwin. I am their only child. And," I added with sadness, "my parents were wonderful people, a teacher and a lawyer. There was no reason for her to keep silent about us."

"No, I'm sure there wasn't. She wasn't... communicative about her early days. But this secretiveness seems to run in the family. Why didn't you let us know who you are? I don't understand. Surely you didn't conceal your kinship because..." His brow puckered again. "My dear girl, don't tell me you suspected foul play in your aunt's death?"

This was the second mention of foul play. I shook my head. "I hardly understand it myself," I said, trying to keep my voice steady. "But I certainly didn't come with any intention of playing detective. Sir John, please forgive me. I was beside myself. I lost both parents a few years ago, and Ciara was the only family I had left, though I never had a chance to know her well. But she encouraged me to play, and gave me a wonderful start in my career. When I heard about her death it was as if the last link to my parents had broken. Then last month I was sick, and I think I went a little crazy from the loneliness. I felt I had to see the places where she'd lived and worked, here and in London, but I couldn't impose on a distinguished family of strangers on the strength of such a slender tie."

In that moment I shelved forever the idea of the Englishman as aloof and reserved. John Denham simply held his arms wide and said, "Oh, my dear," and I walked straight into them.

"Put away once and for all the notion that you're going anywhere," he was saying five minutes later, as I blew my nose on his handkerchief. "We'll cancel your car right now. No," he held up a hand to still my protest. "You may not have any family left, but my relatives aren't that thick on the ground, either. There's Richard and Peter and Robin, and Gianna, and two ancient aunts in Devonshire. That rounds out the tally."

I wondered fleetingly who Peter was. Another cousin?

"So we'll hear no more about my new-found niece leaving. You're the only young and pretty female relative I have, anyway, and I'm hanging right on to you."

The dear man actually seems delighted, I thought, as Richard had foreseen he would be. He would have called Robin in at once, but I reminded him that he was away with the other guests.

"Right, I'll find a way to mention it to him in the

79

course of the day. He'll be thrilled, so don't worry about its being awkward. And Richard?"

"Richard knows," I murmured. "He heard me practicing last night, and remembered that we'd once met in New York. We had a talk." What a bland way to describe that curiously disturbing interview. "Sir John, I do think you must be the kindest man I've ever known."

He laughed. "Tell that to my competitors in the antiques trade, and they'll buy you a one-way ticket to Bedlam. Ha!" He was struck by a new thought. "I've just remembered, you can't call your uncle Sir John. Anyway, it makes me sound like Falstaff, and I'm not that much of a Fat Knight–yet. Now let's make that call, and then I think we'd both be better for some very strong coffee."

≈ CHAPTER 9 ≈

Come, sit down on this sunny stone;
Tis wintry light o'er flowless moors;
But sit, for we are all alone,
And clear expand heaven's breathless shores.
Emily Bronte, Poem Thirty

I thought my nerves had survived the confrontation with John fairly well, but by mid afternoon I was still taut as a wire. He'd overwhelmed me with his gracious and apparently spontaneous warmth, but I was nagged by guilt and regret. He was surely the one who'd suffered most from the interview; it must have hurt dreadfully to have memories of Ciara revived.

In the end I acquiesced gratefully to his wish that I stay. I'd spoken truthfully–I loved it here and had no wish to leave and return to my empty house.

Nonetheless I was jittery and depressed. The idea of playing the harp, so seductive only yesterday, now seemed an impossible effort. I couldn't concentrate on a book, and unpacking took only a few minutes, so I decided at last to go out for a walk. Even handling the gentle Fiametto seemed too much of a challenge.

The sun was venturing tentatively through a canopy of grey and the winter afternoon was temperate, so I donned pants and turtleneck, pulled on a fisherman's sweater, and set out on the path behind the house, making for Marden Fell, one of the higher hills.

My mood was one of teeth-on-edge bleakness, and the

81

bracing air wasn't helping as much as I'd hoped. As I left the path and labored up the bare slopes, I thought distractedly of the tangle I'd made. Why on earth had I ever come? I'd made a fool of myself in front of that gentle, civilized man, and he'd reacted with great generosity. It was either that or throw me out, I thought grimly. Strangely, he'd expressed the same concern as Richard–that I might fear foul play in Ciara's death.

Well, melodrama was hardly this New Englander's cup of tea. And Nancy Drew I certainly wasn't. Nor, regrettably, Stephanie Plum. I could have used some of her love life; the mayhem would have been worth it.

How, I wondered tiredly, was I to face Richard again? If I stayed, another meeting would be inevitable. Yet to my annoyance, I couldn't quite suppress a furtive satisfaction that he'd heard me play.

But why had he lied so blatantly about Ciara? It was inconceivable that she'd done what he said. Obviously he hated her; that had been evident from the moment I set foot in Yorkshire. I tried to understand why he wanted me to believe his wild insinuations. What was the point? She was gone; nothing could harm her now. The troubling thing was my conviction that Richard had a fierce purpose in all that he did.

I reached the top of the fell, panting, out of condition and out of breath, and surveyed the stunning scene below with gloomy pleasure: lion-colored hills embracing the Georgian house, sun sparking off the stable clock, the gleaming pewter of the river, thawed for the time, and the long avenue of bare beeches leading to the main road. I turned wearily and wandered on for a few more moments, over a sweet curve of land into a little declivity where there was shelter from the wind. I sank gratefully onto dry, springy bracken. Shading my eyes, I began to relax in the slight warmth of the sun, half-dozing. Last night and this morning had drained my energy; I hadn't slept, and was still a bit weak from the aftermath of the flu. But lying on the earth, watching the little clouds scurrying overhead, I began to feel a quiet healing.

I don't know how much later it was that I became aware of a sort of rhythmic trembling of the earth. Startled, I raised myself on an elbow and turned to look behind me. Through the golden haze that turned the dried grass into a soft screen of light, I saw a horseman cantering slowly toward me down the length of the fell. The graceful, arrogant bearing of the slender figure was recognizable even before I could make out the color of the mare.

The cadence of hooves swelled and sharpened as horse and rider drew near. He had seen me, and slid off the mare's back before she was fully stopped. I noted with a twist of amusement that he was riding bareback, and wearing faded jeans.

Niniane wore only a halter. Richard unbuckled the light rope and set her free to graze. As he dropped to the ground beside me, I was aware of a curious feeling of apprehension mixed with expectation, not unlike what one feels in the moments before stepping onto a stage.

"I hoped I'd find you here," he said, stretching out his legs. "I rode over to the house by way of the road, but neither John nor Robin seemed to know where you'd gone. Are you all right?" I nodded silently. "So you confessed to him, did you?" Humour glinted in his eyes, and I turned my head to gaze out over the moors.

"He was extremely gracious and understanding," I answered stiffly. "He should have thrown me out at once."

"Not at all," he said, leaning back on his elbows and glancing up at me with a little smile. "He'd never do that, I assure you. Believe me, he's happy that you're here. Despite his expertise in antiques and his general air of worldliness, John, as I told you last night, is a simple man in many ways. He tends to see things in black and white. And he has incredibly strong family loyalties. I know–" he forestalled me as I started to speak. "You feel it's a negligible tie. But John doesn't; there are so few of us left now. And marriage was a commitment for him, you see. He's had rather a dreadful year. This gives him something different to think about."

He sat up, turning to me impulsively. "Please do this for us, Felicity. Stay, at least for a while, so John doesn't feel you're leaving Yorkshire because of him. That would be another burden he doesn't need to carry."

"Yes, I'll stay," I replied. "I promised him. He was generous beyond reason, and I couldn't refuse." Something was gnawing at the back of my mind. Richard's words seemed sincere and unstudied, but I had the uneasy feeling that he might have an underlying motive.

His next statement cut into my thoughts, catching me at an unguarded moment.

"Now I have a favor to ask. I hope you'll erase the past and say yes. It's very important to me."

"Of course," I said automatically and unwarily.

"Good. I want you to play in a chamber group I'm getting together. Please–hear me out." This as I started to rise in protest. "It's just a benefit, and the work is a new piece of mine; rather an experimental thing. No, wait–" he said as I got up onto my knees.

"Is this an attempt to make up for the Debussy cancellation?" I asked coldly.

"Of course not. I'm a professional musician, Lissa, not a psychologist."

"Well, I can't!" I cried indignantly, stung by his practicality. "You know that. It's been years since I've played!"

"And all that unpressured practice has made you better than ever. Look, it's not even an important part, I swear it. Nothing complex. The cello is the principal instrument, anyway; I'm just using the harp as tone color. A flute, an oboe, brass, a few strings, percussion–"

"Where will it be? When?" I asked, trying

unsuccessfully to damp down a ridiculous upswing of excitement.

"In York. In about three and a half weeks."

"Three weeks!" I yelped.

"Come on, Felicity," he laughed. "It's easy enough. And I'll wager you're a quick study."

He was right. On many occasions I'd had to work up orchestral parts overnight. Three weeks would have seemed an eternity of time to Lissa Leone. But now...

"You know you're dying to."

I looked directly at him for the first time since he'd come riding along the fell. The candid enthusiasm in the strong brown face reminded me for a moment of John. But this is a very different man, I told myself sharply. A man who'd betrayed my trust, attacked me without compunction, lied about my aunt.

A gust of wind caught me and I shivered, returning to my earlier thought. A man known for having purpose in his actions; and in his actions toward me, the purposes certainly seemed covert.

"Please, Felicity?" He spoke in a light, charming voice. "My local harpist has gone all maternal on me and looks like producing a brace of tubas. And her alternate plays like a suet pudding. Looks like one, too," he finished reflectively.

Unwilling laughter escaped me, and I forbore to mention that any of twenty competent harpists would have run panting up from London at his call.

The wind spat again and my mood shifted. In that case, why had he picked me?

"No. I can't. Think of the risk." I said bitterly.

"I think of the risk every time I step on the stage, Lissa. We all do." He turned away, looking across the moor. When he spoke again his voice was very quiet

"So you honestly mean to give it all up, all the love and care that were poured into you? What do you think Leon would say?"

85

"He'd say..." I searched for the words, aching with a sense of loss. "He'd say I was throwing it away—the heart and the soul he'd given me."

"The heart and soul were already yours, Lissa. All Leon gave you was the means of accessing them."

I felt myself weakening, tears stinging my eyes. Fighting a sense of terror, I resorted to bitterness once more.

"Aren't you forgetting? I'm unreliable. Erratic was the word, I believe." A cold finger of superstition touched me. Saying it doesn't make it so, does it?

"Felicity." He took my arm and turned me toward him. "Why don't you face it? Your little explosion was skillfully engineered. By a notable demolition expert."

This time I was on my feet in earnest, twisting away from his hand.

"That's enough!" I said furiously. "Ciara was my mother's sister, for heaven's sake. She helped me from the start, and just because I managed to wreck it, I'm not going to lay my petty failures at her feet."

He rose to face me with a puzzled look. "My God, I believe you mean it. Don't forget your Old Testament, Felicity. Abel had a sibling, too." He shook his head in exasperation. "Well, I can understand your credulity. She obviously kept up the façade with you. She's had many fools, and believe me, I've not been the least of them."

"Why are you trying to make me believe that my own aunt would deliberately set out to ruin my career when she was on a pinnacle herself? That she'd go to all the trouble to set me up for success over the years, and then just casually smash it? People don't do things like that!" I was shaking all over with rage and confusion.

A look of pity came into his eyes, and he reached out to cup my bruised cheek. "My poor unhatched chick," he murmured. "You really do think that, don't you? How very little you know."

I jerked my head away. "Don't patronize me," I

grated. "I'm not going to discuss this with you. You know nothing about it."

"Felicity, she was a leech!" There was sudden, impatient anger in his voice. "She fed off the admiration of others and returned a superficial warmth, as long as it was to her advantage. You don't know how many bodies she's walked over."

He took a deep, barely controlled breath and made a curiously repressed gesture with one hand. "Well. Perhaps you shouldn't have recorded the Ginastera and Rodrigo Concertos, and played them so much better than she did."

"Stop it! Just stop it!" I was near to shouting. If I lost my faith in Ciara, what did I have left?

Richard seized my shoulders roughly. "You purblind little fool, do you think she'd listen with complaisance to Leon's talk of 'the unsurpassed freshness of Lissa's musical vision?' Damn it, do you think she'd hear him call anyone–anyone other than herself–the greatest talent he'd ever taught, and let them survive?"

Stunned at his words, I burst into tears and started down the slope, swiping at my blurry eyes. He caught up with me and pulled my hands forcibly from my face. Then he was kissing me with a sort of lyrical savagery as I stood unresisting and unbelieving in his arms.

The kiss skidded on my tears and I turned my face into his shoulder. With a soft laugh, he pressed his lips gently to the top of my head.

In an attempt to put some starch into my buckling knees, I searched for something to say and came up with a brilliant non sequitur.

"What are you calling it–your new piece, I mean?"

He was stroking the wind-whipped hair back from my wet face and replied absently.

"Mm? Oh, that." His casual reply turned my overheated blood to ice. *The Merchant of Dreams.*

We were following a steeply winding track down the far side of the fell. A valley I'd never seen before lay at our feet. A small flock of sheep stood near an ice-fringed stream, and the faint sound of their bleating drifted up to us.

"Can you spare an hour or so? There's something I want to show you," he'd said, returning yet another snowy handkerchief to his pocket.

I was past reasoning now, past curiosity about his actions. I'd pushed Ciara to the back of my mind. Doubts, suspicions and resentments had, for the time, lost the battle to my dizzy remembrance of that brief embrace.

Great, I told myself. Now you're not just a hysterically romantic liar, you're a sex-starved fool, panting to fall into the arms of a famous roué and...assassin?

We crossed the graveled shelf road that wound up from the valley below, and he halted, pointing to the left, where a cliff fell sheer to a meadow gleaming gold in the last afternoon light.

"Delving Drop. We're apt to lose a sheep or two over that each year, poor silly beasts."

He walked beside me, leading the mare. We were lower on the hill now, and sheltered from the wind. Dry stone walls intersected winter-sere fields with the random quality of a child's drawing. I felt a sudden pang of guilt that I'd so rapidly dismissed Ciara from my thoughts; so easily succumbed to the attraction of a man who detested her.

And just why did he, anyway?

"Richard–" It was the first time I'd called him by his name. "You... you really hated her, didn't you? No, don't spare my feelings. I'm trying to understand your point of view. You have to realize she's been my idol since I was a child."

Niniane slipped on a patch of frost-flattened grass and Richard held up, patting her neck. "I know it's hard. Well... I'd known her for years, of course. At one time we were students together, at Curtis. That was before my graduate work at Juilliard. Certainly I was attracted; who wouldn't have been? She was stunningly beautiful, brilliant, and she had a great sense of fun and recklessness. And extraordinary musicianship. We skied occasionally in Vermont, and later in Switzerland. There was always excitement where Ciara was. But of course you know that." He threw me a quick look, caught my involuntary lift of the shoulders. "Did she never take you on any of her jaunts?"

"Once," I smiled. "I couldn't keep up, skiing, drinking, or bed-hopping. Too much the country mouse, I guess. Anyway, the invitation was never repeated."

"Hm. I might posit a different reason for that. Well, at any rate our flings at that time were brief and fairly casual. Our careers were too demanding for anything else. Then, a little more than seven years ago, I married Anna."

I stumbled on a stone, and he glanced over quickly.

"Okay?" he asked, and I nodded.

My heart was doing something strange, and the dry stone walls jumped out at me like neon grids, pulsing crazily. Married. He had been married when I saw him backstage in New York. No one had ever mentioned that. Not even Time magazine.

"You didn't know?" I shook my head, trying to look indifferent. He had kissed me passionately. I was following him without question, presumably to his house at Hawthorns.

"Not likely you would. We kept it very quiet; my wife insisted. She hated publicity and the social round. It was a condition of my giving interviews. But I had the distinct impression that Ciara wasn't pleased by the marriage. Our names had been bandied about a good bit; my being a conductor had given her a lot of opportunities, and I suppose the marriage annoyed her. She managed to act as if Anna didn't exist. Well, Anna was an artist in her own right: a portrait painter, and a damned fine one. She was Austrian, eight years older than I, quiet and loving. I didn't deserve such luck."

He stopped and turned toward me; I saw his mouth tighten. "I've wondered sometimes if she died for my sins. It was leukemia, Felicity. Diagnosed three years after we were married, and it took three years to kill her. They didn't have such advanced treatments for adult leukemia as they do now. She never had a real remission."

I stood speechless, aghast.

He turned back and resumed his downward course. "At the end," he finished bleakly, "she didn't even know me."

"Oh, Richard. I'm so truly sorry." I was bitterly ashamed of my first thoughtless reaction. This story cast a floodlight on my appalling selfishness.

He sketched a deprecatory gesture. "*Machts nicht*. I didn't mean to burden you with an old, sad tale. It's just that– well, I think I went a little mad for a while. Not, perhaps, for the first time in my life. I allowed it to turn me into that worst of things, a true cynic. There were plenty of available people who wanted to help me forget. And I was all too willing." There was self-loathing in his tone. "Too much drink, too many parties, too much jetting around. And too much Ciara. I told you I was one of her chief fools."

We'd fetched up on a tiny level plateau near the bottom of the fell, and he faced me across the mare's back.

"John had met her a couple of years earlier. Thank God I wasn't responsible for that. It was a long pursuit, and she never let the mask slip with him. Just like you, he wouldn't hear a word against her. Oh, I know how you feel about her, how loyal you are. That's because of your own goodness, your own honesty. But a true megalomaniac is capable of machinations you couldn't even imagine."

I looked at him without speaking. It was all too alien to my youthful memory of Ciara; there was nothing I could say.

He sighed, stroking Niniane's neck.

"Well. The marriage was pretty dreadful. I can't tell it all, Felicity, it wouldn't be fair to John. And given his antediluvian ideas of honor and circumspection, I'm dead certain he'd never mention it to you. Suffice it to say she thought there was money to be had from my brother; money enough for her to live on the grand scale she coveted. I suppose she was attracted by the title, the prestige of the London-Paris business, the London house, even the Yorkshire estate, though it was far too remote for her liking. She was vitriolic enough, later on, about the fact that John had converted it to a country hotel, and furious when she realized how much of his income he plowed back into it. After that little discovery she made herself scarce here. But there was more than acquisitiveness behind her determination to marry John; almost a queer kind of spite."

I realized with a mental start that he meant Ciara, not John, had done the pursuing.

"And when her conquest was a *fait accompli*... well, the marriage contract meant nothing to her, of course. She was far more faithful to her musical agreements. At first she was simply incredulous that I wouldn't succumb to her charms again. But that turned to rage when I refused to join in her games, just as if John weren't in the picture at all. They weren't married long, but though he doesn't talk about it, I think he knew what she was, early on. She gave him ample cause."

The repressed deadliness was back in his voice. "I've even, God help me, sometimes wondered if he drowned her himself."

He met my horrified eyes and pulled himself up with an effort. "That's nonsense, of course. Forgive me; I'm raving. And it's getting cold. Let's go. We're almost there; look."

He pointed to the hill that rose opposite us, and there, nestled into a little bay of meadow between the arms of its base, was an old rectangular farmhouse of grey stone, surrounded by a courtyard and outbuildings.

"Not Georgian," he laughed, "but it serves."

I wondered if the lissome Marjorie was still "in charge."

Soon we were at the bottom of the fell. The broad amber meadow, serene in the evening light, stretched between us and the house. Richard gave me a leg up onto Niniane and I sighed with the satisfaction of feeling a horse's bare back under me again. He handed over the rope, vaulting up behind me.

I had a curiously unreal sense of peace. He had alternately bullied and charmed me into a promise of playing his music. He had calumniated my aunt. He had voiced the most terrible suspicions of his brother to me, a virtual stranger. And here we were, riding through the twilight in a restful silence, in perfect amity.

Niniane's hoof struck a stone and he placed his hands lightly upon my waist. I had a vision of those hands, brilliantly spotlit, as he stood on the podium in a darkened hall; heard with my inner hearing the *Faustus* spearing its terror into the dimness.

"One thing more and I'm done." I was back in the meadow, guiding the mare over a bit of crumbling wall. "That night when I first saw you, on the road..."

A tiny frisson shook me and his hands tightened on my waist. If he does that again, I thought, I shall simply fall off Niniane and lie hopefully in the grass. *And how many fools before you do you suppose have done exactly that?*

"Felicity." His use of my real name brought me into focus. "In the dark, with just that fleeting image of you in the headlamps–the cape, the widow's peak, the long, blowing hair; above all, the way you carried yourself, even half-drugged and ill as you were...well. I wasn't expecting it, you see. She was the farthest thing from my mind: the family were getting back to normal and John seemed to be at peace again, at last. When Robin phoned, he was in a panic at the thought of his rich American lodger stranded on a winter night. I'd had a rough day with my composing, and probably downed too much brandy, though not as much as I led you to believe. And I was looking for someone entirely different—the usual American tourist. But when I saw her–you–I knew I wanted her to stay dead, and that made me frantic."

The illusion of peace was gone, and I was cold now, inside and out. A sharp wind was blowing, turning my fingers blue. I clenched my teeth to keep them from chattering. I wanted him to stop, but the beautiful, quietly somber voice went on.

"I was in shock, and a little high on the brandy, not thinking straight. It struck me that John might have lied about her death for some crazy purpose of his own, or that she was hiding out through God knows what twisted motive. John and I have so many years between us, and we've never been really close until this year. Sometimes... well, never mind. Ciara had driven him to the wall, that much was certain. All we knew for sure was that she'd gone out on the boat and hadn't returned. The boat was found; her body never was. And it seemed, for a moment there on the road, that she was back. It was simply more than I could handle. But that's over now. Ciara's gone, and you're you. And here we are."

Oats in mind, Niniane jogged briskly around the corner of the barn. A tall grey-haired woman stood in the courtyard, scattering grain for a flock of chickens. And there on a heap of straw, safely out of the wind in the lee of the barn, sat a very small boy in a bright red cap, a large speckled hen on his lap. He jumped to his feet as we came into view, and the hen fluttered squawking to the cobblestones.

"And," Richard finished, the light and music coming back into his voice as he slid off Niniane and reached up to help me down, "this is my son Peter."

CHAPTER 10

To keep the house from rascals was my charge;
The task was great, and the commission large.
      The Dog and His Master, A.E. Finch

Oh dearest, dearest boy! My heart
For better lore could seldom yearn
Could I but teach the hundredth part
Of what from thee I learn.
      William Wordsworth, Anecdote for Fathers

I hadn't time to take in that unforeseen statement before I was brought up rigid by the most appalling noise: half bay, half howl. I'd never had any fear of animals, but at the awful sound I retreated judiciously to Niniane's off-side. She had started slightly but seemed otherwise unimpressed, lipping at the pile of straw. Suddenly out of the barn shot the biggest dog I'd ever seen, a good five feet from outstretched nose to extended tail-tip, with paws the size of dessert plates.

"G.P.!" Richard's voice cracked through the frosty air. "Sit down at once! What the devil do you mean, raising such a racket?"

The monster, gleaming red-gold in the last rays of the sun, dropped to his haunches as if he'd been shot. A pleased and proud smile spread over his foolish face, and his tail beat furiously against the cobbles as Richard walked over and began to pull his silky, drooping ears.

"That's better. Good boy, G.P.," he murmured. "G.P. tries to be a good boy; it's just that he has a cog missing, poor soul. He tends to forget who I am when I'm gone for more than an hour. And as that happens far more often than not–"

94

He shrugged, smiled, and turned to the elderly tweed-coated woman who had left her chickens and now had Peter by the hand.

"My dear, this is John's niece, Felicity Godwin. Felicity, Mrs. Chidester, who so kindly looks after Peter and me."

I made a polite response and took the strong, thin hand, but with total abstraction. Good God, I was thinking, how many more shocks can my system sustain? A mongrel dog and lap chickens. And a tiny son, with straw on his cap. I glanced cautiously from the grouping of child, nanny and animals to Richard, standing at my side. No. It was impossible to look at the man and imagine him in any setting short of Renaissance splendor.

"I know—where's my Borzoi; that's it, isn't it?" He had picked up on it with lightning speed. "Well, let me tell you, my good woman, this is only a small part of the picture. There's my villa at Asolo, my chateau in the Medoc, my Regency house in London, my secret rendezvous in the Casbah…oh, yes, my yali on the Bosphorus…"

"And your pig sty at Hawthorns," broke in Mrs. Chidester's dryly good-humoured Yorkshire voice. "I told you last week, Richard, it needs hammer and nails, and Hamish can't do it, he's abed with the flu. Agamemnon's gotten himself out twice today."

"Where is he now?"

"Peter and I coaxed him into a stall in the barn, but he's not happy. If you'll take care of it I'll get Miss Godwin and Peter in by the fire before they freeze. The kettle's on for tea."

Richard spread his hands in a quintessentially Italian gesture and headed for the barn. G.P. lumbered up onto his feet and trotted off after him, giving one of the hens a fond swipe with his red tongue as he passed. The chicken staggered and fell over sideways, recovering herself with an indignant cluck.

"He likes chickens, then?" I asked.

"Indeed he does," replied Mrs. Chidester. "He helped himself to two for Christmas dinner."

Peter rushed to his defense. "But he's outgrowing it, Papa says."

"Outgrowing it? You mean he's still growing? Just how old is this beast, anyway?" We were walking briskly toward the side door of the house. The sun had dropped behind the hill and it was very cold now.

"G.P.'s one year and five months old," Peter stated proudly.

"Yes," said Mrs. Chidester, "and it's true, he is a good boy, compared with the way he used to be." She shook her head. "The cabriole legs that dog's eaten, not to speak of the carpets–"

She opened the heavy oak door onto a stone-flagged kitchen. Fireplace flames cast a ruddy blush on the whitewashed walls. Moving to the mantel, she took matches from a little wooden chest and lighted three oil lamps. The blue and white of the curtains and the warm gleam of a big oak refectory table leapt out of the shadows. She set the largest of the lamps in the center of the table, and I fell gratefully into a ladder-backed chair.

"No electricity yet, you see," she was explaining. "The ground's been frozen too hard for the lads to work, and Richard wants the lines buried. But now we've had the thaw... excuse me, I'll just light the lamps in the parlor and make up the fire."

I turned to Peter, who had taken off his cap and gloves and was chafing his hands before the blaze. In the flickering light I could see round patches of red on his cheeks, painted there by the cold. Through the muted crackling of the fire came a distant sound of hammering.

"Do you live here all the time, Peter?" I asked.

"Mostly when Papa's home. Sometimes I'm in London with Gianna. She's my Nonna."

"Oh." I was at a loss until I remembered that nonna

was the Italian word for grandmother.

"But I like it best here," he ran on cheerfully. "I miss Gianna sometimes but there's Marjorie and G.P. and the chickens and Niniane and Sir Bors and the pigs. And the sheep."

He came to perch on the arm of my chair. "Do you live in London, Filcity? Or should I call you Miss Godwin?"

Nothing shy about this one, I thought. Or slow either—he'd caught my name right away, though its complexities stumped him for the moment.

"Let me see if I can get this in the right order, Peter." I smiled into the grey eyes, shining with interest in the dancing light. He had his father's coloring, and a wonderfully natural, unspoiled air about him. "No, I'm an American, and bless you, you're the first Englishman who hasn't accused me of it as soon as I opened my mouth. And no, please don't call me Miss Godwin. It makes me feel like a teacher and I don't really like being a teacher. My name is a bit hard to say, though—Fe-lic-i-ty."

He was trying that out when Mrs.Chidester called, "Peter! Come and wash!"

A door banged somewhere and G.P. came trotting in, head low, tongue lolling.

"Lie down, G.P.!" commanded Peter in a small approximation of his father's voice, and G.P. crashed to the hearth like a marionette whose strings had been cut.

"Excuse me." This child had been taught his manners. "Back in a minute, Filsi—" With a smile and a shake of the head, Peter hurried out the door.

"You know," I said slowly to G.P., marveling at the racket of his precipitate collapse before the fire, "you really ought to learn to lie down a little at a time, the way other dogs do. I shouldn't be surprised if you were one big bone-bruise."

At the sound of my voice he got himself up and came to my chair. An enormous paw slapped down on my knee.

"No," I admonished, removing it gently. "If you wanted to be a lap dog, you should have stopped growing long ago."

He gave a resigned sigh and advanced his huge head, gazing up at me with eyes that held all the intelligence of obsidian. His unwrinkled brow gave him a curiously blank look.

"All right, you are a good boy," I conceded, pulling softly at his ears as he leaned heavily against my knee and sank his leaden head onto my lap. "And you are a clinger. There's something about you, my lad, that reminds me of Tim," I mused, stroking his satiny black muzzle.

"Who is Tim?" asked an incisive voice, and I jumped slightly.

Richard was standing in the door. He'd changed into a clean jersey, and his hair looked damp.

I went on stroking G.P.'s nose. "Oh, it's you," I said. "Are you done with the pigs, then?"

"Indeed I am." He laughed. "But I fear my Brahms will never sound the same to you."

"I haven't heard your Brahms," I replied repressively.

"Ah. Pity. Your loss. Yes, the swine are safely closeted for the evening. I see you've made friends with G.P. Where's Peter?"

"Gone to wash. And it was the other way around. G.P.'s a very friendly dog."

He looked at me thoughtfully. "Not to everyone. And you never answered my first question. Who's Tim?"

"Oh." I gave G.P.'s head a final pat and held my hands out to the fire. "Just a school friend."

"Who reminded you of G.P.? Why? A little light in the upper story?"

I smiled. "Hardly. He's a cellist... a very good one."

"Why like G.P?" he persisted. "Dog-like devotion?"

I shifted irritably in my chair. "You might say that."

"And... 'at school.' That little private institution of

yours, somewhere in the East?"

My face grew hot, and not from the fire. "Yes, he was at Curtis," I replied shortly.

"You wouldn't be speaking of Timothy Willman, by any chance?"

I gave up. "Yes. Do you know him?"

"Very little personally, but certainly by reputation--- one of the leading young cellists in the concert field, isn't he? Had a smashing triumph in London this fall, playing the Dvorák concerto. As a matter of fact, you'll–"

Here he broke off as Mrs. Chidester and Peter came back in.

"Richard," she said briskly, "if you'll take Miss Godwin into the parlor, I'll just get supper on."

"Oh!" I jumped out of my chair, and glanced at my bare wrist. "What time is it? I forgot my watch today. Six o'clock? Oh, murder, I've got to be getting back. They'll think I fell into a rabbit hole."

"Not to worry," said Richard. "I told Robin you'd be with me. Stay for supper, and then I'll run you back in the car."

I looked at him, puzzled. There was no telephone, and no cell service in this area. So he had taken my company for granted even before he found me on the fell! One part of me bristled with resentment at this cool assumption of authority. Another, yearning for the companionship of a like mind, spoke with mild acquiescence.

"Well, that's very kind, if you're sure it's not an imposition."

"Nonsense. Shall we get out from underfoot? Let's move on from tea and have some wine. Come along, Peter."

With G.P. padding behind, the three of us hurried down the cold unlit hall to the parlor, where more oil lamps and a roaring blaze shed brightness and warmth over the long, beautiful room. The wainscoting was paneled to the height of the wooden mantel, with the upper walls painted a soft ivory. Over the mantel hung a portrait of a child of about three. Peter's merry grey eyes laughed out at me. Yes, she had been a painter of remarkable gifts. This must have been done the year before she died.

The room was furnished with an austerity that reminded me of Denham house. But here was the same sense of money lavished: antique Kerman and Belouchistan rugs glowed on the wide, newly polished floorboards, and a nine-foot grand piano, this one a Steinway, stood near tall narrow windows curtained against the chill darkness outside. There was a smell of new paint, and the room had the look of one that had just been moved into. I walked about, looking at some paintings of the Sienese school—I supposed, half incredulously, that they were real—and at one long wall of shelves full of books and scores. The room was still very cold away from the fire. I sank onto a sofa near the hearth, idly wondering if Marjorie would appear. Richard was busy at a table in the corner.

"Wine? There's scotch and bourbon if you'd rather."

"Wine, please—red, if you have it. What were you saying about Tim?"

"Just that he's developed into a major artist. One who's truly fulfilled his potential."

Unlike me, I thought. Thanks partly to your efforts. Suddenly I didn't want to talk about Tim anymore.

Richard handed me a crystal glass brimming with merlot. It was etched with birds, glimmering against the wine. I sat for a moment looking around the room, while he poured orange juice for Peter.

"This is a lovely house, Richard." I leaned against the cushions, compelling myself to relax and shelve my hurt feelings. "And what a wonderful room to practice in. Is the house very old?"

"Mid seventeen hundreds. It was the home farm. The head shepherd moved to a more modern place about twenty years ago, and it had been falling into ruin ever since."

"Well, it's looking superb now." The great dog stood nearby, staring into the flames, his coat shining red in the wavering light. "By the way, what does G.P. stand for?"

"Hadn't you guessed? Grand Pause, of course." He laughed into my uncomprehending eyes. G.P. was an abbreviation for the grand, or dramatic, pause used in musical composition, but...

"I'm afraid I don't quite–oh. Oh!" I choked on the wine, remembering the monstrous foot laid in my lap. "Of course–Grand Paws. Richard, that's terrible! Did you name him?" It was a relief to laugh freely. "Peter, how could he?"

I took another sip of wine. Richard had put some Corelli on a battery-operated player hidden in a tall old armoire, and the room was beginning to sparkle with gaiety– music, firelight, and wine. He came to sit beside me on the sofa, pulling Peter into his lap.

"Agreed. It is a terrible name. But then he's a terrible dog. Right, old Peter?"

"Right. But he's getting to be a good boy," insisted Peter loyally, looking at the object of our musings, who had clattered to the floor and lay with his chin clamped firmly onto Richard's boot.

"Where did you get this behemoth, anyway?"

"Oh, he just appeared."

I gave Peter a doubting look and he shook his head wisely. "Papa saved his life," he explained with pride. "He was going to be given euthasia."

"Euthanasia, lad. Yes, a friend of mine owned a boxer bitch, a show dog, that had an ill-advised romance with an Alsatian. There were only two enormous pups, and one died at birth. This fellow was for the water bucket, but I needed a farm dog, and so... funny, isn't it, how he's grown to twice the size of either parent?"

He was refilling my glass, lifting the bottle from a silver wine coaster set on a low table in front of us. A Meissen bowl planted with paper-white narcissus stood there, sending the fragrance of spring into the air. I sighed contentedly and settled deeper into the cushions, taking the glass from his hand. I could feel the emotional stresses of the last days ebbing away. It had been longer than I cared to remember since I'd enjoyed an evening's companionship, free from worry or depression.

"Do you like dogs, Fellicy? Jiggers!" he said, screwing up his button nose. "You have a very un-sayish name." Embarrassed, he slid off Richard's lap and did a slow somersault on the rug.

Just as I was about to avow my devotion to anything with four legs, Richard corrected Peter quietly. "Miss Godwin, son."

"No, please, Richard. You don't know how that takes me back to the schoolroom. And I have leave for the whole rest of the year! No more milk breaks, lines and spaces, Pawpaw Patches, Nick-Nack Paddywhacks, and, thank God, Nutcracker Suites!"

Peter caught my eye and snorted with laughter at what he supposed to be a collection of absurdities.

But Richard looked startled.

"Good God. You don't mean you actually–"

"Oh, didn't I."

"Why? For how long?"

"To stay sane. And for about thirty years, I think. No, really just two and a half."

"Was it that bad?" He glanced at Peter. "Yet I would have said you like children."

"I adore children!" I protested. "It's just the job itself. It's like drinking imitation strawberry soda when you're longing for wine."

"I see. Of course, it would be. I'd never thought about it before. Well, I think I can offer you some wine, strong wine, very soon."

I stared at him, bewildered. Then I sat up with a little jerk. I'd completely forgotten! Had it been only this afternoon that he'd proposed–no, demanded that I take a part in *Merchant of Dreams*? I was losing all sense of time. Well, it was far from being a re-entry into the concert world, but at least it meant contact with the real music for which I hungered so achingly.

But Peter's mind was back on names. "Your name's too long, Licity, that's why I can't say it."

"Peter–" admonished Richard gently.

"It's all right. He's not the first man to have thought so; remember Leon?"

"But it is, Papa, see? Lissy said so herself. You're Papa, or Richard. Two." He was counting on his fingers. "And Mar-jo-rie–that's three parts."

"Syllables," murmured Richard.

"Syllables. Fe-lic-i-ty–" He'd gotten it at last, the fingers still in play. "Four parts–syllables. That's too long. G.P. and Gianna have just two, like you, Papa, and Robin and me. Maybe that's because we're all related. But no, John has just one."

"How about Uncle John?" Richard laughed.

"Mmm–too long. Almost as long as Felicity." He was lying on his back at our feet, eyes searching the ceiling. Then he sat up abruptly. "It's pretty," he said apologetically, at his father's somewhat dubious look, "but it's too long. Maybe she could be Lissa."

I turned wide eyes on Richard, and saw him looking equally incredulous.

"No." The word held finality; it was impossible to doubt. "I swear, my dear, he's never heard it from me. On my oath!"

I gave my head a little shake to clear it. Hunger, lack of sleep, and the long walk in the cold air, followed by wine and the fire's warmth, had all combined to make me both giddy and ridiculously happy. The Corelli bubbled through the room like a sunlit stream over colored pebbles. My laughter rose to meet it.

"All right, that's settled. Without a doubt, Peter, I'm Lissa!"

Without a doubt. Could I ever play that way again, without a doubt? The new life I felt welling up almost made it seem possible. Well, before God, I would try.

Over his glass, Richard was watching me with an unreadable look in his eyes, and Peter was crowing with triumph. "I named her a new name, didn't I, Papa?"

"You and someone else, Peter. A great man. Lissa's teacher."

Peter looked at me askance. "Do you still go to school?"

"No, Peter. Mr. Lemaitre was my teacher a long time ago. And it wasn't school, exactly. He taught me to play the harp."

Peter's animated face became rather still. "Oh," he said in a small voice.

G.P. collected his joints under him and lurched to his feet, turning hopefully to face the door as Mrs. Chidester came in with a tray.

"Come along, Peter, G.P. Time for supper and bed. I've brought yours in here, Richard, Miss Godwin. The dining room's cold as the grave."

G.P.'s tail scythed back and forth in frantic joy at the sound of his name. I leaned forward with a gasp and caught the precious Meissen bowl just as it skidded wildly off the polished surface of the table.

"Almost scored another one, didn't you, old boy?" Richard took the bowl from my hands and set it in the middle of the table. "Thanks, Lissa. Good fielding."

Mrs. Chidester expelled her breath in relief. "If there's a stone left standing by the time that dog is full-grown—no, Peter, I see you behind the curtains. You've had a nice visit with Papa and his company and now it's supper and bed time. Give your Papa a kiss and say good night to Miss Godwin and then come on to the kitchen."

Emerging amiably from his hiding place, Peter leapt onto Richard's knee, grasped both ears, and pulled his head down, administering a hearty smack on the forehead. Richard, with a convincing rendition of a growling bear, held his son tightly for a moment. Then Peter jumped down and offered himself a bit warily for my attentions. Does he always allow himself to be kissed by Richard's women? I wondered. Marjorie, for instance? And did Ciara kiss him goodnight? The thought vanished as his arms stole around my neck and a cheek, soft and warm as peach-down, was pressed to mine.

"Goodnight, Lissa. When it's warmer we can go riding on my pony." Then he looked at me doubtfully, having second thoughts about my size. "Or–can you ride alone? Could you manage Niniane? I don't think Sir Bors could carry both of us."

"She rides Fiametto," Richard smiled. "And it will be warmer soon. We're nearly into March, you know."

Promising Peter an outing on the next good day, I realized with surprise that spring was near. It had been the third week of February when I'd arrived, and already seven days had passed. And only three and a half weeks to go before the York performance.

Richard took the tray from Mrs. Chidester and kissed her on the cheek. "Good night, my dear. And thank you. It looks delectable."

I seconded him. The supper before us would have tempted an eremite. It amazed me that it had been produced in a kitchen so remote from supermarkets. She had prepared shrimp, steaming rosily up from a flaky pot pie; broccoli, dark green, flanked by diagonally sliced carrots in a shining sauce; and pears, red grapes, and cheese, their colors mellow in the lamplight. I'd missed lunch, and I was ravenous.

Richard set the tray on the table before us, and with a flourish, spread a large linen napkin in my lap. "Buon appetito!"

I laughed. I'd finished my wine and was casting off restraints with the speed of sound. "Or, 'enjoy your dinner'? You certainly have the proper air. Maybe Robin could use you in capacities other than driving the wagon." It was appalling sacrilege, but at the moment I didn't care.

Richard wasn't offended. He merely said, "There was a time when I wouldn't have thought that beyond the realm of possibility. I had a youthful fit of kicking and screaming to escape the demands of music. I tried just about everything except the food industry."

"Yes, that's right, you took some years off, didn't you? And what about Robin: why did he stop playing? Oh, by the way, Richard..." With the volubility of the well-wined non-drinker, I charged on.

He bent to hand me a plate, and his grey eyes slanted up, strangely guarded.

"A rather odd thing happened. I meant to ask you." Had I meant to? Certainly not until today, when mutual confidences had begun pouring forth.

"Odd? About Robin, you mean?"

"Well, maybe odd isn't the right word. Probably it was my imagination, but–I was practicing in the salon, playing on the Bösendorfer, since I didn't dare touch the harp. It was...before, you see. Suddenly I thought what fun it would be to try the harpsichord. I'd had a summer of lessons in Philadelphia; not much, but I'd grasped the fundamentals of touch."

"Mmm. Along with the organ, I believe, and... wasn't it the guitar?"

"Stop that! Well, what I told you was true, after a fashion. I did play the organ at church during holidays. Anyway–has Robin told you this? No? There I was, ripping through the Bach–"

He was buttering a roll, and the movement of his hand was arrested for a moment. "What Bach?"

"I don't know. Oh, the Goldberg, I think." I was aware

again of his eyes, lifting to mine with a cool kind of watchfulness.

"Yes. Leon said you were a genuine piano virtuoso as well."

"That was charitable. But at least I'm closer to it now. I've had lots of time to practice in the past few years." To my surprise, there was no irony in my voice.

"So you were playing the Goldberg Variations, on the harpsichord, and my cousin Robin walked in."

"Yes. I got... carried away. I didn't intend really to play them, but–you know how you lose yourself in the glory of the music, and the devil take the hindmost?"

He didn't answer directly. "I see. So you forgot to maintain your role of Mendelssohn-cum-Gottschalk dilettante, and cut loose with a real performance. How much did he hear?"

"I don't know. I was playing the twenty-sixth variation, I think. The one between the G minor and the Canone alla Nona."

He closed his eyes briefly and nodded. "Horribly difficult."

"It is. But fun!" I held my glass up to the light, entranced by the flames burning in its garnet depths. "Well, the thing is, he turned–oh, this sounds silly and overstated, but I could swear to it. He turned quite white, and stiff, and... dear heaven, Richard, I just happened to think. Does the harpsichord belong to him, and I was sitting there tearing it up without his leave?"

Richard set his plate on the table, rose, and went to stand with his back to the fire.

"The harpsichord is John's; he acquired it as beautiful piece of antique furniture. Also perhaps in the hope that Robin might someday want to play again. He sold his own long ago."

He hesitated for a moment. "Certainly it's all right for you to play it." Again the pause. "But Felicity, be careful of

Robin. Be very careful." His voice was low and strained.

I stared at him, genuinely fuddled now. "Careful? But–oh, I didn't tell you. Robin already knows about me, or he will soon. Your brother said he'd tell him, just casually, when he had an opportunity."

Slowly, Richard pushed himself away from the mantel. "Of course, you're right. But perhaps I should explain his sensitivity. Robin did play, professionally, I suppose you could say, for a time. He'd wanted to be a musician since... well, since his early teens. He managed to get into the Royal Conservatory, with Gianna's help. And to eke out a diploma. But when he graduated, there was nothing for him. He played a debut recital; Lissa, it was a disaster."

"Oh, poor Robin!" I cried. "Performance nerves, or–"

"That, and worse. He's just not truly musical, you see. And though he's very athletic, his hands are poorly coordinated." He turned back to stare into the fire. "And for the major work on his recital the poor devil picked the Goldberg Variations."

So I'd twisted two knives in his heart that day. Not only had I taunted him, unwittingly, with his present job; I'd treated him to the spectacle of a self-acclaimed dilettante, not even a properly trained harpsichordist, unconcernedly navigating through the pitfalls of a piece that was his *bete noire*.

"He should never have attempted it, of course, but he wouldn't be dissuaded. After that he tried to latch onto one early music group after another, always without success. I tried my damnedest, but I couldn't help him; he never got past the auditions. Finally he landed a job in a recording studio. It didn't take them long to find out he couldn't handle it."

"Oh, no! Poor Robin." All the gaiety had gone out of the room. The Corelli had died into its final cadence and there was only the hiss and crackle of the waning fire.

"It was a bitter disappointment for him, of course."

"It must have been awful! Believe me, I can identify with it. And I revived it... no wonder he looked so terrible."

Ruefully, I remembered John's shock when I'd turned to face him under Ciara's portrait. "I hurt your brother, too. Oh, God. I never should have come here."

He looked at me soberly. "Not your fault; you couldn't have known about Robin. With the best intentions in the world, we can't get through life without hurting one another sometimes." His eyes held mine for a moment, and I wondered if he was thinking about canceling my performance years before.

He stooped, picked up a poker, and stirred the remains of the fire. When he spoke again, I thought for a moment that he was changing the subject.

"Have you read *The Alien Corn*? Maugham's story?"

"Yes." Then it hit me. "Oh, dear. Well, at least Robin didn't shoot himself."

"No. But I sometimes wonder if that would have been much worse than what he actually did."

A burnt-out log buckled and fell with a muffled crash. I leaned forward, waiting.

"The young fool did what I'd done years before; what many young men do, when they're at odds with life. And many times it's their salvation—it's probably done the trick often enough in the past with the Denham men—our version of the French Foreign Legion, I guess. Unfortunately, it didn't seem to work out so well for either of us. At any rate, Robin joined the service, in his case the Royal Navy. He trained in the elite underwater corps—the equivalent of your U.S. Navy Seals, or perhaps you call them frogmen. From all accounts, and to his family's surprise, he was quite good at it. But the rigors of training, which are said to be draconian, along with the pressures of such an alien way of life, did what one might fear to an ultra-sensitive boy, fresh from a crushing disappointment. He was discharged a year before his tour of duty was up, on grounds of emotional instability."

I'd once seen a TV special on the Seals training, and remembered how shaken I'd been by what those young men had to endure.

He sighed and came back to the sofa. I saw for the first time that he looked very tired. Picking up the bottle, he poured the last of the wine into my glass.

"Robin had been more or less on his own for a long time. His father, my father's younger brother Basil, died when he was a child, and his mother went off to the Continent, leaving Robin behind. So my father brought him up. It wasn't the most cheerful of households. Unfortunately, he had little patience with Robin's musical leanings... or mine. *Alien Corn* again, with far less sympathy than the character in the story displayed." He paused, rubbing his forehead. "But in the long run, Robin was stronger than we'd thought. After a few months out of the Navy he enrolled in a Swiss hotel school. When he got out he started as a desk clerk, moved on to the kitchens, and managed two inns in Devonshire, very successfully, before he came back here to the Shepherd's Crook and moved on to Denham House."

"And he's never played again?"

"Not to my knowledge."

I watched the embers, winking and glowing like the eyes of some fabulous beast. So Robin had been through it, too. I felt a new kinship with him. But his failure had been actual–in the playing itself–and thus more painful than mine. At least I could console myself with thoughts of what my career might have been, if it hadn't been for factors that even now I didn't understand. At least, I told myself, I knew I'd been a first-class performer. Didn't I have the reviews and a recording to prove it? *Yes, gibed a wicked voice. And now you're Turnerville Elementary's very best.*

Again Richard seemed to read my thoughts. "I'll get that harp score to you. I'm going to Rome tomorrow, but I promise you'll have it as soon as I return... Friday, I think. And now I'd better get you home."

He pulled me up from the sofa, dimmed the lamps, and opened the front door. The cold wind sped my steps toward the Aston, standing on a semi-circle of cobble.

We made the trip back in silence, running slowly, but it seemed to me, sitting on the outside, perilously close to the edge of the narrow shelf road that took us around the fell to Denham House. Still, I supposed, it was safe enough; at least there was no ice now. The waning moon shone through a veil of overcast cloud. I felt curiously drained and morose; reaction, I thought, to wine and unaccustomed happiness.

When he took me to the door he didn't touch me at all. The afternoon on the fell might never have happened. "Sleep well," he said. "And tomorrow you'd better start building up some calluses on those fingers."

"I will. Thank you for the evening, and especially for letting me meet Peter. He's an extraordinary child–so bright and unaffected! Please thank Mrs. Chidester again for the wonderful dinner. Oh, and have a good trip to Rome! Are you playing or conducting?"

"Both." He smiled, waved, and was gone, the gravel crunching under the Aston's tires. I stood there a moment, feeling forlorn, left out of everything that really mattered to me.

It was late, and there was no one in the parlor or the dimly lit hall. As I trailed slowly up the stairs, I heard a little purring cry, and Hishi came out from under the steps and shot past me, waiting at my door. I picked him up and carried him into my room, reflecting that it might be a very good thing if I could develop some calluses on my heart, as well.

⚭CHAPTER 11⚯

Memory is the diary that we all carry about with us.
Oscar Wilde, The Importance of Being Earnest

The next morning my only thought was to get my fingers moving again. I meant to be ready for Richard's music when it came. I went to the salon very early, forcing myself to practice softly, as a blister at this stage would mean disaster.

After three hours of playing from memory, a thought struck me. What I sorely needed was conditioning exercises, but I was bored with the ones I knew. Could Ciara's things have been moved to Denham House after the accident, or could she have kept some duplicate scores here? I'd seen nothing in the salon, but perhaps her music had been stored away. I wanted some really challenging studies.

I was almost glad when my perfunctory search through the hall and public rooms failed to turn up Robin. The awkwardness of broaching the subject of my identity seemed, at the moment, too much; the thought of facing his intent blue gaze sapped my resolve. I decided to try Merrin instead. She was in the kitchen, slicing fruit into sections of awesome uniformity. Wiping her hands on a towel, she turned to me with a smile.

"Miss Godwin! I heard you playing when I was outside the salon this morning. It was beautiful. I didn't know you were a harpist!"

"Thank you. Yes, a harpist of sorts. Merrin, may I speak with you for a moment?" I gestured toward the hall. A young girl from the village was washing up the breakfast dishes, and I preferred privacy for this interview.

Merrin followed me through the hall into the salon, faint bewilderment and apprehension on her face. I hoped she didn't think I was going to complain about the food or the service.

I closed the door and turned to her. "Merrin, I need your help. Ciara Rossi–Lady Denham–was my aunt. Robin didn't tell you, or Sir John? No? Well... no one knew until yesterday. I suppose I was just too shy to identify myself. Americans stand in awe of titles, you know. Things haven't changed that much since Henry James!" Funny how this didn't get any easier, even on the third repetition.

She was standing speechless, staring at me with large blue eyes. "You–you're Lady Denham's niece?" She drew a breath, searching my face. "Why yes, I can see it now. There's quite a strong resemblance. But not knowing, I... excuse me, Miss Godwin. I'm just so surprised."

And not very pleased, I thought. "Merrin, you'll be doing me a big favor if you call me Lissa. I'll be here for a few more weeks, and since I'm almost family and everyone else is on a first-name basis–"

She smiled then, and warmth came into her lovely eyes. "Thank you. But surely that's not the favor you wanted to ask of me."

"No," I laughed. "You see, I'm in a bit of a bind. Richard has asked me to play in York in a few weeks, and I desperately need some conditioning exercises. I've been out of circulation for the last few years. I could order the pieces from London, but if my aunt's music is here, I thought it would save time. And having her markings would be helpful."

"Oh, yes! There's tons of music; I boxed it up myself when I helped her maid clear her clothes out of the London house. It's in the attic with the rest of the things, all labeled. Half a moment, I'll get the key and a torch and take you up."

We mounted the stairs to the second story and walked

113

to the very end of the main wing, where she unlocked an oak door. A steep flight led to the chill and dusty spaces of the attic. It was immense, running, as it did, the entire breadth of the house. Cold light from an overcast sky seeped in through high windows. Merrin flipped several switches on a rank of wall plates, and the huge room became fractionally less grey.

She led me down through rows of draped Victorian furniture and brown-paper wrapped paintings to the far end, where heavy pasteboard boxes were piled and metal racks held a long line of plastic-covered dresses.

"It's somewhere here. Let's see: shoes, books, clippings–ah. Music. This one. And this, and this. All marked. Here," she handed me a knife. "You can cut the tape with that. It's cold up here, though. Should we carry the boxes downstairs where it's warm?"

"No, I won't be long. But I would just like to look at some of her things. Thanks so much, Merrin. You don't know what a help this is."

She gave me a curious look. "Well, if she was your aunt, you should have what you want of them. Sir John said we were to dispose of them however we liked; we just haven't gotten around to it, it's been so beastly cold up here. We understood there was no one else in her family," she ended apologetically.

"That's right. Sir John didn't know," I said quickly. "Thanks again, Merrin. I'll lock up when I'm done."

As she closed the door at the foot of the stairs, I picked up the knife. But for some reason, after all my efforts to find the music, I was reluctant to open the boxes. I sighed and sat back on my heels. A little way down the aisle of furniture stood a battered bookcase full of rejects from the library. I rose and went to examine them, fascinated as always by old books, even bad ones. In spite of the ceiling lights, I needed the flashlight in the dim, cavernous room.

It must have been thirty minutes later that I rose, cold, stiff and dusty, and replaced the last volume on the shelf.

Between the bookcase and the wall was a clutter of objects: a broken hockey stick, an old umbrella with bent spines, a corrugated black rubber tube, a grotesque Victorian lamp. I turned back to the boxes of music, dusting my hands, and as I did so, a transient sunbeam struck a glint of pale fire from a dress hanging on the rack. Curious, I lifted the thin plastic cover and saw, with a shock of recognition, the panel of embroidery, medieval in design, lit by silver-gilt threads.

My dress, here in this Yorkshire attic. My Melisande dress, designed by Leon. I picked up a fold of soft black fabric, and memory flooded over me, sweeping me back to Lynton.

Ciara's letter had arrived soon after I returned home from hearing the D'Annunzio *Faustus*. It was, I remembered, the last letter I'd ever had from her, and the longest. It came at a time when I was made vulnerable by that first renewed contact with music and the resultant overwhelming emotion.

"*Darling,*" she had written, "*I've been a dreadful correspondent though I've thought of you more than you know. Life on the international concert circuit is not all champagne and caviar, or even beer and skittles for that matter. I've been doing tremendous amounts of playing and recording, and it all means work, work, work, as you know. Marten aller arten, and all that! By the way, I hear by the grapevine that you're taking a rest, and believe me I envy you.*

My big news—I know I should have written ages ago—is that I have at last taken the leap! I'm married to an Englishman—titled!—I met in Rome some time ago. His name is Sir John Denham (Baronet!). He's quite famous in the antiques field, and has converted his estate in Yorkshire into a first-class hotel, though of course we have a very private suite reserved for our exclusive use. So now your humble aunt is Lady Denham.

You'll know John's half-brother, of course (as who doesn't)—the rather flamboyant and ofttimes disagreeable Richard D'Annunzio. He and I used to be a bit of an item—all water under the bridge now, of course. He's fixing up a little old farmhouse near

Denham House but we don't see much of him. God deliver me from musicians as relatives or friends (present company excepted, love!). Especially those involved in shady dealings, as one hears R. is. I really don't know how he gets away with it, with such a public persona as he has. They say there are Mafia connections on the Italian side, and sadly the drug rumours persist—strictly entre nous, *yes? So of course I keep my distance, except when we're collaborating professionally. One can't really fault him there.*

Anyway, babe, I have a most monumental favor to ask. Remember that stunning dress—costume, almost—that you wore for your Town Hall recital? Well, if you still have it, could you possibly send it so I could wear it, or have it copied? If you're not using it, of course. I'm playing the Villa-Lobos Concerto in Naples this summer and that dress simply shouts Villa-Lobos, don't you agree?

Must rush to rehearsal. Playing the Milhaud Concerto with the London Symphony this weekend. Here's my address when rusticating, and our town house one too."

She went on to give the Yorkshire and London addresses and to fill the bottom of the page with her customary line of x's and o's. I'd put the letter down rather sadly. No invitation, no hope expressed that I might someday visit Yorkshire or London. No mention or memories of Mother. Oddly, no description of her husband, either. And not even the package of her newest CDs and concert reviews that I'd learned to expect.

I leaned back in my chair, looking out the window at the New England hills. Did I remember the dress? How could I forget it? I grimaced at the thought of the sum Daddy had forked out for it.

I'd worn it only once, for my New York debut recital. I could still see the look of triumph in Leon's eyes as he embraced me afterwards. I'd put the dress away with reverence, almost as if it were a bridal gown, but always intending to wear it again, for the right place and the right music. I shelved those thoughts and obediently headed for

116

the little attic to fill Ciara's request.

The spring chill had still been on the attic, that other attic across the ocean in the Greek Revival house. The dresses hung on a rod along the wall, safely encased in their plastic palls: all those corpses of dreams in velvet and silk and Indian gauze. And there, glowing darkly at the end of the row, hung the gown that epitomized Villa-Lobos to Ciara.

The fluid black fabric was cut with stark simplicity, dropping straight from a low square neckline framed with medieval embroidery: satin threads twining their rose and mauve and green into stylized flowers and leaves, enlivened by touches of silver-gilt. The sleeves were long and loose, ending in closely fitting cuffs; the waist caught by a girdle of the same embroidery, with narrow ribbons falling chatelaine-like to the hem. Deep concealed pockets in the side seams provided the ideal hiding places for lipstick and tuning fork. As I toyed with the soft bright ribbons, the past wheeled over into the present, the enclosing walls fell away, and I stood shivering in the enormous, coldly lit attic of Denham House.

No, I didn't think the dress "shouted Villa-Lobos." It spoke of Tintagel: Ygraine waiting for Uther to come sweeping in, disguised in Gorlois' rain-wet cloak; Isolde dreaming of Tristan, watching the restless heaving of a cold Cornish sea. Or perhaps Melisande, weeping by the well in the forest. There was too much mystery in it for the hot primary colors of Villa-Lobos. I wondered if Ciara had ever worn it. She'd never acknowledged its receipt, nor, I realized, that of the wedding present I'd sent. For the first time I felt a stirring of anger and resentment against her.

It remained to be seen whether the dress would shout, or whisper, D'Annunzio. But I resolved that if it did, I'd ask John's permission to wear it in York, unless the orchestra was restricted to uniform, unadorned black.

Blowing on my fingers, I knelt at last to the boxes. Fifteen minutes later, carrying enough music to condition twenty rusty harpists, I left the attic and its disturbing memories, and went down to face the practical problems of the salon.

I came out of the salon just before lunch, feeling a little off balance. The etudes were coming along. But I was beginning to doubt my emotional stability. I could have sworn I'd left the harp tuned to an absolute 440 A. When I'd started my scales, it sounded almost a quarter tone higher. Even if the salon had been colder than usual, it was unlikely the pitch would have risen consistently enough to keep the harp perfectly in tune with itself, not with the different properties of its nylon, gut, and wire strings. I remembered that Ciara's ear had caused her to tune a little high; she'd had to be very disciplined when tuning for ensemble playing so that her instrument wouldn't sound sharp.

What are you saying, Lissa? That you think she's hiding out somewhere in this house?

I shook my head like a dog coming out of water, just as the Bonnets came down the hall. They were on their way to the drawing room to sip coffee and pore over maps of the Lake District, apparently caring not at all that the weather would probably be even worse there.

"Miss Godwin!" Robin was on their heels. Putting a hand on my arm and looking about with a mock conspiratorial air, he spoke in a whisper. "May I call you Felicity? John told me all about it, and it goes without saying that I'm delighted. I suppose we're cousins-in-law, aren't we?" The twinkle in his keen blue eyes was irresistible.

I sighed with relief. "I'd be happy to think so. Thank you, Robin. You've all been kind beyond belief."

He laughed heartily. "You've hardly committed a crime, after all. I can easily understand why you'd want to slip in here quietly instead of marching up with massed trumpets. But now that we've found you, I hope you're going to stay for a while. Some new companionship would be good for us all; it's been a dreary year."

"I know... it must have been terrible." I wondered

118

whether he'd been fond of Ciara, or even known her well. He didn't seem the sort of person she'd bother with; there was no profit in it. Watch it, Lissa, you're sounding like Richard. Curiously, Robin was the only one who hadn't commented on my resemblance to her.

"Felicity–" he had the appearance of a man who's been struck by a happy thought. "How's your head now?"

"My head?" I asked, bewildered.

"Head, stomach, whatever is afflicted. I've got some errands to run in Richmond today. Why don't you come with me? You've been housebound ever since you got here. Besides," he added lightly, "we can foster our quasi-cousinship."

I hesitated. I wasn't really worried about nausea; I felt fine and was usually all right in the front seat of a car. I did want to practice, but on the other hand my fingers were getting sore again. As yet I'd seen so little of Yorkshire, and Robin's sunny enthusiasm and amiable offhand air acted as a tonic.

"My head's in good shape, Robin. I'm sure I'll be okay in the car. I'd love to come, thanks."

"Good. We'll be back before dinner, and I promise to go easy around the curves." He glanced at his watch. "Say in thirty minutes? We'll have a late lunch in Richmond."

"You're on," I replied, and headed for the stairs.

It was a short drive, and I took it in raptly. The mists began to lift as we crossed a stone bridge spanning the Ure, running swiftly with the early thaw. The great fell looming above us still had traces of snow on its crest, like a dusting of confectioner's sugar.

"Would you like a view of Castle Bolton?" asked Robin. "It's only a few kilometres off our route; we'll make a loop."

I wanted to see everything. The sharp air and Robin's careful driving banished any anxiety about car sickness. And we were talking easily, as if we really were cousins; almost as if we'd grown up together. It was odd how smoothly conversation flowed with all the Denham men.

"We've never had any girls in our family, you know," remarked Robin, throwing me a quick smile. He drove smoothly through a sharp left turn. "There was only John and Richard, and me. I lost my parents when I was a kid, and my Uncle James, Richard's father, took me in. I suppose Richard and I were both cuckoos in the nest," he laughed. "John was the only boy who seemed normal to Uncle James. Fortunate that he was the heir."

"You mean... because of the music?"

"Yes. That and other things. Uncle James found it hard to accept Richard's Italian side, for one, though God knows what else he expected when he married Gianna. She was his second wife, you know." A little shrug. "Or perhaps you didn't. You probably don't want to be hearing these boring things, but since you're here, and virtually family—"

A rabbit bounded across the road and he braked gently.

"Well, it's true that I have a very foggy picture of it all," I rejoined. "Ciara didn't go into details; only that she was married to Richard's half-brother. Is John very much like his father?"

"Superficially, yes; otherwise no, thank God. Oh, John's the stereotypical English gentleman, a bit bluff but sophisticated. He's kind, though, without old Sir James' ferocious temper and inflexibility. And he's far more savvy financially. James very nearly succeeded in ruining the estate before he died. It's taken John fifteen years of hard work to get things back in shape. Look—there across the dale."

Bolton Castle, its towers stark and formidable, loomed ahead. A single leafless tree stood in front, lifting twisted black arms to the sky.

"Fourteenth century," added Robin, "and still standing four-square. They've done a lot of work on it lately."

"What a fortress! It looks more like a prison than a

castle."

"Exactly. Good enough to keep Mary Queen of Scots out of mischief for six months, anyway," he agreed.

The castle fixed its baleful eye on us as we drove along. With oddly mingled sensations of oppression and exhilaration, I turned back to Robin and the subject of the Denhams.

"Did you all grow up in Denham House?"

"Off and on. We weren't allowed to go to school here, of course. Heaven forfend that we should catch the dread Yorkshire accent from our classmates. But we spent holidays at the estate."

"And Richard's mother–Gianna–did she leave Yorkshire soon after Sir James died?"

"Oh, years before that. She walked out on him when Richard was in his young teens. I don't know how she stuck it that long. He'd bullied her into abandoning her opera career after Richard was born. All that glamour and independence was fine while he was courting her, but it wouldn't do at all when she became Lady Denham and the mother of his second son." His amusement was tinged with acid.

"What did she do? Leave the country?"

"Yes, went back to Venice, and took Richard with her. That was a spectacular battle, as you may well imagine. Only Uncle James' loathing of notoriety kept him out of the courts. That, and his conviction that Richard had already been corrupted past saving by Gianna and her music. 'When will you forget that poppycock and learn to be a man, my son?' That sort of thing, you know. And Richard was already making a reputation as a pianist. Well, anyway, after a few years in Italy, they moved to New York. Gianna wanted Richard to go to Curtis and Juilliard. By that time old James had written him off completely."

"Whew! So... not such a happy childhood?"

"No, not such a happy childhood," came the quiet echo.

"And you..." I asked tentatively. "How did you fare in the midst of all this?"

He smiled, strong even teeth gleaming above the trim beard. "Not too badly. I was four years younger than Richard, so he took the brunt. Besides, I was only a nephew, so the burden of keeping the family escutcheon bright didn't fall so heavily on me. But I was your prototypical hero-worshipper. Richard read Pascal, so I read Pascal, wondering what the hell it all meant. Richard rode, so I fell off horses. Richard was a pianist, so Robin had to be one too. Then one night in Manchester I heard a harpsichord concert. That was it for me; I never wanted to do anything else. Uncle James was apoplectic––he had visions of me in international banking––but before he had a chance to throw me out for good, he... well, actually he was apoplectic at the best of times. He overdid it once too often, and died of a stroke."

"Heavens, Robin. I'm beginning to realize how sedate my own family life was. But what did you do, with Gianna and Richard gone?"

"I stayed on with John, in the holidays, until I was old enough for the conservatory. He saw to it that I had harpsichord lessons at school. He was almost thirty by then, and well launched in the antiques trade. Of course he was away much of the time, but we rubbed along nicely together."

We'd taken a right turn and were traveling northeast, with the River Swale silvering the stones on our left. The mists had burned off, and the sky deepened to an intense blue.

Robin lifted an inquiring eyebrow. "Are you all right? We're almost there."

"More than all right. I feel wonderful! It's mostly trains and planes that make me ill."

"Good. Still, we'll lunch first and do errands after."

We'd run down to the bottom of the dale, and the country was more wooded now, with here and there a hint of buds on the bushes, brought out by the early thaw.

Richmond Castle's square tower soared above the river, a battlement at each corner, looking for all the world as if it had been built of old ivory dominoes standing on end. Through the huddle of tall stone houses and smoking chimneys rose a smaller church tower, crowned with spear-shaped projections. Robin parked the car in the market square and we walked up a steep cobblestone alley to a tiny restaurant tucked in beside a hotel.

Over barley soup I took my courage in hand and broached the subject that had nagged at me for so long.

"Robin, I haven't wanted to upset John by asking, but exactly how did Ciara's accident happen? The papers said so little."

"Ah." He set down his spoon, momentarily closed his eyes, and with a wry little nod, began. "Of course you want to know. Well, we kept the details as quiet as possible out of deference to John's feelings, and also, frankly, for the sake of his businesses. She was in the Mediterranean, you know, partly for a holiday, but she was playing in Naples as well. She'd rented a little boat for the duration of her stay, and had taken to sailing some of the tiny bays along the Amalfi coast. She was staying at a hotel up in Ravello. It was a quiet place to practice." He paused reflectively. "At least as much as she ever practiced. Have you been there? No? It's perched above Amalfi a thousand feet or so; it's hell driving up there, but she didn't seem to mind. You know, by the way, that Ciara was quite a good sailor?"

I nodded. A silver-framed photograph of her still stood on my mother's desk. Taken during her New York years, it showed her smiling, the wind in her hair, leaning on the mast of the sailboat she'd kept at Southampton.

"How well did you know her, anyway?"

"Not as well as you might expect, considering that she was my parents' only living relative. But that wasn't her fault. We lived a very quiet life in rural Connecticut–Daddy commuted to the city–and there really wasn't much to interest her there. Besides," I said defensively, "she was the most active concert harpist in the world. She hadn't had time in the last ten years... and she introduced me to Leon, and made it really easy for me to get started..."

There was a small silence. "I see," Robin said, picking up his coffee cup and sipping at the steaming brew. "Well, if you know she sailed, you're probably aware that she went out alone, day or night. She seemed to have no physical fears at all."

"Yes, she was that way about performing, too."

Robin set the cup in its saucer and looked at me unhappily.

"This is the difficult part." He hesitated, then plunged in. "Felicity, the police think she'd been meeting a lover in one of those bays. It was the sort of romantic, dramatic thing she'd do. Then John came to Italy, ostensibly to hear her Naples concert, but really in a last-ditch effort to patch things up."

He looked down at his hands. "It hadn't been going well between them, you see. She wasn't living the life she'd expected with John; the money she'd counted on simply wasn't there. She was retaliating with affairs, not even bothering to conceal them."

More confirmation of Richard's tales. Of course, I reminded myself, they were cousins, and shared a strong loyalty to John.

"After the concert and reception they came back to Ravello. She and John had words and she left in a rage. John wasn't unduly worried when she didn't return; it had happened before. But when there was no sign of her and no message by the next afternoon, he called the police. It wasn't until the following day that someone reported her boat, sunk in shallow water near the little bay where she often swam."

He looked out the window, his face grim. "They never found her, as you know. But it wasn't difficult to see what had happened. She was speeding along in a brisk wind, in the dark, and struck a reef–the hull was smashed in–and was flung out, stunned." He raised his eyes. "Felicity, don't look so bleak!" he pleaded. "She can't have known what hit her." He laid a warm hand over mine.

"It's okay, Robin. I'm the one who wanted to know. It's just the thought of all that genius, that vitality, quenched for nothing." I dredged up a shaky smile. "Well, at least there are lots of recordings. She left her testimony behind her. And thank you, dear Robin. I couldn't have asked John, and Richard seemed so vague."

"Vague?" He looked at me blankly.

"Yes. The only time we talked about it, I could see that he knew only what John had told him."

My thoughts slipped back to the night at the Shepherd's Crook, lit with fire and softly shining lamps, and to the utter unreality of sitting opposite Richard D'Annunzio.

"But... Felicity." Robin was speaking slowly, as if feeling his way through a maze. "Richard couldn't possibly have been vague about Ciara's accident."

I stared at him in bewilderment. The laughing chatter of a group of uniformed schoolchildren on the street outside filtered through the window.

"Didn't you know?" he asked, speaking with careful concern. "My dear, Richard was there. He conducted Ciara's last concert."

I spent the next morning practicing etudes, fretting over the wait for the new music, and puzzling over what Robin had told me about Richard. What was it Richard had said in the inn that night? Robin's own words, that "they" had never found the body. Well, of course that referred to the police. I'd mistakenly assumed, from his detached air, that Richard hadn't been there himself. It meant nothing. I set the harp down irritably. I was getting nowhere; time for a break.

I'd resolved to wear the Melisande dress, if John approved and if Richard allowed its deviation from the orchestral uniform. Practicality had prevailed over aesthetics. Even if Richard's composition turned out to be neo-jazz-age, I didn't mean to waste valuable practice time gallivanting to York in search of a gown. The dress was mine, after all; it suited me very well, and its presence in this house was surely fortuitous. That was one matter I could settle, anyway, as John was working in the library.

In a moment he was answering my tap on the paneled door.

"This is a pleasure, Lissa!" he exclaimed. "How goes the practicing?"

"A bit slowly this morning, I'm afraid," I replied ruefully. "John, I'd like to ask a favor." I launched into a tentative explanation about the dress, fearing again to hurt him. It occurred to me that even the sound of the harp must scrape at his wounds.

"But Lissa, of course you must wear it. It's yours, after all, you know! And have anything else of Ciara's that you like as well. Look, my dear," he said, leading me to the big leather sofa. "I don't wish to sound hard, but please don't think I have any sentimental feelings about this. Things are just things, after all–I've dealt with them, in my trade, long enough to be sure of that."

He rubbed his chin thoughtfully. "Your aunt was a brilliant woman, Lissa, and a beautiful and famous one. I'm afraid I was already too much the old bachelor to make her happy. Our ways of life were so different, you see." He gave a rather sad little laugh. "Talk of compulsions–I did exactly what my father did before me, and I'd seen how that worked out. But she was like a thousand-watt light bulb."

"I know," I murmured.

He laughed again, gently sardonic this time. "And I was the moth. Yes, I suppose, in an odd sort of way, that I equated her with Gianna. I was always a bit in love with her, you know, for all that she was my father's wife and fifteen years older than I! You can't know what it meant when I was

126

a boy, her sweetness and laughter in this dreary house."

He broke off and took my hand. "And now, God bless you, you've brought it back. Lissa, do what you like with any of Ciara's things. Believe me, I'm glad for you to have them." His gaze went to the window, to the moors rising into nacreous mists. "I've put it all behind me, I promise you."

Warmed by his praise, I gave his hand a grateful squeeze and rose to go to my room. But as I climbed the stairs, recollection hit and I halted, grasping the rail. I saw Richard standing, somber and unguarded, on the fell, and his voice rang in my ears as if he were on the step beside me: "I've even, God forgive me, sometimes wondered if John drowned her himself."

∽CHAPTER 12∼

If you want to understand today, you have to search yesterday.
Pearl Buck

Out of the mouth of babes--
Psalm 8:2

On Thursday after lunch I decided to take Fiametto over to Hawthorns to see if Peter wanted a ride. The mists had blown away in a keen breeze, and the sun was stronger than I had yet felt it, with a promise of spring warmth to come. Any Yorkshireman could have told me it was a fool's promise, that winter was toying with us like a cat with its prey, but I embraced the day with gratitude.

I dismounted before I reached the farm, and led Fiametto in to the yard. Placid though he was, I wasn't sure how any horse other than Niniane would react to G.P.'s ravening mock assaults.

But there was no sign of the enormous dog. Looping Fiametto's reins around a post, I tapped on the kitchen door. Mrs Chidester appeared promptly, dusting flour from her hands.

"Miss Godwin! Come in. Though if it's Richard you're looking for, I don't expect him back until tomorrow."

"No, I came to see if Peter could go for a short ride. I promise to take great care of him."

"Well, now. That's thoughtful of you, Miss, I'm sure. The boy does get lonely, with his father away, and only an old woman for company. Let's see... Peter and G.P. have gone with Hamish up to the sheepfold in the high meadow to see if it needs repairs before lambing time. Sit down and have a cup of tea, and they'll be back by the time you've finished, I don't doubt."

She'd thrown me a swift speculative glance when she mentioned Peter's loneliness, and I wondered whether she suspected me of trying to get to Richard through his son. Well, one could hardly blame her; it probably happened often enough. I pulled up a chair and soon had my nose buried in a scalding mug. With a comfortable little sigh Mrs. Chidester settled opposite me.

"There now, that's the bread set to rise. My, but this is nice, Miss Godwin. With us it's feast or famine; when we're in London it's about as quiet as Victoria Station, but we hardly see a soul here."

I felt a tug of sympathy toward her. It couldn't be easy for a woman of her age, carting the lively and precocious Peter between city and country, looking after the livestock, and catering to Richard's vagaries as well.

"It's nice for me too, Mrs. Chidester. I don't really know anyone here, and other than practicing, I have nothing useful to do."

"Practicing! There now, of course. Richard told me you're a harpist, like your aunt."

I laughed. "Well, not quite like my aunt, you know. She was a great one, and very famous."

Mrs. Chidester gave the suspicion of a sniff. "There's ways and ways of getting famous, is what I say, and in my years with this family I've seen most of them. No disrespect to the dead, dear, her being your aunt and all, but it might have been better for this family if she hadn't been so famous. Then maybe they never would have met her at all."

She set her mug down rather hard, and looked straight into my stunned face. "Excuse me, Miss Godwin. I'm speaking out of turn and no doubt I'm offending you, though I wouldn't want to do so. But when I think of the troubles she brought!" Her mouth tightened with disapproval and resentment. "I don't scruple to tell you, though I'm sorry for your feelings, that if I knew by Holy Gospel that one of my boys had drowned her, I'd never say a word."

I set my mug down too, but soundlessly. "I'm not offended, Mrs. Chidester," I said slowly. "And I'm sorry if trouble should have come about through my aunt. But what... I really didn't know her very well, you see," I finished lamely, feeling horribly disloyal all over again.

"Didn't you then?" she asked in genuine surprise. "Miss Godwin, you'll think I'm a gossiping old hen, with nothing to do out here in the wilds but conjure up evil thoughts and be rude to Richard's friends. But when I think of my boys–I raised all three of them, you know: John and Richard and Robin."

"I hadn't realized that," I murmured, intrigued.

"Well, John's mother died when he was born, poor girl. That was Helena, and I came into the family with her, you see. And that Gianna, Richard's mother, she had no more idea how to be a mother than a cat. Oh, kind she was, and gay, just like she is this very day, when Sir James wasn't around to put the damper on, but for all she was twenty-nine years old when Richard was born, she was more like a playfellow to him than a mother, if you ask me. It was music, music, music all day long, him playing and her singing, and picnics, and art galleries, and horseback rides. If she ever said him nay about anything I didn't hear it. And him, he treated her like she was the Queen of Sheba, and still does. And my poor little Robin, left all alone, when that no-good mother of his ran off after his father committed suicide–"

I had been sitting at ease, fascinated, making no attempt to stem her flood tide of recollection. But at this last revelation I sat up straight. The tale was starting to assume all the characteristics of a soap-opera. And I had assumed this family to be, with the exception of Richard, a most staid example of the English aristocracy.

"Suicide! Good heavens, Mrs. Chidester, how terrible!

Was it depression, or–"

She laughed shortly. "Yes, I suppose it would be depressing to be caught embezzling three hundred thousand pounds. But I can tell you this, Miss Godwin; if William Denham hadn't been caught, he wouldn't have been one bit depressed, not he. He'd have been merry as a grig, and made straight for the Riviera, most likely. As it was, he couldn't face up to what he'd done; took the coward's way out, if you ask me."

"Mercy! Poor Robin hasn't had an easy time of it, has he?"

"No, and nor has my Richard, no matter he's that famous now. When your own father despises you, and says to your face he doubts you're his son, never mind that he had his very own eyes, and poor Gianna for all her light-headedness putting up with his wicked jealousy so patiently...."

She trailed off as I was still trying to sort out the pronouns. I was silent, my amusement at a bit of gossip having turned to an odd sadness.

Mrs. Chidester must have sensed it right away, for she said, "Miss Godwin, I don't know what you'll think of me, blurting out all this to a stranger, though you're not really that, being almost part of the family, even though it's through that–oh, my; don't mind what I say. Here I've been quiet as a churchmouse for forty-odd years about our troubles, and now I go on to you like the dam was broken. There's something about you... well," she brushed the corner of her eye angrily with her sleeve. "It doesn't seem right, Richard just getting back on his feet after his poor Anna dying, and Peter without any mother, just an old woman like me, and then that serpent of a woman–excuse me, Miss Godwin– coming along and turning things all topsy-turvy."

"But what did she do?" I cried, goaded beyond all discretion. "I know that Richard disliked her, and felt she was double-dealing in some ways, but..Mrs. Chidester," I drew a shaky breath. "You have to realize that although I didn't know my aunt very well, partly because her career took her all over the world, still I'm very grateful to her. She was my mother's sister, after all. She gave me my start in music, encouraged me..." For a while, I thought unwillingly. For a while. The repetitiousness of my defense was beginning to weary even me.

"Oh, aye, she'll have done that for many, I don't doubt."

I frowned, realizing it was true: Ciara had indeed sponsored several young harpists.

"There's nobody in this world, be they black as the devil, who hasn't got some good to them. Besides," she continued with a sound very like a snort, "a goddess has to have her worshippers."

Yes, that was what we had been, I thought, wondering at Mrs. Chidester's perception.

"But I still don't understand what she did that was so dreadful," I persisted. "When I was a child, Ciara seemed so warm and generous–filled with love."

"Oh, aye, she was filled with love all right," agreed Mrs. Chidester dryly, "but it was love for herself. No doubt you know best about how she treated you, but what I saw in her isn't that uncommon among the great ones. When someone loved or admired Lady Denham, she could reflect that warmth back, just like a mirror reflects the sun without having any heat of its own. But what you might call unselfish love now; the love of a woman for a child, that couldn't bring her money or position, or for a suffering animal that couldn't help itself; well, if she had that, she never showed it when I was about, and I saw her over ten or so years, when she was always pushing herself in on Richard. And the way she used her love... Miss Godwin, I'm no prude, though I am an old woman. I've lived around musicians since Gianna walked through the door of Denham House almost forty years ago. And I know many of them are different from ordinary folk.

Their feelings run deeper, you might say, but at the same time they're closer to the surface; kept alive, and feverish, like, by all that singing and playing, and whatever it is they find in it. So with what I've seen, it would take a bit of doing to shock me. But when that kind of feeling is used to turn people against each other, and in such a cold-blooded way..." A look of contrition passed over her face. "Here I am talking about musicians just like you're not one yourself. And you better than your aunt even, Richard says."

"R-Richard said that?" I stammered, caught unaware.

"Not only said it, sat me down and made me listen to one of your pieces. Not that it wasn't a pleasure, dear. I've always thought harp music was pretty."

I murmured thanks, trying to gather my wits. "Richard has my CD---here?"

Somehow that staggered me more than anything I'd heard in this warm, sunny kitchen.

I had just one recording, made between my sweep of the international competitions and Leon's death. At that time I'd never doubted it would be the first of many. Two concertos, performed with the Orchestre Philharmonique du Luxembourg: the Villa-Lobos and the Ginastera.

They were the conductor's choices, not mine; Ciara had recorded them five years previously. The reviews had been so good that I'd laughed, realizing that if I were foolish enough to believe what I read about myself, I'd never again undergo the relentless struggle for perfection.

"Well, now, he has hundreds of records that he's moved here from London."

I took a mental grip on myself.

The next instant the door burst open and we were transfixed by G.P.'s awful roar. For the first time I realized that his aggression sprang from sheer terror. This gargantuan creature was, in the depths of his muddled brain, afraid of anything or anyone even slightly unfamiliar. And his memory was very short. He stood now canted forward, stiff

133

as a bronze statue, hackles up and baying mouth stretched.

We all shouted at once. "G.P.!" Instantly the tense body relaxed and he trotted to my side, grinning and wagging his tail. I stood to greet Peter and the large, red-faced Yorkshireman who accompanied him, and was immediately lashed by G.P.'s robust appendage, effective as a rubber hose.

"Ow. Ow! If you must be happy, you great beast, can't you do it with your nose pointing in the other direction?"

Peter broke into laughter. "Hallo, Lissa. It's my birthday in two days, I'll be seven. Did you come over for a ride?"

"Perceptive juvenile, I did just that. And Mrs. Chidester says we may go. Allow me to congratulate you on your birthday."

"You're talking just like Papa. I'll get my riding boots and be right back."

"Peter," admonished Mrs. Chidester, "aren't you forgetting something?"

"Oh! Sorry, Hamish. Miss Godwin, this is Mr. Oxley. He takes care of the sheep and cows."

"And a great deal more," added Mrs. Chidester. "All right, Peter, you go and get your things now."

"Cheeky little bugger," said Hamish with a look of amusement, as Peter skipped into the hall and up the stairs. He turned a level gaze on me. "So, Miss Godwin, what are you thinking of Yorkshire?"

"I love it! I've wanted to come here ever since I was a child. I can't wait to see the new lambs, and hear the cuckoos..."

"Ay, well, if you had to be out in the fields while the bloody things are nattering on, you'd gladly wait till Doomsday," he said crisply, ignoring Mrs. Chidester's repressive look. "Dawn to dark—it's 'cuckoo, cuckoo, cuckoo' until you figure it's not the bird that's cuckoo, it's you."

"Oh..." I began, realizing how silly my own romantic

nattering must sound to this hard-working man.

"Goodbye to you then. I'll be off." Without ceremony, he exited the kitchen.

Mrs. Chidester sighed. "You'll have to excuse him, Miss Godwin. Hamish has been with the family since he was a lad, and he's very protective of Richard. He's seen so many women set their snares that he's suspicious of any attractive young person who shows her face around here."

"Oh." Again, I was speechless. I wondered if Hamish's suspicions included Marjorie, or if he approved and wanted to fend off any other contenders. Still reeling, I tried to pull my thoughts together. "Well, Mrs. Chidester, he needn't worry about me. I'll have Peter back in an hour. Thank you for the tea, and for... telling me things. I admit to being very confused. You see, Ciara was all the family I had left."

"Oh, poor lamb. Well, losing a relative would be sad for anyone." She was searching for something sympathetic to say. "I kept thinking myself she'd be back, watching in the hotel lobby all that day."

"You were there?" I was taken completely by surprise.

"We were all there, except for Robin. Gianna knew Ciara from early days, and she'd done her best to warn John off the marriage. She had us packed up as soon as she found out John and Richard were both going to be there–she smelled trouble. So we took Peter and flew down to Italy. Gianna gave out that it was a holiday for Peter, and to hear Ciara play, but she was that worried about Richard. She knew Ciara once had him in her toils, see, and," she lowered her voice to a whisper as Peter's feet clattered on the stairs. "Gianna was afraid he'd do something foolish, I don't know what; run off after her, I suppose, or, if she pushed him too far–"

She broke off and gave me a warning look. I hardly saw it; something was clicking into place. Italy. Of course, it had happened in Italy. What had Tim said, all those long years ago, about Richard's Mafia connections? And Ciara herself, in her letter? If he'd wanted her dead, he need never have raised a hand except to pick up a telephone.

But hadn't Richard said his relationship with Ciara ended before she married John?

G.P. stood up and shook his head, his ears flapping with the sound of a week's laundry on the line.

"Let's go, Lissa!"

I turned to see Peter standing in the door.

"All right, imperious one. We'll be back soon, Mrs. Chidester, and I'll take good care of him."

The sun afforded a faint warmth as we trotted sedately up the meadow. Peter was mounted on his well-mannered little pony, Sir Bors. He managed very nicely indeed for a boy just turning seven; he had light hands and a natural confidence.

Spotting a glimmer of water, I pulled up beside a tiny stream meandering through the dry grass. Shards of ice lay in delicate pleats along the edge of the water.

"Peter, is it safe to drink?"

"No, Papa says not. The sheep graze above here."

"Well, let's stay for a moment anyway. It's so pretty. You can't drink out of the streams in Connecticut, either, but sometimes you can in Colorado."

We slid down by the water. Peter flung himself on his stomach, chin propped on elbows. "Colorado and Conn... Connecticut. Is that like London and Yorkshire?"

"Well, in a way, but not quite. Colorado's where I used to spend holidays, and Connecticut's where I grew up. They're both states, though, like...like Yorkshire is, you might say. Like shires. But they're much farther apart than going all the way across England."

"That must take a long time. Which place did you go to school?" he inquired politely.

Concealing my amusement at the adult *savoir faire* of

136

the question, an exact echo of his father's on our first meeting, I replied, "In Connecticut, in my own home town, till I was fifteen. Then I went to Pennsylvania, and New York. That's both a city and a state; New York, I mean."

"I know," he said. "I've been there with Papa and Gianna. Is that where you got taught by that man who changed your name?"

I nodded, surprised that he remembered.

"Well, I'm not to be sent away to school, not until I'm much bigger. Papa hated being sent away to school, and he doesn't want me to hate anything. So he teaches me when he's home, and Marjorie when he's not, and next year maybe I'll have a tutor. I don't want to go away, so I'm glad. I like being with my people. Papa, and John and Robin, and G.P. and Sir Bors and Gianna and the chickens and you–you're my people now too, aren't you?"

"I can't really lay claim to that honor, love, though I'd like to. I'm only a sort of distant cousin by marriage. An un-cousin, really."

He laughed, his merry eyes sparkling at the nonsense. "Anyway, you're related. John says so. You won't go away, will you?"

I was silent for a moment and he watched me amicably, chewing on a stalk of grass.

"I can't promise that, Peter." There was a queer constriction in my throat. "My home is in the States, you know."

"You're a musician, Papa says. Musicians spend a lot of time going away." He sighed resignedly. "Well, I shan't be one. Maybe I'll be a painter, like Mama was. I love to paint. Or–Papa says I shall probably be a phil... what do you call it? A philosopher."

Laughing, I pulled him to his feet. "You already are, my pet."

After a gentle canter up to the sheepfold and a return

through the meadow, we turned Sir Bors out to pasture. Dismounting from Fiametto outside the kitchen, I didn't see the Aston parked in front of the house. When Richard opened the door, I was transfixed once again by that odd feeling of unreality. But I could see at once that he was in tearing spirits.

"I... I thought you weren't coming back until tomorrow," I murmured, like some apologetic, incoherent fool.

"So you felt safe kidnapping my son?" he laughed, hugging Peter, who had flung himself at Richard's legs. "No, I don't have a present for you, you infant extortionist. You'll have to wait for your proper birthday."

I laughed too, catching the contagion of his good humour.

"Lissa and I have been for a ride, Papa. We jumped, big jumps, didn't we, Lissa?"

"Tremendous. How was the concert, Richard?"

"Mmm... *comme ci, comme ca*," he replied, tilting an equivocal hand. But the fierce exultation blazing from his eyes told me he was still riding high on his triumph.

I began to relax, seeing again the human element behind the figurehead. "Why this sudden modesty? Afraid the gods will strike you down for hubris? Maybe they'll just melt your wings a little, for flying so close to the sun."

"Avaunt, Cassandra!" he laughed protestingly. "Pax. Here, let me pour out a sacrificial libation. Tea? A drink?" Peter's eyes were flashing between us, trying to take it in, puzzled but happy.

"No, truly, thank you. This time I really must get back. Oh–is the harp score ready? For... for your new work?" Mrs. Chidester's last words came rushing back, ominous as a thundercloud, and I found I couldn't utter the title of the piece.

"Yes, I finished it in Rome. There's just a little touching up to do; I promise you'll have it tomorrow. Here, Peter." He took the reins from my hands. "Hold Fiametto for a moment, will you please?"

With a hand on my arm, he turned me about and we walked a few paces toward the front of the house.

"Look, I've got to go to Harrogate tomorrow. I didn't have time in Rome to shop, and the chief desire of Peter's heart is a set of lead soldiers. Harrogate's strong on Victoria toys. Why don't you come with me; maybe you can help me pick out something else for him. And you might like to do some shopping of your own. I'll bring the music along. We'll have lunch, and be back early."

I wanted very much to go, yet I had a plethora of reasons for feeling I ought not to see too much of Richard. "Well..."

"Why not? *Mal de* road?"

"No. I'm quite all right in the front seat, unless I'm already sick. Yes. I'd like to go, thank you. And I do need a pair of shoes for the York concert."

"And a gown? Perhaps we won't be back early, after all."

"No, I'm wearing one of my own that I sent to Ciara last year. It was brought here after...."

"Ah." His voice was light, politely detached. "How fortuitous."

"If it's appropriate, that is. It's not entirely black; it has some colored trim. I think she wore it for her last concert, in Naples."

"It sounds fine. York won't be that formal. Very well, I'll pick you up. At nine, then?"

"At nine," I agreed. "*Mit* score, don't forget."

His teeth gleamed. "*Mit, con, avec,* and with score, I promise."

≫CHAPTER 13≪

I will tell you all Circe's fatal wiles.
Homer, The Odyssey

---That though I knew not in what time or place, Methought
that I had often met with you
And each had lived in either's heart and speech.
Sonnet, Alfred, Lord Tennyson

The brisk March breeze was driving feathery clouds across a blue sky as Richard handed me into the car. He cocked an appreciative brow at my rose wool dress.

"'Shall I compare thee to a summer's day?'"

"Well," I considered, "I suppose you could. Certainly I'm more temperate. At least, more temperate than I was at our first meeting. In fact, we both are."

"Let us hope so. And you're certainly more lovely. Now–magic slippers, is it? And lead soldiers. So we're off to Harrogate."

I tossed my coat into the back of the Aston. A sun that was all brilliance and little warmth lit the golden hills as we drove down the avenue of bare beeches. Inside the car it was comfortable and quiet, but not for long. At the end of the drive Richard paused, switching on the radio. Immediately there arose a cacophony all too familiar to me: one of the *avant-garde* chamber works that sounded like a chemistry lab gone berserk.

"Two tomcats, a pogo stick, and a washing machine."

"Exactly. Here, pick a CD, will you?

He handed me a leather carrier, and after a moment's

consideration I slipped in a Vivaldi flute concerto: *Il Gardellino.* I had grown a little tired of hearing Vivaldi in every elevator, but this was the marvelous one that always put me in mind of a feckless bird who, flying over a garden party, had fallen into the martini pitcher and taken its time getting out.

I said as much to Richard, and he burst into involuntary laughter. To the ridiculously joyous effervescence of the music we shot from under the beeches into the crystalline day.

"You're certainly merry this morning," he observed.

"Yes, I suppose I am." I stretched contentedly. "I'm happy," I added, in some surprise.

He gave me a considering look. "You sound as if that's not the usual state of things."

"It isn't," I said frankly, "and I should be ashamed of myself. I have so much–a house, a job, good health. Yet since I stopped playing..." I trailed off, remembering an acquaintance who had commented rather acidly on my depression. "A fellow teacher once told me I should snap out of it; that she'd thought there was 'more to me' than that."

His hands tightened on the wheel, and he made a wordless, angry sound. "I hope she was thoroughly trampled at the next recess."

It was my turn to laugh. "No, she was right."

"She was stupidly, criminally wrong. If you'd been distressed over a divorce or an alcoholic husband, she probably would have condoled with you. But she couldn't have known, I suppose, how much more music can be a part of one. And that the artist has a great need to see himself reflected in those around him. When your peers don't have even the faintest comprehension of what it is you do..." He lifted his hands from the wheel. "I remember, Lissa. I had my years away from music, too."

His understanding put me pleasantly off guard. I relaxed into the leather seat. Soaring and dipping with

Vivaldi's mad, inebriated bird, I reflected dreamily on how quickly my life had changed from drab gray blanket to vivid tapestry.

I was awakened from this blissful reverie by a thought that jabbed me with icy and metallic reality. I had remembered one of the purposes of this delightful jaunt. Magic slippers, indeed!

"Oh!" I croaked, sitting bolt upright. "The score! You said you'd bring it."

"And so I did. I finished it in Rome, and did the markings last night. The pedal indications are just suggestions; you must put your own in, of course. It's in the back."

I wasn't sure whether the churning in my stomach was caused by the thought of performing again or by the sharp bend the road took as I turned to reach into the seat behind me. Rummaging under my coat, I seized the heavy portfolio with HARP stamped in funereal block letters on the front, and opened it to a thick sheaf of manuscript paper, covered in a neat but assertive hand with what looked to be millions of black notes.

"Oh!" I cried again. You... you said it was easy." Anger and distress leapt up like sulfurous little flames. "'Unimportant' was the word you used. This is just 'tone color?'"

"It... grew. Seemed to take its own direction somehow. But have a heart, Lissa! Give it a try before you panic; I think you'll find it lies under the hands. Anyway, you'd better not look at it while the car's moving." He took the score from my hands and dropped it carelessly into the back. "I don't want a swooning damsel on my hands again," he concluded euphemistically. "Here, have an apple."

He reached into his jacket pocket and handed me a shiny russet fruit.

I looked at him suspiciously. "Richard," I said, "is this a test?"

142

He burst into spontaneous laughter again.

"Absolutely not. Anyway, I don't think I could devise one you couldn't pass." He gave me a swift glance and dropped his hand over mine. "Don't worry, my dear," he said softly. "You're a quick study. It'll be all right, you'll see."

We were winding through a tiny village, grey stone walls channeling the narrow road like a river. More dry stone walls ran up toward the moor above, dividing the tree-bordered fields into long tilted planes. The wind had freshened, blowing cloud shadows across the moor at a dizzying speed. The cluster of houses and barns flowed gently by. It was the exact embodiment of my childhood dreams.

The village was behind us and we'd resumed our speed when I summoned the nerve to ask what I had to know.

"Richard, why are you doing this? I mean, truthfully, with all the established harpists within calling distance, why are you giving the part to me?"

"You don't consider yourself established? A recording with Radio Luxembourg? Concerts all over New York? First prize in the Israel competition? And the Brussels competition? And Munich?"

"That was years ago. I fled the field under pretty murky circumstances."

"You were driven from the field, Lissa, by a master of egocentrism and manipulation. And remember, you were what–twenty-one? Twenty-two? Very young, and you'd just lost your parents and your mentor. Has it occurred to you that if someone tried that on you now, it might not be so easy for them? You might approach the problem head on, and fight like the devil."

I mulled that one over. "Well... maybe. What I'm trying to say is–oh, hell! All right, I'll just say it. Are you letting me play now because of what happened back then? The Debussy program?"

With a keen look at me, Richard pulled the car onto the narrow verge and braked. "Because I owe you one, you mean? Look, Lissa." He laid a hand on my arm. "To tell the truth, there's something of that in it, I suppose. If you think I feel guilty for my part in bringing your career to a temporary halt, and want to assuage my guilt, I won't deny it. But–look at me, Lissa." He raised a hand and turned my face toward him. "Even if I'd never wronged you; never even heard of your brilliance, for that matter–I'd have wanted you after you played in the salon that night."

Wanted me? The words, even misconstrued, sent shivers down my spine. At the same time a singing began in my heart, drowning out the Vivaldi. I saw the cloud shadows, still racing, through a blur of tears, and took refuge in irritability.

"How much did you hear, anyway? Just how long had you been sitting in that blasted chair?"

"Long enough. More than an hour. You were certainly absorbed; I could have walked out with the harpsichord and you'd never have known. I heard Reinecke, Ravel, Milhaud, Rota. And the Tournier. Enough to make me sure you were the one for *Le Marchand*."

And enough for you to see to the very bottom of my soul, I thought. Well, if I had been able to hold D'Annunzio's musical interest for that long, I certainly should be able to handle a part in a chamber work. I hauled the portfolio back over the seat and flipped through the pages. At the sight of the wildly tumbling notes a painful doubt thrust in its barbed shaft.

"And if I spoil it?"

He shut his eyes and let out a soft, short, vehement Italianism. I didn't know the phrase, but its meaning was unmistakable.

"For God's sake, Lissa, don't go all broody on me, like one of Peter's speckled hens. It's just a part, after all, and you're a virtuoso and a professional. What's the fuss? Here,

144

give me the bloody thing–" He seized the score and lobbed it once more into the back. "Let's go and have some fun."

I drew a long and shaky breath. Viewed in the cool clear light of his professionalism, my attitude stood revealed as one of adolescent dithering. He did these things every day as a matter of course; he regarded me as a competent musician who would do the same. I vowed I would maunder no more. I'd do my best with the part, and if my rainbow bubble of glass was crushed again, I'd do the sweeping up by myself–again.

"Right." I answered. "End of subject."

We lunched amid the Victorian splendors of the Majestic Hotel. I drank one more glass of wine than was advisable, and was feeling very carefree indeed as we set out in search of Peter's soldiers.

Peter's armies was more like it, I thought, as the clerk swathed the purchases in opulent wrappings. Richard had selected two magnificent sets of belligerent lead warriors, while I bought my own present for Peter, a big box of Spanish *castillo* blocks like the ones I'd played with as a child.

"He has to have something for all those battalions to defend," I explained as we stepped out into the windy afternoon.

"He'll love it, and so will I."

We went into Ogden's, a quietly elegant jeweler's on Cambridge Street. Nineteenth-century wood cabinets of beautiful workmanship lined the walls to the ceiling, displaying silver, clocks, and jewels of all descriptions.

"What a beautiful opal!" I exclaimed, taking a closer look at a ring, its fiery depths circled by small diamonds. "Such a mysterious stone."

"I've always thought so. Oh, hello, Lucia," he said, turning. "Now, what brings you to Yorkshire?"

"Diamonds of course, Riccardo," she replied, waving a small velvet box under his nose.

She was tall, slim, and beautiful, with Titian hair and

the sort of coolly amused, appraising look that the rich and sophisticated carry off with ease. She wore soft leather boots under a long black coat, with a beautiful violet wool shawl draped over her shoulders. Oh no, I thought. No. This was too much. Her eyes were emerald green, like those of the Scarlett O'Hara doll I'd adored in childhood. Or Ciara's. The combination of red hair, green eyes, and violet shawl was glorious. Her voice was pitched seductively low, slightly and charmingly accented.

"Lucia, may I present Lissa Leone. Lissa, this is Lucia Pavesi, a most important agent, so smile nicely at her. Lucia, I thought you were in Rome."

"So I was, *caro*, and so were you, as you should remember. That doesn't mean I have to stay there."

"And you're here to shop? Don't you find Harrogate a bit limiting?" He held the door open and we stepped out onto the street.

"Perhaps. But it's much easier than a big city, and there are some wonderful old print galleries. Though I must say the climate could stand some improvement. Fit for nothing but your everlasting sheep–brrr!" She shivered dramatically and drew her shawl more closely around her shoulders.

"Well, it's not the tourist season, you know," he said blandly. "You should wear warmer clothing, or try it in May or June."

She swung abruptly toward me. "And you, Miss... Leone, you are a Yorkshire native?" It was plain that, quite correctly, she considered my use of a foreign name spurious. I hadn't yet opened my mouth, so at least she hadn't identified me as American.

"No." Richard's gently sardonic voice forestalled my answer. "Lissa's seeing the sights. She likes touring the hinterlands in March."

"Excuse me," I murmured, feeling hopelessly *de trop*, as if a time-traveling Louisa May Alcott had accidentally inserted me into one of Noel Coward's scripts. "I think I left my handkerchief inside."

Richard's eyebrows shot up in amused disbelief as I turned away. Damn, I thought, my cheeks hot. Did he never forget anything? Twice before he'd been forced to reach into his pocket to supply my needs. Well, I could hardly say I'd left my keys. I didn't have a car any more than I had a handkerchief.

Waiting until their *tête-à-tête* was finished, I stood near a display of clocks at the front of the store. As customers came and went, the two voices, torn by the wind, sounded fitfully through the door. They were conversing in Italian, the woman's speech rapid and agitated, Richard's collected and cold. At length she spat out what was obviously a gutter word, turned on her expensive heel and strode down the street.

I saw Richard throw back his head and laugh. There was something almost lupine in it, and I repressed a shiver. Heading for the door, I met him as he entered. He took my arm and we were on the street again, going in the opposite direction from that in which the red-haired woman had departed.

"Find your handkerchief?" he asked, with charming concern.

"Yes. No! Damn it, Richard, you know I didn't. To be truthful, I just felt a bit in the way."

"Because of the Pavesi? My dear girl, I was counting on your protection."

"Protection? Are you sure you wanted it? From that gorgeous creature? Anyway, I should think you could protect yourself."

"I begin to wonder. She's very persevering–witness the trip to Yorkshire. It's a desirable quality in an agent, but unfortunately she carries it into other areas. And she's a dead bore."

"You mean she came here to see you? In a professional

capacity? She's after your music, then. Or is it your body?" This popped out without premeditation. *Lissa, Lissa, why will you drink too much wine?* Oh, well, it isn't as if he were Muti or Levine, I countered recklessly. After all, he's only a decade older than I; surely I don't have to consider him a monument quite yet.

He burst into laughter. "A little of each, I think. Anyway, I've forestalled her coming to Hawthorns, so it was a fortuitous meeting. Lucia may be gorgeous, but she has all the depth of a sheet of plastic wrap."

"Nevertheless, I've never seen such fabulous eyes. And with that glorious hair–"

"Lissa. Have you never heard of colored contact lenses?"

"You mean–oh." Remembering, I was silenced.

"Now... shoes, right? Ah, there's a purveyor of female footwear just across the street. I'll find some books for Peter while you're looking."

Ten minutes later I was carrying out a sleek parcel containing heels high enough for glamour yet practical enough for managing the harp pedals; confections that could indeed serve as magic slippers. Though I'd blinked at the price, I was delighted to find shoes of the same silver-gilt as the embroidery on my gown.

"Good God, woman," exclaimed Richard, eyeing my parcel in amazement as I entered the bookstore. "You don't mean to tell me that you're done? I was prepared to spend the afternoon here until you were properly shod. Well..." he picked up a small stack of volumes and moved to the counter. "Any more errands? No? In that case, would you like to see something very special? It's a bit out of our way, but it's early yet."

"I'd love to, Richard, but–" I stopped, my gaze riveted by a poster on the wall behind the cash register. It was a stark portrait of Richard, a negative image in black on a red ground, and it had the brutal power of a mailed fist. Below, in bold letters, I read:

Benefit for York Minster
PREMIERE PERFORMANCE
THE MERCHANT OF DREAMS
Richard D'Annunzio, Composer and Pianist
Conducting the York Guildhall Chamber Orchestra
Works of Bach and Beethoven
York Barbican

Then the date and hour.

"I need to practice," I finished weakly.

"Yes, well, I was going to suggest I run over the part with you tomorrow. That will answer any questions about tempo, and we'll know if anything I've written will work. I have most of the day free before—my dear girl, are you ill? What is it?"

He followed my gaze, and laughed. "Oh, that. Yes, it is a bit Mephisthophelean, isn't it? The choice of color is eye-catching, to put it charitably. And there's nothing to draw a crowd like a performer with a speaking likeness to an X-ray film. Sorry it seems to be a one-man show, but none of the principal performers were engaged when it was designed. It's just advance publicity, anyway. It'll be replaced by a more detailed one next week. Ready?"

He picked up the parcels, took my arm, and steered me out the door.

So much for my professional resolve, I thought gloomily. The moment I was confronted by the actuality of the performance, simple fear drained the blood from my face. From what seemed an incalculable distance, I was surprised to hear the ordinary tone of my voice.

"Where are we going?"

"Rievaulx Abbey. Look, about tomorrow—we'll just blunder through the score together. I understand the difficulties of sight-reading on the harp, so don't worry. I'll be grateful for your suggestions; it's a tricky instrument to write for. Shall we say one o'clock?"

He was talking rather fast and very smoothly as he helped me into the car. It occurred to me that he had seen my genuine and spontaneous terror. Perversely, that made me feel confident, and I laughed.

"Okay. One o'clock. But I warn you, that's a lot of ink. I'm not promising a thing."

"She asks for wine, and I give her ink. Very well, I'm exacting no promises."

We drew away from the curb and headed northeast for Rievaulx.

We came out of the trees onto a little crescent of terrace. In the tawny afternoon light the pointed arches of the choir gleamed, tier on tier, from the valley floor. None of the pictures I had pored over, back in the States, had prepared me for this great ruin's heart-lifting purity and ineffable benison of peace. I simply sat down where I was, and said, "Oh."

"Quite," agreed Richard softly.

I was caught up in the combination of laughter and tears that true beauty, whether in nature, music, poetry or art, always brought. Fleetingly I remembered verses from art songs I'd once accompanied. "Beauty has filled my heart; it can hold no more." And "Beauty, more than bitterness, makes the heart ache."

Part of it, I knew, was sorrow for the ephemeral nature of a loveliness that must pass. But I thought, with a swell of elation, that here my heart certainly ached in vain. Though its lonely glory might be diminished, Rievaulx had stood, through all weathers, since the early 1100s.

"No wonder they call architecture frozen music," I mused, as Richard sank onto the dry grass at my side.

"This one's a fugue, I think," he replied. "Incomparable, isn't it? I never tire of seeing it."

I turned to him impulsively, all defenses and fears forgotten in the experience of shared wonder. "Thank you for bringing me here, Richard! I'm so glad I came to Yorkshire, in spite of all that nonsense at the beginning. And... I'm glad I'm going to play again. I know I sound like Pollyanna, but never mind that."

He smiled. "I don't mind at all seeing you in the role of Glad Girl. And I'm happy, too, that you're back behind the harp, Lissa. You shouldn't hide your light under a bushel. It won't do, you know."

With a sigh, he lay back in the dry grass. He must be very tired, I realized. He'd flown in from a demanding performance in Rome only yesterday, and he'd be off again tomorrow.

"Not only because practicing your art is necessary to you, yourself," he continued, "but because you must give something back. I think you have an obligation; we all do. If one really loves music and has a God-given gift, as I know you have, it's hypocrisy to profess that love without giving service to it in some way. There. Close of moralizing."

"'Love without service,'" I quoted slowly, searching my memory, feeling my way, "'is like the emotion of a playgoer who weeps in the theater at sufferings that would leave him unmoved in the street.' That, or something like it, was said in this very place, I believe, long ago. In another context, of course."

"Ailred of Rievaulx." The words were uttered in an amazed whisper. "'To love is one thing; to love with self-surrender is another and a harder thing.'"

He sat up and looked at me with startled eyes. "Lissa, where on earth did you come across that?"

"In a book on Arthurian legend–'the matter of Britain,' isn't it called? I read it when I had flu. So you know it too."

"Yes. I'm working on an Arthurian song cycle, and I've been researching for months. Those phrases stuck in my memory, somehow." More matter-of-factly, he went on.

"And in yours as well. You're a constant surprise to me, Lissa."

"Why?" I tried to keep bitterness out of my tone. "Because I read books, because I have some sort of life of the mind? It's no credit to me. What other sort has there been for me?" I hated the self-pity seeping into my voice, but I was suddenly overwhelmed by frustration. Why can't you take me in your arms again so that once, just once, I can live the kind of life I want?

"You could have done as I did, I suppose," he was saying. "I didn't stop at a life of the mind. I just plunged ahead and compromised myself in–oh, God knows how many ways."

His honesty touched me, and thinking of Anna, I wanted to assuage his regret.

"But never musically," I said firmly.

"Never musically, thank God. And thank you, Lissa, for reminding me of that."

For once I took the initiative, and, getting to my feet, held out my hand. I looked down into eyes that were dark with some obscure pain. In that brief moment, overcome with sympathy and flooded with a sense of kinship, I stood firmly with Mrs. Chidester. If my own eyes had seen him pitch my once-adored aunt overboard, I might have kept silent.

"On your feet, Dr. D'Annunzio," I smiled. "Down the hill, and no tarrying. You're taking me on a conducted–or is it conductor's?–tour of Rievaulx."

That night I stayed up until long past midnight, softly working my way through Richard's harp score. It was, at bottom, what Leon had always referred to as "a good piece of roast beef": something to get one's teeth into. Above and beyond that, it held the passion and dark enchantment I'd sought long and vainly in harp literature. There was violence, though the piece was less dissonant than some of his earlier works. And there was the soaring lyricism, even more intense, that had torn at me in the *Faustus*. It was also far longer than I'd anticipated; I'd have to work fast and efficiently to learn it at all.

Curiously, the harp part seemed almost to stand on its own. The playing was virtually continuous, and as far as I could tell, melodically important. Technically it was a marvel. The most coruscating virtuoso passages were written with an idiomatic understanding of the instrument that made them feel right and reasonable. Though the work was demanding, one wouldn't be teetering on the edge of impossibility. In short, it was difficult enough, sounded formidable, but felt comfortable. My respect for Richard's musicianship overleapt its already towering height.

His knowledge of the harp was remarkable. In writing for an instrument upon which every string has three pitches, controlled by the use of one of seven three-notched pedals, even harpist-composers were known to make errors and omissions. But this score was completely and correctly marked. Richard had done his homework with a vengeance.

I set the harp down, stilled its ringing, and rose to turn out the salon lights. Time for sleep if I were to be smart tomorrow, and smart I must be.

Hishi scratched at the door as I stepped out of my bath, and I picked him up, holding him on his back like a baby as I gently stroked his stomach. His purring deepened to an ecstatic snore.

I sighed as I sank onto the bed. Nice to be a cat, I thought. I'd be one in my next life, perhaps. Then I'd have warmth and affection.

I pulled up the comforter. Warmth and affection–it had been a long time since I'd known them in any form. I thought briefly of the young science teacher at Turnerville who'd asked me out, just once. He was normally intelligent, good natured, and, in the opinion of the faculty women, handsome enough to die for. He was also utterly prosaic, obsessed by college football and the amount of chrome on late-model pickups. It had taken me exactly ten minutes, on our first date, to realize we had virtually nothing to say to each other. The time might have been shorter for him.

Julia had seen it immediately. "Well, of course, Felicity. It couldn't be easy for you to feel romantic about a man who starts every other sentence with 'irregardless'!" For Julia, that was a paradigm of the vapidity behind his suspiciously regular features. But at a deeper level, the whole experience had brought home the terrible loneliness of the artist exiled from her community. It had nothing to do with elitism; it was a painful longing for like minds.

The bedside lamp spilled its light over the pillows, gilding the guard-hairs on Hishi's ears. No matter what happened at the concert, I thought; no matter what Richard had done, whether he had misjudged Ciara, lied to me, or even, I thought half-facetiously, killed her himself; for a little while I'd been given this: this touching of mind and spirit. And it had been nothing short of resurrection.

⋙CHAPTER 14⋘

I cried for madder music, and for stronger wine.
Ernest Dowson,
Non sum qualis eram bonae sub regno Cynarae

I rose at dawn, and by one o'clock I'd mastered the complexities of the score sufficiently to read slowly but fairly steadily through it. I was reviewing a tricky passage when the door opened and Richard came in. He was dressed for travel in a dark suit. I set the harp down and turned toward him.

"Hard at work, I see. How's the... er, lot of ink?"

"I cry pardon, Dr. D'Annunzio. I was mistaken. It truly is written in wine."

He looked, for the first time since I'd known him, somewhat disconcerted, and I wondered if he thought me presumptuous. But he merely said, very softly, "*Merci du compliment,*" and pulled a chair close by my side. We played and talked through the score for an hour, confirming my first impression. The music was difficult but not unreasonably so.

"This bit is tough, I know," said Richard, pointing out a long passage that was particularly black with notes. "If it's not workable, we'll do something else, but I'd like to keep it if you think it'll do."

I studied the page for a moment without speaking. All at once I had a sharp physical awareness of him. He was leaning very close, intent on the music, his tanned face standing out in strong relief against a white shirt. Beautifully cut hair, thick and black, swept across his brow, and there was the same slight aroma of sandalwood I'd noticed on his

155

handkerchiefs. Since that day on the moor he'd never touched me except in the most casual fashion. He slanted an inquiring glance out of the dark-rimmed, lavishly lashed eyes.

"*C'est possible?*" he murmured.

"Certainly," I replied from a dry throat, and giving myself a figurative pinch I launched into the passage, tentatively at first, then with growing confidence.

"Ah." He sat back in the chair. "Unquestionably. I'm impressed. And grateful."

I gave a small laugh. "I'm the one who's grateful. You can't know what it means to be learning a score again."

"Yes, I can. I remember: meat and drink." He rose and took my hands. "Peter thanks you for the castle blocks. He's writing an enthusiastic and illegible letter, and would like you to come and play–his words–soon. And now I'll have to hot-foot it to Manchester; I'm cutting it close now for my flight. I'll be back in five days. If you have any problems, we'll make revisions. But I'm leaving with a tranquil mind, knowing the score's in your hands. And look..." he hesitated, drawing a long breath. "When you practice, try not to think of Ciara, will you?"

For a moment I was bewildered. I heard Leon saying, "You must not play like her! You must not try to be her!"

"It's difficult, I know," he went on, gesturing toward the portrait, "with that hanging there, and having to use her harp. Why doesn't John take the damned thing down, anyway?" he said in sudden exasperation. "There's hardly any need to make this the Ciara Rossi Memorial music room."

His meaning was quite different from what I had thought.

"Her death was an accident; you've accepted that, so don't spoil your tranquility by speculating on it. Just practice, try to rest, and have a good time. It's not too long since you were ill, remember, so don't overdo it. I want you at York."

156

There were those words again. He gripped my shoulder, released it, and was gone. I was standing in the middle of the great room, feeling a little desolate, when Robin came in.

"Ha!" he cried, throwing out his arms in triumph. "They're gone, gone, gone, my dear un-cousin, and I'm free as a bird!"

"Who's gone?" I asked, coming back to earth.

"The Bonnets, of course; the very last of the lodgers. There's no one else until the grand reopening next month, thank God." He was laughing like a child let out of school.

"I'm glad. Nonetheless, you love it, don't you? The work, I mean."

He looked a little surprised. "Why, yes; yes, I suppose I do."

"It must be a great satisfaction, running a beautiful place like this to perfection."

"It's not exactly what I'd planned for my life," he confessed with a grin, "but it's better than cooking burgers."

"Ah, those proverbial plans. Mine didn't work out so wonderfully, either. Though–did Richard tell you? I have a chance to play at the end of the month. It's certainly the last thing I ever expected."

"Yes, the *Merchant* piece. Good for you, Lissa. How's the part?"

"Challenging, to say the least. And full of fire and brimstone, of course, but so much more... oh, you'll just have to hear it, Robin. Will you be coming to York?"

"Certainly I'll come, if I'm in Yorkshire. I've planned a few small getaways, since you've turned out to be family. But we'll have someone in to get meals for you."

"Mmm... thanks, but it's not necessary. I'm a dab hand in the kitchen. That's something we say in Lynton–it means I'm good. Oh, you say it too? Anyway, Robin, I've been thinking about getting back into my training routine for performance: mostly uncooked foods plus lots of exercise. So please don't give the kitchen another thought. I'll shop in Richmond and dice vegetables to my heart's content."

"Done. You can eat celery and carrots all day and night; better you than I. Well, now that I'm no longer in thrall to the culinary arts, and you're determined to be so blooming healthy, how about a walk? It's a rare day."

I looked at the eager, humorous face, the lively blue eyes. Robin was so human, so much of this earth. By contrast, Richard sometimes called up the uneasiness of an enigmatic dream.

"Race you up the fell?"

"Good Lord, no! I'm game for a sedate ramble, but I don't have your American propensity for seeking out difficulties, please remember."

"All right, my staid English un-relative. But you're not fooling me. You're a Yorkshireman. You'd leave me panting in the field." I knew he could; his wiry form gave the impression of coiled strength in reserve.

So we walked that afternoon, on the swell of the hills. The sun smiled down from a sky which bore occasional tatters of cloud, creaming over in the wind like surf at the edge of a strand. We talked nonsense, laughed as heedlessly as children, and I forgot, for an hour, that there was such a thing as music to be played on my dead aunt's harp. Or such a person as the man who had written it in wine.

Or in blood.

≈CHAPTER 15≈

A multitude of small delights constitute happiness.
Charles Baudelaire

Do we stand in our own light, wherever we go,
and fight our own shadows forever?
Edward Bulwer-Lytton

For the next ten days I lived, breathed and slept *Merchant of Dreams*. Having mastered the notes in record time by sheer diligence and willpower, I set out to make them a part of me, to get inside every phrase. At night I'd fall into slumber while running over the difficult passages in my mind, and wake in the same way.

When I wasn't practicing, I had plenty of time for reflection. I was beginning to see myself in a most unflattering light. My conversations with Richard had opened my eyes, at least partially, to a disturbing view of my life over the past five years.

Putting the sorrow of my parents' death aside, I could see that my behavior had fallen far short of being admirable. Through my teens and early twenties all I'd wished for had simply fallen into my lap. Yes, I'd worked hard at my chosen profession, but so had many others. I had musical gifts far beyond the normal. I had contacts and opportunities that other young harpists would have killed for. I had Leon, the most respected concert harpist of the century, as my teacher. I had ample money, loving support from my mother and father, and yes, encouragement from Ciara. And at the first sign of difficulty, what had I done?

Simply fallen apart, totally and unresistingly. Crumbled. Slunk away whining, gone home and turned up my toes. Accepted a teaching job I didn't want–one that was ridiculous, given my accomplishments–as a new form of martyrdom. I hadn't fought one moment for what I knew, in my heart, to be my rightful work.

Richard had tried to justify my passivity on the way to Harrogate, pleading youth, inexperience, and grief. In my present mood of self-flagellation, I wasn't buying that. But I was, for the first time, ready to put it behind me. Well, now I've faced that, I thought, what I want is a challenge.

I wasn't sure I'd ever had a real challenge before. It was always just assumed, among my family and colleagues, that I'd excel, and I did. With my abilities and joy in the work, it was easy. Now no one assumed that I'd excel, but by God I was going to.

Realizing that I was still a bit weakened from the flu, I plotted a regimen that would build up my strength–or utterly deplete it, I thought with wry amusement.

In the early morning, in the quiet of the empty house, I practiced for two hours. Then I rode Fiametto, if the weather allowed, for an hour, practiced for another hour and a half, packed a lunch and made for the fells. Robin accompanied me twice before leaving for a short holiday in London.

When I walked alone, I climbed to the top of the big fell behind the house. At first it was an exhausting struggle; on the extremely steep parts, I would sometimes climb only a dozen steps and rest for six breaths. But as my endurance increased, I cut minutes off my time, and soon was taking only a few short breaks to get my wind back. Once at the top, I lay on a great flat stone, deeply cleft, where a few blades of grass, nurtured by the warmth of sporadic sunlight, were thrusting up to the sky. A tiny spring, brown and clear as ale, issued from the ground and sang its tuneful way around the base of the rock.

As I watched the grey clouds above, I often saw birds

flying into the wind, hanging utterly motionless for long moments. Returning to the house, I would nap for a while, then closet myself with the harp. And after an early supper I'd practice for another two or three hours. I suppose it was a lonely way to spend the days, but they were some of the most joyous and purposeful I'd ever known.

I'd been following this routine for the better part of two weeks when, on Thursday morning, Richard walked in. In the midst of playing a complex, cadenza-like passage I realized two things simultaneously. The salon door was opening, and there was an ominous pain in the pad of my left fourth finger.

"Oh... Richard!" For once, in his presence, I spoke almost abstractedly, the sharp little stab of dread overpowering any other feelings. "Good trip?"

"Very satisfactory. I'm off again tonight. What's wrong?" He'd noted my quick, almost furtive glance at my hand.

"Nothing... oh, damn. I've done it now. I'm beginning a blood blister."

He came to look, lifting my hand in his own firm brown one, cool from the air outside.

"Mm... yes. You'll have to go softly on that for awhile. I thought you weren't going to overdo it."

"Well, I tried not to. Drat it all, Richard, I've been so careful! But I keep getting carried away. Don't laugh, it's all your fault anyway. How can you write a passage like that and expect me to play it at a tame mezzo forte?"

He was still laughing, with a barely veiled triumph in the sound. "No more for you this morning, Madame Liszt. And I suppose you'll have to practice at a whisper for the next few days, whatever your pyrotechnical inclinations. But it couldn't matter less. From the sound of things you have the notes mastered inside out."

I looked at him critically. "Have you been listening outside that door?"

"*Mea culpa*, Lissa. The ego of the composer, you know. Hearing you play–it's like seeing one's own child trotted out in its very best clothes, hair brushed and shining. It's perfect, even in that passage I had doubts about: the close one with the repeated figures. I was sure there would be some buzzing there."

I couldn't keep from beaming at him. I felt as if I'd walked magically into a bright and cloudless day. "It's the wide spacing of the strings, I expect. I've never played anything else, and I'm lucky Ciara's harp has it."

He sat down in the Queen Anne chair. "Look, Lissa, I've just had a brainstorm. You're letter-perfect on that score; it only needs time to develop in your mind. And you need to retrench, give your finger time to recover. Let me propose a plan: I've a concert in Geneva this Saturday night, and on Sunday Robin and I are going on to Zermatt for some early spring skiing. It'll be a matter of three or four days at most. Come with us."

I sat frozen on the bench, trying to quiet the unlooked-for thrill of anticipation. "But... I can't, Richard! I'd love it, but I really can't. I have to stay and work; there's so little time. I can practice very softly. It's nice of you to think of me–"

He brushed this aside impatiently. "*Dio*, Lissa! Sometimes you remind me of Charlotte Brontë."

"Thanks," I responded, puzzled. "Any particular reason, other than our lack of dates?"

A little explosion of laughter. "Yes, damn it! You seem to share her idea that she was unworthy to have fun. Be sensible. You know that score backward."

"Yes, and that's probably exactly the way I'd play it, if I took the time to go to Switzerland. Besides, have you considered my *mal de* air?"

"I have," he answered unexpectedly. "Have you ever heard of a transdermal patch?"

I shook my head.

162

"Gianna uses them. She's been increasingly subject to motion sickness, and she had the prescription from her doctor in Rome. It's a tiny pad permeated with scopolamine, an anti-nausea drug. One just pops it on behind the ear and goes winging off without a care. The medication is absorbed through the skin. And according to Gianna, it's totally effective, far more than the old pills. As a matter of fact, I have some at Hawthorns; I carry them in case she forgets when we travel together." He smiled wryly. "Her mind is always on higher things."

"It sounds wonderful, Richard. I really shouldn't... oh, but it's tempting!" Was I really getting spinsterish, I wondered. Yes, undoubtedly I was; in fact, I'd already arrived. The reference to my beloved Charlotte had caused me an unpleasant twinge. Repressed passions, expressed only through one's art. No wonder I'd felt such a kinship to her.

"Of course you should," he was saying reasonably. "Otherwise you'll have a bloody great hole in your finger, and you'll go stale on the music as well. Come on, Lissa, your flight won't leave until tomorrow night, and when you return you'll still have another full week to practice, plus the three days of rehearsal. It's only the one piece to prepare. Besides, you said you'd never heard my Brahms."

"Oh... are you playing in Geneva?" I'd assumed, somehow, that he was conducting.

"Yes, the Brahms One and the Mozart Twenty-one. And I'm vain enough to want you to hear them."

That really surprised me. "Good heavens, two concertos. Well, I certainly would like to. As you said, it's been my loss."

He winced. "Did I indeed? Oh, well. That definitely settles it; we're off to the slopes. Do you ski as well as you ride?"

I gave a suppressed moan. "You've discovered my Achilles heel. I haven't skied for years, and what I really do best is get up from falls–I've had so much practice. No, I'm a rotten skier and a coward to boot. I've never gotten past being a low intermediate. And yet–it's odd–I absolutely adore it. The feeling of flying, even at my snail's pace. And simply being on the mountain. I just never took time for enough lessons, and I'm not what you'd call a natural."

"Perhaps Robin and I can help you a bit. Anyway, we'll have sunshine, a change of scene, and fun. Tomorrow, then. Robin will see to the reservations, and I'll give him the transdermal patches to pass on to you. Dear God," he finished, tilting back his head and closing his eyes, "it will be good to get out of the concert hall and onto the mountains for a few days."

"You're very tired, aren't you?" The shadows under his eyes were deeper today. It was a terrific schedule to maintain; only someone with enormous natural vitality could survive it. But I knew that his was great–so great that I wondered, for a moment, if some other strain contributed to his look of exhaustion.

"Tired?" His head came forward and he looked at me with brooding eyes. "A bit. I'm behind on my Beethoven for the York affair. That and... ah, well, things will slow down soon. The summer will be relatively quiet, except for festivals." With an effort, he smiled. "I don't suppose you've any ski clothes with you."

"No, but I can pick some up in Switzerland." Ciara's things were in the attic, but somehow I balked at the thought of using them. The Melisande dress was different; it was mine. I realized how much my feelings toward Ciara had been altered by the Denham family.

"They'll cost the earth," he was saying.

"What? Oh, it doesn't matter. I haven't exactly been extravagant on this trip so far."

"Right. You and Robin will fly to Geneva on Friday–tomorrow night. Let's see... I rehearse tomorrow afternoon and Saturday morning. The concert's Saturday night, at

Victoria Hall. Superb acoustics, by the way. So Robin will book a room for you at the Richemond for Friday and Saturday. Sunday morning we'll buzz off to Zermatt." He smiled at me, easily this time. "Or would you rather go somewhere else? Zermatt's a bit passé, I suppose; I go because I loved it as a child, but I have friends who wouldn't be caught dead there."

"Great heavens," I laughed. "I grew up watching old Sonja Henie movies. And reading Heidi. I used to think all chairs should have hearts carved into the backs, and one couldn't go skiing without arriving by sleigh, preferably with Tyrone Power. Just lead me to it!"

"Okay, *liebchen*." Kissing his hand to me, he exited.

I had volunteered to cook dinner that night. John was in residence, and Robin was touching base between his brief holidays. I loved to cook, and, to be honest, I wanted to show off a little.

Robin looked into the kitchen, where I was removing brown paper from my carefully piped meringue shell. He would have stayed, offering witty asides on my outmoded New England techniques, but I shooed him out.

When I judged things to be well in hand, I went upstairs to bathe and dress in heathery green wool. It took less time than I'd thought, so I ran down to the salon to squeeze in a few more minutes of practice. The harp was faintly, almost imperceptibly sharp again, except for the middle C, which was extremely flat. I frowned, pulled it up, and played a long passage. It went flat again. I stopped, set the harp down, and took a close look at the bright red string. It was very bright indeed. I'd thought perhaps it was old and perishing, but now I realized it was brand new.

The hairs prickled on the back of my neck. "Be logical, not emotional, Felicity." The memory of Leon's words steadied me a little. All right. I certainly hadn't changed the string, unless I'd been walking in my sleep. So who was left?

John and Robin were both in the house. Richard, although he'd begged off dinner to spend time with Peter tonight, was conveniently close. But why on earth–it was extremely unlikely that either of the two musicians would have changed the string, even if they had found it broken, on an instrument they didn't play. That left what? Rather, who? I found I didn't want to say Ciara's name, even silently.

Thoughtfully, I entered the library.

"Well, Lissa!" John got to his feet and came to greet me with a hearty kiss. "How lovely you look. And what a treat, my dear! Robin says you've made something delectable for us tonight."

"Robin surmises, optimistically as usual," I smiled. "You can be sure that my barbaric New World cuisine will be a comedown by his standards. But the wines will be good–I asked him to choose. Anyway, I thought it was time I contributed something to this household!"

"Now my dear," John began gently. He and I had argued amicably about my status in Denham House, he insisting I was family, I maintaining that I had begun, and would end, as a paying guest.

"No, I won't spoil our evening with such prosaic matters, but you haven't heard the last from me, my genial host. If we must lock horns–"

John spread his hands helplessly and turned to Robin. "Stubborn, isn't she?"

"A family trait, no doubt," replied Robin casually. John looked taken aback, and I felt surprise at Robin's lack of tact. Probably he just hadn't made the connection to Ciara.

But John, ever gracious, summoned a smile and continued smoothly. "Well, and a very commendable one, after all. The way she perseveres in her practice! Such discipline."

"It isn't discipline, it's lust." This was the time to mention the changed string and the sharped tuning, but somehow I veered away from it, reluctant to turn the light conversation into an inquiry. "Furthermore, I've persevered myself right into a blood blister. And so–did you know?–I'm to fly off to Zermatt with Robin and Richard for a round of *sitzmarks*."

And this time, strangely, John did almost lose his composure. Something flared behind his eyes. "Skiing? With Robin and Richard?" He rose abruptly from his chair and went to refill his glass. When he turned back it was with his usual kind smile. "Well, you'll have some sunshine, and that will be a good thing. Are you quite sure you're strong enough, my dear? One forgets that you came here to rest after an illness."

"Oh, yes." I wondered briefly if the remark had been pointed. Did John feel I was capitalizing on my position to further a relationship with either, or both, of his relatives? I dismissed the thought. "I've been more or less in training, climbing the fells and riding Fiametto, thanks to you. I'm getting stronger every day, truly I am! Besides, you don't know how I ski. It's not a very strenuous procedure, I assure you."

"And you don't worry about accidents to your hands? Or a broken arm, for instance?"

"I know lots of musicians who do, but I've never let it stop me from riding or skiing. Carpal tunnel syndrome is a much more likely injury."

"I'm sure you're right. It's just that we don't want you getting sick or hurt before the York concert, you know. Richard is counting on you so."

"No, I won't. Honestly, John, I'm feeling like an Amazon; I could slay dragons! It must be the Yorkshire air."

I realized I'd actually heard a mention of the York concert without that familiar and dreadful contraction of the stomach. On an upswing of confidence I added, "And I'm really getting to know that score inside out. All it needs it time to 'cook,' and there'll be enough of that when we come back."

"Fortunate that you're a quick study," said Robin.

John shot him a level look and murmured, "Indeed."

Straightforward on the surface, but there was an undercurrent between them that I didn't understand. Feeling a little out of my depth, I said, "By the way, John, I've meant to thank you for letting me use Ciara's harp."

"My dear, of course you're more than welcome. It's wonderful to have it properly cared for. Is it adequate to your purposes?"

"Adequate! I should hope so! It's the finest instrument I've ever played. I'm having a little trouble keeping it in tune, but that's natural, since it hasn't been played for so long." Again I backed away. I could either accuse one of them, or Richard, or make them think I was completely insane by suggesting Ciara had replaced the string. Except for two daily cleaning girls from the village, there was no one else in the house; Merrin was on vacation. In this bright, civilized room, it was all too impossible. "And what a superlative sound! Ciara must have had it specially built, with the Rococo design and the wide string spacing–that hasn't been generally available for a long time."

"Yes, I think she did. She ordered it some years ago, soon after we met. She was very particular about the specifications, I remember."

"Does the wide spacing work for you, Lissa?" asked Robin.

"It's a Godsend, since it's all I've ever played. For those of us with long fingers who can handle the extra reach," I explained to John, "it virtually eliminates buzzing against an adjacent string. It's a marvelous stroke of luck for me that it's built that way."

I looked at my watch, got to my feet and said lightly, "Well. Time to assuage the pangs. Shall we go in, gentlemen?"

They sprang up as one, and each taking an arm, escorted me into the dining room with easy gallantry.

168

"Lissa," said Robin, "you don't know how happy I am that you're going with us."

The clearing-up was done, and John had retired to his rooms to read, so he said, an assistant's evaluation of a newly acquired double stool attributed to Benjamin Goodison.

Robin had built up the library fire and its light flickered cheerfully on the library paneling. I gave a murmur of pleasure and sank deeper into the sofa. In the ruddy shifting glow, the muted colors of hundreds of bindings made a soft rich frieze along the wall.

"So am I, Robin. Though I don't know what could be lovelier than this! Talk about cups running over. I was thinking the other day... everything has gone from grey to technicolor, like that moment in 'The Wizard' when Dorothy opens the door and steps out into Oz." I turned to him with a laugh. "Do you know how many years it's been since I've done anything for pure fun?"

"Far too long, I'd guess." Turning to look into my eyes, he spoke softly. "We're going to change that, Lissa."

"I think I've just begun to realize how futile, and how boring to others, my self-assumed martyr rôle has become."

He dropped an arm casually about my shoulder, and, relaxed and happy with wine and the praise my dinner had elicited, I leaned back into its curve as if it were the most natural thing in the world.

"You know," I continued languidly, "it's really strange to think back over my reasons for coming here. I was obsessed with Ciara, I suppose."

I was starting to add that I sometimes felt appalled at how easily I put her out of my mind when Robin said, "Lissa, you don't think there was anything... not right about her death?"

It occurred to me that now all three Denham men had asked me that question, and I felt my hackles rise.

"I think there was everything wrong about it," I replied, and all at once had the sensation that my neck was resting against a band of steel.

I sat up and looked at him. The black-rimmed irises, so like Richard's except for their brilliant blue color, were wide and strained.

"Robin," I said with sudden passion, "I know how you all felt about her, from Richard right down to Mrs. Chidester. Of course she had her faults–faults that I imagine are standard equipment for almost any international figure: egotism, selfishness, imperiousness. But she had such a tremendous gift to share! She was young, creative, brilliant, and absolutely fearless. There haven't been five harpists of her caliber in the last century. And you have to remember, she'd done so much for me."

I continued more quietly. "She sent me a letter, Robin, not long before she died. I still have it. Perhaps it wasn't the most thoughtfully written epistle in the world; nothing like my mother would have done. Still, after all the trouble she'd invested in me, there wasn't a hint of criticism that I'd let my career lapse; she simply skirted the issue. So I feel her loss, though I never knew her that well. And however it happened," I finished, "it was a stupid tragic quirk of fate, and I didn't think I could ever accept it..." My voice trailed off, "...until I came here."

I sat there, my own words ringing in my ears. I saw, as if looking at another person, how my perception of loss had been dulled by the pleasures and excitements of this house. There was no one left to mourn Ciara, no one to defend her save myself. Anger and guilt fed one another, urging me on.

"If indeed it was a quirk of fate. Robin, do you really think it was an accident? Oh, I know what the Italian police said. But she was such a good sailor! A strong swimmer too. And there seem to have been so many people around who would just as soon have had her dead." Richard and John among them, I thought, and subsided.

170

But it was too late. Robin was looking at me intently.

"So you do realize that." His voice was different, no longer lighthearted and frivolous. He sounded as if he'd struggled with himself and come to a difficult decision. "Well, I suppose you could include me in that unhappy little company, though I didn't have the opportunity. I was on holiday with a friend in Ischia."

I turned to face him, feeling weak. My words had been childish, malicious even; a mere striking out at the injustice I felt everyone, including myself, was doing to Ciara's memory. "Robin," I whispered, "you mean... you think..."

"I'll tell you what I don't think," he broke in with unexpected vehemence. "I don't think for one moment that Ciara died accidentally. As you say, there was too much hatred all around her. And she was too good a sailor to run into a reef, even at night. The weather was calm, and she knew that little bay like the back of her hand. God, if only I'd been there." He struck the sofa arm with a clenched fist.

A new trap door had opened under my feet. Mrs. Chidester's reminiscences had given me some bad moments, but nothing like these irrevocable words. A wave of sickness washed over me.

"Robin." My voice sounded ragged. "Who was there?" I had to hear it again, from someone besides Mrs. Chidester. I could make no sense of any of it; there were too many people who wanted her gone for me to focus on a single subject.

"In the family? Damn near everyone. Richard, of course, conducting the concert. John flew in from London, and at the last moment Gianna came, with Nanny Chidester and Peter. So, the full complement, save yours truly."

"You don't really think, surely, that any of them–" I broke off, finding it difficult to continue.

He rose abruptly and went to stand before the fire, his back toward me. "Oh God, Lissa, I don't know what I think. No, I suppose not. Though it's gnawed at me all these

171

months; there's something wrong, in spite of the police having shelved it. Something bloody wrong." He turned to face me. "Who knows what her life was really like, or what enemies she'd made? It might have been a hired assassination, for one thing. But it didn't have to be outright murder either. There could have been an argument: God knows she provoked enough of those. A shove, a blow; then panic. Unintentional killing disguised to look like an accident. It would have been easy to sink the body, knock a hole in the boat."

"Didn't they already do that in *Rebecca*?"

He stopped, perhaps taken aback at what he thought to be my flippancy. I know I was, myself.

He stared at me for a moment. "Look, dear, you know that according to the police there was a man who met her in that little bay. They'd been seen at a distance, several times, by fishermen, though none of them could identify him. It was always in the evening, when the boats were coming in. Her sailboat was familiar to them, though, and it would have been hard to mistake that hair and that body, even at dusk. It was the sort of knife-edge situation that would appeal to her, satisfy her crazy need for risk. Another day or so and the paparazzi would have been onto it in a feeding frenzy with their zoom lenses. Can't you see it at the supermarket? 'International jet-setting harpist betrays English baronet husband–dot dot dot–seen nude with mystery man at secret island hideout!'"

"Perhaps that was it," I said, grasping the proffered straw. "An argument with her Italian lover."

"Oh, yes." He spoke with bitter amusement. "Her Italian lover." Seeing my dawning horror, he moved quickly to my side. "Don't, Lissa. Oh, my dear, I'm sorry."

The first tear splashed onto his hand as he gently cupped my chin. Then he pulled me up into his arms and tenderly kissed the wetness away. When his lips, salty with tears, met mine, I leaned gratefully into the comfort of his

172

embrace; anodyne to the pain and shock I'd felt when he put my troubling doubts into words.

After a long moment he held me at arms' length, studying me with grave concern.

"Lissa," he said with a sigh. "You're such a lovely girl." He gave me a reassuring little shake. "Forget what I've said, please. I've been talking wildly. We're all a little crazy just now, and I've been working far too hard. But I won't say I'm sorry, since it's put you into my arms."

I wiped away the last traces of tears and looked up at him. "Dear Robin. Thank you for holding me together. I think I'll go up to my room and get some sleep now. I seem to be very confused."

He laughed lightly, confidently. "You weren't at all confused when I kissed you just now."

There was some truth in what he said. I'd certainly responded without hesitation to the tenderness, safety, and pleasure of his embrace.

I smiled unsteadily. "More confused than you could possibly know, but it was a nice confusion. Goodnight, Robin, and I'm sorry for the tears. I seem to cry a lot in Yorkshire."

"Then we're right to get you out of Yorkshire for a bit. And speaking of that, Lissa, it would be best not to take this up with Richard on our trip."

I looked at him, perplexed. "Well, of course I won't, Robin! What would I say? 'Oh, by the way, Richard, was it you who hit my aunt over the head with a rock? Tied weights to her ankles, perhaps, and smashed in her boat?'"

I thought he looked whiter than ever, and remembered that these two men were probably as close as brothers.

"Robin, have you ever talked, really talked, to Richard about it?"

"Can't be done. He's my cousin, Lissa," he said with finality. "You don't know what hell this has been for us all, John especially. For God's sake, let it lie."

"I'm sorry, Robin. That was callous. I must be tireder than I thought. I really am going to bed. A walk in the morning?"

He nodded, and giving my hand a squeeze, stood in the door watching as I hurried up the stairs.

≪CHAPTER 16≫

Toto, I've a feeling we're not in Kansas anymore.
L. Frank Baum, The Wizard of Oz

The lights of Geneva lay like clustered jewels flung down at the end of the inky lake. Circling Cointrin, I caught myself in a smile of wonderment. For the first time in years, I was landing with a clear head and a serene stomach. The transdermal patch, applied when Robin and I boarded, had lived up to its billing, and I had eaten, drunk, and chatted with Robin as happily as if my feet were firmly on the ground.

Settling beside me in the taxi, Robin gave an abrupt exclamation and struck his forehead dramatically.

"What's the matter?" I asked. "Forget your toothbrush?"

"Worse," he moaned. "Richard charged me with telling you about the party tomorrow night so you could bring a gown, and blunderer that I am, I forgot."

"No damage done," I reassured him. "I don't think I have anything that could live up to a Geneva party anyway. What is it, a reception for Richard?"

"Yes, alas, and it'll probably be a stuffy bore. It's being given by some old friends of Gianna's in their bloody great house. I'd rather cruise Geneva with you, babe." Here he took my hand and dropped into what he fondly imagined to be a Chicago accent. "But the Boss insists. Gianna's flying over for the bash, and he wants the Family there."

"Come off it, Al Capone," I rebuked. "From what I've heard of Gianna, I can't imagine any of her friends being

175

stuffy." The prospect of meeting Richard's mother both intrigued and intimidated me.

"No, but these are old friends, I told you, really old. In their eighties, most likely. God, they'll probably be wheeled out for our delectation. We'll have to stand about for hours sipping champagne and being urbane... and inane..."

"Now you've metamorphosed into Cole Porter. I think I liked Al better. Anyway, what are you complaining about? It shouldn't be an effort for you; you grew up among the elite. Consider the plight of an elementary school music teacher from darkest Connecticut. Well, at least I can buy an urbane dress in Geneva."

"Provided you brought your sack of emeralds."

"I never travel without it. You know, Robin, I think I'll shop first thing in the morning, so there'll be time for seeing sights and a nap before the concert. No, you may not go along, you'd just confuse me." I caught his teasing smile, thought of the night in the library, and went on hurriedly. "Just go and look at frogs and scores and institutional equipment, or whatever frogmen and harpsichordists and hotel managers look at for fun. Do you know," I finished with real enthusiasm, "that you are the most extraordinarily versatile person?"

He looked at me unsmilingly, the lively blue eyes still. Then he flicked a finger lightly against my nose.

"All right, my proud beauty, make your own ill-advised choice. I'll treat you to lunch and no doubt have to suffer your second thoughts on the purchase." He opened the cab door and we stepped out under the canopy of the Richemond.

I was dressed and ready as soon as the shops opened the next morning, which in Geneva was remarkably early. I'd slept without dreams and felt refreshed and eager for my pleasant task. Though I'd always abhorred shopping per se, there was, I had to admit, something exciting about looking

176

out a dress for such a special occasion. So I wandered, that morning, like a wide-eyed child in an enchanted orchard of precious and exotic fruit.

It was past eleven when I found it; a luscious pour of apricot silk, to all appearances simple as a slip, but with the innumerable tiny refinements of good Continental couture. Good; the better or best I wouldn't even think of springing for. I walked out of the velvet-carpeted salon without a backward look, knowing that for once I'd made the right, the only choice. I'd brought an old sable cape of my mother's, packed in Lynton with the thought of attending some London concerts. Though I would never buy a fur myself, not caring to think of the little lives extinguished to feed my vanity, it seemed pointless and wasteful to consign an existing one to the moths. Yes, it would do, I thought. And with it only the beaten gold disc earrings, swinging from tiny stylized fish, that Daddy had brought me from Greece when I was a teenager. With a light heart I jumped into a cab and hurried to meet Robin for lunch.

As the lights darkened in the gilded splendor of Victoria Hall, I was aware of a feeling of excitement, almost turmoil, in my stomach. Strangely, I'd always had this feeling when my friends played, far more acutely than for myself. Striving for calm, and trying not to think about the coming York performance, I smoothed the silken skirt absently over my knees and looked around me. The dimly seen faces reflected an almost uniformly pleasurable anticipation, with here and there the bored or exasperated countenance of the reluctant spouse who'd been dragged from his armchair.

Stealing a glance at Robin, I saw he was looking tense. Was he feeling nervous for Richard, as I was, or was it regret for his own aborted career? The organized chaos of the tuning orchestra was suddenly stilled, putting an end to my musings, and Richard D'Annunzio stepped on the stage to a tumult of applause.

I tried to ignore the little wrenching spasm at my heart as he bowed rather curtly, seating himself without further ado at the concert grand. In the attentive silence he raised his hands, the violinists raised their bows, and the strings bounced the first light-hearted octaves into the audience.

The long, amiable introduction to the Mozart Piano Concerto Number Twenty-One was conducted with quiet authority from the keyboard. There was none of the awkwardness I had often associated with pianist-conductors. Richard made the piano bench seem the one possible spot from which to lead an orchestra.

Now he was into the opening keyboard passages, and any further analytical thought went out the window as the rapturous purity of his playing filled the hall. The concerto made no demands on his prodigious technique. He was literally playing: sporting with the music in undiluted joy. My spirits soared with the piano's irrepressible mirth.

Even the overplayed, often sentimentalized second movement, which had long ago borne the dubious distinction of serving as a film score, was imbued with a freshness and transparency that gave it the aura of a first performance, removing every trace of tarnish from its lines. And I had to restrain myself from laughing aloud at the exhilarating, bubbling passages of the third movement as they danced their way through the hall, creating a sunlit world in which nothing could possibly go wrong. As the last insouciant scales scampered into the dome and the roar of applause began, I turned to Robin.

He took a deep breath and smiled. "Another *tour de force*. Listen to that crowd."

Richard's bows were gracious enough, but tinged with a hint of impatience, as if to say, "Yes, this is all very well, but let's be done with the nonsense and get back to what really matters."

The Mozart was followed by a serene and beautifully nuanced performance of a lengthy new Japanese orchestral work, with Richard on the podium. At intermission we sipped champagne in the lobby, not attempting much talk above the noise. When I retreated to the ladies' room I was startled by what I saw in the gilt-rimmed mirror. This girl, with loose dark hair framing a face of extraordinary vivacity, was a stranger to me. Was this really what a few days of musical gratification, stiff exercise, and unaccustomed excitement had done? The wide grey eyes were full of life, and the apricot tints of the slim silk gown were reflected in the high color of my face. I pushed my hair behind the glint of the swinging gold earrings. If I was not the once-blonde Lissa Leone, neither was I the "pale shadow"of Ciara. All at once I felt ready for anything, even York.

Robin was already in his seat. He rose and gave me a smile of winning sweetness. Taut with anticipation of what was to come, I was finding conversation difficult, but he seemed to understand. Again I studied the faces around me, realizing with difficulty that there were those to whom this was merely a casual pleasure, and not a scalding but absolutely necessary joy.

The second half of the program was devoted to the monumental First Piano Concerto of Johannes Brahms, which would be led by the orchestra's associate conductor. The density, length and complexity of the piece precluded its being conducted from the piano.

I'd often been amused to hear this work described as academic and abstract. To me, it revealed the heights and depths of a passionate young composer's soul.

The lights dimmed once again, and Richard was on stage, striding to the piano and seating himself with an economy of movement, all grace and vitality. I could see, even at this distance, that he was in a state of near exaltation. A combination of superb fitness and adrenaline was carrying him with seeming effortlessness through the feat of playing two concertos and guiding the orchestra through another intricate work. The Brahms alone was forty-five minutes in length, demanding tremendous physical strength as well as harrowing concentration. Some men were indeed Titans. My mother had remembered hearing Artur Rubenstein, in New Haven, play the Mozart G major Concerto, the Liszt E flat, and the Brahms First all on one program, and he hadn't been a young man then.

The demonic, awesome opening trills shattered the still air of the hall, and we were swept into the *Sturm und Drang* of the first movement. The relentless D minor roll of the timpani underscored the terror of the music. And then the piano spoke with deceptive quietness.

Your loss, Richard had commented, when I'd remarked flippantly that I hadn't heard his Brahms. How very right he had been. All the dark passion and revolt were there, speaking through his breathtaking virtuosity, illuminated by fearsome intelligence and held true by a foundation of stern musical integrity.

Shaken by the emotional storm of the first movement, I sat bemused through the nocturnal, yearning languor of the Adagio. "I am painting a lovely portrait of you," the twenty-three year old Brahms had written to Clara Schumann, his forbidden love. It was a portrait which moved, with strange compulsion, from devotional purity to piercingly restless longing.

Brahms had described the last movement as "terribly difficult." Richard played the leaping first theme with stunning virility, and the tender passages that followed breathed Brahms' youthful fervor.

The final passages of this, my favorite concerto, had always had a curious effect on me, one that had occasioned wry comment from family and friends. I found myself literally unable to sit still, and when playing the recording invariably rose to my feet, striding about the room, often weeping and laughing joyously, not caring how crazy I seemed. I simply did not know, as the moment drew near, how I was going to sit sanely and sedately in my plush-covered chair.

With rising excitement I heard the reflective cadenza slipping into a lilting alpine sunniness that broke through the austere Nordic themes. Now the heavenly falling trills, followed by the great thrice-ascending and descending octave scale. And then, then–the tremendous surge of life-affirming energy burst out. This, again, was resurrection. I clutched the arms of my seat for dear life, my eyes beginning to fill. In silent laughter and tears, I turned to Robin and clasped his hand. It was impossible not to share this joy.

There was no answering pressure. I looked at him in wonder and concern. His clean profile was set firmly, eyes fixed on the stage. My fingers slipped away from his. For a moment I felt bleak, rejected; almost as if I didn't exist. But the music lifted me again, the piano matching the orchestra strength for strength in the penultimate chords, the final colossal trills and triumphant horn fifths. Then the audience was on its feet in a thunder of applause and bravos. Richard was bowing, smiling now, his work done and his statement made.

I stole another glance at Robin; he still looked a bit dour, but seemed to be shaking off whatever had frozen him into rigidity. Of course, I thought with remorse. He was seeing himself on that stage, regretting the lost dream. As I would have been if I weren't looking forward to York.

By the time the repeated curtain calls had come to an end, Robin was laughing and cracking jokes.

"Well, the old sinner has done it again," he remarked. "I wonder what portion of his soul he had to barter this time, for that sort of triumph?"

That damned *Faustus* again.

"But Robin," I reasoned. "What about all those years of work and discipline? Isn't that enough?"

"Not for some, apparently. Oh, hell. I'm sorry, Lissa. Grapes frosted with alum," he said, with a rueful smile. "You're right, of course; he deserves it, none better. Let's get

181

backstage and tell him so."

"Another coup, you old *Übermensch*!" Robin called as we pushed in through the backstage crowd. Richard, who'd been listening with indulgently tilted head to the effusions of a mink-swathed matron, murmured an apology and came toward us. He and Robin clapped one another on the back, laughing. For some reason the transfiguring passages of the last movement had started up in my head, and when Richard turned to greet me, I was struggling with tears and an obstruction in my throat. I could only look at him with brimming eyes and compressed lips, and shake my head.

He studied me gravely for a moment, then pulled me into a brief embrace. Almost at once he held me away from him, smiling, humorous lines creasing the corners of his eyes.

"That bad, eh?"

When I shook my head again in frantic negation, he said, "No? In spite of pig-sty carpentry? *Grazie Dio!*" and laughing, released me. I began to laugh, too, and reaching into his elegant tailcoat he produced the ubiquitous handkerchief. "I really must buy you a gross or so of these. You're coming to the Grillet's with Robin, right?"

I nodded.

"Good. I'll see you there." He turned back into the waiting crowd.

≈CHAPTER 17≈

The half-shut doors through which we heard that music are
softly closed. Where have we been? What savage chaos of music
whirls through our dreams?
Conrad Aiken, *The House of Dust*

The Grillet's villa, backing up to the shores of Lake
Geneva, more than justified Robin's description. We'd driven
for what seemed blocks along a seven-foot stone wall,
through an imposing gate crowned with griffins, up a long
avenue of poplars, and onto a circular drive jammed with
expensive cars. The "bloody great house" loomed there, the
size of an urban museum, faced with marble and flawlessly
refined in every architectural detail. It was lit brilliantly,
eclipsing the full moon, and as the door opened I caught the
sound of stringed instruments.

Repairing my face in the luxurious powder room, I
admonished myself that these tears were becoming positively
a habit, and a very poor one, too. I hadn't cried for years
before coming to Yorkshire; only once, since Mother and
Daddy died: at the performance of *Faustus*. Oh, well. The
healthy color was still in my face, I saw as I shut off the
elaborately chased faucets, and the flattering overhead
lighting made my hair gleam like a polished chestnut. Good.
I needed all the confidence I could wring from small assets.
The hall was packed with exquisitely gowned and jeweled
women, freely shedding their incandescent wattage. I misted
scent from a tiny bottle and went out to search for Robin.

With the air of getting a dental appointment over with,
he marched me straight up to the Baron and Baroness de

Grillet. She was tiny, thin, white-haired and bone-beautiful; he tall, balding, and amazingly robust for a man in his eighties. Robin introduced me. We were greeted with gentle grace, and soon yielded our places to a group of new arrivals. Neatly removing two glasses of champagne from a passing tray, Robin started off in in search of Richard and Gianna.

I'd looked forward to meeting Richard's mother, but as the encounter approached my nervousness intensified. From all reports, she had every reason to resent me as Ciara's niece. What, I wondered, had Richard told her?

"Aha!" cried Robin. "Here you are!"

Then he was embracing a slender, beautiful, dark-haired woman. I felt a shock of disbelief. Surely this couldn't be Richard's mother? Mrs. Chidester had said she was twenty-nine when Richard was born, and Richard was now what? Thirty-seven? But that would make her sixty-six! It was impossible to think of age in connection with such a face. All one saw was the radiance, the generosity and liveliness. Laughing, mischievous black eyes, soft dark hair drawn into a Psyche-knot, a stunningly simple black gown, low-cut and long-sleeved. She wore emerald earrings, rimmed with a flash of diamonds. Robin released her and she turned to me in a subtle wave of expensive scent.

"Gianna," Richard was saying in a voice which perfectly suited this room with its crystal prisms and Chinese rugs, "let me present Lissa Leone. Lissa, my mother, the Contessa del Marchi." That was all; no more help. He stood there watching us, eyes unfathomable. I felt as if I were standing on a tightrope over some primal abyss.

Her lovely smile faded as she contemplated me. The dark eyes widened in something like alarm, and she looked quickly from Richard to Robin, then back to me. "Miss Leone..." she murmured, uncertainly, extending a wary, jeweled hand.

"Yes." Richard stepped closer. "You're right, of course. She's Ciara's niece; she's visiting John at Denham

184

House." I winced. Thanks, Richard. Now she'll be sure I'm taking advantage of family connections.

"But–" Collecting herself, Gianna called on her beautiful manners. "How fortunate that you could come to Geneva, Miss Leone. John said he had a surprise for me, but..." She broke off and looked about her. "Where is that rogue?"

"John is here?" asked Robin quickly.

I hadn't realized that John planned to make the trip to Geneva; he'd never mentioned it in our talk about skiing.

"Yes, he decided at the last minute to come. It's quite a family party," smiled Richard.

A suspicion crossed my mind. Had Richard told John to keep quiet about my kinship to Ciara until he'd sprung me on his mother? It would be like his Machiavellian tactics, I thought testily.

He turned to Gianna again. "You saw the resemblance, then."

"Of course, Riccardo. Who wouldn't? It's in the bones. Yet..." She broke into rapid Italian. Richard gave a short, pleased laugh. Recalling herself, Gianna said, "Forgive me, Miss Leone. I'm being dreadfully rude."

"No need," said Richard. "It was a compliment, Lissa. She said–ah, Elizabeth!" He turned to embrace a thin grey-haired woman who was plucking imperiously at his sleeve.

"This was all very well tonight, Richard," she chided in crisp English accents, casually dismissing a performance that would be legend tomorrow. "But when are we to hear something of your own?"

"Not for a while, unless you're willing to come to York, Elisabetta *mia*. I'm sending up a trial balloon there in a couple of weeks. And may I present Lissa Leone, who has kindly consented to rise or sink with said balloon. Lissa, Signora Carducci. And of course you know Robin."

She nodded and smiled at me, the long, bony face breaking into kind lines. "I'm delighted, Miss Leone. Hello,

185

Robin! But Yorkshire in March, Richard–good God, boy, no; not even for you."

"No, Elisabetta's made her escape to the sun. Why do you think she married Guido?" twinkled Gianna.

"Well, there were a number of reasons, but I won't deny that the prospect of thawing out was one of the more powerful lures. Why you linger in that savage hinterland, Richard, is more than I can understand."

She stopped abruptly, and her friendly, acute eyes swiveled back to me. "Miss Leone. I believe I've seen you before."

Here it comes again, I sighed inwardly, wearily preparing myself; I thought she was referring to my resemblance to Ciara. But she continued, "Heard you, I should have said. With the London Philharmonic. But you looked different, somehow."

She turned to Gianna, excited now. "My God, Gianna, you were with me! Don't you remember? The harpist?" She peered at me more closely. "I know now–you were a blonde!"

I winced again. Gianna was nodding, wonder dawning in her eyes.

"A harpist of the first magnitude," interjected Richard, who'd nobly declined to smile at the mention of my hair.

"Don't I know it," Elizabeth continued devoutly. "Remember, Gianna, we were ecstatic. It was one of those musical experiences you can count on the fingers of two hands. We went home in a kind of happy cloud. And we didn't even like the harp; we went to hear a Schumann symphony, I think, and were prepared to sit patiently through the other works. Don't you recall, Gianna, you scored a hit on Ciara with that one. Oh, I know–" she said, in response to Gianna's frown and shake of the head. "*De mortuis* and all that. But it was so funny! She simply turned to stone!"

"What's all this?" inquired Robin.

"Well," Gianna began, looking rather childishly defiant, but with a glint of repressed laughter in her eyes, "it was—oh, about three months later, in Rome. Ciara had just performed the same concerto that Miss Leone had played so superbly. I only said that when I heard the Reinecke in London I'd failed to recognize what a second-rate work it was. Well, she'd angered me, Riccardo," she finished defensively.

Richard had closed his eyes and put a hand to his brow. "*Dio mio,*" he breathed. Raising his head, he met my look of startled speculation with grim, pained certainty.

Signora Carducci was laughing. "She deserved it. And I think you're a marvelous musician, Miss Leone. When can we have the pleasure of hearing you play again?"

I spoke for the first time in this rapid-fire exchange. "Thank you kindly, Signora, but I'm afraid I'm a bit of a has-been."

Richard cut briskly through my words. "Nonsense. She's just recovered from an illness, but she's playing in my new piece in York, as I told you. You'll just have to bundle up and come, Elizabeth. Combine it with a visit to Gianna in London."

"Perhaps I will," she replied.

Gianna stepped forward, putting her hand gently on my arm and drawing me aside.

"Miss Leone, I'm so sorry! I was dreadfully rude to speak so about your aunt. We had our differences in the past, but that's no excuse. Can you forgive me?"

I sighed and managed a somewhat wry smile. "The truth is, Contessa, that I knew my aunt very little. She was a sort of goddess to me when I was young, and she did further my career for a while. Now for the first time I'm seeing her through the eyes of others, and it's a bit confusing. But please —there's nothing to forgive."

"I still hope you can forget my pettiness. You are a good person, Miss Leone."

She would have said more, but Robin appeared at my side.

"Let's get some supper, Lissa. Aren't you hungry?"

Gianna turned away with a smile.

"Famished," I lied, and with polite murmurs we merged into the crowd.

After an interlude of browsing the intriguing dishes on long, flower-strewn tables, I returned to the powder room. Looking about for Robin as I exited, I saw him standing with his back to me, engaged in lively conversation with three young people. He'd more than done his duty by me, and I intended to let him off the hook. Besides, I was a little tired, and wanted to sit down by myself for a bit.

Feeling rather stealthy, I closed the door softly behind me and slipped down a long corridor. There were a few scattered groups standing about in conversation, but when I turned left at the end into an intersecting hall, I found myself alone.

I paused at the first open door, which led into a spacious, brightly lit drawing room. Though I saw no one, I heard voices, and passed on. The next door was closed, but the third, under its delicately carved lintel, gave onto a small empty sitting room. It was lit only by the moon and the flickering remnants of a fire. Lavish brocade draperies, silvered by moonlight flooding in over the threshold, moved fitfully in the breeze from a half-open French door.

I sank into a wing chair on the outside wall, relishing the cold air and respite from brilliant light. I felt almost feverish from wine and the press of the crowd. Oddly, the voices I'd heard were louder here; the speakers must be on the marble terrace running along this wing. Then they moved closer, near the curtained door. Startled, I recognized the angry masculine voice, aggressively clear now. Uncharacteristic though it seemed, it was John Denham.

"Damn it, Richard! You can't! I came here to warn

you, not to help precipitate a family disaster. What you're proposing is wrong as well as dangerous: dreadfully, criminally wrong. Use your mind, man; think of the risk." He paused, resuming in a calmer, more reasonable tone. "Don't you realize that the ultimate outcome may be another death? You haven't any right–" John broke off abruptly.. When he resumed, it was in a tone of pleading. "Haven't we had enough grief? Leave it alone, Richard; somehow you have to cancel the trip. My God, anything could happen. It would mean ruin for the family. And if all this came out, it would be as terrible for you as for me."

Richard's coolly implacable voice cut in. "There's no room for that kind of emotion, John. I've been over it from all angles, believe me, and I think this is the way to handle it. Don't worry; I'm not going to sleepwalk through this. As for the other matter, I'm putting it in Carlo's hands. You know his discretion."

Another silence as they took a few steps toward the railing. I could actually hear the sound of their shoes on the marble. Then Richard again. The voices were a little fainter now.

"We've already lost so much. Let me try to salvage what I can, see if we can deal with it ourselves."

John sounded agitated, almost frantic. "Richard, I can't believe you'd actually go through with this. It's as if human life has no value to you. Christ Almighty! I'm begging you–"

"*Basta*, John." Richard said, with repressed savagery. "It's not an easy course for me."

"For God's sake, must you be so relentlessly Italian?"

Richard's voice was so low that I could barely make the words out. "I *am* Italian, John. It will be better for both of us if you remember that."

A long silence, during which my heart tried to hammer a way out of its prison. Then John spoke again, sounding exhausted with defeat.

189

"Very well. But the girl... she'll be injured however it turns out. And she's been through several kinds of hell already. You said yourself that you were far from blameless in that respect."

The level coolness of Richard's voice started an ache in my chest. "Better that she should be hurt now than later."

They turned their steps away left toward the drawing room door, voices fading.

I don't know how long I sat there, unable to move. In the excitement of the trip, the fears born from Robin's and Mrs. Chidester's revelations had been laid to rest. Now they rose again, still unformed but no longer to be ignored. This wasn't mere hearsay; I could hardly deny the evidence of my ears.

The room had become very cold, but I stayed in my chair in a sort of dead bewilderment. Had they been talking of Ciara's death, of silencing someone? Or of drug dealing? What trip did they mean–the trip to Zermatt? These people's lives were so busy; they never stopped moving. And "the girl"... was that me? Of course it must be. Don't be presumptuous, Lissa, you're hardly the only woman Richard has been "far from blameless" in injuring. John feared an unethical–no, a criminal act; something that would bring ruin to the family if it were known. And–I came back to it again– injury to "the girl." What kind of injury? Emotional? Physical? Well, wake up. Death sounds pretty physical.

The barely audible strains of a Haydn string quartet drifted in from the hall. The dying fire crackled softly, settling with a sigh. I lifted my hands with a tremendous effort and pressed them hard against my temples. It was too much for my spinning, wine-fuddled brain. The unaccustomed thrills and nervous tensions of the concert and party had drained my energies. And I'd done it again: knowing one glass of champagne was my safe limit, I'd drunk three–or was it four?–in my fascination with meeting Gianna

190

and my delight in the intoxicating gaiety all around me.

And now this. I had the most peculiar sense of detachment, of inevitability. I now understood why the brainless heroines of horror films never left those dark, decaying houses when they had the chance. Whether from wine or weariness, or in a willing trade of danger for the dullness of my life, I had absolutely no desire to run. Whatever Richard was planning, no matter how immoral or even demonic it might be; no matter whether it was indeed I who stood to be injured; there was simply nothing, at that moment, that I could do about it.

I wasn't even surprised when he appeared silently in the door, a black silhouette against the brightly lit hall. There was no mistaking the height and slender grace of his figure. He reached out and the wall sconces leaped into brilliance.

"Lissa?" I'd involuntarily covered my eyes with a cold hand. "I've been looking for you. Headache, my dear?" He turned the lights off.

I accepted the excuse gratefully. "Yes," I replied. "A bit too much champagne, I'm afraid."

With a sympathetic murmur, he moved to close the French doors. "It's freezing in here," he said, laying a log on the fire. He shut the corridor door, and the Haydn was silenced as if a switch had been flipped. Approaching soundlessly across the heavy carpet, he sat on the arm of my chair. A tiny claw skittered its way along my spine and was gone.

Dropping my hand, I leaned against the damasked back of the chair with a sigh. The mental fuzziness brought on by the champagne was dissipating, and with it, curiously, the heart-pounding fear I'd felt when the two men were arguing. I spoke the first thing that came to mind.

"I didn't realize your mother had married again."

"Yes. He was much older. He lived only two years after the wedding."

"She's incredibly lovely. What was she saying, by the

way—in Italian, I mean?"

He hesitated, searching his memory. "Ah. Yes." There was a smile in his voice. "I asked her if she saw the resemblance between you and Ciara. She affirmed it and said, 'But this one has a soul in her eyes. She hasn't sold it, like the other one.'"

It seemed too much of an effort to answer. He touched my bare shoulder. "You're cold, Lissa," he said, and taking off his jacket, put it around my shoulders. It was warm from the heat of his body, and I accepted it silently.

When Richard spoke again, it was with diffidence, as if he hesitated to broach an unpleasant subject.

"Did you understand what Gianna and Elizabeth were saying? I'm terribly afraid my mother helped ring your professional death knell."

"Please, Richard," I said wearily. "Do you mind if we don't talk about it? I really don't care."

"Poor little one," came the quiet response. "Of course. It's been a strenuous day for you."

This, coming from a man who'd just performed Herculean marvels, made me laugh aloud. He looked at me in surprise, the strong planes of his face softened by firelight and moonlight. The grim altercation I'd overheard dissolved easily into the realm of nightmare. This was the only reality. I was conscious once again of the scent of sandalwood.

"I'm hardly the one who's had a strenuous day. Richard, please forgive me for not saying anything when I came backstage. I couldn't. It was..." I shook my head. "It was the most—"

He placed his fingers softly across my lips. "No, cara. Please don't. Believe me, all the extravagant and probably untrue compliments I heard tonight were nothing beside what you told me."

"But I couldn't even talk." My lips moved against his hand.

"I knew exactly what you were saying." He stood,

192

lifting me to my feet, and took my face in his hands. Where his fingers had silenced me a moment ago, firm lips pressed a slow kiss.

I shivered with longing and a sudden bleak terror, and with an indrawn breath he clasped me in the warm circle of his arms, the gentle deliberation of the kiss flaring into a kind of desperation. I could feel the tremendous tensions of the evening, still rigidly leashed, in his arms and shoulders. Then I forgot everything but the persuasion of his embrace. The dark restless yearning of the Brahms Adagio sang relentlessly through my head.

When he lifted his mouth from mine he had to support me for a moment. Running a finger lightly along my collarbone, he spoke into my hair.

"Purest Brahms."

My eyes flew open unbelievingly. Dear God, yes, I thought.

He traced the line of my cheek. "What, no tears?"

"No; no." I drew a long and shaky breath. "You must think I'm a perpetual waterspout."

Strong fingers thrust gently through the hair at my neck, and I shivered again with longing, remembering their power and art.

He released me abruptly. "It's much better for you not to know what I think."

I stood silent and uncertain.

He looked at me thoughtfully, the light grey eyes luminous in a cold shaft of moonlight. "You're tired, Lissa. It's after two. We'd better get you off to bed if we're going to take the golden road to Samarkand tomorrow. Why don't we breakfast at the Richemond, say at ten. Can you be ready?"

I nodded automatically, thrown off balance by this abrupt shift from passion to logistics.

"Of course. Are you staying here?"

He nodded. "I'll find Robin and we'll get your coat; oh, you'd better give me mine. Meet us in the foyer, will

193

you?"

"I haven't seen John at all," I said inconsequentially.

"He's spending tonight and tomorrow with friends in the country. He said to give you his best, and he'll see you in Yorkshire."

The door opened and closed. Without the coat I was instantly cold again.

Passionate chance encounters might be commonplace for Richard; they certainly were not for me. To have such piercing rapture awakened, then terminated so casually, left me limp and bewildered. Feeling summarily dismissed, I collapsed into the chair, trying to recover my badly shaken equilibrium.

Why was I, the sensible and dutiful New Englander, deliberately suppressing all the troubling things I knew about this man? My God, was I so hungry for love that I'd fall into the arms of a cynical womanizer to whom I meant nothing; blithely forgetting his vehement hatred of my own kin; even putting aside that blackly ominous exchange on the terrace? An exchange I'd heard not half an hour before I was responding fervently to his kiss? With the words still fresh in my head, words that hinted at drug dealing, or worse, murder. And at injury, probably to myself.

The answer was obviously a resounding yes. In spite of Robin's sweetness and cheer, I'd let myself give way to an immature and dangerous infatuation for a public idol. Made vulnerable by loneliness, renewed immersion in passionate music, and an informed awe of great performers (not to mention Richard's formidable personal attractions), it seemed I couldn't wait to immolate myself on the pyre.

Perhaps, I excused myself, it was just the contact with a truly civilized man after all those arid years. Dear heaven, I was off again! Richard D'Annunzio might be aristocratic, quintilingual, gifted and accomplished beyond the aspirations of human males, but there was nothing civilized about drugs, Mafia connections—would that be the discreet

Carlo?–and, possibly, murder.

No. Robin was a civilized man; Richard was not. I castigated myself, for the most recent of uncounted times, for being a birdbrained fool.

Perhaps the clear cold air of Zermatt and the counterbalancing presence of Robin would bring me to my senses. Perhaps I'd see what, if anything, I could do to free myself from this Gordian knot.

The sensible alternative of returning to Connecticut never even entered my mind.

⚜CHAPTER 18⚜

The devil pulls the strings which make us dance.
Charles Baudelaire, Fleurs du mal

We were bucketing along through the Rhône Valley, the three of us; that most exciting and dangerous combination, two men and a girl. The brilliant sun beamed down from a sky of flawless blue.

Richard and Robin seemed to be in roaring good spirits, and I was caught up in their reckless gaiety. We laughed, sang rounds and French songs of moderate impropriety, and in general behaved like children let out of school. We'd lingered over lunch under the castles of Sion, looming from their twin hills, and now were making for Visp.

"I don't know how you have the strength to drive, let along sing," I remarked to Richard. How different he was today! The almost somber European grace had turned to English good cheer. Other than a darkness under his eyes, there was no mark of last night's exhausting performance.

"It's part of his pact with Mephistopheles," explained Robin with mock gravity. "Didn't you realize that *Faustus* is an autobiographical work?"

"Right," agreed Richard promptly. "Wrested from the cauldron of personal experience."

"I'd never doubt it," I said, joining in the silly banter. Our headlong progress through the beautiful valley was exhilarating, and I felt carefree and deliciously irresponsible.

"When are you descending, if I may ask?"

"Descending?" queried Richard.

"She means to the nether regions, Cousin mine."

Richard threw me a quizzical look. "How do you know I haven't already been there? Perhaps I made a shrewder pact than the good Doctor. After all, you know—better to reign in hell than serve in heaven."

My laughter sounded a bit hollow. The flippancy of the moment faded as I recalled the chill I'd felt at Robin's post-concert reference to bartered souls. It seemed a favorite family topic. A few more miles of light-hearted repartee were required to restore my buoyancy.

Fresh snow had fallen at higher altitudes the night before, so we decided to leave the car in Visp and take the train for the entire trip to Zermatt, rather than risking the drive as far as Tasch.

Crowds of skiers and big-boned, Nordic-looking snowshoers had already filled the cars, and we were unable to find seats together. I sat contentedly amidst the laughter and singing of a loden-hatted Austrian group, eyes riveted to the window. I never gave my stomach a thought; I'd even skipped the transdermal patch.

As we ran into the Saas Valley, the unreeling panorama held my fascinated gaze: wooden chalets perched on the mountainsides, wisps of smoke rising to the rapidly dimming sky; narrow silver torrents flinging themselves exultantly down the heights through frozen channels. It was just like the hand-tinted pictures in the old "Lands and Peoples" books my mother had kept from her childhood.

By the time we reached Tasch, what one could see of the heavens was a sapphire blue. We rounded a bend and with shocking abruptness the Matterhorn reared its appalling threat into the gathering darkness, at once terrible and beautiful in its icy power. I turned impulsively to share the thrill of its impact, but Robin was in earnest conversation with a sunburned girl. And Richard was sound asleep.

At last we stepped out into the clear star-scattered night of Zermatt, braced by the thin cold air. The encircling mountains loomed massive and black against a sky nearly as

197

dark but less opaque. Moving with practiced alacrity, Robin snagged a horse-cab. Soon, bells jingling, we were trotting along to the Mont Cervin Hotel, where we settled for fondue and salad and an early night. We all wanted to make the most of the day ahead.

At seven the next morning I was up. After coffee and a roll, I strolled along the main street and through the market square, reveling in the crisp, pine-scented air. I stood for a while on the bridge over the Vispa, watching the noisy headlong roistering of the river, swollen from an early thaw. Channeling had robbed it of its wild beauty, but the water was clean and transparent.

I paused at the little cemetery, reading the markers of those young men who'd died trying to conquer the Matterhorn. Crossed ice axes and other symbols of mountaineering adorned the stones. The graves seemed particularly poignant in light of the current "walk in the park" view that many climbers now held of the mountain's difficulty.

When the shops opened I picked a sober navy parka and a bib overall from the wild array of colors and styles. Woolen socks, a red cap, the warmest gloves I could find, and a pair of sunglasses completed my purchases. Richard had been right about the prices. Gulping as I paid the tab, I hurried out onto the street and back to the hotel, where I found Richard and Robin stamping impatiently around the lobby in their great boots, which looked to me, who hadn't skied in years, like something out of an Arthur Clarke novel.

Renting equipment posed something of a problem, I found when I submitted myself for a fitting. Although I'd skied off and on over a long period of years, I'd never done enough to make it seem worthwhile to buy boots or skis of my own; I'd always used Mother's. And hers were veritable antiques–old, comfortable German leather ones, ankle-high, with multiple buckles. The modern, high-tech boots looked impossibly tall and forward-tilted. I finally convinced the cheerful attendant, who kept trying to do things for my own good, to find a pair that wouldn't decant me onto my nose. Then, to his chagrin, I settled on a far shorter length of ski than he recommended.

All this was accompanied by much gratuitous laughter from Richard and Robin. Sleekly outfitted and equipped with impenetrably black goggles, they looked like a suave pair of international assassins. Annoyed at their Olympian amusement, I absently told them just that. This had the effect of sending them into fresh gales of laughter and me into a prickle of cold sweat. For the first time I wondered whether Robin might share Richard's rumored involvement with organized crime.

But I didn't have much time for thought. Soon we were up the cableway and onto a shining mountain. Robin suggested that I ski down an easy slope so they could evaluate my ability. Taking a deep breath, I pushed off, skiing self-consciously but in what I judged to be my most creditable form. When I pulled up beside them, rather satisfied with myself, I was met with stunned silence. Finally Richard broke it.

"My God," he breathed. "You really did watch old Sonja Henie movies."

Robin stepped in tactfully. "Just a few minor corrections of technique, Lissa, and you'll be zooming along."

But Richard refused to be muzzled; his laughter rang across the crystalline air. "You were supposed to emulate her skating, Lissa, not her skiing. She was an advocate of the school of right angles, and you, I imagine, are her last living disciple. First of all, stand up. No, my good woman, stand up! And pull in that derriere."

I did so as if stung by a hornet, and he collapsed into laughter again. There was no trace of malice in his merriment; he seemed genuinely delighted.

"Now, bend your knees; get those poles back from the ski-tips. Ah. Much better!"

The cousins worked me over for almost an hour, bullying and encouraging, before they departed to their suicidal runs high above, leaving me to practice my newly learned form on the baby slope. At noon we met for sandwiches and *apfelsaft* in the noisy lodge. To my horror, they kindly pronounced me ready for a challenge, and we headed for an intermediate trail.

"Let's do some short turns. At least you can parallel, God alone knows how. Whatever prompted that remarkable stance, anyway?" asked Richard.

For the first time, I realized I'd always skied bent over from the waist, knees locked. "Well, as you said, I really did watch Sonja's movies. But mostly I worked it out myself, I guess. It keeps me from falling over backward," I explained reasonably.

"No doubt. Well, let's go!"

As we started a series of tight turns down the gentle slope, Robin called, "Rhythm, Lissa!"

"Sing!" prompted Richard. "It really will help."

"Sing what?" I cried helplessly, too focused on my form to extract a melody from the thousands stored in my brain.

"Strauss waltzes!" laughed Robin.

I couldn't think of a single one. The only thing that came into my head was the banal "It's the Loveliest Night of the Year." And it worked. By some miracle I was swooping at a respectable speed down the broad run between them, relaxed and in harmony with myself. We came to a stop at the base in a shower of snow crystals.

"Now all you need is lots of practice, and for goodness' sake hang onto your form," Robin urged.

We agreed to meet for a swim at five, and they skated off toward the cablecar that would carry them to their accustomed hair-raising heights. Practice, I thought. Good Lord, more practice, even here. With a resigned sigh, I herring-boned back to the lift.

Dressing for the pool in the mirrored changing room, I was surprised to see how thin I still was. Always slim, but softly so, I'd lost ten pounds to the flu, and the exercise in Yorkshire had kept it off despite Robin's sumptuous meals. I thought enviously of Ciara's slender but voluptuous form, then censured myself sharply. You're alive, Felicity, not lying under the cold sea. Alive and well; uninjured... oh, hell.

I banged the dressing-room door and walked to the pool, its steam rising into the Alpine air. It was littered with the bodies of glamorous women and lithe, tanned men. I lowered myself beside two gorgeous blonde Valkyries who perched on the edge, dangling long legs into the heated water.

"*Liebchen*, look! Isn't that D'Annunzio?" one of them whispered.

"*Ach, ja! Gott*, he is beautiful. And the devil with women, they say."

At the mention of his name I'd unsheathed my rusty German. What was the exact phrase she'd used? *Eingefleischter Teufel*–the devil incarnate.

"Olga says–" she broke off breathlessly as Richard, clad in black trunks and towel, sauntered directly toward her, and me.

"Where's Robin?" I asked.

"Having a drink with a skiing buddy. He'll be out soon." There was a momentary hush in the multilingual buzz around the pool, and the perfectly modulated voice was clearly audible. The pause drew out for a moment, to be swamped by self-conscious chatter.

"Can't escape, can you?"

He took off the sunglasses and peered at them musingly. "I thought these might help."

"Now who's naïve?" I chaffed him. "They just put the icing on the cake."

With a rueful smile he dropped them onto his towel

and sliced cleanly into the water. I slipped in too. He swam a few laps and then surfaced beside me, treading easily. Through the water I saw a gleam of gold on his chest.

"It's all nonsense, you know," he said, appropriating an empty float. I clung to the opposite side of it, tension washing out of my muscles.

"What's nonsense?" I asked dreamily.

"This absurd puffing up of performers, conductors, as if they were movie stars. It's all the media, of course. We're made to assume far more importance than we can humanly support. One's least word or gesture is impossibly magnified to the public. And it's bad for us, sinfully so. Start to believe the publicity, and it's fatal. It may be all right for entertainers; in a way their persona is their art. But it's a terrible pitfall for the classical artist. Instead of being servants to the music, we begin to perceive ourselves as masters."

"Well, perhaps. Still," I went on, "it's been happening for centuries. Think of Liszt. And I don't entirely agree. Don't you think–"

My ruminations were shattered by a noisy splash and a deluge of water, as Robin belly-flopped onto the float between us.

"Robin, you beast!" I cried, wiping water from my eyes.

I ducked to pull him under. He came up spluttering and laughing. "King's X! I had no idea you were so fierce. No, leave the fine Italian revenges to Richard. Come on, I'll race you to the end of the pool." Robin was in his element, sporting like a dolphin, far surpassing his cousin's grace and strength in the water.

"Well, farewell, *Kinder*," said Richard, heaving himself out of the pool. "Cavort to your heart's delight; the old one is having a nap. As your apparently beloved Stendahl would say, I'm *terzo incomodo*–quite superfluous. Meet you at nine?"

For dinner I'd donned an old and loved dress of

burgundy merino, sophisticated yet simple. It was cut like an elongated sweater and cinched with a broad suede belt. Half-moon silver earrings and a bracelet of Navajo make completed the outfit. After the day of all-out exercise, wearing anything structured seemed far too difficult.

Robin hinted unkindly that I might have to unbuckle a bit. He and Richard watched in unconcealed awe as I ate steadily through five courses and didn't stint on the wine.

I was determined to enjoy this night as if it were my last. Dressing for dinner, I'd told myself that the conversation between John and Richard probably involved nothing more sinister than a family business situation. I would put suspicions, shadowy fears of danger, and nagging memories of innuendo–in which I myself had perilously engaged–out of my mind. No matter what social situations developed, I would eschew displaying the unnatural horror shown by Charlotte Brontë upon meeting a stranger. I would not whine, or be prickly; in short, I was overflowing with good intentions, all of which lasted almost two hours.

Sitting over coffee and brandy, we were approached by a pleasant-faced woman in early middle age. She had the sort of countenance that gets better with the years: comfortable, generous, and honest.

"Dr. D'Annunzio?" she ventured tentatively, as if expecting a rebuff. I looked at Richard, a bit nervous for her.

But he was on his feet at once, the role of Italian-English public figure settling about him like a cloak.

"*Desidera*, Signora?"

"My name is Anne O'Neal. Please forgive me, I don't do this sort of thing as a rule, but I just wanted..."

Richard pulled the empty fourth chair out. "Sit down, Mrs. O'Neal." I gave a belated glance at her left hand and saw the rings. No wonder Peter was so sharp; he had a short lifetime of watching his father file away details.

"Oh, I couldn't impose." She looked genuinely

embarrassed.

"Please." He raised his hand for a waiter, who materialized with uncanny speed.

"Si, Maestro?"

"Mrs. O'Neal is joining us for coffee and brandy, Paolo."

Masterful, I thought with the cynicism I'd meant to leave locked in my room. Now I see why those female symphony board members on three continents are so passionate about engaging him.

Mrs. O'Neal was clearly overwhelmed. She pressed her palms to flushed cheeks for a moment, murmuring, "You're too kind. I really had no intention of intruding myself."

"There's no question of that. Mrs. O'Neal, may I introduce Lissa Leone, the concert harpist, and my cousin Robin Denham."

So now I was "the" concert harpist.

She turned to us, her smile full of half-humorous apology. There was something in her expression that I liked at once, and I wrested myself away from my petty thoughts, responding eagerly, letting Richard's mendacious description pass, while Robin said something charming. Somehow I didn't feel that Mrs.O'Neal was the ordinary celebrity seeker. She took a fortifying sip of her newly arrived coffee, and plunged in.

"What I wanted to tell you, although I planned to do it standing up, is... oh, drat it, you'll think I'm insufferably presumptuous and gushing. Well, never mind. Here it is, I'll just say it right out." She closed her eyes for a moment, then sat rigidly erect and looked straight at Richard. I could tell it was taking all her courage.

"Dr. D'Annunzio, I don't know of many things in life that have given me more lasting pleasure than your recording of the Brahms First Concerto. No, pleasure is a pale word. I've worn out one cassette, and I'm starting on a new CD. I'm a Brahms fanatic, I guess. And I've heard it played by many artists, some of whom sound as if they're trying to give birth to a whale... breech, at that."

Here Richard snorted with laughter in a most un-Continental fashion.

"After all," she continued, gaining confidence, "it is the work of a very young and ardent man, isn't it? Well, Saturday night I heard you in Geneva and I can't tell you how..." She broke off in honest wonder and switched to the brandy glass. "How in heaven's name can you breathe new life into every phrase–make every note say what I'm convinced Brahms meant it to say? And why am I so utterly sure of that; that you know precisely what he intended, I mean? Lord, I hope that doesn't sound as egotistical to you as it does to me."

"You're sure because it's true," I said, my cynicism evaporated.

They all turned to look at me as if the cream pitcher had spoken.

"I can't explain it logically either," I went on, with a helpless gesture. "It just is, that's all. It's truth, pure and simple. Any musician worthy of the name would tell you that."

"Amen, Lissa," said Robin.

Mrs. O'Neal looked at me, eyes shining. "So I'm not nuts, after all. And even if life held just one of those moments of terror, and the answering beauty and redemption..."

"It would be enough," I finished.

"Then you do understand," she said softly.

"Absolutely."

"I'll just retire under the table now, if no one objects," murmured Richard.

Mrs. O'Neal and I laughed guiltily, having forgotten the subject of the conversation in the pleasure of shared feelings. Robin laughed too, brightly.

"There, I've said it," smiled Mrs. O'Neal, getting to her

feet, "and I feel better, which is decidedly selfish of me, I suppose. Thanks for letting me interrupt; I'll leave you to enjoy your evening. Good night, Miss Leone, Mr. Denham. Thank you, Dr. D'Annunzio."

"Wait." Richard put a hand on her arm. "You haven't finished your brandy. And I haven't thanked you."

"Thanked me?" she asked.

"Of course. Tell me frankly: you considered approaching me a sort of intrusion, didn't you?"

She nodded. "I certainly did. I felt like an aging groupie. But you've been so gracious.."

"Dear lady, it's like a gift from the gods. Can you imagine what it would be like for an artist to play, year after year, in a vacuum?"

I felt a little twist near my heart.

"But you have your audiences, and the critics," she countered.

"An audience's opinions are articulated by the striking together of palms, if one's lucky and they don't hiss. And critics often speak for their own self-aggrandizement and intellectual display. But an appreciation that comes from the heart–that could never be an intrusion."

I saw that he meant what he said; she'd moved him deeply.

"Lissa did the same for me two nights ago," he went on, nodding toward me. I felt my face grow warm. Robin, left out of the conversation, was looking bored and a bit grim.

"Well, thank you again." Mrs. O'Neal had seen Robin's face and was on her feet. "I'll always remember this evening. I've followed your playing for years. Good night!"

"You don't think we're letting you off that easily, do you?" laughed Richard. "Are you alone?"

"Yes, just now I am. My two teenage girls are on spring break, so they came with me, but they're with friends tonight."

"Then join us."

"But," she faltered, looking down at her perfectly good jersey dress, "I'm not properly... I couldn't possibly..."

"Why on earth not? What do you suppose we're going to do–waltz in a candlelit salon? Play chamber music from parchment manuscripts set on baroque stands? No, we're going to emulate Horace. *'Nunc est bibendum, nunc pede libero pulsanda tellus.'* "

"I'm afraid my parochial school Latin isn't up to that," she said dubiously. "Is it fearfully decadent?"

"Fearfully. 'Now for drinks, now for some dancing with a good beat.' Let's go, Signora O'Neal. We're headed for a disco."

"*Disco*?" I squeaked incredulously.

"Still alive and well in Zermatt," he smiled.

Looking around the warm, smoky, action-filled room, I felt impossibly old and out of things. Yet there was Anne O'Neal, in her mid-forties, comfortably stout, looking perfectly at ease and simply radiating fun as she gyrated to the music with Richard.

I'd always felt self-conscious and stiff about dancing, probably because I'd done so little of it. And perhaps, I thought, moving reluctantly out onto the floor with Robin, because I'd assumed that, like music, it was something to be approached with discipline and dedication. Only in the waltz and Latin dances was I confident, at home with specific patterns. Daddy had taught those to me. And who ever waltzed in the real world?

I took a quick look at the people dancing on the tiny lighted square of floor. They weren't all under twenty, or even thirty. And most of them didn't seem to be doing anything special; just moving as the music took them.

Great heavens, who did I think was watching, anyway? If the matronly Mrs. O'Neal could indulge in such uninhibited play, so could I.

And I did. Making a face at Robin, who was doing

comical things with his eyebrows, I let myself enter the flow of the music. It was envelopingly loud, but not the deafening roar one heard in the States, and it absorbed my nervousness as I started to move.

"If you intellectualize this, I'll hit you," he threatened, and our merriment washed the last stiffness out of my body.

Richard stuck to Mrs. O'Neal like a leech. Pushing aside a feeling of childish hurt, I gave myself up to Robin's witty attentions, and we spun through the evening on a tide of music and movement, laughing as we went.

But at some time late in the revelry we changed partners. Without quite knowing how it happened, I found myself facing Richard, who was dancing with a strange mixture of sophisticated grace and primitive athleticism.

"Good thing the ceiling is high," I shouted over the music, as he executed an improbable jump.

Just as I was tiring from the exertion and noise, the lights dimmed and the music changed to a ballad, softly played. Then I was in his arms, moving languidly across the floor through shifting beams of color.

"You're a wonderful dancer," he commented into my ear.

"Be serious, Richard. I've never really danced at a disco before. I didn't know they still existed–maybe only in Switzerland? And even with this, the slow dancing, my partners always said I was stiff. As a matter of fact, my high school dance teacher said that too, on my report card: too stiff."

He laughed quietly. "The more fools they."

"You're kind…" I began conventionally. Realization struck me. "You know, you really *are* kind."

He held me off, a quizzical look on his face. "Thanks. I guess. Is it that much of a surprise?"

"I was thinking about Mrs. O'Neal. That was a lovely gesture, but surely you can't encourage people to approach you that way; you'd be swamped."

He shrugged. "Circumstances alter cases, to quote Gilbert and Sullivan. I'd been watching her a bit, earlier. She was sitting alone, and she looked sad. Besides, I meant what I said to her. She's a widow, by the way; her husband died five months ago."

"Oh, poor lady. I like her; her passion for music is so real."

"Yes. Well, she has a right. She's from Philadelphia."

"Hmm. How come you didn't accuse her of being American the minute she opened her mouth?"

"Dear Lissa." I could feel him smile against my cheek. "Are you having a good time?"

"That's right, ignore my question. Yes, as a matter of fact, I'm having a marvelous time. I've never done anything like this before."

"What, danced? Or skied? Amazing. Although, seeing you on the slopes this morning–"

"*Silenzio, Dottore, per piacere!* See, I've been reading up Italian. No...never had a trip just for fun, except sometimes to Colorado with Mother and Daddy. All my travels, and they haven't been that many, were for contests or concerts. Business trips, you might say."

"Ah. And tell me, Miss Brontë, how is your conscience holding up through this mad orgy?" His hands tightened ever so slightly.

I answered truthfully. "It expired days ago–trampled to death by a herd of irresistible impulses."

He held me away from him again and looked gravely into my eyes. Then with a little sigh he pulled me close again.

"Do you mind being alone in the morning? Robin and I thought we might do some heli-skiing on the glacier. After lunch we'll introduce you to some more interesting terrain. On our last day we'll all ski the Trockener Steg."

There it was again, the tantalizing closeness, then the withdrawal into practicality. I scrabbled my thoughts together.

"That sounds wonderful. But you needn't baby-sit me, you know. I think I'll have a lesson in the morning."

"Good idea. Lissa—"

"Mm?"

The quiet music stopped. The lights went up and the frenetic beat began once more.

He shook his head, and his hands fell away. *"Niente."*

Richard and Robin left early for the heliport. I breakfasted alone and reported for a lesson at ten. The young Swiss instructor kept his amusement professionally under control; at least he didn't let me see it. At the end of two hours he expressed pleasure at my progress.

"Now," he ordered, "ski. Try to be more aggressive. Always you must work to improve, but it is not done by standing on the sidelines. And please do not try to ski horizontally. Get down the mountain!"

It sounded much like Leon's admonitions. I bade him goodbye and skied off for lunch with Anne, an arrangement we'd made the night before.

She and I had struck up an easy companionship. Among other things, her connection with Philadelphia appealed to me.

"Well, the girls and I will be off this afternoon," she volunteered.

We were dipping into bowls of steaming soup flanked by slabs of moist black bread.

"So soon? Are you going back to the States?"

"Yes, and I'll be glad to get home. Brian and I had planned this trip for all of us a year ago. When he got sick, he made me promise to go ahead and take the girls after he was gone." She smiled, lowering her eyes, and when she looked up they were brilliant with tears. "And it has been good for all of us," she went on, briskly spearing lettuce. "Switzerland is a healthy dose of unreality. The girls have adored the skiing, and I've loved just being out here in the sun, watching."

"You don't ski?"

"Good grief, no! I can hardly get down a mountain on my feet, let alone two slippery pieces of fiberglass!" she laughed. "I suppose you're an expert?"

"If you only knew! My strong point is providing comic relief on the slopes. Richard says my skiing is straight out of an old Sonja Henie movie."

"Is that bad?"

"Terrible! And worse, he and Robin are coming after lunch to take me to what he euphemistically describes as 'more interesting terrain.' This may be positively my last appearance without crutches."

"Well, I wouldn't worry if I were you. You couldn't be in better hands; they wouldn't risk a hair of your head. It's obvious that both those young men are in love with you."

I stared at her blankly, spoon halfway to my mouth.

She burst out laughing. "Surely you know that? Even a perfect stranger couldn't miss it, the way they look at you. How in the world do you keep them from murdering each other?"

"It... it's not like that at all, Anne," I stammered. "We're actually distant relatives of a sort." Oh, blast. Now I'd made it sound like a *menage a trois.*

"Really? I guess my famous intuition has failed me. I'd hoped–well, I've followed Richard's career for years. Strange to think I'm calling him that! I have friends in Philadelphia who knew him long ago, and after that tragic marriage..."

She fell silent for a moment. Then, pursing her lips, she pressed her palms together with a little shake of the head. "I don't know whether I should tell you this. In a way, I guess, it's invasion of privacy, just as my approaching your table was. But somehow, especially as you're his relative, I think you should know. I saw Richard at Mass this morning, and–"

"At Mass!"

211

"Yes. I don't think he saw me; I came in late and sat behind a pillar. I still cry a lot, you know, and at the oddest times. There were only a handful of us. It was the six o'clock service." She hesitated, then went on in a rush. "Do you think he's still grieving dreadfully for his wife? If ever I've seen a man in anguish, it was Richard. I know my eyes were supposed to be shut, but somehow they never are. I looked up and saw him—he was kneeling, of course—and he put his hand to his eyes with a sort of—well, savage despair. It sounds terribly melodramatic but I don't know how else to put it. He looked absolutely at the end of his tether."

My eyes were fixed unseeingly on the table. That glint of gold I'd seen in the pool: it was a cross, of course.

The Mafia, I remembered from my novel reading, were often devout Catholics, never missing church, offering masses for the souls of their dead. Their dead. I shivered and forced myself to speak.

"Well, Anne, he's been under a tremendous strain. This winter's concert schedule has been unusually demanding, I believe. I expect he's just exhausted."

Richard at Mass. Richard, the—what was it—the *eingefleischter Teufel*. The devil in the flesh. But no, that Teutonic mermaid had used the term in connection with womanizing. Not that I'd seen that demonstrated, as yet. His squiring of Anne last night hardly qualified.

"Of course you're right," she was saying. "That's probably it. He's bound to be terribly tired." Her kind, worried eyes belied the words. She hastened to change the subject.

"The other young man, Richard's cousin, I think he said? Does he live in England too?"

"Yes. Robin started out as a harpsichordist, but now he's managing a country house hotel for Richard's brother."

"I bet he's good at it; he's certainly a charmer. It sounds as if the family is very close."

"Yes. Yes, I believe it is."

"Now let's get back to you for a moment. You're a harpist! Such a musical family."

I didn't try to deny the connection, since I'd just falsified it. "Yes, I was a harpist. Actually, I studied in your home town."

"One of Leon Lemaitre's students? Oh!" She struck her forehead. "Of course! I've heard you play with the Philadelphia Orchestra...I've been a subscriber for twenty years and get to every concert I can. I knew there was something familiar about you. You were the big contest winner, weren't you?"

"My sins are catching up with me," I smiled weakly.

"Some sins! My dear child, it was glorious. One doesn't get to hear many harpists, and frankly, most of them are eminently forgettable. The name was familiar, but it's been–what–six, seven years? And I think your hair's different."

"One of Leon's famous transformations," I said resignedly. "I was a blonde back then."

"Well, it was a stunning performance, and I want to hear you again. What did you mean by using the past tense, by the way? Oh! There are your men. Looks as if your pre-crutch time is running out," she laughed, seeing the apprehension on my face.

There was a flurry of goodbyes, a quick exchange of addresses with Anne.

"If you're ever in Philadelphia," she whispered, "let me know how it turns out."

So much for my attempts at camouflage.

Then we were out in the midday sunshine, their perfect teeth flashing white against tanned faces as they began to regale me with an account of the morning's adventure.

The cable car took us up and up, past the last straggling pines that marched in ever diminishing files;

stunted and gnarled, yet holding the snow in little cupped branches like apple blossoms born from the ice. Heavy clouds were rising over the rim of the mountains, but the cold wasn't bitter.

I concentrated on everything I'd learned in the past two days, and as the afternoon went on I gained confidence on the intermediate slopes. Richard and Robin took turns skiing with me, one patiently slowing his pace to mine while the other shot repeatedly past us to the lift. We skied late into the day, until the snow began to fall too thickly for good visibility.

"Good show, Lissa," said Robin. "You were really skiing on that last run."

"You certainly were," assented Richard. "You're going to enjoy the Trockener Steg tomorrow."

Tomorrow. Our last day.

"Well, I'll try it as long as you promise not to spoil your skiing by hanging around with me. That is, if you really think I'm up to it."

"We had plenty of excitement this morning; we'll be ready to take it easy tomorrow. And you're going to be fine."

I kicked off my skis with a sigh of relief.

"Here, I'll carry those," offered Richard. "You're tired."

"What's up for tonight?"

"How about supper–let's not dress–and a walk in the snow through the village afterward? Maybe a drink and an early bed. We want to get a lot of skiing in tomorrow, and this morning wiped me out."

That was well enough, I mused. But where was all the glorious nightlife, not to speak of sex life, that was reputed to go on in an international resort? It was an unworthy and uncharacteristic thought, followed immediately by another: Miss Brontë sees her last chance of romance fade away.

"Don't fret, Lissa." I started, and looked up to see Richard's gently quizzical gaze. "We'll go out in a burst of

214

glory tomorrow night."

✎CHAPTER 19✎

In vino veritas. Pliny the Elder

After a long hot bath I felt beautifully revived; even the stiffness in my legs was bearable. I pulled on warm trousers and a pine-colored sweater, finishing with a spray of my favorite out-of-doors perfume, tinged with western scents of sage and pine. No use wasting the heavy artillery on an occasion like this, I decided ruefully. Anne O'Neal's comments must have colored my attitude; I was wondering how two purportedly smitten men could be so thoroughly platonic. Heavens, I thought, locking my bedroom door, I really have turned into a bitter old maid.

Robin and Richard were waiting in the lobby, and we strolled down to a *Bierstube* through gently blowing snow, sparkling in the soft lights. Laughter and music floated out into the street through opening and closing doors, and my spirits took a buoyant leap. Whatever the situation, I was lucky beyond reason to be here in Zermatt. It was Heidi, the Snow Queen, my favorite Christmas card, and, yes, Sonja Henie, all wrapped up in one.

In the restaurant I addressed myself with gusto to raclette and dark beer. The little room was very warm, and noisy with conversation in German, English, French and Italian. It would have been impossible to harbor gloomy thoughts, even if I hadn't resolved, yet again, to dismiss them. I'd delivered a commendably logical lecture to myself on the folly of an infatuation which vacillated between fearful suspicion and uncritical adoration.

We were lingering over Armagnac when a handsome,

216

fair-haired man in his early thirties appeared at our table.

"Robin, you old rascal! I haven't seen you since Ischia."

Robin turned abruptly as his shoulder was caught in a friendly grip. The flash of recognition in his eyes wasn't entirely welcoming.

But he jumped to his feet, enthusiastically clapping the new arrival on the back. I must have misinterpreted his look, I thought.

"Kit! Lissa, I want you to meet Kit Ingram, an old friend of mine and a fine antiquarian. We were in the Navy together, and now he's working for John in London. Lissa's a harpist, Kit; Ciara Rossi's niece, as a matter of fact. And you know Richard, of course. Have you been here long?"

"About a week. God, but the skiing's great, isn't it? And the weather, until today. What have you been up to?"

"Shivering in Yorkshire, *mon vieux*," laughed Robin. He was completely at ease now, eyes dancing.

Something was rapping softly at the back of my mind. I knew I'd never met this trim young man before, but he reminded me of someone. No, it wasn't even as concrete as that. He was stirring up a recollection that refused to crystallize. I suppose I was staring at him, in an all too apparent way.

"*Deja vu*, Lissa?" Richard queried softly. Involuntarily, my head jerked around toward him. This mind-reading was happening too frequently for comfort. I hoped to heaven he couldn't see my thoughts about him with such alarming clarity.

The other two men were looking at us now, their light banter arrested.

"It's just that you look familiar," I explained. "But I don't think we've met."

"It's my generic face, I expect. It happens all the time."

"It's too much beer on my part, more likely," I laughed. "You know, I think I will take that walk now. It's very warm in here."

"I'll join you," said Richard, rising smoothly. "You two carry on with old boy week and we'll catch you later. Good to see you, Ingram."

It was snowing harder now, and the icy flakes prickled on my hot, sunburned cheeks. Richard slipped a gloved hand through the crook of my arm, and spoke conversationally.

"What struck you so about Robin's friend?"

"You're far too acute. Oh, I don't know, really. There was something that rang a distant bell. Perhaps, as he said, he's just a type....a pretty stunning one! Anyway, it was some quality I couldn't quite identify."

"Other than his being gay, you mean?"

I stopped dead and turned to look at him. "Maybe that's it. But how did you pick it up so quickly? Oh, I forgot– you know him, don't you? But still there's something more, some connection my mind won't make." I stood frowning in concentration.

"He's John's chief assistant, and very good at his work. Shall we try for a happier subject?" He walked on, towing me briskly down the street.

Was this homophobia? I reminded myself that there were men who found it difficult even to acknowledge the existence of homosexuality. I would have thought Richard incapable of such an attitude. Still, perhaps a certain Latin machismo–

"You know, I tried to get Peter to come along on this jaunt," he was saying as pleasantly as if he hadn't cut me off in mid-thought. "He loves to ski, and he's very adept. But he's found a new kitten, and chose to stay with her. He said it was more important for her to feel safe in her new home than for him to go skiing."

"And to be kept out of the jaws of G.P., no doubt. What a lovely child he is, Richard. Quite rare. You've done a beautiful job with him."

"Can't take much credit, I fear. It's a bloody miracle he even remembers who I am when I come driving in. G.P. certainly doesn't." His voice held self-recrimination, and I remembered what Anne had said about his appearance at Mass. Was this a part of his misery?

"G.P. wouldn't remember his own mother. And surely you can't blame yourself for that, Richard," I reasoned. "It goes with the territory. Anyway, Peter is enormously proud of you; he looks up to you in every way."

"God help him, then. And grant he finds a better role model than I am."

Stopping to look in a shop window, I tried to shift him from his suddenly dark mood. "So Peter is a good skier?"

"Amazingly so–he's very gifted. And he's mad for it. We were here for a week at Christmas."

"Then he realizes exactly what he's giving up for the sake of playing father to a kitten. He didn't get that concept of paternity out of thin air, you know."

He was silent for a moment. Smiling, he squeezed my arm and said, as he had at Rievaulx, "Bless you, Lissa."

We walked onto the wooden bridge over the Vispa and stood leaning on the rail, listening to the river's dark rushing passage.

"How lovely not to have cars," I mused. "You hear such wonderful sounds without them."

"You used to hear more," he mused. "And less music blaring out from the doors. Damned engineers, had to canalize the river, too, God knows why. Because they could, I suppose."

We crossed the bridge in silence. When he spoke, it was almost diffidently.

"Lissa, could I ask a favor? When you get back, if you have time, would you just look in on Peter?"

"Of course! I'd love any excuse to do that. You're not coming back to Yorkshire, then?"

"Not right away. I have a concert in Vienna, at the

Musikverein. All Beethoven. And God, I'm not ready." He pressed both hands to his eyes for a moment, then laughed. "Sorry. Sometimes it's like trying to stay two paces in front of a locomotive. Are you cold?"

"Freezing."

"Let's go have a drink, then."

"Okay. Richard, I'm sure your Beethoven is ready, but how you do it is beyond me. How can there be enough hours in the day? How can you possibly find time to practice, let alone compose and learn scores? Especially living so far from London, or from anywhere you work."

"It is a dilemma. But keeping the house in Yorkshire, and being there when I can, is the top priority. Peter loves it, and I want him to know his family, to have the security that—" He broke off momentarily. "I don't particularly want him to grow up in the city, and I'll be damned if he's going to be shipped off to a boarding school."

The security you never had, I finished for him silently. And are too proud, or still too hurt, to talk about the want of.

"Actually," he was saying, "the driving and flying time is very productive for me. I can listen to CDs, memorize scores, work out problems..."

What kinds of problems, I wondered, as my mind made another of those unsettling leaps from defense to attack. Problems that you put in the hands of Carlo, whoever he might be?

"Well," I said, striving to get my thoughts back on neutral ground, "it's an incredible pace. I don't know how you maintain it."

We'd entered another little candlelit cafe, almost deserted at this hour. He pulled out a chair for me next to the wood stove.

"Brandy?"

I nodded. It was getting to be an insidiously pleasant habit.

"Actually, I take excellent care of myself," he said,

220

picking up the subject again. "It's just that things have caught up with me at the moment. I feel as if I were on a galloping horse and had gotten a bit behind his motion. God, I'm full of bad transportation metaphors tonight. Well. I'll catch up, never fear."

"Of course you will." I swallowed some brandy; it seemed to flow directly into my veins, driving the chill before it. Warming to the subject, I leaned across the tiny round table. "In the smallest way, you know, I understand the strain, which by the way never seems to show. Don't you ever feel fear–before you perform, I mean?"

The grey eyes looked straight into mine. "Every time. Blind, deaf, paralyzing, unreasoning terror."

I looked at him in astonishment. "Are you serious?"

"Unfortunately yes."

"And yet you go on, night after night."

"Everything has a price, Lissa. It's part of the tariff for the superb life I lead, doing what I love. You don't feel it?"

I shook my head. "I didn't... not like that. Of course I never dealt with the enormous amounts of music that you do, or so many exalted venues. But when I played–" I searched for the right words. "It was more like a slightly dangerous, almost sensual intoxication."

He raised a hand and two more brandies appeared.

"Iron calm must run in your family. Ciara's the only major performer I've ever known who felt, literally, absolutely nothing at all––no difference between practice and performance."

"I don't think that's good," I mused with tipsy wisdom, sipping at the dark amber liquid. Its aromatic fumes were stinging my eyes.

"No," he said shortly. "It wasn't good."

"She didn't play well that last night, did she? I read somewhere that the performance wasn't up to her usual standard." I realized dimly that I was treading on dangerous ground, but couldn't remember why it was dangerous.

221

"She wasn't happy about it, no. It wasn't obvious to the audience, but the piece didn't cohere." I could sense his withdrawal. He sounded stony, indifferent.

"Why not?"

"I really don't remember, Lissa. Can we talk about something else?"

"And you conducted." I was shocked to hear the resentful, answering coldness in my voice. It sounded like an accusation.

"Lissa." He put down his brandy glass with a thump and took mine firmly from my hand. "Acquit me, I pray. Yes, I conducted, and no, I did not sabotage your aunt's performance, if that's what you're thinking. I may have despised her personally, but kindly give me credit for professionalism."

"It was a bad performance. You conducted. And she died." My voice was flat with challenge. The altitude, the heat from the stove, and the brandy, after the exertions of the day, had worked their awful alchemy. With my one remaining vestige of sobriety, tipping merrily over to join its former companions on a rapidly descending slope, I realized I was walking into a trap of my own making. Perversely set on one last defense of Ciara, I didn't even want to stop.

Apparently, neither did Richard.

"Lissa, do you know how Leon died?"

Why was he bringing this up now? I felt the old pang of loss.

"Of course I do. He was judging Metropolitan auditions, and when he returned from lunch, his heart just stopped."

"Exactly."

I stared at him in bewilderment.

"I want you to think back. What had changed in his life, in the months before?"

I tried to focus, pushing my resentment into the background.

222

"Well—he'd been doing much less teaching and composing. It was as if he'd revived his passion for performing."

"Did you read the reviews?"

"Of course. He was lauded as a superman, having elevated his instrument to heights never imagined. We were all so proud; it made us work even harder."

"And Ciara was in New York; she had a series of solo concerts there."

"Yes, I remember. Actually, she lunched with Leon the day he died."

"Did you read her reviews?"

"What?"

"Don't drift, Lissa. Did you read her reviews?"

My head was spinning, and I didn't answer.

"Did you read her reviews?" Quiet but inexorable.

"Yes–I must have, but I've forgotten."

"What did they say, Lissa?"

"I told you I've forgotten." I heard the panic in my voice.

"Then I'll refresh your memory. They said her performances were disappointing, almost robotic. The amazing technique was still there, but the interpretation was mere nuance, without fire or soul. They compared her to her mentor; one reviewer said that hearing her play after Leon was like comparing a cardboard silhouette to a living being."

"Richard–no. What are you suggesting? That my aunt poisoned Leon out of jealousy?"

"Was there an autopsy?"

"There was no need!" My voice was rising uncontrollably; people were casting uneasy glances at us. "Leon had a heart problem; everyone knew about it. And what you're hinting at sounds like a 1930's crime novel. Things like that just don't happen anymore!"

"Lissa, do you know how many fatal substances can be administered in a drink?"

"No!" I grated furiously. "Do you?"

"Certainly. Have you forgotten, if you ever knew, that I was with black ops?"

Then Tim had been right. I was shivering now.

"Did you go to Leon's funeral?"

"Richard, what is this interrogation? Of course I did. But I didn't see you there."

"Was Ciara there?"

"That's enough, Richard!" I was almost shouting now, goaded past any hope of control. "Were you there, on the beach, the night she died? It seems that someone of your description was!"

"Now we have it." Richard's eyes were like clear ice. "*In vino veritas*. You may as well let me hear it all. I undermined Ciara's performance, as I undermined your career, and drove her to suicide. Is that it?"

I got unsteadily to my feet. I was only dimly aware of Richard's hand reaching out, rescuing the glass I'd precipitated toward the table edge. The moonlit terrace in Geneva swam before my eyes, and I heard the agitated voices, clamoring one on another. *Haven't we had enough grief? This is no time for emotion.* And, ominously, *I am Italian.*

"No. No, that isn't it. I don't think it was suicide at all. I think it was murder."

Somehow I found myself out in the street, stumbling through the snow, now ankle-deep. I was crying, hot tears getting mixed up with the stinging flakes that fell thickly onto my face. And my knees were stiff. Everything hurt.

I felt Richard's hand on my shoulder and wrenched away. He exhaled a soft Italian oath, and grasping my shoulder again, turned me around and pointed me in the other direction. Without knowing how I got there, I felt the heat and queasy upward rush of the elevator, mercifully empty except for the two of us. Standing in a deserted corridor in front of what was presumably my room, I solemnly attempted to insert the key a good three inches above the keyhole.

With a sigh Richard took it from me and opened the door. He pressed the wall switch and a table lamp glowed. Moving me to one side with dogged patience, he closed the door and leaned wearily against it.

"You can't come in here," I protested in watery indignation.

His sigh was very short this time, and his voice curt. "If ever again I am guilty of plying you with alcohol, my *soi-disant* Bacchante, I hope I may develop rheumatoid arthritis in both hands. Whoever said 'whiskey on beer, never fear,' ought to be shot," he finished reflectively, turning on his heel to grasp the doorknob.

At that moment I was certain I was dying. I could barely stand, and the room was spinning hideously.

"Don't leave me!" I gasped, with stunning illogic.

He seized my arms, holding me upright. "You little fool," he grated softly between clenched teeth. Then he lifted me effortlessly in his arms, kissed me with violent, bruising exasperation, and carried me to the bed.

Dropping me unceremoniously, he turned and stalked to the door. He switched off the light, and through the pounding of my heart and the roaring of my ears I heard the spring latch click. In the dim light from the window I watched him return to the bed and closed my eyes, desire brushing away the alcoholic cobwebs.

He reached down and jerked the eiderdown up to my chin.

"I was in Portugal when Leon was buried, playing the Prokofiev Second."

The door slammed behind him and I was alone in the darkened room.

It was a very fragmented night. I remember tears, violent illness, a bath, during which I thought I might drown, more tears, and finally, broken slumber. If this were a novel, I

225

thought in one miserably wakeful moment, Richard would come back to my room, tender and contrite. He would prove his innocence to me. He would swear never again to do... whatever it was he had done. I would forgive him. And there would be a wild and glorious night of love.

As it was, I, Felicity Godwin, unsuccessful harpist and lapsed public school music teacher, was paying the price for absent-mindedly trying to keep up with people who had a normal, decent metabolism.

I changed my plans for my next life. I no longer aspired to be a cat. I would be a truck driver with an enormous capacity for alcohol and no finer feelings at all.

≫CHAPTER 20≪

For sweetest things turn sour by their deeds;
Lilies that fester smell far worse than weeds
William Shakespeare, Sonnet 94

"Summertime, and the living is easy..."

A light tenor carried the melody while the burnished baritone provided harmonies more adventurous than any Gershwin ever imagined.

I raised my head with experimental caution. Outside the window snow was falling in the grey morning light. Moaning, I pulled the pillow over my ears.

"Fish are jumping... and the cotton is high..."

With a stifled scream I jumped out of bed, only to fall back immediately, clutching my head.

Now they were well into the May Day Carol.

"Awake, awake, my pretty pretty maid, out of your drowsy dream; and step into your dairy below, and fetch us a bowl of cream."

"It's going to be Mayday sooner than they think," I muttered, belting my robe with vicious emphasis.

"If you two guys don't get out of here, I'll fetch you more than a bowl of cream," I snarled, yanking the door open.

They fell laughing into the room, and I surveyed them

with cold distaste.

"Thank goodness we're not really related," I added crushingly.

"I'll vote for that," agreed Robin, leering down at my dishabille.

"Come on, Lissa." Richard spoke in his best rallying style. "Breakfast, then we're off to the Trockener Steg."

My voice shot up. "Breakfast! Are you trying to kill me? Besides, there's a blizzard out there."

"It's breaking. You'll feel better after some coffee. We'll give you fifteen minutes. Come on, Robin, we'll go on down and order. Croissants, Lissa? Or bacon and eggs?"

I slammed the door on their merriment.

It was considerably more than fifteen minutes later that I joined them below. As we sat over our coffee, I was aware of a strong sense of disorientation. Last night I'd all but accused Richard of being instrumental in Ciara's death. *In vino veritas,* he'd said. And Robin had hinted reluctantly at his own suspicions before we left Yorkshire. Yet it seemed, in spite of their obvious closeness, that he'd kept silent with Richard. Then there was John–what was his place in all this? Was Richard's "unguarded" statement about him merely a red herring? I wished fleetingly that I'd seen him in Geneva.

And here was Richard, treating me with the same light, humorously civilized charm he'd employed before I turned my brandy-spawned candor on him. What kind of people were these? What was I doing here with them?

And how, I wondered, would my own New England family have reacted to Ciara's questionable death? I tried to imagine Mother and Daddy in veiled verbal intrigue over the breakfast table, and the idea was so incongruous that I laughed aloud, causing the cousins to remark kindly that they were delighted to see me feeling so much better.

Richard had been right about the weather. By eleven

the snow clouds were gone and we were on top of a world of brilliant blue and white.

We'd decided to avoid the big restaurant, and plunged hungrily into the excellent picnic packed by the hotel.

To my amazement, I felt almost completely restored. As I reached for a roasted chicken leg, Robin extended a glass of white wine.

"Good God, don't give her that," exclaimed Richard, neatly intercepting it. "Not at this altitude. Not at sea level, for that matter." He downed the wine unfeelingly.

"Hangover, Lissa?" grinned Robin.

"Just pass the bread, and kindly shut up. I suppose I can always melt snow." Turning to Richard, I asked sweetly, "You did bring a candle and a saucepan?"

"Better than that." He reached into the basket and handed me an icy bottle of *apfelsaft*.

"Oh. Oh, thank you." The wind died out of my sails.

"I'd just like the ski patrol to have an easy day."

"Well," I sighed. "Frankly, I don't think they'll have to bother with me. I believe I'm even slower than usual today. It's unfair to hold you two back." I subsided onto a snow bank, closing my eyes against the glorious sun.

"Actually, you're picking up quite a bit of speed," said Robin. "You're far more in control, so it doesn't feel so fast to you, but we can tell; you're getting down the mountain much more quickly now."

"Do you really think so? Oh, I hope you're right." I stretched luxuriously. "I'm awfully tired of always being the last down."

"One has to be willing to take some risks," Richard remarked quietly.

That piqued me a bit. I'd always had a fear of speed, of going out of control. But I didn't consider myself a physical coward. And I had been a daring performer; caution didn't enter into my playing.

"There are all sorts of risks," I answered coldly,

opening my eyes and sitting up. And you've probably taken most of them, I added silently. I felt a twinge of envy for his life of certainty and bravura courage.

"True." His tone was uncompromising. The challenge of the York concert flashed into my vision. I put my plate in the basket, already neatly packed, and got to my feet.

"Yes, well, I think I'll be off to seek some of them, in my own milquetoast fashion."

"Don't be so prickly, Lissa," Richard laughed. "I only meant that if you want to ski fast, you have to accept the fact that you're going to fall harder. But I do think you're ready to speed up a bit more and still stay in easy control, don't you, Robin?"

"Heavens, yes. In my opinion she's a natural. Really, Lissa, your progress has been phenomenal."

Mollified and secretly pleased, I stamped my boots into their bindings.

We'd made several runs with gradually increasing speed. I was beginning to feel genuine relaxation and rhythm, and had stopped fighting my own forward momentum. At last, I thought gleefully, I'm skiing, really skiing.

At about two o'clock, with the Alpine sun high above, we found ourselves at the head of a long, narrow chute which broadened into a wider slope, merging into a long flat runout before it plunged down again.

"I can't do that," I said with conviction, watching the brightly clad skiers slip casually into that elevator drop.

"You can't miss," chaffed Robin. "It's dead easy. Just keep your knees bent and your weight forward."

"But it's too steep, I can't turn," I protested.

"No, of course not," agreed Richard. "You're not supposed to. Just schuss down and slow yourself by traversing when the slope broadens." He looked at me, challenge in his eyes. "Okay?"

"Okay," I said uncertainly.

Then they were over the lip, dropping with heart-stopping speed, and already out on the broader slope, timing their turns so that they crossed with razor-edged closeness, skimming downhill in lovely dangerous horseplay. They turned and waited for me below the runout.

One must be willing to take some risks, Richard had said. Besides, what was I going to do, sit down and slide?

Steeling myself, I pushed off and plummeted down the near-vertical drop.

It was easy. I was conscious only of exhilaration, of the blue and white world flashing past and the crisp air rushing up to meet me. Without panic, I slowed myself with a smooth series of turns on the wide slope below. Before I knew it, I was flying down the runout far above them. I'd done it! From here on the day would be child's play.

Then my left ski shot out in a wide involuntary arc. I felt a moment of disbelief before my body began describing awful, jarring cartwheels. I could hear the brutal crack of the skis against hard-packed snow. I'd fallen many times before, but never like this. My bindings will release, I thought desperately.

But they didn't. I came to a jolting halt with my left ski tip jammed into the snow at a strange angle, and a fierce pain lancing through my knee.

An anxious flow of German was coming from somewhere behind my head. There was snow down my back, up my cuffs, in my face. I wiped it out of my eyes with a wet glove and bit my lip, trying to reach the release on my left binding.

The elderly Swiss, his weathered face creased with concern, sprung the catches for me, and I fell back on the snow.

"*Danke schön*," I whispered. "Ich..."

"Are you quite all right?" he asked in flawless English.

I sighed. So much for my German accent. "I think so,

just shaken up. I fall a lot," I babbled on, "and I always have been all right. But I've never fallen quite so fast before."

He put an arm around me, helping me to my feet.

I tried my weight on the left leg and sank immediately back onto the snow.

"No," I murmured, feeling the film of perspiration on my face. "I'm sorry. I don't think I can stand up."

"Ah." He spoke regretfully. "I will get help."

"Yes. Thank you. Because," I spoke to his rapidly receding back, "I sure as hell don't think I'm going to walk away from this one."

The pain was pressing in on me now, mounting in waves. I bit my lip again but abandoned that quickly; it had suffered enough from Richard's exasperation the night before. I tried deep breathing instead. An eternity passed. Oh, Lord, I thought. If I've sacrificed York for this foolish escapade... even if I were so fortunate as not to have broken anything, would a sprain mend in time for me to use the harp pedals?

There was a sound like tearing silk above my head, and Richard and Robin pulled up beside me in a rooster-tail of spraying snow. They looked immensely tall against the sun's glare, their eyes hidden behind the black goggles.

Robin knelt at my side.

"Lissa, are you all right? Where are you hurt? We saw you fall, but it was too steep for us to get back up. We had to ski down and take the lift again. God, we were fools to push you into this."

"No, it was fine. It's just my knee... probably sprained."

Robin looked back up the mountain. "You made it down the chute in great style. What happened?"

"Caught an edge, I guess. I got my weight on the outside, somehow, when I was running straight. Just carelessness. I've done it before, but not at that speed. The whole ski just arced out, incredibly fast." I closed my mouth abruptly; my teeth were chattering uncontrollably from chill, shock and pain.

"Thank God your bindings released. It could have been a bad break."

"Well, they didn't. If they had I'd be fine. But I did at least three windmills. Or two and a half." The chattering was worse, and I put a sodden glove to my mouth.

A sled hissed to a stop at my side. Soon two blonde young men were carefully splinting my knee, lifting me onto the sled, tucking me up with blankets, and joking gently and reassuringly all the while. Just before the protective tinted plastic bubble descended over my head, I looked at Richard. His face beneath the goggles was rigid, expressionless. And he hadn't spoken a word.

The car sped west toward Geneva, but Robin drove with considerate care around the bends. Thanks to the painkillers, I felt tranquil, floating, and indifferent. I gazed dreamily out the window at the valley, watching intimations of an early spring nurtured by the warm winds of the Rhône.

The knee was wrenched, no more. Fortunately it was the left one; that meant one less pedal to cope with on the harp, and the radius of movement was smaller. The doctor had cautiously predicted that with the home treatment he prescribed, I'd be able to walk, carefully, within a week.

Robin turned to me and for the tenth time said, "Lissa, I'm so sorry."

"Doesn't matter, really, Robin. I only regret putting a pall on our last day."

"Never think that," he chided, giving my hand a quick squeeze. "You're the one who had all the pain. Anyway, Richard needs the time to practice. I'm just bewildered about your bindings. Did you have any falls in the morning? Or the day before?"

I tried to remember, and found I really didn't care. But politeness prevailed. "None in the morning. The day before... about three. The bindings released once; the other falls weren't fast or hard enough."

"Then they were set properly. I suppose they just jammed. Rotten luck, but it happens."

"Do you, Robin?"

"Do I what, love?" I saw an amused smile touch his mouth. No wonder; I was groggy and incoherent enough to be moderately diverting, I supposed.

"Do you really think that? That they jammed, I mean? Can they jam?"

He turned to me again, puzzlement on his face.

"Of course I do. What else could have happened?"

"Well, they–they might have been reset. For somebody who was heavier."

His eyes widened in disbelief. "But nobody else used them. Do you mean someone else might have mistaken them for their own? But that couldn't have happened; Richard had them. Why on earth–"

"That's what I ask myself." I yawned uncontrollably. "It's not the first odd thing that's happened. Why do I feel like Poe's raven?" I added, tucking the hotel's generously donated pillow between shoulder and ear.

Robin was waiting in a worried silence.

"Well, remember the billet strap?"

He nodded. "Yes, of course. But tack wears out. I've broken reins–"

"It didn't wear out, Robin. I remembered, just last night when I was half awake, where I'd smelled that curious odor on the leather. I think the strap had been etched with muriatic acid. We used it at home to clean the fireplace brick. Very dangerous stuff; you have to use heavy gloves and goggles."

He pulled abruptly over to the verge and looked me in the eye. "What are you saying, Lissa?"

"It's obvious, isn't it? Someone has been setting little traps for me. Nothing fatal, with luck; just enough to hurt me, perhaps make sure I go back to the States."

The rims around his irises looked very black, and his face was carefully expressionless.

"Why, Robin?" I spoke without emotion, out of simple curiosity. I felt as though I were sitting on a big soft grey cloud, looking down on the foibles of humanity with gentle detachment.

"Why would he do these things–a man who has every gift, everything that life can offer? I can see him committing murder, perhaps, in a rage, but why this petty malice?"

Robin dropped his head into his hands for a moment. When he looked up, his face was white and drawn.

"But that's just it, Lissa, don't you see? Too many talents, too much complexity. Is it surprising that he's not perhaps sane in every way? Besides, you don't know that it wasn't just a mechanical failure."

"Not this, perhaps. But the saddle... unless you want me to believe that John did it, or Merrin. Or that Ciara's still alive, hiding out, trying to complete that professional destruction Richard's so fond about talking about. Not that she'd exactly find me a threat to her career these days," I added dryly.

Robin pulled the car back onto the road, driving more slowly now.

"Lissa," he asked, almost reluctantly, "just how much do you know about Richard?"

"Very little. Only a trifle more," I went on with unsparing honesty, "than I know about you or John."

"Fair enough. There's no reason for you to trust me."

"Perhaps not. But there it is... you just inspire trust, Robin."

"Thanks, my dear," he said, with a smile that managed to be wry and grateful all at once. "Lissa, back at Denham House you mentioned you'd had a letter from Ciara not long before she died. Did she tell you anything about her situation with the family?"

"Not really. It was mostly about Richard, and that was

all innuendo. She hinted at drugs."

"Oh, God." There was regret in his voice. "I was hoping you wouldn't have to know that part."

"Robin, I think I'd rather know than keep wondering." Mendacious, I thought. I'd far rather know nothing at all.

"Well, first of all there's the money." He exhaled a little sigh. "He makes a great deal, of course, with the music: concert appearances, recording contracts. But not that sort of money. The cars, the residences he maintains around the world, the investments, and yes, the charities. The outflow is staggering, I can tell you."

"Truly? I thought he was joking when he–no, never mind. And the money comes from drugs? Wait, Robin. You're telling me he's in the trade?" I smiled involuntarily at the incongruity of it.

"I think I'd better start at the beginning. That way you can understand better; maybe you won't condemn him so utterly. Did you know that his father denied, toward the end of his life, that Richard was his son, and left him absolutely nothing when he died?"

"Mrs. Chidester said something..."

"Did she? Well, old Sir James was a bastard and a half. He was Richard's father all right; there's no mistaking the resemblance. But when he couldn't crush Gianna's independence, he began to hate her. And, of course, there was the matter of Richard's refusal to model himself upon James. Richard was a renegade: a musician, which set him outside the pale as unmanly, and confoundedly Italian to boot. Ergo, he couldn't be James' son. It was just like the son of a bitch to repudiate utterly all the things that had attracted him to Gianna in the first place. When Richard left England with Gianna, James had the perfect excuse to disinherit him."

"But he was only a boy!"

"Yes, but he'd long ago earned James' contempt. It started early, when Richard let him see how he loathed public school. Oh, he excelled, he couldn't keep from doing that with his brain, but he made no bones about detesting the petty rites, the bullying, all that chilly regimentation. Not that I was that fond of it either." His mouth crooked up sardonically.

"All James' interests–and they were few: hunting, politics, the estate–left Richard cold. They were opposed at every point, and tolerance wasn't James' strong point; as a matter of fact he was choleric to a fault. He was hardly a doting father to John, either–he had very little notion of how to be a father at all. But he upheld John as a model to Richard. John was away at Cambridge, or he might have defended Richard.

"Of course, Gianna's *idée fixe* about Richard didn't ameliorate things. She had him in a positive fever of music from the time he could sit at a keyboard, and during holidays they were always at it. She saw his genuine talent, but it was also her escape from the dullness of her life, and perhaps her way of getting back at James as well. James feared and resented their closeness, and felt that Gianna was robbing Richard of his masculinity."

This time it was I who gave a humorless laugh.

"Yes. Well, they finally cut and ran, after God knows how many ugly scenes. Richard studied in a number of places–Italy, France, New York. Both of them took out American citizenship. Then one year, in the middle of term at Juilliard, he dropped out and simply disappeared. I think he was burned out from the years of work, and he'd been brooding since Uncle James died, God knows why. Anyway, he joined the CIA; I suppose it was his substitute for the French Foreign Legion."

I remembered the evening at Hawthorns; Richard had said much the same.

"He was the perfect candidate, of course: steel-trap brain, photographic memory and phenomenal retention, excellent grounding in history, languages, knowledge of the Continent. The whole package."

"I've heard the rumors."

"Have you? Well, he went in as a linguist and propaganda writer. The position was more than nominal, and I imagine he was very good at it. But ultimately he was assigned to get rid of a double agent."

"Get rid of..." my voice came faintly. So it was true.

"Don't be naïve, Lissa," he said brusquely. "Governments are governments, even yours. Yes, get rid of. But this particular agent was a moral imbecile, and had left such a trail of gratuitous destruction that Richard says he felt no compunction–at least not then. After all, the concept of vendetta is nothing new to an Italian. God knows Gianna's family..." He took a long, controlled breath.

"Richard's code name was 'le Marchand de Sable': the Sandman. Hard to believe he's using it for the title of a composition title, isn't it? It just shows... well. I don't know how many 'assignments' there were after that, but within three years he'd left the organization, returned to his musical studies, and damn near killed himself with overwork and practice. It was haunting him, you can bet on that, the things he'd done. But they say once you've killed, it's easy." He accelerated to pull around a van.

"After a time he married Anna. She was an artistic, wonderfully serene woman, and a great comfort to him. We all hoped the marriage would settle him. But you know how that ended. Her death just about devastated him, though he never stopped performing. In the meantime the successes started piling up, and he took to high living. The drug thing– I honestly think he was forced into it by blackmail, to begin with. Can you imagine the effect on his career if he'd been exposed as a professional assassin? The humanitarian organizations would have had full-page blackballing petitions in all the major newspapers and periodicals, signed by every figure in the arts they could muster."

"But what would be the point? Why would a drug ring single out Richard?"

"International contacts, for one thing. His would be invaluable. So would much of the knowledge he'd gained in intelligence. Did you know that clandestine operators can traffic in narcotics with impunity, as long as it's done in pursuit of their goals? And of course there's that aura of invulnerability that great artists have. Somehow, Lissa, he got the upper hand in those dealings. He's so damned smart. And don't forget he had the help of his family's Mafia connections. Anyway, it all turned to his own advantage in a big way."

"I'm sorry–I don't believe it. Robin, I just can't. It's too ludicrous!"

But was it? I could think of several exalted personages who'd been exposed in cocaine deals. The warm blanket effect of the painkiller was wearing off, and I tried to clutch its remnants to me. But the familiar ache stirring in my knee was nothing to the one in my chest.

"Believe it or not as you like. Hell, Lissa," he cried angrily. "I'm not exactly crazy about it myself. He's my cousin, you know." He lifted his hand in a gesture of helpless frustration, and dropped it with a thud onto the wheel. "Sorry. Well, when Ciara found out about his extra-musical career, and his addiction–"

"Addiction?" This was worse than anything. "No, Robin. He couldn't be addicted. It's just not possible. No one could do what he does and be addicted!"

"Come on, my dear," chided Robin gently. "Do you really think every drug makes the user bug-eyed, or violent, or causes him to stagger about in a euphoric trance? We're talking about sophisticated drugs, sophisticated usage. His intellect, his reflexes would be subtly heightened, that's all; for a time, anyway. But sometimes it distorts his judgment. He does erratic and irresponsible things, though I don't doubt he hates himself afterward."

Or before, I thought, remembering Anne O'Neal's description of the Mass.

"Even before the drugs..." he continued, as if to himself. He shook his head. "But that could be a concomitant of genius, I suppose." He went on in his normal tone. "Haven't you noticed his shifts of mood?"

Haven't I just, I thought sadly. "So you think he killed Ciara?"

"God knows. We never will. It might have been an accident, it might have been... once, for a moment, I even thought it might have been John. She'd played them off against one another, pushed them both beyond human endurance. John with sex and jealousy, Richard with taunting about the drugs. But do you think Richard, already hating her for having betrayed John, would have accepted it meekly if she'd threatened to blow the whistle on him? Not bloody likely," he finished grimly.

"And you've said nothing? Done nothing?"

"Lissa, what could I do? I wasn't even there. The verdict, remember, was death by accidental drowning. There wasn't a shred of proof to the contrary. Besides, it would have killed John; he's had more than enough grief. And," he said again, "Richard's my cousin."

I was silent.

He looked at me, appealing for support.

"Think about it, Lissa. What would you have done?"

I'd been lying in my room in Zermatt with only a night light on, pillows propping my knee, groggy with painkillers. The curtains were open and the mountains looked like shapes cut from black paper and pasted against the darkly translucent sky. Earlier, I'd watched as an *alpenglow* turned the peaks to glorious apricot radiance. Soon, cooling, they faded from rose through amethyst into mauve.

As if all light and warmth had been bled out of the world, they hung brooding there, dead stones, smudged across the horizon in chilly, lifeless grey.

Richard came in quietly. Through the haze of drugs I

wondered, without much curiosity, how he'd unlocked the door.

He moved across the room and pulled up a chair between the windows and the bed.

Another idea drifted into my head with that detached, cushioned quality the drug produced. I'd completely misinterpreted the Adagio of the Brahms Concerto. My perception of it had been badly at fault. It wasn't tender devotion melting into sensual longing. It was the grave, grey crepuscular hush of a sick-room, broken by the feverishly distorted musings of a disturbed mind. Musings that were gently hushed into silence again by that same grave greyness.

Well, it had happened. I was "the girl," and I had been injured. And Richard had taken my skis last night.

His eyes, grown accustomed to the gloom, met my own wide-open ones. He spoke softly.

"Ah... you're awake, Lissa."

I nodded, unable to speak past the tightness in my throat.

"The doctor says you can travel tomorrow. Unless you'd rather stay until you're in less pain; we can cancel the flight."

"No." It came out husky and cracked. "No, I want to go home. I mean, back to Yorkshire." I was not going to cry.

"Thank God it was just a wrench and not a break. Dr. Busch says you'll have moderate use of it in a few days, with proper treatment. So you'll be able to play at York after all, if you're careful."

I looked at him with incredulity. His head was silhouetted sharply against the night sky, features obliterated, unreadable.

He had engineered this accident, as he said Ciara had engineered the decline of my career.

I thought with difficulty back to the day before, that wonderful afternoon on the mountain when I began to feel real confidence. At the end of the last run, Richard offered to

241

carry my skis. Robin and I returned to the hotel while Richard stopped to speak with a ski instructor he knew.

It would have been a quick and simple matter for him to reset the bindings to, say, one hundred and fifty pounds, so they wouldn't release for a fall by someone who weighed one twenty-five.

And now he was expecting me to play for him. Was he insane, or was I?

I wondered for a moment whether it was really Ciara who'd been responsible for discrediting me professionally. How easy to cast the blame on a dead woman! But why on earth would Richard want to hurt me now? Was it some kind of mad vendetta triggered by grief at her loss? Maybe he only pretended to loathe her. I gave up. Even fearing and half-despising him, I longed for him to lay his hand on my head, and I hated myself for it.

In spite of the drug's blanketing effect, the ache in my knee was beginning to eat through like slow acid. And with it, my rage flared up against this man who'd repeatedly set me up and knocked me down, as if I'd been one of Peter's toy soldiers. But I was aware now—it had taken long enough—and I'd be alert. He wouldn't find such an easy mark this time. Hadn't I wanted a challenge? Here it was. I'd wrest back what he'd stolen from me, and be damned to all his strength and cunning.

I raised myself on the pillow.

"Of course I'll play, Richard. It would take more than a wrenched knee to keep me away from that concert." Better luck next time.

"Good woman." And now, rising, he did put his hand on my forehead. Cool though it was, it felt like a brand. "I'm so sorry, Lissa."

When I looked at him blankly, he continued.

"About your accident, you know. I'd give anything for it not to have happened." I heard him draw a deep, careful breath and let it out slowly.

My God, he really is mad, I thought desolately.
Schizophrenia? Drugs? Had he truly deceived himself,
compartmented his actions this effectively?

"So you'll fly out tomorrow," he was saying, "and
we'll start rehearsal in ten days. I'm staying over until Friday;
I've located a piano. After that I'll be in Vienna, at the
Imperial Hotel if you need me. The concert's at the
Musikverein on Sunday. Lissa?"

I was staring at the wall. He gave my shoulder a little
shake. "At the Imperial. In Vienna," he repeated, slowly and
distinctly. "Have you got that?"

I nodded silently.

"I'm calling John to tell him what happened. He'll
meet you at the airport in Leeds." He bent swiftly, pressing
his lips to my cheek. "Take care, little one. And rest well."

The door closed before the first weak, baffled tear slid
down my cheek.

And now, speeding along the road to Geneva, Robin
was asking what I would have done in his place.

A curious succession of images raced through my
mind in a kaleidoscopic whirl.

Father Francis, in the little white frame Anglican
church in Lynton, his slightly nasal voice intoning the Ten
Commandments.

"Thou shalt not kill."

Ciara's beautiful, vivacious face, dissolving to the
bones, stirring gently with the secret currents under that dark
blue sea; her evil–and somehow I could almost accept that
now–finally laid to rest.

The double agent, faceless to me; a man who had
callously destroyed life, destroyed in his turn by–what?
Gun? Stiletto? Garrote? There would have been no need.
Just hands. Pianist's hands.

Drugs, their horror and devastation seeping into
countless lives. "Better to reign in hell than serve in heaven."

A broken billet strap. An oddly altered musical instrument. The crack of skis on hard-packed snow–and suddenly the dull accustomed pain in my knee flared into fierce life.

Then, a darkened concert hall, with thousands of transfixed faces raised to the God-given, life-affirming music that lifted them in the purity of its joy. Listeners whose view of life would never be quite the same again.

And Peter, who'd given up three glorious days of skiing and sunshine to comfort and reassure a newly weaned kitten. Peter, who worshiped his father. Who had no mother. John. Mrs. Chidester. Gianna. And yes, Robin.

So little to set against death and corruption.

I leaned my head against the seat, closing my eyes. I knew what I would do in Robin's place. Without the most irrefutable proofs, I would do what he had done, what Mrs. Chidester had done.

Which was to say precisely nothing. And resolutely shutting out the spectacle of my ruined, decaying conscience, I let myself drift into sleep.

Robin helped me into the aisle seat, taking my crutches. As we began to taxi down the runway, he turned to me in alarm.

"Oh, my God! I'm so sorry, Lissa. I completely forgot." He reached into his pocket. "Here's the patch Richard left for you."

"It's all right, Robin. I forgot, too. It's not a very long flight."

He had the foil envelope open. "So...do you want to put it on?"

And so dead were my emotions, so dulled my brain, that I applied the flesh-colored disc behind my ear without another thought.

John's face went white with alarm when he met us at

the terminal. He was almost as pale as I must be, I thought with listless amusement.

"My poor Lissa! Here, sit down. Richard said it was only a minor injury. I didn't realize..."

His comforting arm was supporting me, and I felt the betraying sting of tears. Why must I feel so bound to these people? Their unexpected kindnesses muddied every clear perception. The only possible thing was to remove myself from their sphere, and that I was resolved to do, immediately after York.

"I'm all right, John, really. Bless you for meeting us. No, my knee isn't bad, truly, just a wrench. But I could do with a cup of tea and some toast before we start back."

When they helped me into the Bentley, I sank limply into the leather cushions. John tucked a blanket around me and slid under the wheel, while Robin settled himself and the crutches in the back seat.

"How was the skiing?" asked John.

"Beautiful. You tell him, Robin." I closed my eyes.

It was all one to me whether or not Robin unfolded the story. Physically and emotionally I was beyond caring.

Because not twenty minutes after applying the transdermal patch, I'd been seized by the most violent attack of nausea I'd ever known.

✑CHAPTER 21✑

Float, golden note,
From the harp strings all in tune.
Climb, quivering chime,
Up the moonbeams to the moon.
William Percy French, Fairy Song

It was easier than I'd hoped to operate the harp pedals. The radius of movement for the left foot was small, and most of the harp's weight was borne on the right side. Robin had driven me to Richmond for a cortisone shot, I'd been applying icepacks, and the discomfort was rapidly waning, though I still hopped a bit. My incipient blood blister had morphed into a conveniently tough pad.

At my request, two of the workmen moved the harp upstairs to my bedroom. This eliminated the strain of going up and down several times a day. I'd practiced since early morning, impatient to pin down every aspect of the score. Richard had been right; the time away had actually been beneficial, giving the music time to soak into mind and spirit without the distraction of mere mechanics.

With an upward run of insistent force and passionate fury I concluded the cadenza–was it really a cadenza? I'd been thinking of it that way for some time–and set the harp down, looking out the window. Birds were flying over the fell, and there was a merry headlong carelessness to the stream that flowed down through a copse of trees. Soon all the beauty of spring would wake on the hills, but I wouldn't be here to see it. I pushed that thought away, and tried to shut out all speculation about the past weeks.

I could make nothing of the bizarre events and bits of information known to me. Sometimes I felt like a little boat dashing itself repeatedly against giant rocks. I couldn't practice if I continued to worry myself into a frenzy. And all I wanted to do now was play, as well as I could, at York, and then go home. But I would be careful. Very careful indeed.

I glanced at the enamel face of the antique Dutton table-clock. Two pm... almost time for Peter. When I'd mentioned Richard's request that I look in on his son, John arranged to bring him to Denham House for a visit. I was so fond of Peter that the irony implicit in my concern for the child of a man who'd attempted twice–no, three times–to injure me barely brushed at my consciousness.

Hearing a car, I hopped to the window, supporting myself on the dressing table in passing. A quick glimpse in the mirror showed me that the tan imparted by three days of brilliant Swiss sun was already fading.

The car door slammed. I heard John's voice and Peter's quick laughter, their footsteps running up the stairs.

"Here's Peter the Incorrigible," announced John. "Are you quite sure you're ready for this?"

"Ready and willing," I declared, returning Peter's hug.

"Then I'll leave you two for the nonce, and rejoin you for tea."

Peter divested himself of several parcels, which turned out to be a seedcake from Mrs. Chidester; his own hand-drawn get-well card (decorated with violently orange and purple pansies); the box of *castillos* I'd given him; and a little covered wicker basket.

Eyes shining, he pulled up a chair for me, seated me with great aplomb, and placed the basket on my lap.

"Cleo wanted to visit, too," he explained. I opened the hinged lid and lifted out a tiny kitten.

She was marmalade-colored, soft as thistledown, with a perfectly square face and great round aquamarine eyes. Her chin and throat were snowy white; the minute raspberry nose as flat as if she'd run headlong into a stone wall.

"Oh! Peter, she's beautiful!" I held the warm, weightless body up to my cheek and listened to her disproportionately loud purr.

"She's the most beautiful kitten in the world!"

"Wherever did you find her?"

His small face contracted with anger. "Near the road. Someone had put her in a shoe box and thrown her out of a car. She was starving, and her shoulder was out of joint. Papa put it right again. I'd like to kill them."

"Well," I said, seeing the thunderclouds swell, "she's certainly not starving now." I stroked the round little sides gently. "You've done a beautiful job of fattening her up."

But he was not to be distracted. "I hate people like that."

"I know, love," I murmured. "I'm with you. But if you can't catch them, the best thing to do is pick up the pieces, and that's what you've done."

He muttered something in a low voice and turned to look out the window.

"What did you say, Peter?"

"I said people like that, people who're cruel to animals, are like the Snow Queen."

"Oh, the Anderson story. Heartless, you mean. Yes, you're perfectly right."

"No, I mean the real Snow Queen. She's dead now."

"Peter..." I was appalled at the practical satisfaction in his voice.

"That's what my Nanny always called her. After Hishi, anyway."

"I'm lost, pumpkin. Explain, *prego*."

Peter laughed, his fiercely creased brow clearing. "Oho, Italian! You've been around Papa too much."

Out of the mouths of babes, I thought.

"Come on, Peter. You've left me far behind."

"Well, it was winter. Not this one but last." Soon after

Ciara's marriage to John. I noticed that Peter wouldn't use Ciara's name.

"Hishi Ono had been climbing up under the hood of her car because the motor made it warm. My Uncle John gave him to her, for a present," he explained. "And one day when she started the car he was in there. John had told her always to honk the horn so he'd come out, but she didn't. So the motor cut his tail off," he explained pragmatically.

My mouth fell open. I'd always assumed that Hishi was a genetically tailless Manx.

"He was cut in other places, too, and all bloody," he continued. "She wouldn't even take him to the vet, John did that right away, and she wanted to have him put down. And she never let him come in her room again. She wouldn't pet him or comfort him, Lissa! And Papa says Hishi has always hated women since then. Well, I hate her. She's like those people who throw kittens out of cars," he began again, in circular fashion.

"Yes, I quite see," I said hastily. "And I can't say I blame you. But she's gone, Peter. And it's absolutely no good hating people, you know, it hurts only yourself."

"Prrrtt?" My knees sank under the weight of Hishi, who, overcome by curiosity, had slipped out from under the bed and sprung onto my lap.

"Gently, love," I said apprehensively, as he stood stiff-legged, staring at Cleo with unblinking eyes. "She's just a baby."

Arching her back, Cleo spat at him, cuffing him accurately on the nose. He retreated to the other side of my chair, where he stood gazing intently at her for a moment, slowly narrowing and widening his eyes. Then with another little trill he leapt into the middle of the bed, yawned in an elaborate show of boredom, and commenced to wash.

Peter was staring at me. "How did you ever get him to come in here?"

"I didn't. Honestly, Peter. He sort of adopted me the

249

first night I came."

Peter shook his head, baffled.

"Anyway, Hishi's far too intelligent to be a misogynist–
a woman-hater," I explained. "He probably judges on
character alone. And he doesn't sleep in car engines now, he
sleeps properly under the covers, with his head on my pillow.
By the way, how did he get a Japanese name?"

"It's not Japanese. When we got him we didn't know if
he was a boy or a girl. She didn't name him, so we called him
He-She. And he was such a bad little kitten that we were
always saying 'Oh, no!' So John named him Hishi Ono."

I laughed. "Well, I should have known no animal in
this family would be called Fluffy or Mittens. Now, do you
have a pocket knife on you? I can't wait till teatime, I'm
ravenous. Let's have some of that lovely seedcake and build a
royal palace for Cleo."

After we'd completed the last turret and hung the
banners in place, making serious inroads on the cake as we
worked, Peter's interest turned to the harp. He stood up,
brushing off crumbs, and traced the carvings with a small
finger. Lying on his back, he looked into the sound-holes and
carefully moved the pedals up and down. At last, his
mechanical curiosity satisfied, he asked me to play. He
helped me gallantly to my feet and I hopped to the
instrument, accompanied by his laughter.

"You look like a kangaroo!"

After a moment's thought, sifting through my
repertoire for something age-appropriate, I launched into a
bouncy French folksong. Peter nodded and clapped silently
to the rhythm of the music.

"That was fun," he conceded, "and short. Do you have
anything with more meat to it?"

If this kept up, I thought, I was going to have a
permanently dislocated lower jaw. Then I remembered. Of
course. This child had heard Brahms, Beethoven,
Rachmaninoff, Mozart and who knew what else from his

cradle days.

"Well," I began, and cleared my throat. "Well, you know, I haven't been practicing much besides your Papa's *Merchant* lately…I don't really like the C.P.E Bach, or the Handel, and I'm afraid there isn't anything that comes up to piano repertoire…" I couldn't believe I was having this conversation with a six—now seven–year-old boy. He was approximately the age of my students in Lynton.

He nodded understandingly. "How about *Feerie* then?"

I looked at him keenly. "Peter, do you know that piece? Did you hear Ciara play it?"

"No. I didn't listen to her play." A pause, as the former darling of international reviewers was neatly shelved. "But Papa told me you played it, and that it's about Fairyland. I want to hear it, if you please. I like stories about Fairyland; Marjorie and I read them out of the Blue Fairy Book. And the Red Fairy Book," he said, impish mischief in his eyes. "And the Yellow Fairy Book. And the Green Fairy Book. And the Orange…"

"Okay, okay, I get it!" I laughed. "But I warn you, it's a rather long piece. Oh, jiggers," I said, unconsciously borrowing his favorite expletive, "that's right; you won't care. You've probably been listening to Mahler for years."

"I like Mahler. But not when he's being sarcastic."

A little punch-drunk, I pulled the harp onto my shoulder.

The opening harmonics rang out clear and pure. Why on earth, I thought distractedly, had Richard been discussing, with his juvenile son, the playing of a woman he took pleasure in tormenting? I botched an arpeggio, stifled a curse, and settled down to play as seriously as if I were in Alice Tully Hall. None of it made any sense. Maybe nothing in my life did, except music.

When I finished, he sat silent, gazing at me with grave eyes. Then he simply said, "Wow," and came to give me a kiss.

"You liked it, then?"

"Yes. It gets wild, almost scary at the end, doesn't it? Like some of the things Papa plays." The little boy was back.

"I wish! But yes, it does. I guess these aren't very tame fairies. It certainly didn't scare the cats, though. Look."

And there on the bed, curled close to Hishi's outstretched and snoring form, was Cleo, fast asleep.

≋CHAPTER 22≋

Thou droop'st in dreary silence now,
With shivered frame and broken string.
George Borrow, The Broken Harp

I walked into the Barbican concert hall an hour early, its empty spaces echoing about me. For the first time in years, I was overcome by a powerful feeling, a feeling I'd almost forgotten.

It was like entering a deserted corridor, its coolly lit length stretching into infinity. Everything was in suspension, silenced, waiting. Nothing had happened–yet. Anything was possible; it was a *tabula rasa*. This was the pre-rehearsal feeling, the vacuum that one rushed to fill with brisk action and sound. Taking the padded canvas cover off the harp, storing it in the trunk, tuning, riffling through the score. Playing scales and arpeggios. Holding the detached, clinical, as yet uncritical silences of the hall at bay.

I ran rather frantically over the music. Several string players and a flautist wandered in, nodded, settled themselves and began to warm up. The percussionists arrived, tuned, and launched into a passage in which the rhythms were cerebrally complex, with dynamics ranging from a raging fortissimo to the thinnest pianissimo whisper. Delicate sounds of cymbal and snare-rim floated in the air, to be shattered by the visceral, gut-wrenching tempest of descending timpani rolls.

My heart started to pound. I began resolutely to work on the cadenza-like passage. Out of the corner of my eye I saw Richard walk in and place his score on the stand. I hadn't seen him since that last night in Zermatt. Robin had driven me, and the harp, to York in the estate wagon this morning.

Richard stepped onto the podium, and in the ensuing silence, I looked around. One chair was empty in the string section, directly to the right of the conductor. Hurried footsteps sounded behind me, and a tall young man, holding his cello high, strode out of the wings.

"Sorry, Dr. D'Annunzio," apologized a pleasant American voice. "My plane was late."

I leaned forward incredulously. Tim? Here?

"I only just got here myself. Shall we begin, and have our introductions later? Forgive my haste, but I'm itching to hear how this sounds–on the outside of my head, for a change."

The ripple of general laughter was transfixed by the oboist's A, and ebbed away into sounds of tuning.

Then Richard raised his hands, and we focused every iota of attention on him. The *tabula rasa* was prepared. His hands would descend, and this particular slate would never be blank again.

An hour and fifteen minutes later, he put down his baton with a sigh. "Beautifully done, ladies and gentlemen. More than I could have hoped for. We've a long way to go, but the groundwork is done. You're remarkably well prepared. Shall we break, and acquaint ourselves?"

Ironic, I thought. We were playing as if we'd been together a lifetime, and many of us didn't even know our neighbors' names. But it was obvious that I was flying in high company: these were superlative musicians.

I was elated and relieved. It had gone well, and I'd muffed no more cues than anyone else. Well, I shouldn't have. Uncharacteristically for a harpist, I played almost continuously through the work. The music was as I'd anticipated: frighteningly powerful and intoxicatingly beautiful.

Without warning, I found myself enveloped in a fervent bear hug. Good heavens, how could I have forgotten about Tim?

"It's really you, Lissa? I can't believe this." He pulled me off the bench, held me away from him, and gave me a long look. "You sound great. And you look great, too! Thinner—and no longer the blonde harpie, eh? I like it!" He touched my hair lightly. "What on earth are you doing in Yorkshire, and where have you been hiding? God, it's been years! Let's get some coffee while you tell me. Hey, Cador!" He called to the oboist, who was fussing despairingly over his reed. "Have you met our harpist? She just happens to be my old flame from Philadelphia!"

We sat in the wings near the coffee machine, laughing in disbelief. "What a terrific surprise, Tim! And before I say one more word, I want to congratulate you. I see your smiling face, ten times the normal size, every time I go into a record shop. But of course you always made the cello seem like child's play, not to speak of that gorgeous tone and—what did the Washington Post say?—'the uncanny impression that the instrument is speaking words, not notes.'"

Tim reddened in pleasure. "You're one to talk. This piece is a perfect virtuoso showcase for you, by the way."

And so much more than that, I thought. "It's very well written—not that terribly hard. But Tim," I went on, only half teasing, "the last thing I expected was to see you playing under Richard D'Annunzio. Change of heart?"

He looked slightly discomfited. "If you're in this business, Lissa," (thus implying, I supposed, and correctly so, that I was not) "you can't always pick and choose. There's no denying the man is a genius, and certainly one of the most powerful in the field. He's talking of writing a cello concerto..." Tim trailed off, his strongly-beaked face growing still pinker. "Anyway, enough of that. How about dinner? Oh, damn, rehearsals. Well, day after tomorrow, the night before the concert, okay?"

I nodded as we started back to the stage. My evenings were free enough. It seemed exceedingly unlikely that I'd be seeing Richard again outside the concert hall.

I'd arranged to get into the concert hall at eight the next morning. After three hours of practice, back aching, I decided to allow myself a look at York. I had five hours before rehearsal started; the piece was going very well, and I could afford to break for lunch and some sight-seeing.

I wandered through York Minster, staggered by the sheer size of it, exhilarated by the beauty of the medieval stained glass. The glorious transept, damaged by fire in the 80s, had been meticulously restored. The proceeds of our concert were to aid in the cleaning and repair of the windows, which were said to represent more than half the surviving medieval glass in England.

After lunch, walking slowly along the streets, I came upon the library. My knee was hurting again and I decided to go in and sit for a bit before returning to the hall.

Browsing along a shelf of new books, I came upon one about British Intelligence, written by a former official. I stood there a moment, my attention caught, then went to the card catalog. Yes, they had a few books on the corresponding American agency, though none of them were current. Nonetheless, I'd have a look. Perhaps I'd learn something that would help me understand Richard.

An hour later I sat at the long table, trying to summon the energy to get back to the harp. Even in my superficial grazing through the books, I'd immediately come upon several descriptions that could have been written to specification for what I knew about Richard.

As Robin had pointed out, Richard had been the perfect recruit. The Agency had a history of social and intellectual elitism which fitted him like a second skin.

The clandestine mentality of the covert operator, it seemed, battened on deception and secrecy, and developed a sort of professional amorality: the credo that righteous goals can be attained by unethical means. This was referred to as "the right to lie." Operators in training were graded on how effectively they could deceive their colleagues. Tortuous, convoluted plans were preferred to straightforward ones. Few agents, it seemed, saw a dichotomy between a moral private life and an amoral career. But it was noted that, unsurprisingly, the work tactics often carried over into relationships with friends and even family. And a former head of the CIA was quoted as saying that in all his years with the Agency, he recalled only one operator who felt some scruples about the activities he was assigned to.

Just before I closed the last book, I came upon one passage of justification. There was, the writer maintained, no possible defense of a free society without adequate intelligence gathering. There were tigers on the loose, and we must guard ourselves or perish.

The afternoon rehearsal was tougher than yesterday's euphoric beginning, demanding even more intense concentration. We were getting down to fine points now, and Richard's points, like God's, were exceeding fine. At the beginning of the break he caught me before I left the harp.

He spoke with impersonal friendliness. "May I have a moment, Lissa? One passage... ah, here it is. The one leading into this *tutti*. Can you make it just a bit more deliberate, with perhaps a little *luftpause* here? You're rushing me the merest trifle; I'd like to broaden if we can. Otherwise it's perfection."

"Of course. I do that... rush. It's one of my worst habits. Look, Richard, you don't have to temper the wind to the shorn lamb, or ewe, or whatever. When it comes to rehearsals I'm tough as old leather. Just rip away at me like you would at anyone else."

He looked genuinely shocked. "Rip away? I never do that!"

"No?"

He shook his head emphatically.

Reflecting, I saw it was true. Richard was demanding but never hurtful, as were some of the tartars I'd played under, particularly toward the lesser orchestra members. His demands were always phrased as courteous, amicable requests. A wry but gentle humor kept us smiling. And he had an uncanny knack for word pictures, which we all seemed to interpret with one mind.

On the third and final day of rehearsal I arrived earlier than usual for the post-lunch session. I took the opportunity to practice whenever I could get into the hall, but I wanted extra time today; something was troubling me.

I'd been putting the cover on the harp after *Merchant* the afternoon before. Most of the other players were staying on as usual to rehearse another work. As I reached for my string case, Cador, the oboist, inquired, "Will we be doing the harp work first tomorrow, Dr. D'Annunzio?"

The harp work. Oddly disturbed, I'd gone back to my hotel. I sat down with my score and went back mentally over the two rehearsals. Yes. It was most definitely a "harp work." A chamber concerto, in fact.

Why had I been in such denial? I'd hidden mentally behind Richard's description of my part as "tone color," the conscious, wary part of my brain not wanting my playing to be prominent. But in actual performance, I realized, caught up the music's passion and forgetting all caution, I'd been pulling out all the stops; playing it, in glorious abandonment, like the solo work it was. It was the case of the Goldberg Variations all over again. I shook my head in hopeless bewilderment at my obtuseness.

No, I'd never allowed myself to admit that I was, in fact, the soloist in this piece. Nor had I ever been referred to as such. Richard, that day on the moor, had cited the cello as principal instrument; obviously he'd made drastic revisions to the score.

But yesterday he'd moved the harp to the front center of the orchestra, just at his right hand. "The sonorities are lost with you way over there, Lissa. Let's see if this will improve the balance." Even then my mind's protective mechanism had set up a screen: I hadn't grasped it at all. I should have; with my strength as a performer, no conductor had ever complained before of losing my sonorities. It was usually "A little less harp, please."

Well, it was done now. In for a penny, in for a pound. And in the meantime, I didn't have to do anything differently. Richard seemed very pleased, and I was in a fever of enjoyment.

Entering from the wings, I caught a gleam of gilt on the stage, and broke step. Something was dreadfully wrong. Running toward the harp, which for all its stately height looked small and vulnerable against the expanse of the stage, I gave a gasp of dismay and stood still, unbelieving.

The canvas cover was off, flung down into the murkiness of the pit. Beside the harp, like a felled soldier, lay the conductor's massive stand. But the loser in this encounter had been the harp. It stood erect still, in mute, injured dignity; but the scrolled soundboard was riven by a great jagged hole, its edges cruelly splintered.

I sank onto the bench, my whole body flinching as if I'd received the wound myself. I couldn't even take in, for a moment, what it meant; all I could see was the beautiful instrument and the ugly, incongruous hole. Then Ciara's face overlaid the harp like a double exposure.

I heard voices off-stage, and Richard, accompanied by Tim, walked out of the wings.

"Lissa! You're early today. What–oh, my God. What happened? Did you knock the stand over?"

"No." Anger bubbled up, seethingly hot and volatile. The middle of my chest felt like the saucepan of praline candies I'd made last Christmas. I remembered abstractedly

259

that they'd never set. "No, I walked in just before you. It was already done." Knees suddenly weak, I leaned my head on the harp.

"How in God's name–did you see anyone or hear anything?" cried Tim, aghast.

I shook my head.

"It's my own damned fault," said Richard, righting the stand. "If my brain had been functioning I would have arranged for you to have a key of your own instead of simply telling Harry to unlock at one o'clock."

"I should have put it in the case when I left for lunch."

He made an impatient gesture. "The piano is here, unprotected. What's the difference? And I told you no one but the orchestra was using the hall until tonight; I thought it would be safe. Don't blame yourself."

Tim spoke up. "But who? A vandal? Some crazy kid who wanted to destroy something?"

"It could have been an accident," I broke in quickly. "Perhaps a child wandered in, wanted to see what was under that canvas, stepped onto the podium... pretended to conduct, maybe, and knocked the stand over." Anything, anything other than the awful conjectures forming in my mind.

"It would have to be a kid, or some lousy drunk," raged Tim.

Or a drug addict. Here it comes. I shivered as it broke over me. Or simply someone who hated me. Not, oh, please not Richard; surely he wouldn't sabotage his own work, unless he was psychotic enough to have doubts about it. And when had he ever had doubts? Another idea stabbed me, more unsettling than the first. Maybe his doubts were about me; maybe I hadn't really fulfilled his expectations. Did he have another harpist in reserve, and this was his way of jettisoning me, knowing I needed an instrument with wide spacing? Remembering the passage I'd read about the means justifying the end, I looked up in sudden speculation.

"Come on," said Richard briskly, taking my arm.

"Where are we going?"

"To the telephone. We'll get a harp flown in from London, and Harry can pick it up in his truck. We'll rehearse the other works this afternoon, and reschedule Merchant for tonight. It'll have to be somewhere else, though; there's a lecture here."

"Do you think it's possible to get it here in time? I need wide spacing–I hope they'll have something...."

He was unlocking the conductor's dressing room. I leaned against the wall. The ambiguities were beyond me. He was saving the situation. That should have made me happy and relieved, if it weren't for the maelstrom of doubts I'd felt just before he went into action.

Richard rang information, dialed the London harp salesroom, identified himself, and described the situation with an economy of words. Then he handed the phone to me.

"Here. Tell them exactly what you want, and they'll get it out at once. I'll give Harry the arrival time." He turned and left the room.

"Thank God. ... Hello. Yes, please. Yes, a concert grand. Do you–do you have any of Ciara Rossi's harps? One left? Oh, that's wonderful! It has wide spacing, hasn't it? Good, that's essential. And the condition: it's been regulated and restrung? With first quality strings? Perfect! Send that one, please. Thanks so very much!"

I found Richard onstage. "You have that airport schedule memorized, don't you?"

He smiled wryly. "I should. I live by it. Everything okay?"

I nodded. "It'll be on its way. And what a stroke of luck: it's a concert grand of Ciara's, with wide spacing, that hasn't sold yet. Thank you, Richard." I sat down abruptly. "I... I suppose I hadn't realized how much I really do want to play."

He clasped my shoulder. "We all want that. Now go and get some rest; relax till tonight. Don't worry about this...

261

it was just somebody's stupid meddling. I'll get a message to you at the hotel about rehearsal time and place. We'll do the Bach now instead."

I slipped into my coat and headed for the door. Then I turned back to the dressing room. I'd have to call Robin; he'd planned to meet me and Tim for dinner at seven, on what was to have been our free night.

Robin was both shocked and supportive. He had to meet Richard directly after rehearsal to give him some scores that had arrived at Hawthorns, but he'd pick me up and drive me to the substitute hall, wherever that turned out to be.

"I can't believe my luck, Robin. They actually have one of Ciara's grands, with wide spacing. Otherwise I'd have been up a tree. And I'll have it by six! I never thought," I laughed, "that I'd be thanking God for airplanes."

Rehearsal at eight o'clock, the message had said. By six o'clock Robin and I were at the small school auditorium that served as our rehearsal hall for this last night.

The case was waiting off-stage, and Robin lifted the instrument gently out. I unzipped the cover.

"Oh, it's lovely. I didn't know she had a model eleven." The golden irises, carved in relief near the crown, gleamed softly. "And new strings, as promised. Let's see how it sounds."

I tuned briefly, launched into the first theme and immediately hit a clunker.

"Well, *it* sounds fine," I laughed. The harp had a glorious richness of tone and remarkable clarity. "But as for me...."

I started over, with the same result, and swore mildly. I wasn't used to missing notes. "I guess this whole disastrous episode shook me up. As Leon used to say, 'Relax, damn you, relax!'"

Robin gave me a whimsical smile. For the third time I began the principal theme, with the identical appalling errors.

262

"What the devil?" I gripped the edges of the soundboard and drew a deep breath. Then it hit me, and my hands dropped into my lap. I'd felt bloodless this afternoon; now, it seemed the marrow was being sucked from my bones.

"Robin."

"Mm?"

Tentatively I played an octave, then a tenth.

"I don't believe this." I set the harp down. My voice was flat. "They sent the wrong one."

"What?"

"Yes. This is standard spacing. That's why I'm missing the intervals. The strings are closer together. Oh, it's no big deal if you're used to changing from one to the other. But with our long fingers, Ciara and I have always stuck with wide spacing." Unthinkingly, I'd spoken as if she were alive. "As a matter of fact, I've never even played a standard. Leon's studio harp was wide-spaced, too." Bitter frustration boiled over. "I can't believe they got it wrong. I specified very clearly–oh, the blasted incompetents!"

"Oh, Lord, what a tangle. Well, what's to be done? Do we go through the whole process again? They'll be closed until morning, you know. Oh!" He struck his palm with a clenched fist. "And tomorrow's Sunday."

"It wouldn't do any good anyway," I said slowly. "Tonight's the last rehearsal. Without that... well, I don't know. I might be able to do the performance. If we could find someone to open up the salesroom early in the morning..."

"Lissa." A different quality in Robin's tone brought me to a stop. "I probably shouldn't ask this, but did Richard hear you ordering the harp?"

"Of course," I replied. "He placed the call himself. Oh, no... wait. He went back onstage while I was on the phone. Why?"

He was silent for a long moment. With a short expelled breath, he pulled a chair close to the harp and sat

263

beside me. "I don't know any good way to say this. Are you aware that Richard thinks–has a suspicion–oh, hell."

I sat like a stone. "What does Richard think, Robin?" I asked very quietly.

"Well, I don't mean he actually believes it. It was when I took him the mail and the scores. He was just having a moment of doubt, remembering that you..." He paused, and finished very softly. "Stopped performing, for a while."

"You needn't be so polite," I said brusquely. "You mean Richard thinks I'm so terrified of the actual performance that I'd do anything to get out of it, including destroying the soundboard myself."

"Lissa, please."

"And he'll think, when that failed to get me off the hook, that I deliberately ordered the wrong spacing, knowing I couldn't be expected to give a competent performance without a period of readjustment."

Silence again, while he looked unhappily at his feet.

I stood up. "Robin," I said. "You have to go. I need to practice. And thanks for the ride." I walked with him to the wings.

"But what will you do?"

"Cope." I was past anger now; there was no time for it.

I hurried back to the harp, seated myself, and started playing intervals, pinpointing the problems. Slow, deliberate thirds, fourths, fifths, sixths, sevenths, octaves, ninths, tenths: up and down the strings. I was overreaching mostly in the extreme registers, and with the wider intervals. So. Fifths once more, sixths, sevenths, octaves. I'd wanted a challenge. And again fifths.

"So that's it; now you know it all." I gazed at Tim across the table, picking up my spoon to dispatch the last fig in Madeira cream. It had taken me a great deal longer to relate the events of the past few weeks than it had to tell of the five years past. "We're a long way from the pastrami of Philadelphia, Tim."

The two of us were alone in the restaurant. We'd dined very late, after the rehearsal, and without Robin, who'd had to return unexpectedly to Denham House to supervise an early morning arrival of furniture from London.

"Yes we are, thank the Lord. Speaking of the past, you certainly vanished without a trace. I was going to write you in Connecticut, but the rumor was that you'd gotten married."

This raised my eyebrows. Ciara again?

As if he'd read my thoughts, Tim went on. "I wonder... you know, Lissa, I think D'Annunzio's right about Ciara. I mean, Lord knows he's not one of my favorite people, and ordinarily I wouldn't give much credence to what he says, except musically, but we all knew she was a snake. Except you, of course. Well, she was your aunt, and it was clear that you idolized her, so we kept quiet when you were around. She pulled quite a few cute little numbers in her time. Toppling harpists from the ladder was a specialty of hers. Not only when they were beginning to look like a threat; sometimes she dislodged the smaller talents just for fun. She seems to have reserved the grand scale treatment for you. But no matter. She's gone, and you're back, better than ever, from what I've heard in the last three days."

"I'm not 'back,' Tim. This is just a one-shot job, a freakish bit of luck for me. I'll be teaching in Turnerville again next fall."

His heavy brows drew together. "Balls!" he said rudely. "When there are plenty of harpists playing major performances who aren't fit to tie your shoes? Look, Lissa, I could help. I have a few useful contacts."

"Thanks, Tim." My smile felt a bit strained. "Right now I just want to concentrate on doing this one piece right. After that, I'm heading back to Connecticut."

"Really? When?"

"Less than a week. I have to pack up my things at Denham House, and I want one more day there to climb on the fells." I stared morosely at my rapidly filming coffee.

"You don't sound too happy, babe. Listen, are you involved with D'Annunzio?"

With an uncontrollable start, I looked up. "Involved?" I gave a small laugh. "He's my aunt's husband's half-brother, Tim, and he lost his regular harpist, and I happened to be on hand. That's the extent of the involvement."

Tim gave me a thoughtful look, absently signed the bill, and got to his feet. "Let's walk, Lissa. Oh–can you, with your hurt knee? I'd forgotten. You're still limping a little, aren't you?"

"I'm fine as long as we don't go too fast."

He helped me into my coat and we stepped out into a cold and damply gusting night. We were up on the medieval town walls before he spoke again.

"Lissa, Ciara's not the only one who didn't play straight with you. And it seems you're not the only harpist D'Annunzio's jettisoned."

I turned to look at his unsmiling face. "Tim, what are you talking about?"

"Cador was telling me after rehearsal yesterday. D'Annunzio called up Maria Giardino, the harpist he'd originally engaged for this concert, when he was in Rome a few weeks ago. Cador knew because he and Maria were playing in the same chamber group."

"Are you telling me that he canceled her agreement?" I demanded furiously. When he was in Rome. That would have been–when? Just before Peter's birthday. Just after that searing afternoon on the fells. And he'd spoken to me about a "local harpist"!

"Actually, yes, but to be fair, you have to understand that she was delighted. He simply wangled another offer for her, much more lucrative–tacked her onto a string quartet for a tour of Greece. She's there now, as a matter of fact. He has the clout to swing these things, you know."

"Oh!" I stood still, hands clenched at my sides. A light mist was beginning to fall. "Compared to Richard, Machiavelli was playing tic-tac-toe. That man is the most duplicitous, manipulative–"

"Hold on, Lissa. God knows I hold no brief for D'Annunzio, but Cador thinks that in this case he was right. Giardino couldn't begin to handle that piece the way you do; she doesn't have the strength or the fire. Oh, I know you think it's not that difficult, but that's exactly what I'm talking about. That's why Cador told me about it last night. 'Thank God we've got Leone' was the way he prefaced it."

"Tim, let's sit down."

"Won't you freeze? It's beginning to rain."

"Yes, but maybe it'll wash the cobwebs away. I've just realized that John and Robin both knew about this," I mused, thinking back to the night in the library. "I've got to get out of here," I finished helplessly.

"By God, I think you do. I don't know what's going on, but like I said, you don't seem too happy to me."

"Happy? No, I'm not happy." My control was going; it had been a long and disturbing day, culminating in a terrifying rehearsal. "Maybe he had legitimate reasons for dropping Giardino, but Tim–oh, I don't know how to say this without sounding like a fool. I think Richard is a psychopath, or perhaps his emotional balance is affected by drugs. At least two people who knew Ciara think her death wasn't accidental, and one of them is fairly certain that Richard did it. But no, that won't do," I cried, clutching my head. "He thought I was her, and he couldn't if he'd killed her, unless he really was drunk or drugged."

"Whoa! What the hell are you talking about?" Tim put his arms around me, rocking me gently. "You'd better fill me in, Lissa. I think you left a few things out of the first telling."

"Richard saw me on the road at night, when I first

came to Yorkshire, and for a moment he thought I was Ciara. He couldn't have, could he, if he'd killed her? Not unless," I said, harking back to Robin's speculations, "not unless he just hit her and left her for dead, without making sure." I shuddered, sitting silent and drained on the wall.

Tim shook his head. "What kind of people have you gotten mixed up with, Lissa? Well, I guess we shouldn't be surprised after what we've always heard about D'Annunzio." He exhaled a deep breath, took my hand, and spoke with calm good sense. "Damned if I know any answers, sweetie, and the probability is that none of us ever will. But I do know this. Priority number one is to get you out of here. Do you really want to play this infernal concert?"

"Yes. Oh, yes, I do."

"You're sure? Okay. That shouldn't be a problem. I'll stay close, there's a guard on the instruments now, and Robin will be on hand. He seems like a good guy. Priority number two," he went on, "is to forget about Ciara. She's gone, one way or another, and if the police can't unravel it, neither can we. Now. Priority number three. You don't have to spend any more time with this bunch. If you're under attack by an emotionally skewed person, you can just remove yourself, can't you? Walk away from it, Lissa; don't be like those dumb dames in the slasher movies. Maybe in his irrational moments," he theorized neatly, "D'Annunzio wants to hurt you because you remind him of Ciara. In his better times, he sees you as what you are, a great musician and a megawatt performer. You know, I don't think he intends you any real harm. If he wanted you out of the way for some crazy reason, nothing could be easier, with the contacts he's reputed to have. But even if you're in no actual danger, don't ever think for a moment," he said gravely, "that you can change someone like that. The best thing you can do, Lissa," he finished gently, "is cut your losses and run like hell."

⚞CHAPTER 23⚟

I keep such music in my brain
No din this side of earth can quell;
Glory exulting over pain,
And beauty, garlanded in hell.
    Siegfried Sassoon, *Secret Music*

No matter how early a performer arrives on the night of a concert, there's always at least one member of the audience who gets there first. I sometimes wondered if mothers of eight escaped their broods for a pre-concert nap, or if persecuted husbands fled nagging wives by moving curtain time up an hour. Why else would they spend all that time in a silent and empty hall?

I picked up a program at the door, compulsively confirming the position of my piece in the concert. I noted that the work was listed in French, as *Le Marchand de Sable*, and saw, without surprise, that my name was printed below the title: Lissa Leone, harp. Ignoring the scattered few already settled in their seats, I made my way purposefully toward the harp which stood just offstage, securely locked in its huge molded case. Sliding the instrument carefully out onto the floor, I uncovered it, checked it thoroughly, and breathed more easily. All was well–no suspiciously frayed strings or slipped pedal springs. With the ease that came with years of managing my own instrument, I picked up its eighty-odd pounds and, setting it on the dolly, rolled it onto the stage. It wouldn't be positioned right and center until after the Bach Suite, but I wanted to test the harp's sonorities, as I hadn't played it in this hall before.

I set my score on the stand, pulled the tuning fork out of the deep right-hand pocket of my dress, and began to tune. But after a moment I stopped and looked at my fingers; they felt slightly powdery. I rubbed thumb and forefinger down one of the strings, and very tentatively flicked them with my tongue. Laughing with real amusement, I took out my handkerchief–the only time I was sure to have one was at a performance–and wiped the strings down. Alum. Alum, for Pete's sake! Totally harmless; it certainly wasn't going to make my fingers shrivel, or whatever effect had been hoped for. A touch of shellac, on the other hand, would have been very effective. I'd once gotten a film on my fingers from a piece of furniture that Mother and I had been refinishing. Freshly out of solvent, I'd decided to take a chance and practice anyway. The residue from my hands took days to wear off the strings, making my fingers stick in the most unpredictable ways. Well. Someone was cracking, getting childish. Someone, though, who knew how to open locks on harp trunks.

In forty-five minutes' time the other musicians began to drift in. I was perfectly tuned, and as well prepared as possible. Even with the solid hour and a half of work on intervals, there had been a couple of thoughtful looks from Richard at rehearsal last night. I'd gone through the piece with my heart in my mouth, but he'd said nothing, and I'd made no excuses. I'd practiced for five systematic hours today, and the intervals were responding amenably. The readjustment to regular spacing was complete, and far easier than I'd feared. If for some insane reason Richard wanted a scapegoat for this piece, it wasn't going to be Lissa Leone.

I glanced at my watch and rose from the bench, pulling the harp back into the wings. *Merchant of Dreams* came just before intermission, so I had a long wait, always the worst part of a performer's evening. As I headed toward the dressing room, I heard the orchestra tuning for the Bach Suite.

I smoothed the folds of my Melisande dress and fought down a rising tide of giddy lightheadedness. They were into the last movement of the Bach now; it was almost time. Suddenly I wished myself a million miles away, but it was too late. God help me, I thought. Why can't I be a string player, out there on the stage from the first, with the safety of my section all around me? This waiting was terrible. I felt very sick.

Pushing myself out of the hard wooden chair, I reached into the pocket containing the handkerchief and the tuning key, and pulled out a lipstick. I would certainly need the color; I felt bled white.

But looking in the mirror, I had a shock. This was the woman I'd seen in Geneva: eyes sparkling, cheeks flushed like the rose-colored ribbons that hung from the embroidered girdle. I held my hands under the hot water, warming them to the bone. Thrusting them under the dryer, I studied them for a moment: they were steady as a rock. Then it hit me. Expecting to be frightened, I'd almost convinced myself that I was. I met my own eyes in the mirror, and the old confidence and strength flooded over me. This is your milieu, Lissa, I told myself. Thank God, this is your milieu. With a happy and grateful laugh, I hurried back toward the applause.

Harry was there ahead of me, his stocky frame lifting the harp with no apparent effort, carrying it to the center of the stage. I picked up the music stand and followed. The folder, empty and unweighted, slid to the floor. Panic-stricken, I picked it up and whispered to Harry.

"Harry, do you have my music?"

"Your music? No, Miss Leone. I saw it backstage on your stand before the first number, though. Could you have taken it to the dressing room?"

I fled backstage, ignoring the twinge in my knee. The dressing room was bare and empty; all the performers in the small Bach orchestra were playing in the D'Annunzio work, and had stayed on stage. The additional wind and percussion players were already in their places. No, the music wasn't here.

Richard was standing in the wings at stage left, waiting for the audience and the players to settle. Picking up my skirts, I dashed behind the backdrop and touched his sleeve.

"Richard? Do you have my score?"

"Your score? Why, no... have you misplaced it?" He went suddenly dead white under his tan. "My God, Lissa, where could it be?"

"Never mind. It doesn't matter. I know where it is."

I raced back behind the backdrop, stopped to calm my breathing, and walked on stage with the poise born of long practice. I noticed through a red haze that all the women players were wearing stark, unadorned black. That added to my rage. I reached the harp, made a few rapid adjustments to the tuning, sounded my A. It was matched by the oboe, and then the glorious cacophony of tuning flowered around me.

Dear, great God in heaven, I thought desperately. Who am I supposed to be, Patient Griselda?

No. Just a flaming failure. And Richard was barking mad.

In a burst of applause he stepped onto the podium, bowing, collecting us with his upraised hands.

I'll do it, I thought above the hammering of my heart. I'll play this damned work in spite of everything. I don't need the damned music anyway. I'll show Richard, or whatever evil person, or spirit –I took a long breath–is doing this that I'm not quite so easily crushed this time. I grasped the empty music stand, and turning, set it firmly and deliberately behind me.

Richard was holding my glance intently, alarm and consternation in his eyes. Why had I forgotten how bright

272

the stage lights were during performance? I smiled with all the brilliance I could muster, and gave a confident nod.

I never had time to decide whether the answering smile was perfidious or simply relieved, because his hands swept down and we were into *Le Marchand*.

Tim was playing a solo passage with great energy and fervor, the cello's insistent voice enveloping me from behind. One by one the instruments entered, piling dissonance on subtle dissonance in frighteningly controlled stress and confusion. And from this architecturally conceived chaos emerged the harp theme, strong and pure, bringing sanity out of horror and despair. The tremendous chords rang out, filling the hall; the harp strings sang with a life of their own. It was as if a dozen conflicting radio channels had suddenly resolved into one stream of ineffable beauty. And I was making these sounds, through the grace of God.

A great calm descended upon me. I never for one moment allowed myself to think ahead. Richard's face was filled with the most passionate joy, and I didn't care whether it was faked, or even schizophrenic. I was submerged, willingly and irrevocably, in the strange world of *Le Marchand*.

And so were the other musicians. With Richard's sure hands to hold us up, we could do no wrong. I heard myself playing the cadenza, or rather, heard it emerging from the vividly lighted strings. Was it truly my own hands that produced this unearthly glory? The harp was speaking through me. It sounded as if every note were being wrenched from some primal heart of fire. A sweep of rising urgency from the strings, the descending thunder of the timpani, and I joined them in the apotheosis of the principal theme.

Thirty-four minutes had passed in a waking dream. We sat in a long silence, the last vibrations dying in the hall. Then erupted a storm of applause and cheering. I was in a near trance, hardly realizing that Richard was tugging at me, pulling me up. He put his arm around me, presenting me to an audience now surging to its feet, and held my hand high as the applause swelled to a roar.

"Heavenly sound," he grinned. "Now you remember why we do it." I burst into laughter as we bowed again, hand in hand, and returned to my place by the harp while he led Tim forward, finally bringing the orchestra triumphantly to its feet.

"Well, you've done it, my lass," beamed Robin, clasping me in a hearty embrace. "How many curtain calls was that, anyway?"

"Hasn't she, though," said Tim as he squeezed in for a hug. "Good grief, child, you really cut loose tonight. I mean, rehearsals were great, but tonight was just damned brilliant."

"You were pretty incandescent yourself, old buddy."

"A mere accessory. You were the star. I can't wait to see the *Times* tomorrow."

I was speechless for a moment. "The *Times*?"

"Yes, as in London, you idiot. You're not in the Big Apple anymore."

I cuffed him lightly. "I know that, but—you mean the *Times* critic is here tonight?"

"Of course, what did you expect?" High on euphoria, he chattered on. "Maybe not for you and not for me, and not for Uncle Wiggly, but surely you don't think he'd miss a D'Annunzio premiere?"

"No... certainly not. Well, truthfully, Tim, I just didn't think about it at all."

"No wonder. You've done enough thinking for the whole month, playing without the score tonight. That piece is so diabolically complex. Honest to God, Lissa, I almost had a heart attack when I saw you put that stand behind you. You set it down directly on my left foot, by the way."

"Oh, Tim, I'm sorry!"

"Think nothing of it; it was worth every bruise and

broken toenail. I was just lucky it didn't get my Guarnerius. God, what a great night! And it's only half over for D'Annunzio."

"Oh, that's right." He was playing Beethoven on the second half of the program, the Fifth Piano Concerto. Henry and his stagehands had already moved the harp back into the wings and were rolling the piano out, as orchestra members took their seats and began to warm up.

"Lissa."

I turned and he was standing there, a thick sheaf of manuscript paper extended toward me. I took it, bewildered, as Tim moved to speak to Robin.

"I started changing it," Richard said very softly, "from that day in the stable when I was absolutely sure who you were."

My eyes faltered, dropped from his to the title page. It was the full conductor's score, and it said:

Le Marchand de Sable
Richard D'Annunzio
Concerto for Harp and Chamber Orchestra
for Lissa Leone, with gratitude

I clasped it to my breast and closed my eyes for a moment, unbelieving, humble, and triumphant all at once. Then I looked straight at him, thrust the score at Tim, and with a happy shriek flung my arms around Richard, planting a kiss with commendable accuracy.

"Hey!" He gave a mock stagger, swung me around, and set me on my feet. "Steady on. You did it, Lissa; changing ink into wine is no mean trick, and freeing yourself from the score made a miraculous difference to your performance. I'd no idea you intended that–I thought for an awful moment that you'd misplaced the music. I liked the insouciance with which you ignored my incipient heart attack, by the way. But truly," he went on, serious again, "you transformed it, my dear. It was beyond anything I could have dreamed."

At this moment it seemed worse than ridiculous to think he'd taken my score. "No. It was all there to begin with, in black and white. I'll never be able to thank you, Richard." Knowing that he'd understand, I finished, "I'm Lissa again."

"And ever shall be. Ah. Beethoven time. All right, Harry, I'm coming."

Tim, startled out of mesmerized attention, seized his cello and hurried onstage.

"Richard, wait! Your artistic dignity might bè just slightly undercut," –here I ostentatiously extracted the embroidered handkerchief nestling against the lipstick in my pocket–"if you go on stage looking like an advertisement for Love's Flaming Orchid. Besides, it doesn't tone with your white tie."

"Good God," he murmured, contemplating the handkerchief in exaggerated disbelief. "You don't mean this belongs to you?" He swabbed away. "Yes, it might prejudice old Wilding's pen a bit, I suppose, though as for me and my house..." He handed the handkerchief back to me, smiling. "You're coming to the party, of course. The Billings' place." He stepped out onto the stage, and the applause began.

And in my triumph and joy, I repressed, for the moment, the one incontrovertible reason I'd played without the music.

I was stretched as tight as one of my own strings with elation and excitement, and the party was not a help in winding me down.

It was very different from the formal affair in Geneva. Held in a house built on a human scale, it was intimate, noisy, and hilarious. All the orchestral musicians were there, stuffing themselves happily on delectable food and holding a vociferous concert post mortem in front of the fire.

Richard was more exhilarated than I'd ever seen him. Prompted by his friends, he went immediately to the piano, conscripted a violinist, and plunged into wild gypsy airs. He was apparently unable to stop playing. He followed the gypsy music with the Schubert-Liszt *Soiree de Vienne*, bubbling with elegant wit and joie de vivre, and segued into jazz improvisations so pyrotechnical and wickedly cerebral that we were all left gaping. He concluded with a steal from Victor Borge, the '*Pilgrim's Chorus*' from *Tannhäuser*, his left hand thundering out the melody while the right, holding a handkerchief, played the descending figurations in a lunatic parody of dusting the keys. We were limp from laughter when he finished, but I had a twinge of uneasiness. It was abandon bracketed by discipline, but only barely so, and it reminded me of the slashing, razor-edged play he and Robin had indulged in on the slopes at Zermatt.

At two in the morning, with the party still in full cry, I asked Robin to drive me back to the hotel. Before we pulled out of the drive at Billings House, he slipped an arm around me and turned my face up for a kiss. I gave his cheek a fond but absent pat.

"You're a dear, Robin."

"It's been a wonderful night for you, hasn't it?"

"Yes, but I think the sun's about to come up. I want to crawl under a blanket and sleep for five years."

"A triumph," he continued, undistracted. "You've certainly proven yourself beyond question."

Remembering the story of his aborted career, I made light of it. "It was a lucky evening for all of us," I smiled. "But truly, Robin, I'm dead in the water."

He was silent for a moment. When he spoke, his voice was tender.

"Lissa."

"Hm?"

"Are you serious about going back to the States?"

"You bet. I'm leaving while I'm on a roll."

"Don't go," he murmured against my hair. "You mean so much to me, Lissa. We need time, you and I. Stay on... at least until it's really spring."

I looked up at him in the dimness of the car. He was smiling a little.

Stay on? I was fond of Robin, as I was of Tim. Even this comfortable companionship of like minds was very precious to me. But stay in Yorkshire: expose myself to more inexplicable machinations, more hurt and perhaps danger? I thought of Richard, in white tie and tails on the podium; at the party, flinging himself so passionately into gypsy music. And yes, I thought of that night in the dark, moon-shafted room in Geneva. Stay in Yorkshire under that shadow, waiting for the casual, frustrating encounters, the furtively arranged petty cruelties, with my heart and brain warring in sick confusion? No. I'd had enough of vacillating between wild infatuation and bleak puzzlement. I'd leave on the tide of this wonderful night. What had Tim said?–cut your losses and run like hell.

"You've been such a dear friend to me, Robin, and I'll always cherish that. But I have to go. It's the right thing to do. I've made my reservation for Wednesday." I extricated myself gently and squeezed his arm, and he drove me to the hotel with no further protest than a sigh.

Exhausted though I was, I must have played *Le Marchand* ten times through in my head, and the windows of my hotel room were growing grey before I finally slept. I awoke after one in the afternoon and was lying there, listening contentedly to the bustle of Monday traffic, when the phone rang.

It was Richard. Robin was already gone. He'd started back early, after taking both harps to the station for London: Ciara's broken one for repairs and her model eleven to be returned. Richard proposed lunch before we left for Denham House. There was excitement in his voice, carefully damped down.

As it seemed inevitable that I was to ride with him, there was no point in refusing to meet him for lunch. Besides, I suspected that his excitement had something to do with the concert reviews, and I was lusting to read them.

When we were seated comfortably at a flower-decked table, Richard silently handed me two newspapers, folded back to the reviews. With a tiny pang of nervousness, I lowered my eyes to the print. As I read I felt a smile stealing uncontrollably across my face; then I began to laugh. The *Times* spoke first of *Le Marchand*; of its brilliance, lyricism, and new maturity.

"One hesitates," it read, *"to use the term neo-Romanticism, which is a dangerously deceptive label to affix to any serious composition. But in his return to a tonal structure, Richard D'Annunzio has given us access to unimagined beauties, and this without the slightest diminution of strength or originality. If a Sandman is a bringer of dreams, D'Annunzio has every right to take the title to himself.*

Perhaps the greatest surprise of the evening was his treatment of the solo harp. There is a tendency to regard this instrument as feeble and banal, and indeed much of the literature, and regrettably often, the standard of playing, bears out such a view. Last night Miss Leone, who has not been heard in concert for some years, banished that notion from this reviewer's head for all time. In a performance compounded of intellect, phenomenal technique, and a sort of divine fire, she raised her instrument to its rightful place beside the violin and piano as a voice capable of articulating the most demanding musical concepts. Dr. D'Annunzio is to be commended on his choice of soloist for what was unquestionably a concerto in one movement, though rather oddly it was not titled as such. We hope to hear much more from Miss Leone in the months to come."

He went on to comment briefly but positively on Tim's solo passages, and more lengthily, on Richard's brilliant Beethoven.

The York reviewer had written in a like vein; his adjectives were perhaps a trifle more colorful, and to my amusement he mentioned that my slight limp, noticeable when I crossed the stage, was attributable to a recent skiing accident.

With a smile and an incredulous shake of the head, I laid the papers down. I looked up and met Richard's eyes, and they were glowing with that familiar look of triumph.

We loitered over lunch, savoring the reviews and talking through the concert's high points, and late winter darkness was drawing in as we neared home.

"Even John enjoyed it; I do believe he's getting reconciled to music after all these years. He asked me to felicitate you—he had to leave right after intermission. Well, that *Times* review is one to treasure, *cara mia*."

I wondered why it sounded so much more intimate in Italian.

"And did you notice," he smiled, shaking his head in complacent amusement, "how quickly Wilding's pen consigned me to the oubliette the minute you came on the scene?"

"What nonsense! But yes; I'll always cherish the reviews, and all the memories. It's a wonderful valedictory."

The car shot forward with a jerk, then slowed. "Valedictory? What in blazes are you talking about, Lissa?"

I hesitated; I almost wondered myself. After the concert I'd felt like a woman on the brink of a new life. Nothing was impossible. I was ready to slay dragons. Today, in spite of all the euphoria, reaction had set in. It was all very well to play under Richard's aegis: I hadn't sought this appearance, hadn't had to put myself on the line to win it. But just now, with the hourglass running out on my turbulent Yorkshire stay, I wasn't sure I had the energy and drive to re-establish myself on my home turf. I no longer harbored any doubts about my abilities, but somehow the thought of returning to the New York scene seemed inexpressibly dreary. The impending separation from Richard, so necessary to sanity and so wrenching, leached the joy out of the evening.

"Richard," I began. "It was understood from the first that this was a one-time thing. You gave me a heaven sent opportunity to vindicate myself, and I'll always be grateful to you."

His hands were tight on the wheel, but I could see he was striving for a lighter note.

"Quitting while you're ahead, eh? It won't do, Lissa, I told you that before. And—understood by whom? Never by me, I assure you. No; your self-protective mechanisms are overreacting, that's all. You just have to get in there and take your lumps with the rest of us."

Suddenly I was very tired. For the first time I was realistic about what lay ahead; over the past three and a half weeks my thoughts had extended no further than the concert hall in York. Now I saw, with actual physical pain twisting at my heart, what I'd refused to face even when I made my plane reservation. Our parting was truly imminent, and final. I no longer had any reason to stay in Yorkshire; indeed it was mad even to think of it. Walk away, Lissa. It was over, all those moments of verbal fencing, the fun of traveling together, the intense satisfaction of rehearsals. The communion with a mind that shared my most passionate wants: music, beauty, excitement, the pleasure of written and spoken words. It was over. The fears, suspicions, sick doubts were over too. And yes, most searing of all, the embraces, few and brief, that were etched into my memory with aching clarity.

"No. That's not really the reason. Those mechanisms aren't coming out of the closet any more, thanks to you. And perhaps I'll think about auditioning for an orchestra next year. But I'm going back to Lynton Wednesday, Richard. It's been more wonderful than I could ever have expected, but I have to get a grip on reality now."

We were driving up the avenue of beeches, the headlights illuminating the stark tunnel of their bare branches. At the door he braked, not gently. Without another word he strode around the car, opened my door, seized my suitcase, and herded me to the entrance.

The front door closed behind us and he set his back against it. I could see him fighting to control exasperation, and when he began his voice was quiet and reasonable.

"Reality? What is your reality, then? Lissa, you've read the reviews. You heard what everyone said last night, your fellow musicians most of all. In spite of your genuine modesty, your diffidence, you can't help knowing what you are. And you'd bury all this? Teach school again? Play in a symphony, when you're the potential concert harpist of your age? For Christ's sake, Lissa! it would be like trying to hide smoke. Can't you see? Doors will open. Lissa," he went on more urgently, "I can open many of them for you."

"No," I said from a tight throat, turning away. I had to end this insane see-sawing. Get thee behind me, Satan. At the edge of my vision I saw a slight movement at the far end of the hall; in my agitation it hardly registered.

He drew a deep, shaken breath and tried again. "It was all for nothing, then: those hours, those years of care and genius lavished on you. Did it never occur to you, in your blind, criminal selfishness"—his voice was growing harsher—"or rather, have you simply forgotten, once again, that you have an obligation?"

"Obligation?" I queried numbly, facing him again.

"Yes, an obligation. We've talked about it before, if you can trouble yourself to remember." He was working up to a white fury now. "An obligation to your teachers, to your school, to everyone who helped you. Even to Ciara. How many young harpists do you suppose would have given their souls for your place at Curtis; yes, and made something of it, too."

Below the belt, I thought, wincing.

"And you think you owe nothing to Leon?"

Another vicious pain stabbed at my heart.

Richard's voice was reverberating through the empty hall. "Great God, Lissa, you were his white hope! He poured his life's blood into you. An old man, ill, on the edge of heart failure, giving without stint. But I suppose you think you incurred no debt for all you received, all the advantages you've been given. You evidently feel no duty to return anything: not to your teachers, not to the public, not to music itself." And now that golden evening at Rievaulx did swim up, belatedly, into memory.

He seized my arms in a painful grip, and my anger flared up like wildfire. In my vulnerable state, after the tremendous highs and lows of the last few days, it was more than I could support. With the stubbornness of a child who blindly defies an adult, I told myself that I was tired of being pushed around, of having my strings pulled by this great and neurotic man.

"Maybe I don't!" I cried, provoked on every front. "What makes it your business anyway? Just because you condescended to set me up again, after you helped pull me down..."

A voice cut in sharply, making me start. "Lissa, what is this? Take your hands off her, Richard."

He didn't move. I turned to see Robin, intense blue eyes blazing, fierce tension in every line of his body.

"Stay out of it, Robin." Richard's voice was suddenly, lethally quiet. He didn't even spare him a glance.

"Lissa..." pleaded Robin. There was something indefinable in his eyes, but it was just beyond my grasp.

I shook my head, wordless, miserable, and he turned on his heel, fists clenched. After a moment I heard a door slam somewhere in the house. Then silence.

I turned back to Richard with a little sigh. He still hadn't released my arms, and his hands were hurting me. Incredibly, I felt desire flowering through my body. Surely,

surely, I thought, he would relent and pull me into a comforting embrace.

But he did nothing of the kind. His inflection was very crisp. The black-rimmed irises, clear, icy grey, held mine inexorably.

"Are you adamant about this?"

I almost laughed. I adamant! His arrogance infuriated me afresh.

"Call it what you like," I said coldly. "It's a matter of common sense. You don't really know me at all. Perhaps I like a safe life. Perhaps I'm meant to teach second-graders and play at parish guild teas."

His hands dropped from my arms. It couldn't have been clearer if he'd performed the symbolic hand-washing gesture. His voice was quite colorless and level as he delivered the final killing insult.

"As you say." He turned, and the door closed silently behind him.

Having achieved what I'd set out to accomplish, I burst into tears just as the library door opened and John Denham came uncertainly into the hall.

"Lissa?" He put a gentle hand on my arm. "Are you all right, my dear?"

I nodded, rubbing tears away with the heel of my hand.

"Was that Richard?"

"Yes," I sniffed. "I'm sorry. We were–arguing," I added unnecessarily.

"So I gathered. But how extraordinary. No," he smiled sadly. "Not that a man and a woman should argue. But," a sudden frown furrowed his brow. "that Richard should shout. Do you know," he finished slowly, "that even in his blackest rages, I have never, ever, heard Richard raise his voice."

⚞CHAPTER 24⚟

Wandering aimlessly, broken by my thoughts,
Which slowly sharpened daggers at my heart.
Charles Baudelaire, Beatrice

I woke late again after a wretched night. Wearily slipping on my robe, I called the London harp salon to discuss repairs to the sound board of Ciara's harp. I was not in the best of tempers, and the manager sounded so chilly and indifferent that I couldn't resist saying, "You sent me the wrong harp, by the way."

"I beg your pardon?" she said stiffly. "We sent what you ordered, Miss Leone."

"No. I specified an instrument with wide spacing, and you sent a standard model." I felt righteously censorious, seeing that the concert had turned out so well.

Her voice became maddeningly tolerant, reducing me to the status of a first-grader who must be taught her numbers.

"I have the order right here, Miss Leone, and yes, you did request wide spacing. I remember it well. Those models haven't been made for some years, you see."

"Yes, I know." Teach your grandmother to suck eggs, I thought irritably.

"But if you'll recall, you phoned back and changed it to standard spacing. And after we had the harp all packed for shipping, too," she added accusingly.

"I... but I didn't. There's some mistake," I whispered.

"There's no mistake, Miss Leone. It's written right here on the order: concert grand, natural finish, wide spacing; then it's crossed through, and changed to standard spacing, so we substituted the gold eleven. I initialed the change."

"Who made the second call?" There was a bitter taste in my dry mouth. "Was it Dr. D'Annunzio?"

Blank silence spun out along the wire. Then, "Why, you made the call, Miss Leone. Don't you remember?" Her voice had grown far more human at the mention of Richard's name.

"I talked with you myself. I knew it was you right away from your American accent, even before you told me your name. And Miss Leone," she was positively gushing now, "all of us here have read your reviews and want to tell you—"

I set the receiver into its cradle and leaned back in the chair, looking out the window. It had begun to snow in thin, fitful spurts.

I was afraid as I had never been in my whole life, with a superstitious fear, demeaning and enervating. Thinking of the luminous, smiling portrait in the salon, I almost forgot to breathe.

All right, then. Action. My reservation was already made for tomorrow. I didn't have the energy for a walk, so I'd pack instead. I would say goodbye to John and Robin. Peter? I didn't think I could.

Yet I couldn't go without a word, hurting that affectionate child. I'd leave a note for him, and write a long and chatty letter when I got home. He'd forget me soon enough. After all, there was the elusive Marjorie.

Sounds of hammering and the shriek of nails being drawn rose from the dining room directly below, where workmen were unpacking the last of the antiques selected for the refurbishing of Denham House.

Robin had returned from York the night before the concert, I remembered, to supervise the unloading of the van. The pieces had stood crated until he, John, and Kit Ingram could be on hand to oversee their unpacking and place them in the proper rooms.

I covered my ears to shut out the noise, attempting to think. I wasn't hungry. Yes, I'd pack right now, before the last trace of will and energy left me. The onset of depression was something I had ample cause to recognize.

Pulling my trunk from the back of the closet, I turned to the dresses hanging there. The Melisande gown glinted, darkly splendid. I thought of the way in which that promise of splendor had been fulfilled, only two nights ago. Suddenly I couldn't bear the sight of it, and pulled it roughly from its hanger, impatient to bury it at the very bottom of this yawning coffin.

Shaking out the dress, I laid it on the bed to fold it. Then I remembered the lipstick, tuning fork and handkerchief I'd left in the pocket; the handkerchief I'd lent, for a change, to Richard.

I thrust my hand angrily at the side seam, delving deep, and came up with a small roll of paper. Wrong pocket; I kept things on the right. Yes, here they were. But what was this bit of paper, anyway? I didn't remember putting it there; I never even used the left-hand pocket, as it made the skirt on the audience side fall awkwardly when I was seated at the harp. Sinking onto the bed, I picked it up and slowly opened it out.

It was a little rectangle of cream-colored stock. The brief scrawl was in black ink.

"Two a.m. at the cove. Keep it quiet–and forgive me. I want you. R."

I took the key from the kitchen rack and walked numbly to the attic stairs, deliberately detaching myself from the pain in my chest.

The dress had looked fresh when I found it all those weeks ago, and I'd assumed it was cleaned after Ciara's death. But of course it never showed a wrinkle; that was one of the fabric's selling points. I'd just tested it myself, in the bedroom, by a savage and futile attempt to crease it.

So I'd found the dress just as she'd worn it in Naples, simply put back on its padded hanger and shipped to Denham House with the rest of her things.

And Ciara was left-handed.

It was snowing again, and attic was clammily cold. Its spaces loomed before me like the hold of a great ship, glowing with an eerie blue luminescence.

Muffled in sweaters to my ears, I stood over the boxes, searching for a label that said "letters" or "papers," knife ready in my hand. Lethargy gone, I was filled with cold energy as the attic was filled with chilly light. If I had to go through every scrap in every box, I was going to find something to back up the evidence of the card now lying hidden under a corner of my bedroom rug. There must be related letters, a journal, something to confirm their twisted relationship. Walk away, Tim had warned. Well, by heaven, I wasn't going to run out on Ciara, not with the knowledge I had in my hands.

I was certain now that she was dead; the card left little doubt in my mind that her murder had been skillfully planned. My unhealthy fantasy of her lurking somewhere out of sight had evaporated. I still didn't know how the tinkering with the harp tuning had been done, but it must have been easy enough. And I suspected that having a woman with an American accent make the call to the harp salon would have been no problem—not when one knew that many women. Anyway, it was doubtful that Ciara could have reconstructed her painstakingly effaced native accent if she'd wanted to.

My heart still refused to accept what my mind now knew with certainty; every instinct, and, I thought sarcastically, gland, cried out against it. But the scale was weighted, finally and irrevocably. I began to slit the tapes with unnecessary violence.

An hour later I knew there was nothing. I'd opened

every box: more music, scores, shoes, cosmetics, books, though surprisingly few; underclothes, some lovely night things, costume jewelry. Gloves, hats. But not one letter, not even a checkbook. Either John had filed her papers away, or they'd been destroyed. I turned to the books out of defeat and a kind of dull curiosity.

Contemporary novels, mostly, with a few travel books here and there. *How to Make Love to a Man*. She probably could have written that one. One thin, expensively-bound volume of poetry, by Baudelaire: *Les Fleurs du Mal*. This edition boasted several different translations, as well as the French text. I flipped it open idly, remembering Henri Duparc's ravishing song setting of "Invitation to the Voyage," the only one of the poems I knew. I loved the music so much that I'd made a transcription for harp and cello, and performed it once, with Tim.

An inscription on the flyleaf, in Ciara's impetuous, nearly illegible hand, jumped out at me. "From C. to R.," with some French tag scribbled beneath. So it was Ciara's gift to Richard. He must have left it in her flat when he was still "one of her fools." It bore no date. I rose slowly with it in my hand, telling myself I was curious about the other poems; knowing, in nauseated despair, that I was taking it because it had belonged to him.

Moving toward the door, I passed the old bookshelf with the clutter of discarded objects thrust behind it. The awful lamp, the broken hockey stick, the black corrugated rubber tube.

So her papers had been destroyed, probably in London; more than likely, they'd never been here at all. Why had I expected it to be otherwise? And what was I to say to John? My false energy ebbed away, and the descent down the stairs felt like a walk to the scaffold.

But John was on his way to Scarborough to meet a client.

"I'm sorry I can't stop now, my dear, I'm late," he said, planting a hasty kiss on my cheek. "I'll be back in the morning, and we'll have a nice chat before you leave. I hate for you to go... won't you change your mind? Well, you know best. When things settle down you'll be back, and we'll stay in touch. I only wish you had better weather for your last day. By the way, take a look at the things we've uncrated in the dining room, won't you, Lissa? There are some first-rate pieces there; perhaps they'll cheer you up. Must dash!"

Dazedly, I pushed at the half-open doors and entered the dining room. My misery did lift a bit as I walked about, looking at the lovely things. All traces of the packing were removed; only a quilted pad remained, protecting the long dining table's lustrous surface from a number of smaller pieces set upon it.

Near the fireplace stood a delicate Sheraton worktable, elbowed by a gaming and writing table. A walnut chair, early Georgian, boasted lions' heads on its arms and elegant scallop shells fanning across its knees. There was an Irish settee, upholstered in silver-green brocade, and a sinuously graceful cabriole stool. On the dining table a mantel clock with silver fittings reposed next to a double-lidded workbox. How my mother would have loved these things! Suddenly I gave a small cry of recognition and moved toward the center of the table, where the chandelier's light glinted along the brass bindings of a Georgian writing box.

It was almost a duplicate of the one that Daddy had restored for my twentieth birthday. The walnut box was about twelve by sixteen inches, and nine inches deep. Its hinged lid was cut at an angle sloping from front to back, so that when opened, it lay flat on the table, forming an area perfectly slanted for writing.

Turning the tasseled key, I lifted the lid and lowered it to the table with care. The finely tooled leather of the writing surface concealed recesses for holding paper and envelopes. Like mine, this case was fitted: the larger cavity held a narrow removable tray for holding pens, with a shallow storage compartment underneath. Curiously, I lifted the tray. There was nothing there. The tray was flanked by wells for stamps and a sander on one side, and for an inkwell on the other. I remembered our excitement when quite accidentally we'd discovered the secret compartment, which surprisingly the seller hadn't known about. Raising the inner lid, I pulled gently upward on the wooden interstice between the two adjacent wells.

Powered by a spring that was simply a curved piece of steel, the secret panel flew out into the body of the box, revealing two slim drawers under the fittings. I looked around guiltily; the spring had projected the panel against the opposite wall of the box with a noise like a pistol crack in that silent room.

I gave the leather tab on the left drawer a tentative tug. We'd found yellowed newspaper clippings in ours, and a sentimental poem written out in painstaking copperplate.

Nothing so innocuous lay hidden here. I knew at once what the little plastic packets of white powder were; no one could have grown up in our time, reading books and newspapers and watching television, and failed to know.

Oh, God. Oh, God, it needed only this, I thought, as I slammed the drawer and attempted with trembling fingers to lever the panel back into position. It seemed forever before I managed to dovetail the end into its niche. I pushed it flat with a loud click. As I closed the lid and turned the key, something caught my eye, and looking up nervously, I saw a movement in the mirror above the side-board, which reflected the open double doors behind me. But I was too late; it had no more meaning than the final ripple emanating from a stone cast into a pool.

I was standing there frozen, hand still foolishly on the box, when purposeful steps rang on the tiles of the hall. Without turning, I continued to stare into the mirror.

"Oh, Lissa." Richard's voice was cool and

impersonally brisk. "So everything's uncrated. Good. Just tell Robin I'm taking this, will you? It's mine."

Without another word he lifted the box from under my hands and carried it out of the room.

Still gazing blindly at the mirror, I heard the front door close. When I started slowly for my room, I saw Robin on the stairs, a look of blank incredulity on his face. Altering my course, I hurried toward the kitchen door and made for the stables. But not to ride; simply for the bleak comfort of burying my face in a warm mane.

It was after midnight when I laid down *Les Fleurs du Mal* and looked out the window. The freezing rain which followed the snow had stopped, and the moon was out, the clouds torn away by a bitter wind. I touched the pane; it was even colder now.

Almost as cold as my heart. How I wished I'd never opened the covers of this slim and elegant volume. But driven by some perverse compulsion, I'd leafed through the poems, first with weary indifference, then, as horror blossomed, in frantic search, tracing a shaking finger down the faint vertical pencilings that marked the telling passages. Even knowing what I already did, this consolidation of cool deliberate evil made me physically ill. I turned the pages, reading the self-indictments for the last time.

The first were selected portions of *Au Lecteur*.

Who but the Devil pulls our waking-strings!
Abominations lure us to their side;
Each day we take another step to hell,
Descending through the stench, unhorrified.

Here he'd continued with an alternate translation of the same work; presumably it described his condition more specifically.

If poison, arson, sex, narcotics, knives
Have not yet ruined us and stitched their quick,
Loud patterns on the canvas of our lives,
It is because our souls are still too sick.
There's one more ugly and abortive birth.
It makes no gestures, never beats its breast,
Yet it would murder for a moment's rest,
And willingly annihilate the earth.

It's ennui. Tears have glued its eyes together.
You know it well, my Reader. This obscene
Beast chain-smokes yawning for the guillotine—
You—hypocrite Reader—my double—my brother!

The next must have been marked with Ciara in mind:

You'd take to bed the whole world as your prize,
You slut of sluts, by boredom brutalized!
To exercise your jaws at this rare sport
Each day you must be served a fresh-killed heart.

This hideous wrong in which you feel secure,
Has it not made you shrink one step in fear,—
That nature, strong in her concealed designs,
Makes use of you, oh woman, queen of sins,
Vile animal! to mould a genius?

A single line, more heavily underscored, brought an unwilling wrench of pity:

Am I not a dissonant chord in the heavenly symphony?

Now a damning fragment:

Deviless, you're heading for the devil!
I'd gladly keep you company,

293

If only the pace at which you travel
Didn't leave me somewhat dizzy.
So get on, alone, with you to the Devil!

And the last, and worst:

—must he be put in fetters, thrown into the sea.

Worst, because a barely perceptible "s" had been penciled in before the pronoun.

This was what I had sought, and now that it was in my hands all I wanted to do was die. I turned back to the flyleaf, inspecting it with mindless thoroughness, as if I thought the inscription might magically have changed. Then, my attention suddenly riveted, I brought the book closer, inspecting the dedication. "From C. to R." Yes, that was clear enough. Painstakingly, I made out the rest: *—ma cher oiseau de malheur.* My French, like Ciara's, was execrable, but every first-year student would have enough vocabulary to cobble this up: "my dear bird of evil." I sat back in the chair, utterly stunned. Thoughts of my departure, which yesterday brought regretful but overwhelming relief, had been forever tarnished by today's revelations. Now there was absolutely nowhere to turn.

CHAPTER 25

Like sheep, we're doomed to travel o'er
The fated track to all assigned.
On Life, Ebn Alramacram

I longed to crawl into bed and wait for the release of morning, but instead levered myself out of the chair like an old, old woman. I knew what I had to do, and I would do it, just as I always had. It was the last step to be taken before I went back to my own home, and to peace. Peace. One might as well be dead as have that kind of peace, I thought, pulling on my Zermatt parka and pocketing my gloves. But I knew now what had happened, or almost all of it, and supposed I could live with it. I'd have to.

The silver spandrels on the table clock winked in the firelight. Twelve-thirty. I picked up my hiking boots and tiptoed along the hall and down the stairs, past Robin's bedroom. He was asleep; the light was out. Yes, I'd waited long enough. Taking a flashlight from the kitchen closet, I let myself quietly out the back door, where the cold struck me breathless. I sat down on the stoop and laced my boots with rapidly numbing fingers.

The road was too long; I took the sheep track over the fell. But I soon had cause to regret my choice. The thin layer of snow was covered with a sheet of ice formed by the freezing rain, and now it was beginning to snow again. I couldn't use the flash yet, I decided, as I picked myself up from yet another fall. My injured knee felt like a well-advanced toothache, and the rubber soles of my boots had no more grip on this icy mixture than they would have had on polished marble.

When I finally reached the top, I turned the flashlight onto my watch. One twenty-five. It had taken me something over fifty minutes. Walk away, Lissa. You don't have to do this. What possible difference can it make?

Probably none, I realized as I rested there, fighting to draw breath into my cold-seared lungs. But at least I could put one thing right, I thought. And issue a warning. It was wrong to leave without trying. One has to be willing to take some risks. This one threatened nothing worse than a broken leg, I judged, as I began the horrendous slither down the fell. Well, never mind. It would be a good match for my heart.

I gave a sudden gasp of fright; I'd slid down a bank into the midst of a dim confusion of woolly shapes. The drowsily indignant baas began, and I swore mildly, startled into silly tears. It was only a flock of sheep, the ewes heavy with lambs I'd never see.

Swinging the flashlight around, I realized I'd intersected the road that rounded the shoulder of the fell and was standing on its ice-slick graveled surface. Directly to my left was a black abyss plunging to the floor of the valley. I covered my mouth and stood still, heart hammering. Would I have seen it in time if the sheep hadn't stopped me? I'd lost my bearings in the snow, and borne too far west.

If the hill was slippery, the road was a skating rink. I moved with extreme caution to cross it, veering far to the right, away from that awful maw. The sheep were bleating and seething in self-induced panic, and one of the pregnant ewes slipped, struggling back to her feet with difficulty.

"I'm sorry!" I cried out absurdly. "Oh, don't hurt yourself!"

Tossing her head contemptuously, the ewe trotted off to join her flock, and I continued my downward journey. The strain on my knee was getting worse at every step.

At last I could make out Richard's house. Through the fast-falling snow a dim light shone from the front windows.

He must be up still, in the parlor. Probably sorting out his little packets, I thought bitterly. I slipped again, and in the same moment heard a faint concussion. Perhaps it was a backfire from a car on the other side of the fell, though surely no sane person would take a vehicle out tonight.

By the time I reached the front door the snow was blinding, my body was a grinding ache from cold and exhaustion, and my courage had fled. If I hadn't been so tired, I would have turned back. But I simply hadn't the strength; I must at least sit down, first, before a fire.

Could I really confront Richard with all of this? God help me, I thought, knowing I was powerless to help myself. And I suppose He did, for the dogged determination of the Godwins rose up in me. I aimed my flashlight at the door and gave the brass knocker several irritated raps.

"Richard," I croaked, "let me in." My throat was raw from the labored trek through the frosty air. "It's Felicity." In that moment I was, indeed, very much Felicity Godwin.

There was a flurry of hysterical barking, cut short by a sharp command. Then a long silence. At last the light in the window shifted, as someone picked up a lamp and moved toward the door. It opened, just a crack.

"Lissa!" Richard's voice was a harsh whisper. "What the hell are you doing here?"

"I have to see you. Please, Richard."

"Absolutely not. Go home. I can't see you now."

I was suddenly livid with anger at the sheer incivility of it. Go home? Just go home? As if I lived in the next block? Struggle for another hour and a half across the slippery fell when I was already frost-bitten?

"Richard," I mumbled through numb lips, "you don't understand. I'm leaving tomorrow. There are some things I have to tell you." Damn it, was he going to leave me out here to freeze?

"I'm sorry, Lissa. It won't do. There's–someone here with me. Now please go."

297

Someone here with him. Of course. My heart hit my boots and exploded upward in a burst of genuine fury.

"Oh. Terrific. Who is it, Marjorie?" I asked with sarcastic sweetness.

"Marjorie? What--no. Please, Lissa, will you just get out of here?"

"Listen, Don Giovanni," I raged. "I didn't come to here to seduce you, never fear. You can have fifteen women in there for all I care. I came, if it matters, to tell you I'm sorry I believed you killed Ciara, which you probably never really thought I did anyway, and I know now that you didn't do it, damn you, and I know who did. No, just shut up."

This as he tried frantically to silence me. I could see his face through the door now, in the glare from my flashlight. He looked terrible, exhausted, eyes puffy. Well, no wonder.

"I thought you'd better know, so you can take whatever action you want. And," I went on in a flat voice, "I know about your drugs, I found them in the writing box today. Very clever, to use John like that."

"Lissa, for God's sake," he whispered in an anguished voice.

"Don't interrupt her, cousin mine. I want to hear her little story; it sounds intriguing beyond words, if a bit incoherent. Come in, Lissa dear."

The door swung wide. I stared uncomprehendingly. Even my painfully gained knowledge hadn't prepared me for the reality of the black thing gleaming coldly in Robin's hand. He laughed as I lifted my glance to his face. And what I saw in his eyes was Richard's death, and mine.

⤳CHAPTER 26⤳

When I have fears that I may cease to be...
Sonnet, John Keats

He made a mock bow, horrible in its parody of
graciousness, and gestured me inside with the gun, placing
the oil lamp on the Steinway. I saw, with nightmare clarity,
the score of the Rachmaninoff Third Concerto on the music
rack. In the ancient room, the muted light created the
atmosphere of a period movie. Beside the fading fire, G.P.'s
tail struck the hearth with monotonous regularity. He looked
unhappy and bewildered, his tail wagging in a pathetic
attempt to reassure himself that all was well.

There was a second lamp on the low sofa table beside
the Meissen bowl. The narcissus had gone by, and the bowl
was empty. In spite of the fire, the room was freezingly cold.
I raised my eyes to Richard's, and gasped. Out of the
shadows behind him stepped another man, with another gun:
Kit Ingram.

"Well, what a lot of trouble you've saved us, Lissa,"
smiled Robin. "Sit down. We have plenty of time."

"I'll stand, thank you," I said, stiff with terror.

"I think not." He took my arm and pushed me down
onto the sofa with casual brutality. "And I'll have that torch,
if you please. Richard can stand, though, there against the
mantel where he's well lighted. Kit?"

"He's covered."

"Good. Well, now I have my two birds. I couldn't
decide whether it was safe to let you go back to the States,
you know. What a foolish mistake that would have been! I

299

suppose I was less convincing than I thought. That pains me: I expended rather a lot of effort on you. What tipped you off?"

A combination of hurt, anger and contempt made me incautious. "Shakespeare. Baudelaire: she gave *Les Fleurs du Mal* to you, didn't she?"

"Of course. It was so funny, Lissa. I'd mentioned the poems and she bought me a copy, without the faintest idea that my loathing for her was one of the reasons I loved them. I pointed out a few verses that referred to our mutual interests; other than that, I'm sure she never cracked the covers, except for writing her rather sophomoric dedication."

"Yes: her 'dear bird of evil.' Then you marked your credos, probably in John's own London house, while you were still having an affair with her. You knew she'd never find them; she wasn't into serious literature, even if it was perverse. How in God's name, Robin, can you be that person, and then the other one I thought I knew?"

His silent smile of amusement drew me on. "And then there was your deep sea diving equipment." I thought of the rubber tube snaking obscenely behind the bookshelf.

"Not deep sea; scuba. Ciara wasn't a submarine, you know. I didn't need the heavy stuff to take care of her."

"Let's by all means be accurate. Tell me, were you really that careless, leaving it in John's attic, or was it just bravado?"

He and Kit exchanged a quick, private smile that made my legs start to shake.

"Bravado, of course. Part of the fun is living on the edge. You can't imagine how inexpressibly dull it is in this family. It's almost impossible to get a reaction out of one's relatives, now that Uncle James is gone."

"John's forbearance, and mine, hasn't come from lack of energy, Robin."

Robin turned on Richard with savage alacrity. "No, you damned paragon. I suppose you always hoped that the black lamb, son of the black sheep, would outgrow his little peccadilloes and stay quietly in his appointed niche."

"For a long time we both did. In the past few months it's been more a matter of deciding how those 'peccadilloes' must be dealt with."

"Oh?" Robin quirked an eyebrow, suddenly urbane again. "It must be a relief to have the matter so effectively taken out of your hands. And by the way, you ought to show some gratitude, you know. Were it not for me, you might have had to deal with dear Uncle James all these years. If you'd been at Denham House when he had his apoplectic fit, instead of off galvanizing audiences across the Atlantic, you might even have called an ambulance."

In the shifting light Richard's face looked even worse, but he gave Robin no satisfaction. He merely said, "If I'd been there he wouldn't have let me in."

Robin laughed and turned to me. "So the intrepid girl sleuth knows who did it, as they say in the detective books. Very clever. But do you know how it was done?"

"Not entirely."

Paradoxically, the fear was gone again, and the conversation, for the moment, took on a hypothetical aspect. Perhaps it was the surreal quality of the whole affair, or more likely the overload had simply switched off my nervous system.

"Not if you really were in Ischia. That's a long swim, even for a couple of frogmen."

"Oh, we were in Ischia all right. A house party, as Richard's tame spy so dutifully confirmed. Unfortunately for him, dear Carlo just discovered that our host owned a hydrofoil, which Kit and I had quietly borrowed. So you won't be seeing Carlo again, Richard; Kit took care of that—at about the time you were rehearsing in York, I believe."

A sudden bright laugh.

"Wrong; how forgetful I am. Of course...you two will be meeting very soon."

In the last flickering light from the fire, I saw shock and grief register on Richard's face. Then Robin swung back to me, smiling.

"Another correction: you three. You'll like Carlo, Lissa. Richard inherited him from his Italian grandfather. Sort of an elderly human watchdog. You know," he went on with a deprecating gesture, "I had you figured all wrong. I thought perhaps you came here to blackmail me, as your beloved aunt had been doing for so long. That's why I let you book into Denham House at such an awkward time."

I remembered blessing my luck at getting a reservation so easily.

"You knew who I was before I came?" I fought to control the tremor in my voice.

"Of course. When Ciara and I were on more intimate terms, we laughed over her little rearrangement of your life. You put far too much importance on it, by the way. You were a mere annoyance; a gnat to be swatted. But you were still an unknown quantity to me. I had to find out what you knew, and what you were up to, sailing in here incognito."

"Great God," I exclaimed in disgust. "What a pair you were. Well, you were safe enough. She never mentioned you to me. So if I was a gnat, Leon was a falcon?"

"You could say that. She didn't appreciate his rebirth as a performer, especially as her own reputation was getting shaky; he really had been her Svengali, and when she thought she'd outgrown him, it all started going to hell. She was doing tricks instead of music. Same thing with you, Lissa, I imagine."

"You're wrong, Robin." Richard spoke evenly. "Lissa never needed a Svengali."

"It's irrelevant. A few drops from a little vial in his wine, and she thought she'd be on top again."

I felt my brain jumping around among these awful revelations. Imminent death. Ciara---my own blood. My unforgivable suspicions of Richard. And Leon. All that brilliance and accomplishment, his devoted mentoring of scores of young harpists—wiped out casually over a reputation that only a tiny group of listeners knew about anyway. Anger flooded back, sweeping some of the fear away.

Robin was deep into his exposition.

"And when I found you didn't share her more peculiar talents, and what a pure and harmless little lass you were, I thought I'd urge you safely back to the States. But as John remarked, you are so persevering."

"She's a Scorpio," interjected Richard, almost conversationally. Distracted, I stared at him. Then I returned to Robin.

"So you faked up all my little disasters. Fiametto's girth, my ski bindings. Not only that, you added a spot of love-making on the side. For heavens' sake, why?"

"In a word, fun. People are so damned stupid, Lissa. You can do anything you want with them, if only you know how. It keeps the ennui at bay. Kit, by the way, obligingly readjusted your bindings."

"And the harp? You smashed that beautiful instrument? Lifted my score?"

I heard a muffled exclamation from Richard.

"And fiddled with the tuning; I guess you could do that if I was out of the room for five minutes. But why? What did you hope to accomplish by that?"

"Have you gotten the impression that I wanted you out of the way? I was hoping you might flee the spiritual threats, since the physical didn't seem to make any impression on you."

I shook my head silently. "Childish. And putting alum on my strings. That was a silly, useless trick, Robin."

I'd heard on a television special that you should always use your attacker's name, as a means of making him more human. Fat chance, I thought. But incredibly, I was losing patience with Robin's nattering, almost forgetting the way this must end.

"You would have done better to touch them with shellac. Your consulting chemist failed you on that one. Though the transdermal patch was a walloping success. What did you permeate it with, by the way?"

"Ipecac, in a DMSO base. We have Kit to thank for that; he read it up with a doctor friend of his."

"I'm sure you had plenty of supplies on hand."

"No problem. But that was a funny thing. The patch isn't supposed to work unless you put it on hours ahead of time, which I conveniently omitted to tell you. I was hoping you'd be getting out your little sick bag on the way to Geneva, but no. You know, I think our sly Lissa probably faked the whole thing about motion sickness. Anyway I didn't leave it to chance on the return trip."

"No, I didn't fake it. Maybe I was just so happy and carefree–" I broke off. "Who made the call to the harp salon, by the way, to change the specification? Was that your own sweet voice?"

He paled with anger, then laughed again. "An American bar girl Kit knows in York. We told her it was a practical joke, and gave her a healthy tip."

"And all the time you were manipulating me so I lost my faith in Richard. That was a stellar performance on the drive back from Zermatt, by the way–your agony over Richard's instability."

Now I was talking on, desperate to buy time. Robin's gratification in revealing his cleverness made it possible. But it was useless, a mere prolonging of the nightmare. No one was going to come to Richard's isolated house at three o'clock on a stormy morning.

"Ah, well. There's no denying it, the whole family's talented in the arts. Perhaps I'll take up theatre as my next career."

Kit made a sharp movement as Richard leaned exhaustedly against the mantel. A log, crumbling to ashes, sent up a final jet of flame, and for the first time, I realized that the puffiness around his eyes was the result of a blow. Alert now, I saw a dark stain on the leg of his khakis.

"Richard! You're hurt!"

"I'm all right." He smiled grimly. "The pleasure was worth it." He jerked his head at Kit, and my eyes, now adjusted to the dimness, made out an angry bruise across Kit's jaw.

"Ah yes. Richard's single noble attempt. Pity he hasn't kept his assassin's skills honed more effectively."

"He's been practicing more important things," I grated. "It wasn't a backfire, then—what I heard."

"No." Richard spoke very softly. "Not a backfire."

"Changed the plans a bit, our Richard did," came Robin's lilting voice. "We were in something of a dilemma after Kit overreacted to his little attack. He was to have a simple car accident on the road up the fell; an unfortunate excess of brandy—couldn't handle the ice. Consider the loss to the musical world. However, Richard off Delving Drop is one thing; Richard off Delving Drop with a bullet wound, no matter how well we brandied him, quite another. And then you miraculously came along to save the situation. So much more interesting, don't you think? Murder and suicide."

"Haven't you forgotten your car tracks?"

"Kit's, actually. Mine's modestly garaged at Denham House. Not to worry, they'll be covered thirty minutes after we leave; just look how the snow's coming down, dear girl. I shall find you both, of course, when I drive over here in a few hours to ask my cousin why you're not in the drawing room, ready to leave for the airport. How I shall mourn. Not a new idea, really; it crossed my mind last night when you two were quarreling so romantically."

"I'm sorry I shouted at you, Lissa," Richard interjected in a lifeless voice. "I meant what I said, but I thought if Robin believed we weren't talking anymore, he might let you off unscathed."

"Clever of you, Richard. As I was saying, our present plan had crossed my mind. But I shelved it. Such a bloody lot of trouble to get you to Hawthorns, and besides, I knew once back in the States you'd never return to Yorkshire with Richard dead. However, as things worked out, you've expedited the plan quite neatly."

So that was what I'd seen igniting in his eyes, there in John's front hall. Of course. One mark of a natural criminal was opportunism. Seize the moment and turn it to advantage.

"Wonderful," I muttered, and the terror rolled back in. "So who's to be the initiator in this little scene?"

"You, of course. It's generally known you came here after an emotional illness, and on false pretenses; I've made sure of that. We can all testify to your infatuation for Richard–John, Mrs. Chidester, Kit, even Peter. Both John and I heard you quarreling violently last night. You set your sights too high, Lissa, that's all, and failed where many others have failed before you. So–" he took on an expansive, improvisatory tone, "you come here, on your last night, in a desperate attempt to win him over, staking everything on a last throw. He spurns your charms." Robin was enjoying this immensely. "And inflamed with unrequited passion, you shoot him with his own gun, and then tragically despatch yourself."

"I don't have a gun," interposed Richard.

"You do now," Robin assured him, "and here's the purchase slip, in your name, which goes into your desk drawer." Reaching into his coat pocket, he suited the action to the words. "Kit thought it as well to be prepared, and took care of that little task. It's detail that's important, you see. Never take half-measures... well, you'll hardly have the chance. But we've strayed from the subject. I was telling darling Felicity how Ciara met her maker."

Out of the miasma of horror two thoughts struggled to surface. Surely I'd misinterpreted the scene and this was some sort of insane masquerade; it wasn't possible that this bantering killer was the engaging, congenial person I'd hiked and danced with. At any moment now, he'd throw aside the gun and burst into laughter at his own elaborate joke. But if this awful scene was real, as my logical mind knew it was, why was Richard so passive, so defeated?

He swayed suddenly, and Robin and Kit were instantly across the room, their shadows swooping in the light from the oil lamps. He straightened with an effort, pinned between the two guns.

"Let him sit down!" I cried fiercely. "He's losing blood!"

"Nothing to what he's going to lose," laughed Robin. "You couldn't possibly be a very good shot, Lissa. I imagine you will have to perforate the Great Pianist several times, most inaccurately, before you're finally at liberty to turn the gun on yourself."

"You're dead wrong." My brain had clicked in again, icily clear. "I was Connecticut junior revolver range champion, and my house is full of trophies. Daddy taught me. Everyone knows it. You'd never get away with that; detail is important."

Richard gave a quiet laugh, and Robin cursed under his breath. Then he controlled himself and, perching beside me on the sofa arm, went on with the confessional that his raging, twisted ego couldn't contain.

"But back to our principal subject. What was interesting about Ciara's demise is that she bargained for one Denham and got another."

"How did you manage to plant that note? I found it in my dress, the one she'd worn that night."

"That was your dress? I wondered at you, wearing it. I didn't plant the note, love. Ciara must have pocketed it with her own hand. Well, Ciara was careless at the best of times. I'd hoped the note would turn up in Ravello, and make things interesting for Richard. I'm an old pro at forging his hand."

Richard looked increasingly worse, but managed a cynical assent.

"That was the easiest of all, and she swallowed it whole. We believe what we want to, I suppose, and what she fervently wanted to believe in was the manly arms of Richard. I simply stopped in at a florist's in Naples, on the way to Ischia, and left the note to be delivered in an armful of roses during her curtain calls. Money well spent. How her tiny heart must have pounded with delight."

"And the earlier meetings in the cove? Did you fake those rumors? I suppose there really wasn't any 'Italian lover.'"

"My dear Felicity, you astonish me with your naïveté. There was always a lover, or two or three, Italian or no. Yes, she'd been frolicking with a waiter from the hotel; she discovered him the season before. Of course he hardly leapt forward to testify, as it would have meant his job.

"But consider her joy when she thought the Eminent Conductor had once again succumbed to her charms. Imagine her surprise when, happily anchoring for a romantic moonlit rendezvous—though actually there wasn't any moon, fortunately for us—she suddenly feels her foot seized by a black apparition from the sea. Before she knows it, her ankle is enclosed in a cuff, to which is attached a chain. Not hard to procure, my innocent, at certain 'adult' stores. And attached to the other end of the chain is a lead weight, conveniently borne by said apparition on an underwater flotation device. One never knows how one's early training will come in handy. Then hey presto! And a rock to the hull, a bit of a tow, a quick swim back to the waiting hydrofoil—"

"Not quite hey presto," murmured Kit. It was the second time he'd spoken.

"No. To be accurate, some time elapsed before she went overboard. Enough time for the apparition to remove its mask. Because I wanted her to be bloody sure," he finished viciously, "whose face Death wore. Her own was quite a study, I can tell you."

"You're mad," I said flatly.

"Certifiable," added Richard.

"I warned her!" shrilled Robin, out of control again. "She was too damned greedy, she wanted more and more. Blackmailing bitch." He swung his head toward me, blue eyes suddenly troubled and pleading as a child's. "She was going to tell, Lissa. She was going to tell John if I didn't give her more money."

"Tell him what?" I whispered.

"About the drugs." My eyes flew to Richard. "About Edmund Garrett. And about Kit and me. She was going to tell John... about Kit and me. And she said she'd tell him I'd been her lover, too. Well, I'd had enough of her, long before. God, how sick of her I was–her incessant demands turned my stomach. But John would have thrown me out, turned me over to the police–"

This pathetic travesty of the Robin I'd known was making me ill. "The drug business–it's yours, then? And Kit's?" At least I would know the truth about this before I died.

"There isn't any drug business." Now his voice was dull, apathetic. "Not any more, not after Ciara; it was too dangerous. God knows what she'd leaked. We cut the connection."

I closed my eyes for a moment. "Then the cocaine in the writing box–"

"Mine. My own supply. Clever of Richard, wasn't it," he said, malice rising in his voice, "to force the issue by taking it. And to try and draw my fire from you; he knew I'd seen you prying. I do love seeing a spider caught in its own web."

I turned to Richard, heart-stricken.

"Anyway, it doesn't matter, we're on to something better now." There was a frightening finality in his voice. He was gathering himself to rise.

Grasping frantically at any straw, I asked, "Who is

Edmund Garrett?"

Richard answered. "He was Robin and Kit's instructor in the Navy unit. He made the mistake of disciplining them for an infraction of rules. Two weeks later he disappeared."

"He was a little shit. But it was a learning experience for all three of us." Robin smiled crookedly. "One might say it was the ankle cuff's maiden voyage."

"Nothing was ever proven, but there was enough speculation and unease to get these two winners discharged on psychological grounds, which couldn't have been difficult to do. You know, Robin," and pain sounded through the hardness of Richard's voice, "you're wrong about John. He wouldn't have cared that you and Kit were lovers, or even you and Ciara, by that time. He would have been so happy," he finished wearily, "just to think you were capable of love."

The lamp on the piano flared and went out. With an oath, Robin got to his feet.

"Damn you and your everlasting superiority, Richard! Now you're setting up as the authority on love. I've had enough, Kit; this amusement stales."

A terrible thought struck me. "Where's Peter?" The words emerged almost devoid of sound.

"London. I sent him with Marjorie as soon as I left Denham House today."

"And damn her too, the old hag! She always played favorites with you."

"You're wrong there. She cared the most of all for you, Robin, from the day your mother left you."

Marjorie was Mrs. Chidester? I had no chance to think, because Robin was in a fury again.

"Don't you speak about my mother! You had it all: a mother who loved you, audiences falling at your feet from the time you were thirteen. Cars, women, houses—all with the wave of a finger. Oh, yes. The virtuoso. But that wasn't enough. The composer. And that wasn't enough. The conductor." He jabbed the phrases with vicious emphasis.

"And you!" He turned on me in a frenzy, and my heart began to thud in earnest. "God, how I wanted to throttle you that day when you played the Goldberg. 'A mere dilettante, Mr. Denham.'" His voice shifted up an octave, mocking my accent with cruel accuracy. " 'Just a few summer lessons on the harpsichord.' I sweated blood, and for what? But you–it's not enough just to be a harpist, is it?"

"Come, Robin," said Richard. "This is obsessive. Surely you can't be jealous of everyone who can keep both hands together."

I gasped as Robin whirled on Richard, but Richard's voice cut in, cool and bored.

"What was that Shakespeare you mentioned earlier, Lissa?"

I shook my head warningly, but he gave one insistent nod, looking straight into my eyes.

"It–it's from The Merchant of Venice," I faltered, and again gave a tiny shake of the head. But his commanding look overrode me once more.

"Well?" Robin stood as if mesmerized. Then he took hold of himself. "If you're going to recite, you'd better get at it. You're running out of time."

But a different quotation swam up. *If I must die*, I thought, *I will encounter darkness as a bride, and hug it in my arms.* Yes; what the hell. As well go now as later.

"The man who hath no music in himself, nor is not moved with concord of sweet sounds, is fit for treasons, stratagems and spoils."

Something was happening to Robin's face; it seemed to be fragmenting into unrelated features, their juxtaposition subtly wrong. He grasped my arm with bruising savagery, and I gave an involuntary cry.

"Let her go, Rob," rasped Richard.

G.P., who had been dozing uneasily, got warily to his feet, hackles rising, and emitted a low growl, advancing toward us with the slow motion of a bad dream.

And Shakespeare's words kept coming, as if they were a ribbon pulled out of my mouth by a magician; I could do nothing to stop them.

"The motions of his spirit are dull as night, and his affections dark as Erebus: let no such man be trusted."

Robin struck me hard in the face. Richard sprang forward, but Kit's gun was on him. Robin swiveled toward Richard, and I heard the click of a safety catch. And now G.P.'s growl had risen to a horrifying, sustained snarl.

"Shoot that goddamned dog, Kit," snapped Robin, and the gun's muzzle swung toward the floor.

"No!" I cried desperately, and dropped to my knees, my only thought to save the one innocent creature in the room. "Oh, good boy, G.P. Good boy!"

Then several things happened at once. G.P. lowered his head, relaxed into an apologetic smile, and began wagging his great tail back and forth. Transfixed by a minute hope, I extended my hands and he moved toward me, tail still flailing. It caught the lamp on the table and sent it, with the Meissen bowl, shattering on the stones of the hearth. Just before the light went, I saw Richard's right hand lash out in a flat backhanded blow, the edge of his palm catching Kit in the throat. Almost simultaneously he kicked Robin with terrible force. Robin screamed, a shot rang out with deafening impact, and Kit went down without a sound. The guns rattled to the floor.

I felt a burning on the outside of my left forearm, and brought my hand away wet from the parka sleeve.

"Lissa... here, watch out for that broken glass." Richard was at my side, muttering under his breath. "Oh, you blessed dog. I'll buy you a tenderloin, I swear." Then he took my arm. "Are you all right? Oh, my God, it's wet. You're bleeding."

"So are you. It's just a graze, I think. Leave it for now. We'd better tie them up."

"Ingram's dead, I think. Should be, anyway. Can you

312

get some laundry line out of the pantry?"

In the darkness of the room I heard him groping for the guns, then kneeling to touch Robin.

Somehow his matter-of-factness didn't shock me. I'd grieved over many a dead animal, but I could feel no remorse for Kit. I didn't know him, and to me he was an empty façade, a common killer behind a mask of erudition and charm. He'd been perfectly willing to take the life of a woman he'd met only once. Robin...Robin was something else again. It would take me a long time to come to terms with that. But the Robin I thought I knew had simply never existed.

I shifted so that the blood dripped onto the floorboards instead of the Belouchistan.

"Can you get to the kitchen? There's laundry line in the pantry. Wait, here's the torch. And bring a knife."

With G.P. close on my heels, I found the pantry and soon pocketed the clothesline and knife. I picked up a guttering lantern from the kitchen table and made my way back to the scene of bedlam, holding the light high while Richard made a cursory inspection of Robin, who was breathing stertorously.

"He'll keep," he said curtly. Kneeling beside me, he carefully slit my parka sleeve. He probed the wound with gentle and precise fingers, then sat back with a long sigh.

"Good. You're right, it's only a graze. Ricochet from Robin's gun when I kicked him." He pressed thumb and forefinger hard to his brow, then raised his head. "We were both very fortunate tonight."

Now that the cataclysm was over, I started to tremble uncontrollably. "You were certainly cool enough," I said through chattering teeth. "But I forgot, you used to do this sort of thing for a living." An irrelevant question surfaced out of my reaction. "Why did you make me recite that quotation? That was madness, Richard. I thought we'd come to the end."

His voice was thin with exhaustion. "Distraction value. I knew I had to make a move soon, and that I'd only have one chance. I needed Robin's focus off me before I summoned up what little I remembered from the CIA. God knows my first attempt was ineffectual enough–we were trained only to kill, no halfway measures, and I didn't want to kill. But if it hadn't been for G.P.'s brainstorm... Robin is afraid of animals. I foresaw some kind of turmoil when the growling started, but I was terrified Kit would shoot G.P. I could never have hoped for such blind luck."

He looked at me with sudden curiosity, and the casualness of his next sentence made me realize that he was in shock, too. "Were you really–what was it–junior revolver champion of Connecticut?"

"Great heavens no. I've never touched a revolver in my life. Do you have the guns? And shouldn't we tie Robin up?"

"I have them. And yes, we should."

A wave of weakness came over me in a rush, and I dropped my head into my hands. "Richard, I don't believe any of this. But I have to tell you. When I thought you–"

I never finished. With a scrabbling sound, Robin pushed himself up. Bent almost double, he made a break toward the hall. As he passed Kit's body, he gave one small moan of pain.

Richard leapt up with a cry, stumbled as his leg gave way, and forced himself back to his feet. We heard the kitchen door bang against the outer wall, and after a moment the roar of a motor fractured the silence.

"Let him go," said Richard in spent tones, as I ran to the front door. "You're right, I should have tied him up at once. I've obviously forgotten the first principles of an operator. But he won't get far. We'll take my car to Denham House and call the police." His hand went to his eyes, and I wondered how long he and John had been trying to avert this moment.

314

Then he opened the door and limped out onto the cobbled drive, ankle deep in snow. I followed him slowly. Through the heavy snowfall we could see headlights, dimmed by the flurry of wet flakes, snaking up the side of the valley. The whine of the motor rose in pitch as the car accelerated. He was going far too fast, fleeing his demons, I thought, as well as the retribution that must come. But he could never leave those demons behind; he'd embraced them voraciously, and they had become the material of his being.

"Oh, God," Richard was murmuring. "He'd better slow down for that turn, he's coming up to Delving. On this ice—"

The lights crested and swung into the final stretch before the turn above the drop. The cliff, too steep to hold snow, loomed black against the whiteness of the fell. I grasped Richard's arm, hand over my mouth.

"Rob, you fool," he whispered urgently. "Slow down. Dear God, slow down..."

With a distant scream of brakes and a red flash of lights, the car lurched, righted itself, and slithered sideways over the edge, its headlights wheeling into a cloud of whiteness. The snow wasn't deep enough to cover the rocks below. The thunderous crash was followed by reverberations that seemed to take an eternity to die. Then there was only the faint baaing, mournful and foolish, of the flock that had stood between Robin and his escape.

⤳CHAPTER 27⤶

Time goes running, even as we talk.
Take the present, the future's no one's affair.
Horace, Book One, Ode Eleven

I sat beside John, the light of the spring morning flooding through the long salon windows. The glorious silent promise of the harp was gone, and it seemed that the soul of the room had fled with it. A misty Scottish landscape replaced the portrait of Ciara.

The inquest was over, and what I'd feared would be a field day for the tabloids had been somewhat moderated by appeals to friends in high places. Robin's and Kit's psychological discharges and the disappearance of Edmund Garrett were emphasized, and Kit's death named self-defense. It was mentioned that I'd suspected Ciara's murder and attempted to warn Richard.

John's regretful comments added a sort of dignity to the episode. Hopefully, it would eventually fade from the public's consciousness, replaced by even more sensational events.

"Well, Lissa, if you must," John said with genuine sadness.

"I've grown so fond of you, my dear, and I hoped, with Robin gone, that you might stay. But I do understand; it's a pretty bleak outlook just now."

"It's not that, John. I just have to have time to get myself back together. What will you do about running the house?"

"Oh, an old friend and his son are coming to take the job. We'll have our grand opening, though it's been put off for a bit."

"I'm so sorry for coming here and precipitating the whole–" I broke off, unable to continue.

"Lissa, I won't have you thinking that. Richard and I were having inquiries made long before you set foot in Yorkshire. I had my suspicions about Kit, too, but at the time it seemed safer, for Robin's sake, just to keep him under my eye. Besides, he was a damned fine assistant, the best I've ever had. He knew his business, there was no question of that." He gave a gently ironic little laugh.

"Too well, actually. He and Robin were setting up a brilliantly organized antiques forgery racket." He shook his head sadly. "Poor Robin. He was capital in the business here. So much ability."

But not the one ability he'd thirsted for.

"We all knew there was something wrong about the dismissal from the Navy. But the years passed and Robin seemed to be doing so well. Oh, there were occasional problems: we caught him in some minor forgeries, and suspected he might be cooking the inn's books. We convinced ourselves that he'd grow into the responsibilities with time. But Richard caught on to his use of drugs; he was far less naïve than I about that. Also about Ciara, of course, and their connection. When she disappeared and her boat was found, he couldn't shake off the fear that Robin had something to do with it. So he sent Carlo to find out what he could in Ravello and Ischia."

"Who was Carlo, John?"

"Carlo was Sicilian. When Gianna's father was in his thirties, he found a young boy starving on the streets and took him in; Carlo had worked for he family ever since. You're thinking Mafia, I can see. I've heard the stories for years, of course. Well, I honestly don't know, Lissa. Gianna just laughs. What I do know is that Carlo transferred his

317

loyalty to Richard when the old man died, and made himself useful in a variety of ways. But you may be sure that Richard, with his iron-clad concepts of English honor and Catholic morality, kept Carlo very straight indeed. You look surprised, my dear. Well, Richard went off the deep end for awhile after Anna died, it's true. But he's exacted a terrible penance from himself ever since."

Then he smiled and took my hands. "You must promise me never to blame yourself for one iota of what happened, Lissa. The situation was ripe when you arrived; we were just debating a course of action. What we stuck at was Ciara's death. We didn't want to believe Robin capable of killing a woman, I suppose. We truly loved him, you see, in spite of our knowledge." His voice roughened. "At his best, he was..."

"I know," I said, tears spilling over.

"Of course you do." He gave my hands a little shake. "Forgive me, my dear. It must be so awful for you. In my own grief I keep forgetting that you were in love with him."

I stared at him in amazement.

"We both knew, of course, and that was one reason...." He trailed off. "Well, why wouldn't you be? His bisexuality wasn't evident. He was so energetic, so attractive, such good fun–and sharp as a razor. We'll never know why he had to be so dreadfully flawed. But I was afraid for you, Lissa, when I found you cared for him. Especially with the trip to Switzerland on the horizon. I came back to the library, that night you made dinner for us, to get some papers I'd forgotten, and when I saw you in his arms...."

"John! I was not in love with Robin. I thought he was my friend, and I enjoyed all the things about him you've just mentioned. But I never cared for him in that way. How could I, when–oh, never mind." How did one explain total eclipse in terms of the heart? I couldn't even do it in terms of science.

A look of wary hope was transforming on John's face, anxiety giving way to cautious relief. "Lissa... was it... is it

Richard?"

I nodded miserably. "Yes."

"Then it's settled!" he exclaimed heartily. "You shan't go. He loves you most frightfully, Lissa, you must know that."

"He's never given me any reason to think so. And he knows I believed awful things about him, John. Robin led me in that, and I went as tamely as any little lapdog on a string. I wish to heaven I'd listened to my heart instead of my head; it knew all the time, in spite of the evidence. No, Richard's withdrawn from me absolutely. All through that terrible time after Robin and Kit died–the police, the inquest–he never spoke to me unless it was unavoidable."

"Listen to me, Lissa. He was in pain. He tried so hard, for so many years, to redeem Robin. With his overdeveloped conscience, he felt a personal guilt for his own success and Robin's failure, his wealth and Robin's lack of it. We would have settled money on Robin long ago if we hadn't been certain he'd use it to accelerate his own destruction. Now Richard's torturing himself over Robin's death, and Carlo's, and probably Ingram's as well. Whereas someone less sensitive would write off Robin's end as inevitable and well deserved, Richard feels that he should, somehow, have been able to alter the course of events. He was trying to do just that when he got Carlo to go to Ischia, and went with you and Robin to Switzerland. It was part protection, and part, to be honest, trap-baiting, and I didn't like it one bit. We were terrified for you to be with Robin at all, but after the incident with Fiametto, Richard hoped that by watching unremittingly he could catch Robin in one of his spiteful tricks and compel him to be sensible. He was ready to threaten him with violence, and I with dismissal. We didn't have any real evidence, you see, and only our suspicions as to why he wanted you out of the way. And we hadn't admitted to ourselves, even then, how sick he really was. You know how convincing he could be. Oh, my dear," he finished, "I know

319

Richard's been cold to you in his pain, and it's grieved me, but... tell me, Lissa, just how much pride do you carry around with you?"

"I?" I gave a sad little laugh. "Where Richard's concerned, I travel very lightly indeed."

"You have a couple of hours before Mirren takes you to Leeds. Look, Lissa, take my car and get over the fell. I wish I knew Richard's schedule; there's at least a chance he may still be there. Just go! And trust me; I know I'm right."

The snow was long gone, but I took the road slowly, unused to the right-hand drive. I eased the Bentley down the steep turns, deliberately blanking out my thoughts at Delving Drop, and drove along the curving track across the field, drawing up beside the barn.

Marjorie Chidester was unpinning dishtowels from a clothesline.

"Miss Leone! Ah, but you've just missed Richard. He left early this morning for London. He rehearses this afternoon and plays tonight, though how he can, after poor Robin and losing all that blood, and then if you can believe it he goes on to Munich to rehearse the next day. Well, at least he's playing the same piece. Come in, dear, have a cup of tea. You looked dragged out."

"I wish I could, Mrs. Chidester, but I have to get back, I'm leaving for London in about an hour myself." Now that I knew he wasn't here, my knees went weak, and I sank onto the stone wall. "What piece is it?"

"That Rachmaninoff Third Piano Concerto, and the devil's own piece of work it is, not that it doesn't have some pretty parts in it. I wish to the good Lord you'd come over sooner, dear, he needed you."

I looked at her speechlessly.

"Yes, I know I'm speaking out of turn again, but heaven knows what's going to happen to him. Miss Leone, I've heard him practice that piece time and again, and it's always a storm, but I've never heard anything like this since I had ears. It's a marvel there's a key left on that poor piano. You know that place in the first part where it builds up and up till you think it can't go anywhere else and then it just turns on you and tears you up for good?"

Coming from a layman, it was an excellent description. I nodded. "The cadenza. Yes, I know it."

"Well, he just ripped himself up over it, again and again, until I couldn't stand it anymore and had to get out of the house. Every time he did it, it was like he was trying to kill himself a little more through his hands. And then he started playing a quiet part, tender-like, and that was worse, I don't know why. That sun's strong," she said, wiping at her eyes. Then, suddenly, "He never came to see you?"

"No."

She sighed. "He's got the pride, and who can blame him, he comes by it rightly from his mother and father both, not to mention how people have built him up for what he's done himself. But he's grieving to death, dear. Over poor Robin, like we all are, sick and bad though he was, and better out of this world. And over you."

I shook my head. "Not over me, Mrs. Chidester."

"You're wrong there, dear. He said to me, before he left, 'Marjorie, she thought I killed Ciara. She thought I was dealing drugs.' Then he gave a little shrug, and laughed in a way that would break your heart, bitter and resigned-like. 'Well, she knew my past,' he said. 'I can hardly blame her.' I was sure he'd come see you before he left. He went out and started his car twice yesterday morning, but both times he came back in and went to savaging that poor piano again."

The Bentley wavered oddly in the sunshine. I rose from the wall and took the long, bony hand. "Mrs. Chidester, I have to go. Please tell Peter I said goodbye, and give him this letter with my love. Are he and Gianna still in Italy?"

She nodded assent. "She and Richard wanted him out of here till it was all over. I told Gianna I wasn't leaving

321

Richard's side, and she said, 'No, you make sure you don't.'"

"I'm glad you've been with him. I know how he loves you. Well, goodbye, and thank you for your kindness."

"This isn't the way for you to leave, dear. John tells me you're going back to the States."

"It's all I can do, Mrs. Chidester. Richard hasn't even looked at me since Robin died. But thank you. Take care of them."

I hurried to the car and sped back to Denham House, all nervousness about the road's perilous corners lost in my mounting turmoil.

"Gone?"

"Yes. Did he know I was leaving this morning?"

John spoke reluctantly. I'm afraid so." Then, with anger, "Damn that stiff-necked bastard! Sorry, my dear. But Richard's a fool."

I gave a small laugh. "On the contrary, John, he's a very wise man. It would never have worked. He and I have done little but worry at one another since we met."

"That's nonsense. It's been a damned difficult time for both of you. He loves you, Lissa, and you're so right for each other."

"John, I don't think so. Richard is... well, he's Olympian. He's so totally self-determined, so driven. I'd be excess baggage at best."

"Is that the way you really see him?"

I nodded. "What other way is there?"

John sighed. "Musically he's Olympian, yes. He has colossal strengths and inhuman discipline. And he can be imperious, I know; a conductor, by definition, is not a meek man. But Richard *is* a man, Lissa, with human vulnerabilities. He can bleed, just as you and I can. People look at the public image and assume he's Olympian all the time; they don't know how often life has knocked him down. Well, he's always risen like a phoenix, and he hasn't turned his own suffering on others, either. I wish you could believe me when I tell you how terribly he needs you."

I shook my head. "Richard is the most complete man I've ever known; he doesn't need anything I have to give. Anyway, it's out of my hands now. Obviously he didn't want to see me. Here's Merrin to take me to the station. Oh, John." I went into his arms. "I'll never be able to thank you for everything."

"Hush. Next time you come, the harp will be mended and waiting. I'll always keep it for you. I love you, my dear."

I nodded and made for the door, unable to speak. The tacit truth weighed between us, dragging like lead. John and I both knew how unlikely it was that I would ever walk into Denham House again.

CHAPTER 28

---the fall of a dim curtain
over the dark end of a a dark play--
Edward Arlington Robinson, Avon's Harvest

From some abiding source of power,
strong-smitten chords, ye seem to flow—
and yet I cry in anguish as I hear
the long-drawn pageant of your passage
roll magnificently into the night.
Robert Louis Stevenson, Music at the Villa Marina

The train journey passed in a mental fog. As we
hurtled through the fields, copses of trees, their canopies
dressed in fresh young green, rushed up to meet us. I didn't
feel sick, not physically.

Tim had phoned the night before, offering breakfast
and a ride to Gatwick in the morning. I accepted with more
gratitude than enthusiasm; it was still difficult for me to raise
the energy for conversation. We talked briefly about his
upcoming recording of the Dvořák Cello Concerto. Then he
turned the subject to me.

"Well, I'm glad you're out of that tangle, Lissa. It must
have been an awful nightmare; you could have been killed.
But it's over. Now you can leave that bizarre scene and get on
with your real life."

I assented quietly from a million miles away. Yes. My
real life.

I woke with a start in the hotel bed in which I'd cried

myself to sleep. I'd meant to lie down for just a few moments before dinner. My mouth was dry and my head ached, and I was filled with a vague yet rapidly solidifying conviction that there was something urgent I had to do. Snapping on the bedside lamp, I looked at the clock and snatched the phone from its cradle. Ignoring the fluttering in the pit of my stomach, I dialed the concierge's desk with an unsteady hand.

It was late, dreadfully late. I'd never make it by the end of intermission, not unless they were playing some marathon opus on the first half. But I had to try.

I wondered, as the cab moved with maddening slowness through the heavy evening traffic, why I was putting myself through this final test. I'd certainly had no intention of it when I arrived in London, falling on that bed and drifting into a fitful, exhausted doze.

But something had thrust me up out of sleep and into this crazy action. To see him at a distance, to hear him play; wasn't there already enough pain without that? Approaching him backstage was out of the question. John and Mrs. Chidester to the contrary, he'd made his feelings unmistakably clear. He'd remained a distant stranger throughout the police proceedings, and made no attempt to see me since. Yes, he'd certainly washed his hands of me.

Nonetheless, I found myself leaning forward in the taxi. "Please," I begged, "could you drive a little faster? If I'm late they won't let me in."

"I'll try, lady," said the cabby obligingly. "You sound like you really mean it. Favorite performer of yours?"

"What? Oh... yes." He caught the tone of my voice, glanced sharply around at me, and trod on the accelerator. The reflected light from the street lamps gleamed wetly along the pavement.

"You meeting someone?"

"No. No, I just–there's part of this concert I don't want to miss." To my chagrin I was crying openly. He swerved to pass a bus. The glass dome of Royal Albert Hall rose in front of us.

This is all there is, Lissa. This performance, maybe not even this, and then it's back home for you, back to the schoolroom. Just be grateful you came out of it with your life. Of course, he performs in New York; you can always hear him there.

"Hold on, Miss, here we are."

I was staring at the posters: they bore the same stark image of Richard that had advertised the York concert, but in a positive image, black and white.

As we slid to a stop, I thrust a bill at him; it had been ready in my hand since we left the hotel.

"Lady, are you sure you want to go to this concert?" He had seen my look at the poster.

"No, not really. Thank you so much for hurrying." I slammed the door and bolted up the stairs to the entrance. Oh, God. Intermission was over, then; I saw two stragglers hastening toward a door on the orchestra level. As they squeezed through I could hear the orchestra tuning. Now the enormous lobby was bleakly empty. I was too late and I had no ticket; they'd never let me in.

I took the endless steps to the third tier two at a time, regardless of my high heels. The door was barred by a young woman in black, looking as stern as the angel of God at heaven's gate.

"Please—"

She shook her head. "I'm sorry. It's too late, I can't let you in. He's coming on stage right now." Her voice was inexorable.

Sick at heart, I was turning away when the door swung violently open, and a red-faced man exited in a paroxysm of coughing.

I slipped through the opening like an eel.

"You can't do that," she whispered frantically. "It's against the rules!"

326

"I know," I agreed in a contrite whisper, and set about finding one of the very few empty seats. The careful, silent closing of the door behind me was as eloquent as a slam. I'd probably confirmed her idea of Americans as rude, untutored concert-goers.

Richard, in white tie and tails, was walking on stage to a roar of applause. The conductor stood on the podium. Murmuring apologies, I slid hastily into a seat between a well-upholstered dowager and a thin long-tressed youth. Then silence fell, and with it the peculiar pre-performance tension that stretched the air of the hall. As Richard moved to seat himself on the bench, I saw that he was no longer limping.

How complete a world it looked from this distance, three tiers up. It was an island of brilliant light in a sea of darkness. Self-contained, cool and stark, the players and the piano were limned in black and white, like the poster outside. The scene was almost clinical in its look of formal professionalism; there was nothing on the stage that was not absolutely essential to the work ahead. It seemed an unlikely soil for the almost intolerably vital emotions that would soon flower from it.

I looked about me; the huge circular hall was packed. I wondered how many of these people had come out of simple curiosity to see the man who'd been involved in such a sensational episode. Well, perhaps many of them had come for that reason. But I had a strong suspicion that by the time they left, something far less ephemeral would have eclipsed their unhealthy fascination with what had happened in Ravello and at Hawthorns. Perhaps in death Robin was doing something for music that he couldn't in life.

They were ready now. A foreshadowing of peril and disaster nearly suffocated me; I remembered how many great pianists had foundered on the reefs of this particular concerto. Then Richard nodded, the conductor gathered his forces, the orchestra murmured its two-bar introduction.

And now the quiet Slavic melody sang from the piano.

As the first movement progressed, I realized two things. The first was that my cheeks were still wet from the breakdown in the taxi, and that if Richard kept playing like this it wouldn't be worthwhile drying them, even if I had a handkerchief. The second was that his playing was charged with a tremendous intensity that struck almost visible fire from the gleaming black piano. He was racing toward the cadenza with fearful power and dangerous velocity. Yet somehow the music never lost its logic and majesty; it was all making sublime musical sense.

I heard an indrawn breath beside me as he hurtled through a passage with terrifying speed and passion. The principal oboist played a figure faster than he'd ever dreamed of essaying it, and only his thorough professionalism kept it from sounding startled. I glanced over at my white-haired neighbor. She'd clasped her hands together in something very near prayer. Returning my look, she gave a tiny expressive shake of her head, and we stared at one another in awed surmise.

Then our attention was wrenched back to the stage as the cadenza began its ominous, tempestuous surge and fall, building giant step upon giant step.

"I wrote it for elephants," Rachmaninoff had said; mega-virtuoso elephants, presumably. Gods, he had meant. The emotional demands were as superhuman as the technical ones. And Richard had chosen the more difficult of the two cadenzas provided by the composer.

He was playing this finger-breaking concerto–the performance of which had been likened, by one superb American pianist, to climbing the Matterhorn on roller skates–playing, no, attacking it, with the most shocking ferocity and recklessness. He was taking appalling, heart-stopping risks, and they were coming off brilliantly. But my fear for him, as he rushed toward the abyss, was turning my bones to water.

Now I knew what Mrs. Chidester had meant. When Richard came to the climax of the cadenza, the fury and despair encompassing both extremes of the instrument's register, I felt as if I'd never truly heard the piano speak before. Anton Rubenstein had arrogantly stated, "The piano's too small for me. I could use twenty like this." It seemed as if Richard had twenty, and was tearing the heart out of all of them. When the cosmic storm had subsided into the dry finality of its D octaves, my neighbor turned round eyes on me.

"My God," she whispered.

I nodded carefully, trying not to dislodge any tears.

The audience drew a collective, shuddering breath. There was scarcely a stir as they awaited the next movement. Nobody coughed. The conductor, who at that moment would probably have climbed gratefully into a barrel at the lip of Niagara, was making rather a business of sponging his brow.

At last he looked at Richard, poised in cool immobility on the bench. He had catapulted his audience into every extreme of longing, anguish, and fury, wrecked their nerves with his spendthrift daring, and now sat there exactly as if nothing out of the ordinary had happened. After a moment he gave a curt nod, and the strings and oboe grieved their way into the Intermezzo. Richard's entrance was a cry of bewildered desperation.

Then came the achingly beautiful lyrical themes, sung with rending tenderness. And I felt if I lived to be ninety, I would never be able to listen to this music again.

The Intermezzo segued into the Finale without pause, and under Richard's hands–hands that had killed Kit Ingram with an almost casual blow, then explored my wound with the utmost delicacy–the transition was an ironic, disillusioned snarl that cut into my heart. Then he was back at his horrifying game, a game, it seemed, which he couldn't lose.

He was interpreting the scherzando section of the

Finale as a bitter joke; there was a callousness, almost, about his playing that made a mockery of the earlier moments of ardor and tender beauty. I knew instinctively that he didn't give a damn how many notes he dropped, but he was miraculously prevented from missing a single one. He simply couldn't put a finger wrong. I was reminded sharply of Robin's gibes about Dr. Faustus. But this inhuman mastery was a result of towering genius, unrelenting method and discipline, and surely, under the circumstances, sheer blind luck.

Somewhere toward the middle of the Finale I was aware of a subtle change in his playing. It was just as compelling, just as powerful, but the focus had shifted from headlong, suicidal recklessness to a sort of rational working-out process. Indeed, if it hadn't been so beautifully realized, it would have sounded almost dogged. It was as if he were thinking abstractly through the music, his brain function somehow related to the manual touch on the keyboard.

I told myself how ridiculous this was; the music had simply changed character, that was all. The thought was swept away by the brilliant corruscations of the scintillant passages: one could swear that sparks were flying from the great instrument.

But what happened next ended all speculation and completed the devastation of my heart and spirit.

The last pages were played with a triumphant, transforming joy that that was unmistakable. It wasn't just what Rachmaninoff had written, it was the man performing the music.

He's worked through what happened to us and put it behind him, I thought. He's been through all the terror and pain and puzzlement, and taken me with him. And he's emerged into exultation, and left me behind.

The audience was on its feet, roaring, screaming in a frenzy of near hysterical adulation. The plump lady beside me reached down and plucked at my sleeve, surprised to find my concert manners remiss. With an effort, I stood, and she smiled approval. Leaning over, she spoke into my ear over the ocean of noise.

"There's no one like him, dear," she beamed.

"No. No one."

"But even he's never played like this."

I shook my head and escaped to the door.

As the ultimate conclusion to my chain of follies, I went backstage after the repeated curtain calls. "Went" is the wrong word; I simply followed my feet. I even told the guard, God help me, that I was a relative.

I won't speak to him, of course, I won't go all the way in. Just one more glimpse, and then I'll put the accursed Atlantic between us.

My resolution, in the end, was easy to keep. I rounded the corner to see him enveloped in the embrace of Lucia Pavesi. Over her shoulder, his eyes flared with the jubilation I'd heard at the end of the Finale. Then he saw me, and they went blank.

"Lissa–" his voice carried faintly across the chattering, laughing group.

I was pushing my way back to the door.

"Lissa!" At the note of command, I turned in spite of myself. Lucia had swiveled, her arm still about him, the long strands of carefully disarranged Titian hair gleaming against his black jacket. She was smiling with confident amusement.

Then at last I took Tim's advice to heart and ran like hell.

⋙CHAPTER 29⋘

Music, sister of sunrise,
and herald of life to be!
Algernon Charles Swinburne, *Music, an Ode*

"Well, I wish you'd stay, Lissa."

We stood in the first class lounge at Gatwick; Tim was catching a flight to Madrid.

"Heaven knows what opportunities might turn up for you in London. Of course you can always storm New York. But I'll be based here for six more months, and I could introduce you to some people. Not that you need much introduction after that *Times* review."

"Tim, you're a dear soul, and I don't have words to thank you for shepherding me through all this. But now I just want to get home."

"I understand, sweetie. It's been a harrowing experience for you, Lord knows. Talk about crime in high places... well, who ever knows what's going to happen? But it'll pass. You'll probably go back to New York and knock their socks off."

"I think my sock-knocking capacity is somewhat impaired. But I may play some auditions next year," I added, for the sake of forestalling argument.

"Well, if your mind is made up. Oh, they're boarding your flight; better go. Lissa, if you ever change your mind–about playing or about me–" He wound to a halt, lifting his shoulders helplessly.

The line of passengers was moving steadily toward the gate. "You're a love, Tim," I said, hugging him impulsively.

A love, but not my love.

I'd been to my last D'Annunzio concert; I'd never stretch myself on that particular rack again.

A firm hand closed on my arm, pulling me out of Tim's embrace.

"Come on, Lissa. I have your luggage."

My heart jerked violently and I turned to stare at him in stupefaction.

"Let's go," he said, unsmiling. "Tony got your things before they were loaded."

"Tony? Who's that, Carlo's successor? How did he—you're mad," I cried. "I'm going to Connecticut, they're boarding my flight right now. And you're supposed to be in Munich."

"I canceled."

"*Canceled*?" Somehow this capped all the other improbabilities.

"We're going to talk. You're not leaving like this."

After a night during which I hadn't closed my eyes, the shock of his sudden appearance was more than I could take. In an explosion of anger and resentment, I twisted my arm violently in his grasp.

It was if I'd never moved. Pianist's hands, I thought. Yes, and assassin's hands. All my laboriously built strength was useless against them.

I took refuge in bitter words. It never occurred to me what a formula they'd become.

"Will you kindly take your hands off me?"

They were announcing the final call for my flight.

"Let her go, D'Annunzio." Tim's face flamed with anger. "She'll miss her plane."

"That's the plan, Willman," said Richard evenly.

"I'm warning you, D'Annunzio. Take your blasted high-handed tactics back on the stage where they belong. And get your confounded fists off her."

"Do you know, people are always telling me that," said

333

Richard, deadly quiet. "I'm getting a trifle weary of it. I'll let her go if she tells me that's what she really wants."

I nodded my head dumbly, and his hands fell away. The sight of his stony face made me speak gently; I knew, suddenly, what lay behind it.

"It's mostly me who says it. And Robin... once."

He closed his eyes.

"Oh, Richard," I murmured. "I'm sorry."

He looked at me for a moment, levelly, considering. Then, "Let's go," he repeated crisply. "Your bags are in the car."

The uniformed attendant at the gate, who'd been watching us anxiously, gave a little shrug and turned toward the boarding ramp, closing the door behind her.

Richard put an arm about my shoulders and turned me toward the exit.

"Lissa, this is insane," cried Tim furiously. "You don't have any idea what you're doing. Are you going to let him bully you like this?"

I nodded. "Goodbye, Tim," I said with a rueful smile, as we headed down the corridor.

We sat inside the Aston in the short term parking lot. It was raining slowly and unstintingly; the inside of the car was dim and chill. He started the engine and switched on the heater, but made no attempt to move the car.

Finally I could bear it no longer, and turned to him.

"Well?" I asked. "What was that little scene in aid of?"

"Forgive me, Lissa." He was looking straight ahead, watching the rain that coursed steadily down the glass. "I didn't mean it to be like that. After last night–well, I'm a little tired, and not quite in control. Sounds familiar, doesn't it? But when I saw you in Willman's arms–"

"You're wrong. He was in mine. And speaking of last

night, and being in someone's arms..." I reminded him.

"Lucia? You know how predatory she is, and I was so elated that she might as well have been the Albert Memorial. Lissa, I didn't sleep at all last night. I couldn't. I kept thinking about–oh, God, all of it, Robin, John, Kit, but most of all you. I knew what I was going to do, and I couldn't do it until ten o'clock this morning; it drove me nearly wild."

"And what were you going to do?"

"Stop you from leaving, of course. By any means I had to, up to and including kidnapping. Lissa, this is hard, but I have to ask it. You believed my coldness to you after that night–and I freely admit that I withdrew from you–was because I knew you thought me capable of calculated murder and drug-dealing, didn't you?"

"Yes, I suppose so. I was so confused. When we had those few moments together after Kit..." I broke off, bracketed by two deaths.

"I know. Dear Christ, Lissa, your courage that night, the way you refused to let fear paralyze your intellect–it was just like York, when I think about it. Well, to get back to the matter at hand. It wasn't just Robin dying, or what you'd believed about me. It hurt to know you'd picked me as the villain of the piece, but I never blamed you for it; everything you heard was so damning. Robin had the most extraordinary talent for simulating sincerity; no one knows that better than John and I. And God knows I'm hardly white as snow. I've killed, once before your very eyes. Yes, I know," he turned his head as I began to protest. "If I hadn't, we'd both be in our graves. But it wasn't just righteous anger at being cast in Robin's role. It was something far more childish and unjustifiable."

He stopped, absently turned on the windshield wipers, then clicked them off again. The fleeting view of empty cars was at once obscured by a new sheet of water.

Tentatively, I put a hand on his sleeve. "What is it, Richard?"

For the first time he looked directly at me. Then he closed his eyes briefly and gave a tiny, almost inaudible sigh. When he opened them again, he'd assumed a steely control.

"John told me, in Geneva. He came upon you two," he said a matter-of-fact tone, "in the library at Denham House. He feared that you were in love with Robin. And knowing Robin as he did, he realized that you stood to be hurt either way: Robin would betray you emotionally, or–and we both feared this–with his twisted mind, he'd do you some real physical damage. You could have been seriously hurt in that fall from Fiametto, you know.

"I might just as well come out and say it, Lissa, ugly though it is. I was jealous of Robin alive, and more jealous of him dead. The thought that you were grieving over what he really was, and his loss–as a lover–was more than I could stand."

My heart was doing odd things; it felt like a trout leaping upstream against the current.

"And you believed that? That I was in love with Robin?"

"I had to," he said quietly. "You seemed so happy when you were with him. The two of you were so lighthearted, so carefree together, like a couple of children. I even had a faint hope that Robin was changing. And then when I kissed you, there in Geneva," his voice dropped so that I could hardly hear him. "When I kissed you... you shuddered."

My poor, beloved fool, I thought. Your famous perceptions certainly failed you that time. Well, no wonder; they'd had a merciless overload on the concert stage that night.

"Of course," he went on with a resumption of briskness, "John and I never believed that your fall from the horse was anything but another example of Robin's ingenuity. He always made the most of the moment, and looking back, I think he probably hoped that one would be fatal. He must have been in a panic over what Ciara might have told you.

"Then, when he saw you weren't badly hurt, he told me he was planning to invite you to ski in Zermatt. It sounded straightforward enough, but I knew there was a taunt underneath. I suppose he wanted more of a chance to see if Ciara had tipped you off before he decided what to do. When you didn't put the squeeze on him, I think he realized pretty quickly that she hadn't, but you know how carefully he planned. The ski slopes were as good a place as any to get you injured so that, if you didn't break your neck or die of concussion, hopefully you'd at least go back to the States. Well, the whole idea of Zermatt terrified us, but at that stage John and I were still hoping to avert an open scandal; I didn't see how we could forbid you to go. So I quickly made myself one of the party."

"Why on earth did he agree to your coming?"

"He needed cover. He actually wanted me there; he couldn't have risked one of his little accidents with the two of you alone. And he loved walking the tight-wire. He'd never broken his cover with me before Zermatt, by the way, Lissa, even in direct confrontation, except to show amusement. So I think he took my presence as a stimulating challenge; you heard what he said about banishing ennui, at Hawthorns. And you saw it in Zermatt, when Ingram came to our table. Robin was livid at first, afraid that Kit would drop an indiscreet word, that'd I'd figure they were working together. But then, as usual, he got caught up in the spirit of the game."

"*Rope*," I muttered.

"I beg your pardon?"

"*Rope*. Dear Lord, yes. That was the connection I couldn't make in Zermatt that night. Why were you suddenly so anxious to get me off the subject, anyway?"

"Simple fear. I could see your ever-active brain fermenting something, and if you'd let the tiniest suspicion show, Robin wouldn't have hesitated for an instant to rig something lethal. You do have a most open and expressive countenance, my darling."

I passed that one by with no more than an extra thump of the heart.

"But what's this about rope?"

"Did you see the old Hitchcock movie? That's what my brain was trying to tell me when I saw Robin and Kit together. Those two young murderers, killing as an intellectual exercise. They were so attractive and urbane; homosexual, but not obviously so. And they entertained the victim's family and friends literally over the body, remember? They used the trunk where it was hidden as a buffet. I almost had it, until you diverted me. Walking the tight-wire, yes. And speaking of that, Richard, what the devil were you doing last night? If sheer terror can kill, you nearly succeeded in making a corpse out of me."

"Last night. Ah, yes. Well... working things out, you might say." His voice lightened.

As I had thought, then. "Oh. Working things out. With the most formidable piano concerto in the literature as your vehicle?"

"We can't always choose, can we? The programs were already printed."

"And your conclusion, at the expense of several thousand trembling spectators?"

There was a rather long silence. "John called yesterday before the concert and said that you and he had cleared some things up when you said goodbye. I had to make a decision. On the one hand I was, admittedly, still hurt that you'd believed the rumors about me. And I was grieving over Robin. I loved him, Lissa, in spite of everything. We'd prayed against all odds that he hadn't killed Ciara and had no lethal designs on you, that it was all just a sort of unbalanced devilry.

"I was frantic in Zermatt, you know; we felt sure he had something up his sleeve, and I hadn't a clue what, except that it probably involved skiing. But that was the point in

338

being there, of course. Without some kind of proof I couldn't make a move, and I had a crazy hope that I could catch him setting one of his traps and bring him to his senses. John was more realistic; he thought it madness to let you go at all. I should never have let your skis out of my sight; I thought keeping them in my room would be safe enough, but it wasn't, not with those two. It was hell, I can tell you, watching you in the role of sacrificial lamb." I remembered Anne O'Neal's account of Richard at Mass.

"I was on tenterhooks, hoping to hear from Carlo. And the hardest part was to let you go back to Geneva without me, even though I was certain Robin wouldn't risk anything with the two of you alone. I told him I'd kill him if anything happened to you. He may have been a tight-rope walker, but he wasn't suicidal." His mouth was a hard straight line.

"And on the other hand?"

"Yes, I digress. Always clear sighted, aren't you?" he smiled.

"I haven't been exactly famous for it lately."

"Well, on the other hand, Lissa, I knew that if I lost you, nothing would be worth living for. Not even music. So I had to swallow my pride—no small morsel, as you know."

"I didn't notice any great display of humility back there in the terminal," I remarked, over the irregular thudding in my chest. "But never mind. Just when did you come to this decision?"

"About midway through the Finale. And then I felt like all the gods rolled into one, I was so happy. I knew I had to stop you from leaving this morning—*cara*, what's the matter? What have I said to make you cry?"

"Oh, Richard." I bit my lip and waited until my voice was working again. "That was the worst moment of all. Worse even than seeing Robin with a gun in his hand."

"Why on earth?"

"Your joy, your exultation. At first I was sure you were

feeling the same kind of pain I was. And then... all that exultation. I thought you'd left me; put me behind you for good."

"You're bloody right it was exultation." He caught me into his arms with a laugh. "And there won't be any more leaving, on either side. Good God," he said reflectively. "To think I've committed myself to a woman whose idea of fun is the twenty-sixth variation of the Goldberg."

"Why this morning?" I asked, when I could breathe. "Hmmm?"

"Why not last night? I mean, why didn't you–" His lips cut off my question, and the Brahms Adagio slipped back into its rightful perspective.

"Come find you? Because, my dear impulsive love, you flew out of there like a bat out of hell; I knew I'd never catch you in that crowd. Furthermore, you'd omitted to tell John where you were staying; I checked. And even my ardor was somewhat damped by the thought of calling several hundred hotels. But just to show you how resilient it is..."

He kissed me again.

"Richard–Richard, no, wait. Wait. Stop!"

"Why?" he murmured, lips still on mine.

"Where do you intend to go? Now, I mean?"

"Yorkshire, I suppose." That Italian lift of the shoulder. "Or we can stay here. It couldn't matter less. Come here." He reached for me again.

"Wait!"

With a quizzical smile and a spread of the hands, he subsided into his seat.

"When did you call Munich? Quickly, think!"

"Oh... just before I left my flat. I couldn't reach Klaus any earlier. About nine, I suppose. Why?"

"Good heavens, you must have flown this car." I looked at my watch, then opened the door. "Come on."

"May I inquire–"

"All you like, when we have time. Where's your new

340

factotum, gone to ground? Okay. Grab your bags; I've got mine."

"Certainly. Here, give me that. Would you care to tell me where we're going?"

"To Munich, of course. They won't have found anyone to play your brain catalyst by this time, not for tomorrow night, so get on your cell. Come on, hurry. Canceling!" I teased gently. "You're not going to be able to afford that, if you're supporting my tastes. As a matter of curiosity, Richard, where *does* all that money come from?"

"Tires."

"What?"

"My late Italian grandfather's tire factory," he said simply.

I burst into laughter, and he dropped the suitcases and pulled me into his arms.

"No, seriously, I mean to be self-supporting," I continued, through the kiss. "So... Richard, you know those doors you were talking about?"

He drew away a little and looked at me, and I saw a dawning hope in his eyes. He nodded cautiously.

I smiled at him. "Open them."

Libraries
gunnison county
connect.   discover.   imagine.   learn.

Gunnison Library
307 N. Wisconsin, Gunnison, CO 81230
970.641.3485
www.gunnisoncountylibraries.org

CPSIA information can be obtained
at www.ICGtesting.com
Printed in the USA
FSOW03n2115230118
43722FS

9 781533 374653